Anthony Trollope

The Complete Short Stories

VOLUME II

Editors and Writers

Edited, with introduction, by
Betty Jane Slemp Breyer

Texas Christian University Press
Fort Worth, Texas 76129

Published by Texas Christian University Press

Manufactured in the United States of America

Library of Congress Cataloging in Publication Data
Trollope, Anthony, 1815-1882.
    Editors and writers.
    (Anthony Trollope, the complete short stories; v. 2)
    1. Litterateurs — Fiction. I. Breyer, Betty Jane Slemp.
II. Title.
PZ3.T75An 1979 vol. 2 [PR5684] 823'.8s 79-19986
ISBN O-912646-57-8   [823'.8]

Contents

Introduction

THE STORIES IN THIS VOLUME are about writers, editors, and writing; and because they are Anthony Trollope's stories they are about human difficulties, large and small, which plague those whose business is the imagination. Trollope's own career as writer and his experiences as editor of *Saint Pauls Magazine* brought him not only first-hand knowledge of the problems writers can face but also the acquaintance and sometimes the friendship of most of the important literary figures of his time. Always keenly and sympathetically observant of his fellow writers, he saw and understood their difficulties — even though, or perhaps just because, he had early learned the best way of using his own talents.

Much, perhaps quite enough, has been said about Trollope's method of writing, but a brief review of it might be useful here. For Trollope was sometimes fond of prescribing it as a general panacea for literary ills, and it can be supposed to underlie his treatment of the ills that beset the characters in these stories. His method involved two disciplines: that of a rigid schedule and that of constancy. He describes his "scheme of work" in *An Autobiography:* "According to the circumstances of the time, — whether my other business might be then heavy or light, or whether the book which I was writing was or was not wanted with speed, — I have allotted myself so many pages a week. The average number has been about 40. It has been placed as low as 20, and has risen to 112. And as a page is an ambiguous term, my page has been made to contain 250 words; and as words, if not watched, will have a tendency to straggle, I have had every word counted as I went." He learned to rise early and write for three hours before the other business of the day began. Whenever he could, he wrote at home; but he soon learned to complete his self-imposed

allotment of words wherever he was. He wrote on trains, in carriages, and on shipboard; whether travelling to Edinburgh or to
Ceylon, Trollope could be found writing. "I always had," he said,
"a pen in my hand. Whether crossing the seas, or fighting with
American officials, or tramping about the streets of Beverley
[where he stood and was defeated for a parliamentary seat], I
could do a little, and generally more than a little."

T. H. S. Escott recalls in his *Anthony Trollope* an amusing encounter he himself had with Trollope's writing habits:

> One November day, at Euston Station, he entered the com-
> partment of the train in which I was already seated, on some
> journey due north. Just recognising me, he began to talk
> cheerily enough for some little time; then, putting on a
> huge fur cap, part of which fell down over his shoulders, he
> suddenly asked: "Do you ever sleep when you are travelling?
> I always do"; and forthwith, suiting the action to the word,
> sank into that kind of snore compared by Carlyle to a Chal-
> dean trumpet in the new moon. Rousing himself up as we
> entered Grantham, or Preston, Station, he next inquired:
> "Do you ever write when you are travelling?" "No." "I al-
> ways do." Quick as thought out came the tablet and the
> pencil, and the process of putting words on paper continued
> without a break till the point was reached at which, his
> journey done, he left the carriage.

Constancy and routine, then, were his method: so many words
a page, so many pages a day, so many weeks to finish a novel.
There is a touching mixture of pride and humility as he talked of
his accomplishments and his adherence to the disciplines he set
himself. For him hard work, not inspiration, was the quotidaian
reality of the writer. When *An Autobiography* was published
shortly after his death in 1882, the young writers and critics were
horrified by the literary opinions recorded there. The book confirmed all their worst suspicions about their fathers' generation.
Here was a man who described writing as a task to be learned by
practise as a trade might be learned. Here was a man who talked
about practising his craft as a cobbler practises his, who positively
rejected the ennobling pursuit of inspiration, and who spoke with
unconcealed distaste of those whose discipline did not lead them
to habits of industry. "There are those," he said there, "who

would be ashamed to subject themselves to such a taskmaster, and who think that the man who works with his imagination should allow himself to wait till—inspiration moves him. When I have heard such doctrine preached, I have hardly been able to repress my scorn. To me it would not be more absurd if the shoe-maker were to wait for inspiration, or the tallow-chandler for the divine moment of melting."

There are two reasons for such an emphatic dismissal of inspiration, and they lie in the words *wait* and *move*. First, he had little use for those who believed it was their right, indeed their duty, to wait for that "divine moment." He is, after all, talking in this passage not about writing but about excuses for not writing. It is quite easy to imagine that such a man as he — industrious, self-disciplined, and quick-tempered — would feel scorn for those who used inspiration, or rather lack of it, as an excuse for failing to meet such literary obligations as they might have contracted. He even cites with hardly suppressed fury an occasion when the publication of his own work was delayed because an editor had not received the promised work of another writer in time. For such lapses of literary etiquette Trollope had no sympathy. So in his broad and exaggerated way he takes a hearty swat at the divine-moment-of-melting school of writing. Then, secondly, Trollope firmly believed that the work of creation was an active process, not a passive one. The imagination must not wait to be moved; it must be driven to move! In "A Walk in the Wood" he described the arduous task of disciplining and using the imagination. The imagination, he said, is very much like Ariel, who will do his work only under compulsion. Always fond of homely metaphor, especially in speaking of abstractions, he described the imagination in this way: "He will skip hither and thither, with pleasant bright gambols, but will not put his shoulder to the wheel, his neck to the collar, his hand to the plough." Only with "judicious discipline" can this unruly servant be brought to do his master's work. This judicious discipline began for Trollope at an early age when in his lonely and neglected childhood he learned to build "castles in the air," sustaining over weeks and months fictions created by his own imagination. Without this early discipline, he felt, his later novel-writing career would have been impossible. But this discipline once achieved, Trollope can say of his labors, "I have been impreg-' nated with my own creation till it has been my only excitement to sit with the pen in my hand, and drive my team before me at as quick a pace as I could make them travel." If this is not inspi-ration, it is something very much like it. In short, though he would not admit it, Trollope courted and won the Muse in his own brusque fashion.

With the exception of "The Misfortunes of Frederic Pickering" and "Mrs. General Talboys," the stories in this volume were pub-lished in *Saint Pauls Magazine* from October 1869 to May 1870. Trollope was the editor of *Saint Pauls* from its first number in October 1867 until his resignation in the summer of 1870; and the stories that he wrote for the magazine were later collected in a volume he entitled *An Editor's Tales*. Trollope was not success-ful in making *Saint Pauls* a popular and self-supporting magazine. It may have been that the marketplace was not able to support yet another periodical of unexceptional merit. It may have been that Trollope himself, though hard-working and critically hon-est, was not temperamentally suited to conduct such an enter-prise. Or it may have been, as Sadleir suggests in his *Anthony Trollope: A Commentary*, that Trollope had difficulty reconciling those literary works he considered good with what he thought the public would accept. At all events, the failure of *Saint Pauls* not-withstanding, the stories of his own that its editor published there are among his very best. Rarely in his other stories and nov-els do we get such a revealing and intimate look at Trollope as we do in these stories from *Saint Pauls;* for seldom did he write with more feeling about the *cacoethes scribendi* or the agonies of editorship than in these stories. They are in a way the culmina-tion of his experiences and observations as a literary man.

It should be noted, however, that one aspect — call it moti-vation — of the literary life receives very little attention. The stories, it is true, do not explore the impulses that make one want to be a writer. Those Trollope seems to have taken for granted, or as not so very different in most cases from his own: "Over and above the money view of the question," he says bluntly in *An Autobiography*, "I wished from the beginning to be something more than a clerk in the Post Office. To be known as somebody,

— to be Anthony Trollope if it be no more — is to me much."
But whatever may drive men (and women) to become writers,
Trollope wished to record the effect, not study the cause. As
Henry James pointed out in his *Partial Portraits:* "He had no air
of being able to tell you *why* people in a given situation would
conduct themselves in a particular way. It was enough for him
that he felt their feelings and struck the right note, because he
had, as it were, a good ear. If he was a knowing psychologist, he
was so by grace. . . ." He "struck the right note" because he never
falsified what he knew of human nature and because he saw all
the existing paradoxes of human nature with sympathetic amusement and absolute truthfulness. Writers to him were not a breed
apart; if anything, they had more than their share of human faults
and human virtues. It is the sometimes comic, sometimes tragic
battle of wits, talents (or lack of them), feelings, and ambitions
that he records in the stories he wrote for *Saint Pauls.* Moreover,
the stories, he tells us, are based in large part on experiences
which he himself had encountered: ". . . how an ingenious
gentleman got into conversation with me, I not knowing that he
knew me to be an editor, and pressed his little article on my notice; how I was addressed by a lady with a becoming pseudonym
and with much equally becoming audacity; how I was appealed
to by the dearest of little women whom here I have called Mary
Gresley; how in my own early days there was a struggle over an
abortive periodical which was intended to be the best thing ever
done; how terrible was the tragedy of a poor drunkard, who with
infinite learning at his command made one sad final effort to re-
claim himself, and perished while he was making it; and lastly
how a poor weak editor was driven nearly to madness by threatened litigation from a rejected contributor."

Among these stories, two deserve special comment: one of
them because, in it, Trollope has, consciously or unconsciously,
given us a candid and appealing look at the travails of a young
writer whom Trollope himself at the same age must have very
closely resembled; and the other because, in its grim treatment
of intellect and talent degraded, Trollope comes as close as he
ever could to "Naturalism."

The first of this pair, "The Panjandrum," appeared in the January and February, 1870, issues of *Saint Pauls.* It tells of the at-

tempts of several young people to found a magazine — *The Pan-jandrum* — which would astonish the world with its brilliance and become a leading organ of intellectual enlightenment. The young man on whom the story centers is given an allotment of pages to fill for the first issue. As the days pass and the deadline draws near, he begins to despair, for he has written nothing. He resorts to artificial means to stimulate his sluggish Muse. He locks himself in his room; he eats rare meat (which produces only indigestion); he drinks green tea; he gets up at four in the morning and tries to write. Nothing works. He counts the number of words he must write and calculates the time it would take him to fill the pages if only he had something to write. Finally, in desperation, he abandons his room and goes for a walk in the park, wandering aimlessly around and thinking of nothing but his dreadful task and the approaching deadline. Then he sees hurrying along on the path before him a well-dressed servant with her charge, a girl of ten or eleven, and hears the child say, "Oh, Anne, I do so wonder what he's like." That single incident is enough to spark his imagination. As he walks around the park he begins to create a story around the face, the voice, the question of the little girl. Soon he has built a "castle in the air" in which he himself is the unknown brother to whom the girl is rushing so eagerly. The young man reflects upon the power of the imagination: "As I made this castle for myself, as I had sat with this girl at my side . . . I had never once thought of *The Panjandrum* . . . . That very morning it had seemed impossible to get anything written. Now, as I hurried upstairs to get rid of my wet clothes, I felt I could not take the pen quickly enough in my hand, I had a thing to say, and I would say it."

The young author in the story is charmingly and touchingly like Trollope; and he echoes Trollope's own enthusiasm for the task of writing when he says, "I doubt whether any five days in my life were ever happier than those which were devoted to this piece of work." And that is about as far as Trollope's analysis of the creative process ever goes. He probed no deeper into the theory of his art than the successful practise of it required. To him writing meant having "a thing to say" and having the discipline and strength of purpose to say it. At its best this "thing" was the faithful portrayal of his fellow men — thinking, speaking, feeling, interacting; and if in some cases they happened also to be his fellow writers, the intricacies of their characters and relationships are still of far more concern to him than the intricacies of their occupation.

"The Spotted Dog," that grisly chronicle of degradation and despair, is another case in point. For though its protagonist (or, any rate, main agonist) is "so well educated, so ripe in literary acquirements that we know few whom we could call his equal," very little space is devoted to demonstrating these gifts. They are simply *données*. The man who possessed them and abused and wasted them and brought them and his life at last to naught — this man and the scarcely less impressive men (and women and children) whom he involved in his downfall are Trollope's concern. And again his focus is upon effects, not causes. What these people say and do to one another is what Trollope reports. And the result is almost a little Greek tragedy: the long-ago errors of judgment and action hardly more than hinted at, but the "fifth act" from onset to catastrophe told step by painful step relentlessly. Nor does Trollope seem to have indulged himself in this unwonted profusion of naturalistic detail for its own sake. The squalor of Liquorpond Street and Cucumber Court is as appropriate, as dramatically necessary, to the self-destruction of Julius Mackenzie as the bloody palace of Atreus to the murder of Agamemnon, Aegisthus, or Clytemnestra.

But "The Spotted Dog" is only almost a tragedy, and a concluding word needs to be said about the reason why; for it will bear upon all these stories and all the preceding discussion of them: The reason is no other than the narrator, the editor whose tales these are and who, not surprisingly, sounds a lot like Trollope himself. The question of identity is academic. Suffice it to say that they both comment upon life and art in much the same tone of voice. And that tone is not tragic. It is sometimes gloomy, sometimes harshly factual, sometimes heartrendingly sad, often — indeed pervasively — ironic; but always there is the gracious leaven of tenderness and humor even in the most trenchant irony. Ironies abound in "The Spotted Dog," for example, but are they tragic ironies? From the editor's point of view, from Trollope's point of view as editor or as artist, they are emphatically not. It is true that the editor's painstaking efforts to oblige two fellow litterateurs have led to the destruction of one and the irreparable disappointment of the other; but we are left in no doubt that both the destruction and the disappointment were inevitable and that neither represents any serious loss to the world of letters. Mackenzie's literary output, despite his massive education and his self-proclamation as a poet, has consisted exclusively of voluminous contributions to the "penny-dreadfuls" at sixpence a page. And as for those other victims of the editor's good intentions, the dear old Doctor and the precious manuscript he longs to see in print, there is this:

> "At sixty-five, sir," he said to us, "a man has no time to dally with his work." He had been dallying with his work all his life, and we sincerely believed it would be well with him if he continued to dally with it to the end.

These are not the matter nor the language of tragedy.

It may be, of course, that the editor (or Trollope) really means it when he speaks more than once of the dangers of the literary profession — its allurements of money and fame so patent, its years of toil and frustration so hidden. Certainly there are sad failures in these pages. And certainly there is compassion as well as humor in the editor's comment when one of them, in defense of her youthful ambition, reminds him of the early success of Currer Bell: "The injury which Currer Bell did after this fashion," he says to the reader but not to Mary Gresley, "was almost equal to that perpetrated by Jack Sheppard." One suspects, nevertheless, that beneath the compassion here or the irony or satire elsewhere there lies a firm substratum of faith in that clear formula, a thing to say and the self-discipline to say it. Young Mary Gresley lacked the one; the old Doctor lacked the other, or perhaps both. How many other aspirants have been measured against this Trollopian standard and been found wanting?

The Turkish Bath

I T WAS IN THE MONTH OF AUGUST. The world had gone to the moors and the Rhine, but we were still kept in town by the exigencies of our position. We had been worked hard during the preceding year and were not quite as well as our best friends might have wished us; — and we resolved upon taking a Turkish bath. This little story records the experience of one individual man; but our readers, we hope, will, without a grudge, allow us the use of the editorial we. We doubt whether the story could be told at all in any other form. We resolved upon taking a Turkish bath, and at about three o'clock in the day we strutted from the outer to the inner room of the establishment in that light costume and with that air of Arabic dignity which are peculiar to the place.

As everybody has not taken a Turkish bath in Jermyn Street, we will give the shortest possible description of the position. We had entered of course in the usual way, leaving our hat and our boots and our "valuables" among the numerous respectable assistants who throng the approaches; and as we had entered we had observed a stout, middle-aged gentleman on the other side of the street, clad in vestments somewhat the worse for wear, and to our eyes particularly noticeable by reason of the tattered condition of his gloves. A well-to-do man may have no gloves, or may simply carry in his hands those which appertain to him rather as a thing of custom than for any use for which he requires them. But a tattered glove, worn on the hand, is to our eyes the surest sign of a futile attempt at outer respectability. It is melancholy to us beyond expression. Our brother editors, we do not doubt, are acquainted with the tattered glove, and have known the sadness which it produces. If there be an editor whose heart has not been softened by the feminine tattered glove, that editor is not our brother. In this instance the tattered glove was worn by a man; and though the usual indication of poor circumstances was conveyed, there was nevertheless something jaunty in the gentleman's step which preserved him from the desecration of pity. We barely saw him, but still were thinking of him as we passed into the building with the oriental letters on it, and took off our boots, and pulled out our watch and purse.

We were of course accommodated with two checked towels; and, having in vain attempted to show that we were to the manner born by fastening the larger of them satisfactorily round our own otherwise naked person, had obtained the assistance of one of those very skilful eastern boys who glide about the place and create envy by their familiarity with its mysteries. With an absence of all bashfulness which soon grows upon one, we had divested ourselves of our ordinary trappings beneath the gaze of five or six young men lying on surrounding sofas, — among whom we recognised young Walker of the Treasury, and hereby testify on his behalf that he looks almost as fine a fellow without his clothes as he does with them, — and had strutted through the doorway into the bath-room, trailing our second towel behind us. Having observed the matter closely in the course of perhaps half-a-dozen visits, we are prepared to recommend that mode of entry to our young friends as being at the same time easy and oriental. There are those who wear the second towel as a shawl, thereby no doubt achieving a certain decency of garb; but this is done to the utter loss of all dignity; and a feminine appearance is produced, — such as is sometimes that of a lady of fifty looking after her maid servants at seven o'clock in the morning and intending to dress again before breakfast. And some there are who carry it under the arm, — simply as a towel; but these are they who, from English perversity, wilfully rob the institution of that picturesque orientalism which should be its greatest charm. A few are able to wear the article as a turban, and that no doubt should be done by all who are competent to achieve the position. We have observed that men who can do so enter the bath-room with an air and are received there with a respect which no other arrangement of the towel will produce. We have tried this; but as the turban gets over our eyes, and then falls altogether off our brow, we have abandoned it. In regard to personal deportment, depending partly on the step, somewhat on the eye, but chiefly on the costume, it must be acknowledged that "the attempt and not the deed confounds us." It is not every man who can carry a blue towel as a turban, and look like an Arab in the streets of Cairo, as he walks slowly down the room in Jermyn Street with his arms crossed on his naked breast. The attempt and not the deed does confound one shockingly. We, therefore, recommend that the second towel should be trailed. The effect is good, and there is no difficulty in the trailing which may not be overcome.

We had trailed our way into the bath-room, and had slowly walked to one of those arm-chairs in which it is our custom on such occasions to seat ourselves, and to await sudation. There are marble couches; and if a man is able to lie on stone for half-an-hour without a movement beyond that of clapping his hands, or a sound beyond a hollow-voiced demand for water, the effect is not bad. But he loses everything if he tosses himself uneasily on his hard couch, and we acknowledge that our own elbows are always in the way of our own comfort, and that our bones become sore. We think that the marble sofas must be intended for the younger Turks. If a man can stretch himself on stone without suffering for the best part of an hour, — or, more bravely perhaps, without appearing to suffer, let him remember that all is not done even then. Very much will depend on the manner in which he claps his hands, and the hollowness of the voice in which he calls for water. There should, we think, be two blows of the palms. One is very weak, and proclaims its own futility. Even to dull London ears it seems at once to want the eastern tone. We have heard three given effectively, but we think that it requires much practice; and even when it is perfect, the result is that of western impatience rather than of eastern gravity. No word should be pronounced, beyond that one word, — Water. The effect should be as though the whole mind were so devoted to the sudorific process as to admit of no extraneous idea. There should seem to

3

be almost an agony in the effort, — as though the man enduring it, conscious that with success he would come forth a god, was aware that being as yet but mortal he may perish in the attempt. Two claps of the hand and a call for water, and that repeated with an interval of ten minutes, are all the external signs of life that the young Turkish bather may allow to himself while he is stretched upon his marble couch.

We had taken a chair, — well aware that nothing god-like could be thus achieved, and contented to obtain the larger amount of human comfort. The chairs are placed two and two, and a custom has grown up, — of which we scarcely think that the origin has been eastern, — in accordance with which friends occupying these chairs will spend their time in conversation. The true devotee to the Turkish baths will, we think, never speak at all; but when the speaking is low in tone, just something between a whisper and an articulate sound, the slight murmuring hum produced is not disagreeable. We cannot quite make up our mind whether this use of the human voice be or be not oriental; but we think that it adds to the mystery, and upon the whole it gratifies. Let it be understood, however, that harsh, resonant, clearly-expressed speech is damnable. The man who talks aloud to his friend about the trivial affairs of life is selfish, ignorant, unpoetical, — and English in the very worst sense of the word. Who but an ass proud of his own capacity for braying would venture to dispel the illusions of a score of bathers, by observing aloud that the House sat till three o'clock that morning?

But though friends may talk in low voices, a man without a friend will hardly fall into conversation at the Turkish Bath. It is said that our countrymen are unapt to speak to each other without introduction, and this inaptitude is certainly not decreased by the fact that two men meet each other with nothing on but a towel apiece. Finding yourself next to a man in such a garb, you hardly know where to begin. And then there lies upon you the weight of that necessity of maintaining a certain dignity of deportment which has undoubtedly grown upon you since you succeeded in freeing yourself from your socks and trousers. For ourselves, we have to admit that the difficulty is much increased by the fact that we are short-sighted, and are obligated by the sudorific processes and by the shampooing and washing that are to come, to leave our spectacles behind us. The delicious wonder of the place is no doubt increased to us, but our incapability of discerning aught of those around us in that low gloomy light is complete. Jones from Friday Street, or even Walker from the Treasury, are the same to us as one of those Asiatic slaves who administer to our comfort, and flit about the place with admirable decorum and self-respect. On this occasion we had barely seated ourselves, when another bather, with slow, majestic step, came to the other chair; and, with a manner admirably adapted to the place, stretching out his naked legs, and throwing back his naked shoulders, seated himself beside us. We are much given to speculations on the characters and probable circumstances of those with whom we are brought in contact. Our editorial duties require that it should be so. How should we cater for the public did we not observe the public in all its moods? We thought that we could see at once that this was no ordinary man, and we may as well aver here, at the beginning of our story, that subsequent circumstances proved our first conceptions to be correct. The absolute features of the gentleman we did not, indeed, see plainly. The gloom of the place and our own deficiency of sight forbade it. But we could discern the thorough man of the world, the traveller who had seen many climes, the cosmopolitan to whom East and West were alike, in every motion that he made. We confess that we were anxious for conversation, and that we struggled within ourselves for an apt subject, thinking how we might begin. But the apt subject did not occur to us, and we should have passed that half hour of repose in silence had not our companion been more ready than ourselves. "Sir," said he, turning round in his seat with a peculiar and captivating grace, "I shall not, I hope, offend or transgress any rule of politeness by speaking to a stranger." There was ease and dignity in his manner, and at the same time some slight touch of humour which was very charming. I thought that I detected just a hint of an Irish accent in his tone; but if so the dear brogue of his country, which is always delightful to me, had been so nearly banished by intercourse with other tongues as to leave the matter still a suspicion, — a suspicion, or rather a hope

"By no means," we answered, turning round on our left shoulder, but missing the grace with which he had made his movement.

"There is nothing," said he, "to my mind so absurd as that two men should be seated together for an hour without venturing to open their mouths because they do not know each other. And what matter does it make whether a man has his breeches on or is without them?"

My hope had now become an assurance. As he named the article of clothing which peculiarly denotes a man he gave a picturesque emphasis to the word which was certainly Hibernian. Who does not know the dear sound? And, as a chance companion for a few idle minutes, is there any one so likely to prove himself agreeable as a well-informed, travelled Irishman?

"And yet," said we, "men do depend much on their outward paraphernalia."

"Indeed and they do," said our friend. "And why? Because they can trust their tailors when they can't trust themselves. Give me the man who can make a speech without any of the accessories of the pulpit, who can preach what sermon there is in him without a pulpit." His words were energetic, but his voice was just suited to the place. Had he spoken aloud, so that others might have heard him, we should have left our chair, and have retreated to one of the inner and hotter rooms at the moment. His words were perfectly audible, but he spoke in a fitting whisper. "It is a part of my creed," he continued, "that we should never lose even a quarter of an hour. What a strange mass of human beings one finds in this city of London!"

"A mighty mass, but not without a plan," we replied.

"Bedad, — and it's hard enough to find the plan," said he. It struck me that after that he rose into a somewhat higher flight of speech, as though he had remembered and was desirous of dropping his country. It is the customary and perhaps the only fault of an Irishman. "Whether it be there or not, we can expatiate free, as the poet says. How unintelligible is London! New York or Constantinople one can understand, — or even Paris. One knows what the world is doing in these cities, and what men desire."

"What men desire is nearly the same in all cities," we remarked, — and not without truth, as we think.

"Is it money you mane?" he said, again relapsing. "Yes; money, no doubt, is the grand desideratum, — the 'to prepon,' the 'to kalon,' the 'to pan!' " Plato and Pope were evidently at his fingers' ends. We did not conclude from this slight evidence that he was thoroughly imbued with the works either of the poet or the philosopher; but we hold that for the ordinary purposes of conversation a superficial knowledge of many things goes further than an intimacy with one or two. "Money," continued he, "is everything, no doubt; rem, — rem; rem, si possis recte, si non —; you know the rest. I don't complain of that. I like money myself. I know its value. I've had it, and, — I'm not ashamed to say it, sir, — I've been without it."

"Our sympathies are completely with you in reference to the latter position," we said, — remembering, with a humility which we hope is natural to us, that we were not always editors.

"What I complain of is," said our new friend still whispering, as he passed his hand over his arms and legs, to learn whether the temperature of the room was producing its proper effect, "that if a man here in London have a diamond, or a pair of boots, or any special skill at his command, he cannot take his article to the proper mart, and obtain for it the proper price."

"Can he do that in Constantinople?" we inquired.

"Much better and more accurately than he can in London. And so he can in Paris!" We did not believe this; but as we were thinking after what fashion we would express our doubts, he branched off so quickly to a matter of supply and demand with which we were specially interested, that we lost the opportunity of arguing the general question. "A man of letters," he said, "a capable and an instructed man of letters, can always get a market for his wares in Paris."

"A capable and instructed man of letters will do so in London," we said, "as soon as he proved his claims. He must prove them in Paris before they can be allowed."

"Yes; — he must prove them. By-the-bye, will you have a cheroot?" So saying, he stretched out his hand, and took from the marble slab beside him two cheroots, which he had placed there. He then proceeded to explain that he did not bring in his case because of the heat, but that he was always "muni," — that was his phrase, — with a couple, in the hope that he might meet an acquaintance with whom to share them. I accepted his offer, and when we had walked round the chamber to a light provided for the purpose, we reseated ourselves. His manner of moving about the place was so good that I felt it to be a pity that he should ever have on a rag more than he wore at present. His tobacco, I must own, did not appear to me to be of the first class; but then I am not in the habit of smoking cheroots, and am no judge of the merits of the weed as grown in the East. "Yes; — a man in Paris must prove his capability; but then how easily he can do it, if the fact to be proved be there! And how certain is the mart, if he have the thing to sell!"

We immediately denied that in this respect there was any difference between the two capitals, pointing out what we believe to be a fact, — that in one capital as in the other, there exists, and must ever exist, extreme difficulty in proving the possession of an art so difficult to define as capability of writing for the press. "Nothing but success can prove it," we said, as we slapped our thigh with an energy altogether unbecoming our position as a Turkish bather.

"A man may have a talent then, and he cannot use it till he have used it! He may possess a diamond, and cannot sell it till he have it! What is a man to do who wishes to engage himself in any of the multifarious duties of the English press? How is he to begin? In New York I can tell such a one where to go at once. Let him show in conversation that he is an educated man, and they will give him a trial on the staff of any newspaper; — they will let him run his venture for the pages of any magazine. He may write his fingers off here, and not an editor of them all will read a word that he writes."

Here he touched us, and we were indignant. When he spoke of the magazines we knew that he was wrong. "With newspapers," we said, "we imagine it to be impossible that contributors should from the outside world be looked at; but papers sent to the magazines, — at any rate to some of them, — are read."

"I believe," said he, "that a little farce is kept up. They keep a boy to look at a line or two and then return the manuscript. The pages are filled by the old stock-writers, who are sure of the market let them send what they will, — padding-mongers who work eight hours a day and hardly know what they write about." We again loudly expressed our opinion that he was wrong, and that there did exist magazines, the managers of which were sedulously anxious to obtain the assistance of what he called literary capacity, wherever they could find it. Sitting there at the Turkish bath with nothing but a towel round us, we could not declare ourselves to a perfect stranger, and we think that as a rule editors should be impalpable; — but we did express our opinion very strongly.

"And you believe," said he, with something of scorn in his voice, "that if a man who had been writing English for the press in other countries, — in New York say, or in Doblin, — a man of undoubted capacity, mind you, were to make the attempt here, in London, he would get a hearing."

"Certainly he would," said we.

"And would any editor see him unless he came with an introduction from some special friend?"

We paused a moment before we answered this, because the question was to us one having a very special meaning. Let an editor do his duty with ever so pure a conscience, let him spend all his days and half his nights reading manuscripts and holding the balance fairly between the public and those who wish to feed the public, let his industry be never so unwearied and his impartiality never so unflinching, still he will, if possible, avoid the pain of personally repelling those to whom he is obliged to give an unfavourable answer. But we at the Turkish Bath were quite impalpable to the outer world, and might hazard an opinion, as any stranger might have done. And we have seen very many such visitors as those to whom our friend alluded; and may, perhaps, see many more.

"Yes," said we. "An editor might or might not see such a gentleman; but, if pressed, no doubt he would. An English editor would be quite as likely to do so as a French editor." This we declared with energy, having felt ourselves to be ruffled by the assertion that these things are managed better in Paris or in New York than in London.

"Then, Mr. _____, would you give me an interview, if I call with a little manuscript which I have to-morrow morning?" said my Irish friend, addressing us with a beseeching tone, and calling us by the very name by which we are known among our neighbours and tradesmen. We felt that everything was changed between us, and that the man had plunged a dagger into us.

Yes; he had plunged a dagger into us. Had we had our clothes on, had we felt ourselves to possess at the moment our usual form of life, we think that we could have rebuked him. As it was we could only rise from our chair, throw away the fag end of the filthy cheroot which he had given us, and clap our hands half-a-dozen times for the Asiatic to come and shampoo us. But the Irishman was at our elbow. "You will let me see you to-morrow?" he said. "My name is Molloy, — Michael Molloy. I have not a card about me, because my things are outside there."

"A card would do no good at all," we said, again clapping our hands for the shampooer.

"I may call, then?" said Mr. Michael Molloy.

"Certainly; — yes, you can call if you please." Then, having thus ungraciously acceded to the request made to us, we sat down on the marble bench and submitted ourselves to the black attendant. During the whole of the following operation, while the man was pummelling our breast and poking our ribs, and pinching our toes, — while he was washing us down afterwards, and reducing us gradually from the warm water to the cold, —we were thinking of Mr. Michael Molloy, and the manner in which he had entrapped us into a confidential conversation. The scoundrel must have plotted it from the very first, must have followed us into the bath, and taken his seat beside us with a deliberately premeditated scheme. He was, too, just the man whom we should not have chosen to see with a worthless magazine article in his hand. We think that we can be efficacious by letter, but we often feel ourselves to be weak when brought face to face with our enemies. At that moment our anger was hot against Mr. Molloy. And yet we were conscious of a something of pride which mingled with our feelings. It was clear to us that Mr. Molloy was no ordinary person; and it did in some degree gratify our feelings that such a one should have taken so much trouble to encounter us. We had found him to be a well-informed, pleasant gentleman; and the fact that he was called Molloy and desired to write for the magazine over which we presided, could not really be taken as detracting from his merits. There had doubtless been a fraud committed on us, — a palpable fraud. The man had extracted assurances from us by a false pretence that he did not know us. But then the idea, on his part, that anything could be gained by his doing so, was in itself a compliment to us. That such a man should take so much trouble to approach us, — one who could quote Horace and talk about the "to kalon," — was an acknowledgement of our power. As we returned to the outer chamber we looked round to see Mr. Molloy in his usual garments, but he was not as yet there. We waited while we smoked one of our own cigars, but he came not. He had, so far, gained his object; and, as we presumed, preferred to run the risk of too long a course of hot air to risking his object by seeing us again on that afternoon. At last we left the building, and are bound to confess that our mind dwelt much on Mr. Michael Molloy during the remainder of that evening.

It might be that after all we should gain much by the singular mode of introduction which the man had adopted. He was certainly clever, and if he could write as well as he could talk his services might be of value. Punctually at the hour named he was announced, and we did not now for one moment think of declining the interview. Mr. Molloy had so far gained his object that we could not resort to the certainly not unusual practice of declaring ourselves to be too closely engaged to see any one, and of sending him word that he should confide to writing whatever he might have to say to us. It had, too, occurred to us that, as Mr. Molloy had paid his three shillings and sixpence for the Turkish Bath, he would not prove to be one of that class of visitors whose appeals to tender-hearted editors are so peculiarly painful. "I am willing to work day and night for my wife and children; and if you will use this short paper in your next number it will save us from starvation for a month! Yes, sir, from, — starvation!" Who is to resist such an appeal as that, or to resent it. But the editor knows that he is bound in honesty to resist it altogether, — so to steel himself against it that it shall have no effect upon him, at least, as regards the magazine which is in his hands; and yet if the short thing be only decently written, if it be not absurdly bad, what harm will its publication do to any one? If the waste, — let us call it waste, — of half-a-dozen pages will save a family from hunger for a month, will they not be well wasted? But yet, again, such tenderness is absolutely incompatible with common honesty, — and equally so with common prudence. We think that our readers will see the difficulty, and understand how an editor may wish to avoid those interviews with tattered gloves. But my friend, Mr. Michael Molloy, had had three and sixpence to spend on a Turkish Bath, had had money wherewith to buy, — certainly, the very vilest of cigars. We thought of all this as Mr. Michael Molloy was ushered into our room.

The first thing we saw was the tattered glove; and then we immediately recognised the stout middle-aged gentleman whom we had seen on the other side of Jermyn Street as we entered the bathing establishment. It had never before occurred to us that the two persons were the same, — not though the impression made by the poverty-stricken appearance of the man in the street had remained distinct upon our mind. The features of the gentleman we had hardly even yet seen at all. Nevertheless we had known and distinctly recognised his outward gait and mien, both with and without his clothes. One tattered glove he now wore, and the other he carried in his gloved hand. As we saw this we were aware at once that all our preconception had been wrong, that too common appeal would be made, and that we must resist it as best we might.

There was still a certain jauntiness in his air as he addressed us. "I hope thin," said he as we shook hands with him, "ye'll not take amiss the little ruse by which we caught ye."

"It was a ruse then, Mr. Molloy."

"Divil a doubt o' that, Mr. Editor."

"But you were coming to the Turkish Bath independently of our visit there?"

"Sorrow a bath I'd 've cum to at all, only I saw you go into the place. I'd just five and ninepence in my pocket, and says I to myself, Mick, me boy, it's a good investment. There was three and sixpence for them savages to rub me down, and threepence for the two cheroots from the little shop round the corner. I wish they'd been better for your sake."

It had been a plant from beginning to end, and the "to kalon" and the half-dozen words from Horace had all been parts of Mr. Molloy's little game! And how well he had played it! The outward trappings of the man as we now saw them were poor and mean, and he was mean-looking too, because of his trappings. But there had been nothing mean about him as he strutted along with a blue-checked towel round his body. How well the fellow had understood it all, and had known his own capacity! "And now that you are here, Mr. Molloy, what can we do for you?" we said with as pleasant a smile as we were able to assume. Of course we knew what was to follow. Out came the roll of paper of which we had already seen the end projecting from his breast pocket, and we were assured that we should find the contents of it exactly the thing for our magazine. There is no longer any diffidence in such matters, — no reticence in preferring claims and singing one's own praises. All that has gone by since competitive ex-amination has become the order of the day. No man, no woman, no girl, no boy, hesitates now to declare his or her own excel-lence and capability. "It's just a short thing on social manners," said Mr. Molloy, "and if ye'll be so good as to cast ye'r eye over it, I think ye'll find I've hit the nail on the head. 'The Five o'clock Tay-table,' is what I've called it."

"Oh; — the five o-clock tea-table."

"Don't ye like the name?"

"About social manners, is it?"

"Just a rap on the knuckles for some of them. Sharp, short, and decisive! I don't doubt but what ye'll like it."

To declare, as though by instinct, that that was not the kind of thing we wanted, was as much a matter of course as it is for a man buying a horse to say that he does not like the brute's legs or that he falls away in his quarters. And Mr. Molloy treated our objection just as does the horse-dealer those of his customers. He assured us with a smile, — with a smile behind which we could see the craving eagerness of his heart, — that his little article was just the thing for us. Our immediate answer was of course ready. If he would leave the paper with us, we would look at it and re-turn it if it did not seem to suit us. There is a half promise about this reply which too often produces a false satisfaction in the breast of a beginner. With such a one it is the second interview which is to be dreaded. But my friend Mr. Molloy was not new to the work, and was aware that if possible he should make fur-ther use of the occasion which he had earned for himself at so considerable a cost. "Ye'll read it; — will ye?" he said.

"Oh, certainly. We'll read it certainly."

"And ye'll use it if ye can?"

"As to that, Mr. Molloy, we can say nothing. We've got to

look solely to the interest of the periodical."

"And, sure, what can ye do better for the periodical than print a paper like that, which there is not a lady at the West End of the town won't be certain to read?"

"At any rate we'll look at it, Mr. Molloy," said we, standing up from our chair.

But still he hesitated in his going, — and did not go. "I'm a married man, Mr. _____," he said. We simply bowed our head at the announcement. "I wish you could see Mrs. Molloy," he added. We muttered something as to the pleasure it would give us to make the acquaintance of so estimable a lady. "There isn't a better woman than herself this side of heaven, though I say it that oughtn't," said he. "And we've three young ones." We knew the argument that was coming; — knew it so well, and yet were so unable to accept it as any argument! "Sit down one moment, Mr._____ ," he continued, "till I tell you a short story." We pleaded our engagements, averring that they were peculiarly heavy at that moment. "Sure, and we know what that manes," said Mr. Molloy. "It's just, — walk out of this as quick as you came in. It's that what it manes." And yet as he spoke there was a twinkle of humour in his eye that was almost irresistible; and we ourselves, — we could not forbear to smile. When we smiled we knew that we were lost. "Come, now, Mr. Editor; when you think how much it cost me to get the introduction, you'll listen to me for five minutes any way."

"We will listen to you," we said, resuming our chair, — remembering as we did so the three-and-sixpence, the two cigars, the "to kalon," the line from Pope, and the half line from Horace. The man had taken much trouble with the view of placing himself where he now was. When we had been all but naked together I had taken him to be the superior of the two, and what were we that we should refuse him an interview simply because he had wares to sell which we should only be too willing to buy at his price if they were fit for our use?

Then he told his tale. As for Paris, Constantinople, and New York, he frankly admitted that he knew nothing of those capitals. When we reminded him, with some ill-nature as we thought afterwards, that he had assumed an intimacy with the current literature of the three cities, he told us that such remarks were "just

14

the sparkling gims of conversation in which a man shouldn't expect to find rale diamonds." Of "Doblin" he knew every street,
every lane, every newspaper, every editor; but the poverty, dependence, and general poorness of a provincial press had crushed
him, and he had boldly resolved to try a fight in the "methropolis
of litherature." He referred us to the managers of the "Boyne
Bouncer," the "Clontarf Chronicle," the "Donnybrook Debater,"
and the "Echoes of Erin," assuring us that we should find him to
be as well esteemed as known in the offices of those widely-
circulated publications. His reading he told us was unbounded,
and the pen was as ready to his hand as is the plough to the hand
of the husbandman. Did we not think it a noble ambition in him
thus to throw himself into the great "areanay" as he called it, and
try his fortune in the "methropolis of litherature?" He paused for
a reply, and we were driven to acknowledge that whatever might
be said of our friend's prudence, his courage was undoubted. "I've
got it here," said he. "I've got it all here." And he touched his
right breast with the fingers of his left hand, which still wore the
tattered glove.

He had succeeded in moving us. "Mr. Molloy," we said, "we'll
read your paper, and we'll then do the best we can for you. We
must tell you fairly that we hardly like your subject, but if the
writing be good you can try your hand at something else."

"Sure there's nothing under the sun I won't write upon at your
bidding."

"If we can be of service to you, Mr. Molloy, we will." Then the
editor broke down, and the man spoke to the man. "I need not
tell you, Mr. Molloy, that the heart of one man of letters always
warms to another."

"It was because I knew ye was of that sort that I followed ye in
yonder," he said, with a tear in his eye.

The butter-boat of benevolence was in our hand, and we proceeded to pour out its contents freely. It is a vessel which an editor should lock up carefully; and, should he lose the key, he will
not be the worse for the loss. We need not repeat here all the
pretty things that we said to him, explaining to him from a full
heart with how much agony we were often compelled to resist the
entreaties of literary suppliants, declaring to him how we had
longed to publish tons of manuscript, — simply in order that we

might give pleasure to those who brought them to us. We told him how accessible we were to a woman's tear, to a man's struggle, to a girl's face, and assured him of the daily wounds which were inflicted on ourselves by the impossibility of reconciling our duties with our sympathies. "Bedad, thin," said Mr. Molloy, grasping our hand, "you'll find none of that difficulty wid me. If you'll sympathise like a man, I'll work for you like a horse." We assured him that we would, really thinking it probable that he might do some useful work for the magazine; and then we again stood up waiting for his departure.

"Now I'll tell ye a plain truth," said he, "and ye may do just as ye plaise about it. There isn't an ounce of tay or a pound of mait along with Mrs. Molloy this moment; and, what's more, there isn't a shilling between us to buy it. I never begged in my life; — not yet. But if you can advance me a sovereign on that manuscript, it will save me from taking the coat on my back to a pawnbroker's shop for whatever it'll fetch there." We paused a moment as we thought of it all, and then we handed him the coin for which he asked us. If the manuscript should be worthless the loss would be our own. We would not grudge a slice from the wholesome home-made loaf after we had used the butter-boat of benevolence. "It don't become me," said Mr. Molloy, "to thank you for such a thrifle as a loan of twenty shillings; but I'll never forget the feeling that has made you listen to me, and that too after I had been down on you rather at thim baths." We gave him a kindly nod of the head, and then he took his departure. "Ye'll see me again anyways?" he said, and we promised that we would.

We were anxious enough about the manuscript, but we could not examine it at that moment. When our office work was done we walked home with the roll in our pocket, speculating as we went on the probable character of Mr. Molloy. We still believed in him, — still believed in him in spite of the manner in which he had descended in his language, and had fallen into a natural flow of words which alone would not have given much promise of him as a man of letters. But a human being, in regard to his power of production, is the reverse of a rope. He is as strong as his strongest part, and, remembering the effect which Molloy's words had had upon us at the Turkish Bath, we still thought that there must be something in him. If so, how pleasant would it be to us to place such a man on his legs, — modestly on his legs, so that he might earn for his wife and bairns that meat and tea which he had told us that they were now lacking. An editor is always striving to place some one modestly on his legs in literature, — on his or her, — striving, and alas! so often failing. Here had come a man in regard to whom, as I walked home with his manuscript in my pocket, I did feel rather sanguine.

Of all the rubbish that I ever read in my life, that paper on the Five o-clock Tea-table was, I think, the worst. It was not only vulgar, foolish, unconnected, and meaningless; but it was also ungrammatical and unintelligible even in regard to the wording of it. The very spelling was defective. The paper was one with which no editor, sub-editor, or reader would have found it necessary to go beyond the first ten lines before he would have known that to print it would have been quite out of the question. We went through with it because of our interest in the man; but as it was in the beginning, so it was to the end, — a farrago of wretched nonsense, so bad that no one, without experience in such matters, would believe it possible that even the writer should desire the publication of it! It seemed to us to be impossible that Mr. Molloy should ever have written a word for those Hibernian periodicals which he had named to us. He had got our sovereign; and with that, as far as we were concerned, there must be an end of Mr. Molloy. We doubted even whether he would come for his own manuscript.

But he came. He came exactly at the hour appointed, and when we looked at his face we felt convinced that he did not doubt his own success. There was an air of expectant triumph about him which dismayed us. It was clear enough that he was confident that he should take away with him the full price of his article, after deducting the sovereign which he had borrowed. "You like it thin," he said, before we had been able to compose our features to a proper form for the necessary announcement.

"Mr. Molloy," we said, "it will not do. You must believe us that it will not do."

"Not do?"

"No, indeed. We need not explain further; — but, — but, — you had really better turn your hand to some other occupation."

"Some other occupation!" he exclaimed, opening wide his

eyes, and holding up both his hands.

"Indeed we think so, Mr. Molloy."

"And you've read it?"

"Every word of it; — on our honour."

"And you won't have it?"

"Well; — no, Mr. Molloy, certainly we cannot take it."

"Ye reject my article on the Five o'clock Tay-table!" Looking into his face as he spoke, we could not but be certain that its rejection was to him as astonishing as would have been its acceptance to the readers of the magazine. He put his hand up to his head and stood wondering. "I suppose ye'd better choose your own subject for yourself," he said, as though by this great surrender on his own part he was getting rid of all the difficulty on ours.

"Mr. Molloy," we began, "we may as well be candid with you —"

"I'll tell you what it is," said he, "I've taken such a liking to you there's nothing I won't do to plaise ye. I'll just put it in my pocket, and begin another for ye as soon as the children have had their bit of dinner." At last we did succeed, or thought that we succeeded, in making him understand that we regarded the case as being altogether hopeless, and were convinced that it was beyond his powers to serve us. "And I'm to be turned off like that," he said, bursting into open tears as he threw himself into a chair and hid his face upon the table. "Ah! wirra, wirra, what'll I do at all! Sure, and didn't I think it was fixed as firm between us as the Nelson monument! When ye hanselled me with the money, didn't I think it was as good as done and done?" I begged him not to regard the money, assuring him that he was welcome to the sovereign. "There's my wife'll be brought to bed any day," he went on to say, "and not a ha'porth of anything ready for it! "Deed, thin, and the world's hard. The world's very hard!" And this was he who had talked to me about Constantinople and New York at the Baths, and had made me believe that he was a well-informed, well-to-do man of the world!

Even now we did not suspect that he was lying to us. Why he should be such as he seemed to be was a mystery; but even yet we believed in him after a fashion. That he was sorely disappointed and broken-hearted because of his wife, was so evident to us, that we offered him another sovereign, regarding it as the proper price of that butter-boat of benevolence which we had permitted ourselves to use. But he repudiated our offer. "I've never begged," said he, "and, for myself, I'd sooner starve. And Mary Jane would sooner starve than I should beg. It will be best for us both to put an end to ourselves and to have done with it." This was very melancholy; and as he lay with his head upon the table, we did not see how we were to induce him to leave us.

"You'd better take the sovereign, — just for the present," we said.

"Niver!" said he, looking up for a moment, "niver!" And still he continued to sob. About this period of the interview, which before it was ended was a very long interview, we ourselves made a suggestion the imprudence of which we afterwards acknowledged to ourselves. We offered to go to his lodgings and see his wife and children. Though the man could not write a good magazine article, yet he might be a very fitting object for our own personal kindness. And the more we saw of the man, the more we liked him, — in spite of his incapacity. "The place is so poor," he said, objecting to our offer. After what had passed between us, we felt that that could be no reason against our visit, and we began for a moment to fear that he was deceiving us. "Not yet," he cried, "not quite yet. I will try once again; — once again. You will let me see you once more?"

"And you will take the other sovereign," we said, — trying him. He should have had the other sovereign if he would have taken it; but we confess that had he done so then we should have regarded him as an impostor. But he did not take it, and left us in utter ignorance as to his true character.

After an interval of three days he came again, and there was exactly the same appearance. He wore the same tattered gloves. He had not pawned his coat. There was the same hat, — shabby when observed closely, but still carrying a decent appearance when not minutely examined. In his face there was no sign of want, and at moments there was a cheeriness about him which was almost refreshing. "I've got a something this time that I think ye must like, — unless you're harder to plaise then Rhadhamanthus." So saying he tendered me another roll of paper, which I at once opened intending to read the first page of it. The essay was entitled the "Church of England; — a Question for the

People." It was handed to me as having been written within the last three days; and, from its bulk, might have afforded fair work for a fortnight to a writer accustomed to treat of subjects of such weight. As we had expected, the first page was unintelligible, absurd, and farcical. We began to be angry with ourselves for having placed ourselves in such a connection with a man so utterly unable to do that which he pretended to do. "I think I've hit it off now," said he watching our face as we were reading.

The reader need not be troubled with a minute narrative of the circumstances as they occurred during the remainder of the interview. What had happened before was repeated very closely. He wondered, he remonstrated, he complained, and he wept. He talked of his wife and family, and talked as though up to this last moment he had felt confident of success. Judging from his face as he entered the room we did not doubt but that he had been confident. His subsequent despair was unbounded, and we then renewed our offer to call on his wife. After some hesitation he gave us an address in Hoxton, begging us to come after seven in the evening if it were possible. He again declined the offer of money, and left us, understanding that we would visit his wife on the following evening. "You are quite sure about the manuscript," he said as he left us. We replied that we were quite sure.

On the following day we dined early at our club and walked in the evening to the address which Mr. Molloy had given us in Hoxton. It was a fine evening in August, and our walk made us very warm. The street named was a decent little street, decent as far as cleanliness and newness could make it; but there was a melancholy sameness about it, and an apparent absence of object which would have been very depressing to our own spirits. It led no whither, and had been erected solely with the view of accommodating decent people with small incomes. We at once priced the houses in our mind at ten and sixpence a week, and believed them to be inhabited by piano-forte tuners, coach-builders, firemen, and public-office messengers. There was no squalor about the place, but it was melancholy, light-coloured, and depressive. We made our way to No. 14, and finding the door open entered the passage. "Come in," cried the voice of our friend; and in the little front parlour we found him seated with a child on each knee, while a winning little girl of about twelve was sitting in a

corner of the room, mending her stockings. The room itself and
the appearance of all around us were the very opposite of what
we had expected. Everything no doubt was plain, — was, in a
certain sense, poor; but nothing was poverty-stricken. The children were decently clothed, and apparently were well fed. Mr.
Molloy himself, when he saw me, had that twinkle of humour in
his eye which I had before observed, and seemed to be afflicted
at the moment with none of that extreme agony which he had
exhibited more than once in our presence. "Please, sir, mother
ain't in from the hospital, — not yet," said the little girl rising up
from her chair; "but it's past seven and she won't be long." This
announcement created some surprise. We had indeed heard that
of Mrs. Molloy which might make it very expedient that she
should seek the accommodation of an hospital, but we could not
understand that in such circumstances she should be able to come
home regularly at seven o'clock in the evening. Then there was
a twinkle in our friend Molloy's eye which almost made us think
for the moment that we had been made the subject of some, hitherto unintelligible, hoax. And yet there had been the man at the
Baths in Jermyn Street, and the two manuscripts had been in our
hands, and the man had wept as no man weeps for a joke. "You
would come, you know," said Mr. Molloy, who had now put
down the two bairns and had risen from his seat to greet us.

"We are glad to see you so comfortable," we replied.

"Father is quite comfortable, sir," said the little girl. We looked
into Mr. Molloy's face and saw nothing but the twinkle in the
eye. We had certainly been "done" by the most elaborate hoax
that had ever been perpetrated. We did not regret the sovereign
so much as those outpourings from the butter-boat of benevolence of which we felt that we had been cheated. "Here's
mother," said the girl running to the door. Mr. Molloy stood grin-
ning in the middle of the room with the youngest child again in
his arms. He did not seem to be in the least ashamed of what he
had done, and even at that moment conveyed to us more of liking for his affection for the little boy than of anger for the abominable prank that he had played us.

That he had lied throughout was evident as soon as we saw
Mrs. Molloy. Whatever ailment might have made it necessary
that she should visit the hospital, it was not one which could in-

terfere at all with her power of going and returning. She was a strong, hearty-looking woman of about forty, with that mixture in her face of practical kindness with severity in details which we often see in strong-minded women who are forced to take upon themselves the management and government of those around them. She curtseyed, and took off her bonnet and shawl, and put a bottle into a cupboard, as she addressed us. "Mick said as you was coming, sir, and I'm sure we is glad to see you; — only sorry for the trouble, sir."

We were so completely in the dark that we hardly knew how to be civil to her, — hardly knew whether we ought to be civil to her or not. "We don't quite understand why we've been brought here," we said, endeavouring to maintain, at any rate, a tone of good-humour. He was still embracing the little boy, but there had now come a gleam of fun across his whole countenance, and he seemed to be almost shaking his sides with laughter. "Your husband represented himself as being in distress," we said gravely. We were restrained by a certain delicacy from informing the woman of the kind of distress to which Mr. Molloy had especially alluded, — most falsely.

"Lord love you, sir," said the woman, "just step in here." Then she led us into a little back-room in which there were a bedstead, and an old writing-desk, or escritoire, covered with papers. Her story was soon told. Her husband was a madman.

"Mad!" we said, preparing for escape from what might be to us most serious peril.

"He wouldn't hurt a mouse," said Mrs. Molloy. "As for the children, he's that good to them, there ain't a young woman in all London that'd be better at handling 'em." Then we heard her story, in which it appeared to us that downright affection for the man was the predominant characteristic. She herself was, as she told us, head day-nurse at Saint Patrick's Hospital, going there every morning at eight, and remaining till six or seven. For these services she received thirty shillings a week and her board, and she spoke of herself and her husband as being altogether removed from pecuniary distress. Indeed, while the money part of the question was being discussed, she opened a little drawer in the desk and handed us back our sovereign, — almost without an observation. Molloy himself had "come of decent people." On this point she insisted very often, and gave us to understand that he was at this moment in receipt of a pension of a hundred a year from his family. He had been well educated, she said, having been at Trinity College, Dublin, till he had been forced to leave his university for some slight, but repeated irregularity. Early in life he had proclaimed his passion for the press, and when he and she were married absolutely was earning a living in Dublin by some use of the scissors and paste-pot. The whole tenor of his career I could not learn, though Mrs. Molloy would have told us everything had time allowed. Even during the years of his sanity in Dublin he had only been half-sane, treating all the world around him with the effusions of his terribly fertile pen. "He'll write all night if I'll let him have a candle," said Mrs. Molloy. We asked her why she did let him have a candle, and made some inquiry as to the family expenditure in paper. The paper, she said, was given to him from the office of a newspaper which she would not name, and which Molloy visited regularly every day. "There ain't a man in all London works harder," said Mrs. Molloy. "He is mad, I don't say nothing against it. But there is some of it so beautiful, I wonder they don't print it." This was the only word she spoke with which we could not agree. "Ah, sir," said she; "you haven't seen his poetry!" We were obliged to tell her that seeing poetry was the bane of our existence.

There was an easy absence of sham about this woman, and an acceptance of life as it had come to her, which delighted us. She complained of nothing, and was only anxious to explain the little eccentricities of her husband. When we alluded to some of his marvellously untrue assertions, she stopped us at once. "He do lie," she said. "Certainly he do. How he makes 'em all out is wonderful. But he wouldn't hurt a fly." It was evident to us that she not only loved her husband, but admired him. She showed us heaps of manuscript with which the old drawers were crammed; and yet that paper on the Church of England had been new work, done expressly for us.

When the story had been told we went back to him, and he received us with a smile. "Good-bye, Molloy," we said. "Good-bye to you, sir," he replied, shaking hands with us. We looked at him closely, and could hardly believe that it was the man who had sat by us at the Turkish Bath.

He never troubled us again or came to our office, but we have often called on him, and have found that others of our class do the same. We have even helped to supply him with the paper which he continues to use, — we presume for the benefit of other editors.

"The Turkish Bath" appeared first in the October issue of *Saint Pauls Magazine* for 1869.

Mary Gresley

W E HAVE KNOWN MANY PRETTIER girls than Mary Gresley, and many handsomer women, — but we never knew girl or woman gifted with a face which in supplication was more suasive, in grief more sad, in mirth more merry. It was a face that compelled sympathy, and it did so with the conviction on the mind of the sympathiser that the girl was altogether unconscious of her own power. In her intercourse with us there was, alas! much more of sorrow than of mirth, and we may truly say that in her sufferings we suffered; but still there came to us from our intercourse with her much of delight mingled with the sorrow; and that delight arose, partly no doubt from her woman's charms, from the bright eye, the beseeching mouth, the soft little hand, and the feminine grace of her unpretending garments; but chiefly, we think, from the extreme humanity of the girl. She had little, indeed none, of that which the world calls society, but yet she was pre-eminently social. Her troubles were very heavy, but she was making ever an unconscious effort to throw them aside, and to be jocund in spite of their weight. She would even laugh at them, and at herself as bearing them. She was a little fair-haired creature, with broad brow and small nose and dimpled chin, with no brightness of complexion, no luxuriance of hair, no swelling glory of bust and shoulders; but with a pair of eyes which, as they looked at you, would be gemmed always either with a tear or with some spark of

laughter, and with a mouth in the corners of which was ever lurk-
ing some little spark of humour, unless when some unspoken
prayer seemed to be hanging on her lips. Of woman's vanity she
had absolutely none. Of her corporeal self, as having charms to
rivet man's love, she thought no more than does a dog. It was a
fault with her that she lacked that quality of womanhood. To be
loved was to her all the world; unconscious desire for the admiration of men was as strong in her as in other women; and her
instinct taught her, as such instincts do teach all women, that
such love and admiration was to be the fruit of what feminine
gifts she possessed; but the gifts on which she depended, — depending on them without thinking on the matter, — were her
softness, her trust, her woman's weakness, and that power of sup-
plicating by her eye without putting her petition into words
which was absolutely irresistible. Where is the man of fifty, who
in the course of his life has not learned to love some woman simply because it has come in his way to help her, and to be good to
her in her struggles? And if added to that source of affection there
be brightness, some spark of humour, social gifts, and a strong
flavour of that which we have ventured to call humanity, such
love may become almost a passion without the addition of much
real beauty.

But in thus talking of love we must guard ourselves somewhat
from miscomprehension. In love with Mary Gresley, after the
common sense of the word, we never were, nor would it have
become us to be so. Had such a state of being unfortunately be-
fallen us, we certainly should be silent on the subject. We were
married and old; she was very young, and engaged to be married,
always talking to us of her engagement as a thing fixed as the
stars. She looked upon us, no doubt, — after she had ceased to
regard us simply in our editorial capacity, — as a subsidiary old
uncle whom Providence had supplied to her, in order, that if it
were possible, the troubles of her life might be somewhat eased
by assistance to her from that special quarter. We regarded her
first almost as a child, and than as a young woman to whom we
owed that sort of protecting care which a greybeard should ever
be ready to give to the weakness of feminine adolescence. Nevertheless we were in love with her, and we think such a state of
love to be a wholesome and natural condition. We might, in-

deed, have loved her grandmother, — but the love would have been very different. Had circumstances brought us into connection with her grandmother, we hope we should have done our duty, and had that old lady been our friend we should, we trust, have done it with alacrity. But in our intercourse with Mary Gresley there was more than that. She charmed us. We learned to love the hue of that dark grey stuff frock which she seemed always to wear. When she would sit in the low arm-chair opposite to us, looking up into our eyes as we spoke to her words which must often have stabbed her little heart, we were wont to caress her with that inward undemonstrative embrace that one spirit is able to confer upon another. We forgave all her faults. We exaggerated her virtues. We exerted ourselves for her with a zeal that was perhaps fatuous. Though we attempted sometimes to look back at her, telling her that our time was too precious to be wasted in conversation with her, she soon learned to know how welcome she was to us. Her glove, — which, by-the-bye, was never tattered, though she was very poor, — was an object of regard to us. Her grandmother's gloves would have been as unacceptable to us as any other morsel of old kid or cotton. Our heart bled for her. Now the heart may suffer much for the sorrows of a male friend, but it may hardly for such be said to bleed. We loved her, in short, as we should not have loved her, but that she was young and gentle, and could smile, — and, above all, but that she looked at us with those bright, beseeching tear-laden eyes.

Sterne, in his latter days, when very near his end, wrote passionate love-letters to various women, and has been called hard names by Thackeray, — not for writing them, but because he thus showed himself to be incapable of that sincerity which should have bound him to one love. We do not ourselves much admire the sentimentalism of Sterne, finding the expression of it to be mawkish, and thinking that too often he misses the pathos for which he strives from a want of appreciation on his own part of that which is really vigorous in language and touching in sentiment. But we think that Thackeray has been somewhat wrong in throwing that blame on Sterne's heart which should have been attributed to his taste. The love which he declared when he was old and sick and dying, — a worn out wreck of a man, — disgusts us, not because it was felt, or not felt, but because it was told;

— and told as though the teller meant to offer more than that warmth of sympathy which woman's strength and woman's weakness combined will ever produce in the hearts of certain men. This is a sympathy with which neither age, nor crutches, nor matrimony, nor position of any sort need consider itself to be incompatible. It is unreasoning, and perhaps irrational. It gives outward form and grace that which only inward merit can deserve. It is very dangerous because, unless watched, it leads to words which express that which is not intended. But, though it may be controlled, it cannot be killed. He, who is of his nature open to such impression, will feel it while breath remains to him. It was that which destroyed the character and happiness of Swift, and which made Sterne contemptible. We do not doubt that such unreasoning sympathy, exacted by feminine attraction, was always strong in Johnson's heart; — but Johnson was strong all over, and could guard himself equally from misconduct and from ridicule. Such sympathy with women, such incapability of withstanding the feminine magnet was very strong with Goethe, — who could guard himself from ridicule, but not from misconduct. To us the child of whom we are speaking, — for she was so then, — was ever a child. But she bore in her hand the power of that magnet, and we admit that the needle within our bosom was swayed by it. Her story, — such as we have to tell it, — was as follows.

Mary Gresley, at the time when we first knew her, was eighteen years old, and was the daughter of a medical practitioner, who had lived and died in a small town in one of the northern counties. For facility in telling our story we will call that town Cornboro. Dr. Gresley, as he seemed to have been called though without proper claim to the title, had been a diligent man, and fairly successful, — except in this, that he died before he had been able to provide for those whom he left behind him. The widow still had her own modest fortune, amounting to some eighty pounds a year; and that, with the furniture of her house, was her whole wealth, when she found herself thus left with the weight of the world upon her shoulders. There was one other daughter older than Mary, whom we never saw, but who was always mentioned as poor Fanny. There had been no sons, and the family consisted of the mother and the two girls. Mary had been only fifteen when her father died, and up to that time had been regarded quite as a child by all who had known her. Mrs. Gresley, in the hour of her need, did as widows do in such cases. She sought advice from her clergyman and neighbours, and was counselled to take a lodger into her house. No lodger could be found so fitting as the curate, and when Mary was seventeen years old, she and the curate were engaged to be married. The curate paid thirty pounds a year for his lodgings, and on this, with their own little income, the widow and her two daughters had managed to live. The engagement was known to them all as soon as it had been known to Mary. The love-making, indeed, had gone on beneath the eyes of the mother. There had been not only no deceit, no privacy, no separate interests, but, as far as we ever knew, no question as to prudence in the making of the engagement. The two young people had been brought together, had loved each other, as was so natural, and had become engaged as a matter of course. It was an event as easy to be foretold, or at least as easy to be believed, as the pairing of two birds. From what we heard of this curate, the Rev. Arthur Donne, — for we never saw him, — we fancy that he was a simple, pious, commonplace young man, imbued with a strong idea that in being made a priest he had been invested with a nobility and with some special capacity beyond that of other men, slight in body, weak in health, but honest, true, and warm-hearted. Then, the engagement having been completed, there arose the question of matrimony. The salary of the curate was a hundred a year. The whole income of the vicar, an old man, was, after payment made to his curate, two hundred a year. Could the curate, in such circumstances, afford to take to himself a penniless wife of seventeen? Mrs. Gresley was willing that the marriage should take place, and that they should all do as best they might on their joint income. The vicar's wife, who seems to have been a strong-minded, sage, though somewhat hard woman, took Mary aside, and told her that such a thing must not be. There would come, she said, children, and destitution, and ruin. She knew perhaps more than Mary knew when Mary told us her story, sitting opposite to us in the low armchair. It was the advice of the vicar's wife that the engagement should be broken off; but that, if the breaking of the engagement were impossible, there should be an indefinite period of waiting.

Such engagements cannot be broken off. Young hearts will not consent to be thus torn asunder. The vicar's wife was too strong for them to get themselves married in her teeth, and the period of indefinite waiting was commenced.

And now for a moment we will go farther back among Mary's youthful days. Child as she seemed to be, she had in very early years taken a pen in her hand. The reader need hardly be told that had not such been the case there would not have arisen any cause for friendship between her and me. We are telling an Editor's tale, and it was in our editorial capacity that Mary first came to us. Well; — in her earliest attempts, in her very young days, she wrote, — heaven knows what; poetry first no doubt; then, God help her, a tragedy; after that, when the curate-influence first commenced, tales for the conversion of the ungodly; — and at last, before her engagement was a fact, having tried her wing at fiction, in the form of those false little dialogues between Tom the Saint and Bob the Sinner, she had completed a novel in one volume. She was then seventeen, was engaged to be married, and had completed her novel! Passing her in the street you would almost have taken her for a child to whom you might give an orange.

Hitherto her work had come from ambition, — or from a feeling of somewhat restless piety inspired by the curate. Now there arose in her young mind the question whether such talent as she possessed might not be turned to account for ways and means, and used to shorten, perhaps absolutely to annihilate, that uncertain period of waiting. The first novel was seen by "a man of letters" in her neighbourhood, who pronounced it to be very clever; — not indeed fit as yet for publication, faulty in grammar; faulty even in spelling, — how I loved the tear that shone in her eye as she confessed this delinquency! — faulty of course in construction, and faulty in character; — but still clever. The man of letters had told her that she must begin again.

Unfortunate man of letters in having thrust upon him so terrible a task! In such circumstances what is the candid, honest, soft-hearted man of letters to do? "Go, girl, and mend your stockings. Learn to make a pie. If you work hard, it may be that some day your intellect will suffice to you to read a book and understand it. For the writing of a book that shall either interest or instruct a brother human being many gifts are required. Have you just reason to believe that they have been given to you?" That is what the candid, honest man of letters says who is not soft-hearted; — and in ninety-nine cases out of a hundred it will probably be the truth. The soft-hearted man of letters remembers that this case may be the hundredth; and, unless the blotted manuscript submitted to him is conclusive against such possibility, he reconciles it to his conscience to tune his counsel to that hope. Who can say that he is wrong? Unless such evidence be conclusive, who can venture to declare that this aspirant may not be the one who shall succeed? Who in such emergency does not remember the day in which he also was one of the hundred of whom the ninety-and-nine must fail? — and will not remember also the many convictions on his own mind that he certainly would not be the one appointed? The man of letters in the neighbourhood of Cornboro to whom poor Mary's manuscript was shown was not sufficiently hard-hearted to make any strong attempt to deter her. He made no reference to the easy stockings, or the wholesome pie, — pointed out the manifest faults which he saw, and added, — we do not doubt with much more energy than he threw into his words of censure, — his comfortable assurance that there was great promise in the work. Mary Gresley that evening burned the manuscript, and began another, with the dictionary close at her elbow.

Then, during her work, there occurred two circumstances which brought upon her, — and, indeed, upon the household to which she belonged, — intense sorrow and greatly increased trouble. The first of these applied more especially to herself. The Rev. Arthur Donne did not approve of novels, — of other novels than those dialogues between Tom and Bob, of the falsehood of which he was unconscious, — and expressed a desire that the writing of them should be abandoned. How far the lover went in his attempt to enforce obedience we, of course, could not know; but he pronounced the edict, and the edict, though not obeyed, created tribulation. Then there came forth another edict which had to be obeyed, — an edict from the probable successor of the late Dr. Gresley, — ordering the poor curate to seek employment in some clime more congenial to his state of health than that in which he was then living. He was told that his throat and lungs and general apparatus for living and preaching were not strong enough for those hyperborean springs, and that he must seek a southern climate. He did do so, and, before I became acquainted with Mary, had transferred his services to a small town in Dorsetshire. The engagement, of course, was to be as valid as ever, though matrimony must be postponed, more indefinitely even than heretofore. But if Mary could write novels and sell them, then how glorious would it be to follow her lover into Dorsetshire! Rev. Arthur Donne went, and the curate who came in his place was a married man, wanting a house, and not lodgings. So Mary Gresley persevered with her second novel, and completed it before she was eighteen.

The literary friend in the neighbourhood, — to the chance of whose acquaintance I was indebted for my subsequent friendship with Mary Gresley, — found this work to be a great improvement on the first. He was an elderly man who had been engaged nearly all his life in the conduct of a scientific and agricultural periodical, and was the last man whom I should have taken as a sound critic on works of fiction; — but with spelling, grammatical construction, and the composition of sentences he was acquainted; and he assured Mary that her progress had been great. Should she burn that second story? she asked him. She would if he so recommended, and begin another the next day. Such was not his advice. "I have a friend in London," said he, "who has to do with such things, and you shall go to him. I will give you a letter." He gave her the fatal letter, and she came to us.

She came up to town with her novel; but not only with her novel, for she brought her mother with her. So great was her eloquence, so excellent her suasive power either with her tongue or by that look of supplication in her face, that she induced her mother to abandon her home in Cornboro, and trust herself to London lodgings. The house was let furnished to the new curate, and when I first heard of the Gresleys they were living on the second floor in a small street near to the Euston Square station. Poor Fanny, as she was called, was left in some humble home at Cornboro, and Mary travelled up to try her fortune in the great city. When we came to know her well we expressed our doubts as to the wisdom of such a step. Yes; the vicar's wife had been strong against the move. Mary confessed as much. That lady had

32

spoken most forcible words, had uttered terrible predictions, had told sundry truths. But Mary had prevailed, and the journey was made, and the lodgings were taken.

We can now come to the day on which we first saw her. She did not write, but came direct to us with her manuscript in her hand. "A young woman, sir, wants to see you," said the clerk, in that tone to which we were so well accustomed, and which indicated the dislike which he had learned from us to the reception of unknown visitors.

"Young woman! What young woman?"

"Well, sir; she is a very young woman; — quite a girl like."

"I suppose she has got a name. Who sent her? I cannot see any young woman without knowing why. What does she want?"

"Got a manuscript in her hand, sir."

"I've no doubt she has, and a ton of manuscript in drawers and cupboards. Tell her to write. I won't see any woman, young or old, without knowing who she is." The man retired, and soon returned with an envelope belonging to the office, on which was written, "Miss Mary Gresley, late of Cornboro." He also brought me a note from "the man of letters" down in Yorkshire. "Of what sort is she?" I asked, looking at the introduction.

"She ain't amiss as to looks," said the clerk; "and she's modest-like." Now certainly it is the fact that all female literary aspirants are not "modest-like." We read our friend's letter through, while poor Mary was standing at the counter below. How eagerly should we have run to greet her, to save her from the gaze of the public, to welcome her at least with a chair and the warmth of our editorial fire, had we guessed then what were her qualities! It was not long before she knew the way up to our sanctum without any clerk to show her, and not long before we knew well the sound of that low but not timid knock at our door made always with the handle of the parasol, with which her advent was heralded. We will confess that there was always music to our ears in that light tap from the little round wooden knob. The man of letters in Yorkshire, whom we had known well for many years, had been never known to us with intimacy. We had bought with him and sold with him, had talked with him and, perhaps, walked with him; but he was not one with whom we had eaten, or drunk, or prayed. A dull, well-instructed, honest man he was, fond of his money, and, as we had thought, as unlikely as any man to be waked to enthusiasm by the ambitious dreams of a young girl. But Mary had been potent even over him, and he had written to me, saying that Miss Gresley was a young lady of exceeding promise, in respect of whom he had a strong presentiment that she would rise, if not to eminence, at least to a good position as a writer. "But she is very young," he added. Having read this letter, we at last desired our clerk to send the lady up.

We remember her step as she came to the door, timid enough then, — hesitating, but yet with an assumed lightness as though she was determined to show us that she was not ashamed of what she was doing. She had on her head a light straw hat, such as then was very unusual in London, — and is not now, we believe, commonly worn in the streets of the metropolis by ladies who believe themselves to know what they are about. But it was a hat, worn upon her head, and not a straw plate done up with ribbons, and reaching down the incline of the forehead as far as the top of the nose. And she was dressed in a grey stuff frock, with a little black band round her waist. As far as our memory goes, we never saw her in any other dress, or with other hat or bonnet on her head. "And what can we do for you, — Miss Gresley?" we said, standing up and holding the literary gentleman's letter in our hand. We had almost said, "my dear," seeing her youth and remembering our own age. We were afterwards glad that we had not so addressed her; though it came before long that we did call her "my dear," — in quite another spirit.

She recoiled a little from the tone of our voice, but recovered herself at once. "Mr.＿＿＿＿＿＿ thinks that you can do something for me. I have written a novel, and I have brought it to you."

"You are very young, are you not, to have written a novel?"

"I am young," she said, "but perhaps older than you think. I am eighteen." Then for the first time there came into her eye that gleam of a merry humour which never was allowed to dwell there long, but which was so alluring when it showed itself.

"That is a ripe age," we said laughing, and then we bade her seat herself. At once we began to pour forth that long and dull and ugly lesson which is so common to our life, in which we tried to explain to our unwilling pupil that of all respectable profes-

34

sions for young women literature is the most uncertain, the most heart-breaking, and the most dangerous. "You hear of the few who are remunerated," we said; "but you hear nothing of the thousands that fail."

"It is so noble!" she replied.

"But so hopeless."

"There are those who succeed."

"Yes, indeed. Even in a lottery one must gain the prize; but they who trust to lotteries break their hearts."

"But literature is not a lottery. If I am fit, I shall succeed. Mr. _____ thinks I may succeed." Many more words of wisdom we spoke to her, and well do we remember her reply when we had run all our line off the reel, and had completed our sermon. "I shall go on all the same," she said. "I shall try, and try again, — and again."

Her power over us, to a certain extent, was soon established. Of course we promised to read the MS., and turned it over, no doubt with an anxious countenance, to see of what nature was the writing. There is a feminine scrawl of a nature so terrible that the task of reading becomes worse than the treadmill. "I know I can write well, — though I am not quite sure about the spelling," said Mary, as she observed the glance of our eyes. She spoke truly. The writing was good, though the erasures and alterations were very numerous. And then the story was intended to fill only one volume. "I will copy it for you if you wish it," said Mary. "Though there are so many scratchings out, it has been copied once." We would not for worlds have given her such labour, and then we promised to read the tale. We forget how it was brought about, but she told us at that interview that her mother had obtained leave from the pastry-cook round the corner to sit there waiting till Mary should rejoin her. "I thought it would be trouble enough for you to have one of us here," she said with her little laugh when I asked her why she had not brought her mother on with her. I own that I felt that she had been wise; and when I told her that if she would call on me again that day week I would then have read at any rate so much of her work as would enable me to give her my opinion, I did not invite her to bring her mother with her. I knew that I could talk more freely to the girl without the mother's presence. Even when you are past fifty, and intend only to preach a sermon, you do not wish to have a mother present.

When she was gone we took up the roll of paper and examined it. We looked at the division into chapters, at the various mottoes the poor child had chosen, pronounced to ourselves the name of the story, — it was simply the name of the heroine, an easy-going, unaffected, well-chosen name, — and read the last page of it. On such occasions the reader of the work begins his task almost with a conviction that the labour which he is about to undertake will be utterly thrown away. He feels all but sure that the matter will be bad, that it will be better for all parties, writer, intended readers, and intended publisher, that the written words should not be conveyed into type, — that it will be his duty after some fashion to convey that unwelcome opinion to the writer, and that the writer will go away incredulous, and accusing mentally the Mentor of the moment of all manner of literary sins, among which ignorance, jealousy, and falsehood, will, in the poor author's imagination, be most prominent. And yet when the writer was asking for that opinion, declaring his especial desire that the opinion should be candid, protesting that his present wish is to have some gauge of his own capability, and that he has come to you believing you to be above others able to give him that gauge, — while his petition to you was being made, he was in every respect sincere. He had come desirous to measure himself, and had believed that you could measure him. When coming he did not think that you would declare him to be an Apollo. He had told himself, no doubt, how probable it was that you would point out to him that he was a dwarf. You find him to be an ordinary man, measuring perhaps five feet seven, and unable to reach the standard of the particular regiment in which he is ambitious of serving. You tell him so in what civillest words you know, and you are at once convicted in his mind of jealousy, ignorance, and falsehood! And yet he is perhaps a most excellent fellow, — and capable of performing the best of service, only in some other regiment! As we looked at Miss Gresley's manuscript, tumbling it through our hands, we expected even from her some such result. She had gained two things from us already by her outward and inward gifts, such as they were, — first that we would read her story, and secondly that we would read it quickly; but she had not as yet gained from us any belief that by reading it we could serve it.

We did read it, — the most of it before we left our editorial chair on that afternoon, so that we lost altogether the daily walk so essential to our editorial health, and were put to the expense of a cab on our return home. And we incurred some minimum of domestic discomfort from the fact that we did not reach our own door till twenty minutes after our appointed dinner hour. "I have this moment come from the office as hard as a cab could bring me," we said in answer to the mildest of reproaches, explaining nothing as to the nature of the cause which had kept us so long at our work.

We must not allow our readers to suppose that the intensity of our application had arisen from the overwhelming interest of the story. It was not that the story entranced us, but that our feeling for the writer grew as we read the story. It was simple, unaffected, and almost painfully unsensational. It contained, as I came to perceive afterwards, little more than a recital of what her imagination told her might too probably be the result of her own engagement. It was the story of two young people who become engaged and cannot be married. After a course of years the man, with many true arguments, asks to be absolved. The woman yields with an expressed conviction that her lover is right, settles herself down for maiden life, then breaks her heart and dies. The character of the man was utterly untrue to nature. That of the woman was true, but commonplace. Other interest, or other character there was none. The dialogues between the lovers were many and tedious, and hardly a word was spoken between them which two lovers really would have uttered. It was clearly not a work as to which I could tell my little friend that she might depend upon it for fame or fortune. When I had finished it I was obliged to tell myself that I could not advise her even to publish it. But yet I could not say that she had mistaken her own powers or applied herself to a profession beyond her reach. There was a grace and delicacy in her work which were charming. Occasionally she escaped from the trammels of grammar, but only so far that it would be a pleasure to point out to her her errors. There was not a word that a young lady should not have written; and there were throughout the whole evident signs of honest work. We had six days to think it over between our completion of the task and her second visit.

She came exactly at the hour appointed, and seated herself at once in the arm-chair before us as soon as the young man had closed the door behind him. There had been no great occasion for nervousness at her first visit, and she had then, by an evident effort, overcome the diffidence incidental to a meeting with a stranger. But now she did not attempt to conceal her anxiety. "Well," she said, leaning forward, and looking up into our face, with her two hands folded together.

Even though Truth, standing full panoplied at our elbow, had positively demanded it, we could not have told her then to mend her stockings and bake her pies and desert the calling that she had chosen. She was simply irresistible, and would, we fear, have constrained us into falsehood had the question been between falsehood and absolute reprobation of her work. To have spoken hard, heart-breaking words to her, would have been like striking a child when it comes to kiss you. We fear that we were not absolutely true at first, and that by that absence of truth we made subsequent pain more painful. "Well," she said, looking up into our face. "Have you read it?" We told her that we had read every word of it. "And it is no good?"

We fear that we began by telling her that it certainly was good, — after a fashion, very good, — considering her youth and necessary inexperience, very good indeed. As we said this she shook her head, and sent out a spark or two from her eyes, intimating her conviction that excuses or quasi praise founded on her youth would avail her nothing. "Would anybody buy it from me?" she asked. No; — we did not think that any publisher would pay her money for it. "Would they print it for me without costing me anything?" Then we told her the truth as nearly as we could. She lacked experience; and if, as she had declared to us before, she was determined to persevere, she must try again, and must learn more of that lesson of the world's ways which was so necessary to those who attempted to teach that lesson to others. "But I shall try again at once," she said. We shook our head, endeavouring to shake it kindly. "Currer Bell was only a young girl when she succeeded," she added. The injury which Currer Bell did after this fashion was almost equal to that perpetrated by Jack Sheppard.

She remained with us then for above an hour; — for more than two probably, though the time was not specially marked by us; and before her visit was brought to a close she had told us of her engagement with the curate. Indeed, we believe that the greater part of her little history as hitherto narrated was made known to us on that occasion. We asked after her mother early in the interview, and learned that she was not on this occasion kept waiting at the pastry-cook's shop. Mary had come alone, making use of some friendly omnibus, of which she had learned the route. When she told us that she and her mother had come up to London solely with the view of forwarding her views in her intended profession, we ventured to ask whether it would not be wiser for them to return to Cornboro, seeing how improbable it was that she would have matter fit for the press within any short period. Then she explained that they had calculated that they would be able to live in London for twelve months, if they spent nothing except on absolute necessaries. The poor girl seemed to keep back nothing from us. "We have clothes that will carry us through, and we shall be very careful. I came in an omnibus; — but I think I shall walk if you will let me come again." Then she asked me for advice. How was she to set about further work with the best chance of turning it to account?

It had been altogether the fault of that retired literary gentleman down in the North, who had obtained what standing he had in the world of letters by writing about guano and the cattle plague. Divested of all responsibility, and fearing no further trouble to himself, he had ventured to tell this girl that her work was full of promise. Promise means probability, and in this case there was nothing beyond a most remote chance. That she and her mother should have left their little household gods, and come up to London on such a chance, was a thing terrible to the mind. But we felt before these two hours were over that we could not throw her off now. We had become old friends, and there had been that between us which gave her a positive claim upon our time. She had sat in our arm-chair, leaning forward with her elbows on her knees and her hands stretched out, till we, caught by the charm of her unstudied intimacy, had wheeled round our chair, and had placed ourselves, as nearly as the circumstances would admit, in the same position. The magnetism had already

39

begun to act upon us. We soon found ourselves taking it for granted that she was to remain in London and begin another book. It was impossible to resist her. Before the interview was over, we, who had been conversant with all these matters before she was born; we, who had latterly come to regard our own editorial fault as being chiefly that of personal harshness; we, who had repulsed aspirant novelists by the score, — we had consented to be a party to the creation, if not the actual writing, of this new book!

It was to be done after this fashion. She was to fabricate a plot, and to bring it to us, written on two sides of a sheet of letter paper, On the reverse sides we were to criticise this plot, and prepare emendations. Then she was to make out skeletons of the men and women who were afterwards to be clothed with flesh and made alive with blood, and covered with cuticles. After that she was to arrange her proportions; and at last, before she began to write the story, she was to describe in detail such part of it as was to be told in each chapter, On every advancing wavelet of the work we were to give her our written remarks. All this we promised to do because of the quiver in her lip, and the alternate tear and sparkle in her eye. "Now that I have found a friend, I feel sure that I can do it," she said, as she held our hand tightly before she left us.

In about a month, during which she had twice written to us, and twice been answered, she came with her plot. It was the old story, with some additions and some change. There was matrimony instead of death at the end, and an old aunt was brought in for the purpose of relenting and producing an income. We added a few details, feeling as we did so that we were the very worst of botchers. We doubt now whether the old, sad, simple story was not the better of the two. Then, after another lengthened interview, we sent our pupil back to create her skeletons. When she came with the skeletons we were dear friends, and we had learned to call her Mary. Then it was that she first sat at our editorial table, and wrote a love-letter to the curate. It was then mid-winter, wanting but a few days to Christmas, and Arthur, as she called him, did not like the cold weather. "He does not say so," she said, "but I fear he is ill. Don't you think there are some people with whom everything is unfortunate?" She wrote her letter, and had recovered her spirits before she took her leave.

We then proposed to her to bring her mother to dine with us on Christmas Day. We had made a clean breast of it at home in regard to our heart-flutterings, and had been met with a suggestion that some kindness might with propriety be shown to the old lady as well as to the young one. We had felt grateful to the old lady for not coming to our office with her daughter, and had at once assented. When we made the suggestion to Mary there came first a blush over all her face, and then there followed the well-known smile before the blush was gone. "You'll all be dressed fine," she said. We protested that not a garment would be changed by any of the family after the decent church-going in the morning. "Just as I am?" she asked. "Just as you are," we said, looking at the dear grey frock, adding some mocking assertion that no possible combination of millinery could improve her. "And mamma will be just the same? Then we will come," she said. We told her an absolute falsehood, as to some necessity which would take us in a cab to Euston Square on the afternoon of that Christmas Day, so that we could call and bring them both to our house without trouble or expense. "You shan't do anything of the kind," she said. However we swore to our falsehood, — perceiving, as we did so, that she did not believe a word of it; but in the matter of the cab we had our own way.

We found the mother to be what we had expected, — a weak, lady-like, lachrymose old lady, endowed with a profound admiration for her dauther, and so bashful that she could not at all enjoy her plum-pudding. We think that Mary did enjoy hers thoroughly. She made a little speech to the mistress of the house, praising ourselves with warm words and tearful eyes, and immediately won the heart of a new friend. She allied herself warmly to our daughters, put up with the schoolboy pleasantries of our sons, and before the evening was over was dressed up as a ghost for the amusement of some neighbouring children who were brought in to play snapdragon. Mrs. Gresley, as she drank her tea and crumbled her bit of cake, seated on a distant sofa, was not so happy, partly because she remembered her old gown, and partly because our wife was a stranger to her. Mary had forgotten both circumstances before the dinner was half over. She was the sweetest ghost that ever was seen. How pleasant would be our ideas of departed spirits if such ghosts would visit us frequently!

They repeated their visits to us not unfrequently during the twelve-months; but as the whole interest attaching to our intercourse had reference to circumstances which took place in that editorial room of ours, it will not be necessary to refer further to the hours, very pleasant to ourselves, which she spent with us in our domestic life. She was ever made welcome when she came, and was known by us as a dear, well-bred, modest, clever little girl. The novel went on. That catalogue of the skeletons gave us more trouble than all the rest, and many were the tears which she shed over it, and sad were the misgivings by which she was afflicted, though never vanquished! How was it to be expected that a girl of eighteen should portray characters such as she had never known? In her intercourse with the curate all the intellect had been on her side. She had loved him because it was requisite to her to love some one; and now, as she had loved him, she was as true as steel to him. But there had been almost nothing for her to learn from him. The plan of the novel went on, and as it did so we became more and more despondent as to its success. And through it all we knew how contrary it was to our own judgment to expect, even to dream of, anything but failure. Though we went on working with her, finding it to be quite impossible to resist her entreaties, we did tell her from day to day that, even presuming she were entitled to hope for ultimate success, she must go through an apprenticeship of ten years before she could reach it. Then she would sit silent, repressing her tears, and searching for arguments with which to support her cause.

"Working hard is apprenticeship," she said to us once.

"Yes, Mary; but the work will be more useful, and the apprenticeship more wholesome, if you will take them for what they are worth."

"I shall be dead in ten years," she said.

"If you thought so you would not intend to marry Mr. Donne. But even, were it certain that such would be your fate, how can that alter the state of things? The world will know nothing of that; and if it did, would the world buy your book out of pity?"

"I want no one to pity me," she said; "but I want you to help me." So we went on helping her. At the end of four months she had not put pen to paper on the absolute body of her projected novel; and yet she had worked daily at it, arranging its future construction.

During the next month, when we were in the middle of March, a gleam of real success came to her. We had told her frankly that we would publish nothing of hers in the periodical which we were ourselves conducting. She had become too dear to us for us not to feel that were we to do so, we should be doing it rather for her sake than for that of our readers. But we did procure for her the publication of two short stories elsewhere. For these she received twelve guineas, and it seemed to her that she had found an El Dorado of literary wealth. I shall never forget her ecstasy when she knew that her work would be printed, or her renewed triumph when the first humble cheque was given into her hands. There are those who will think that such a triumph, as connected with literature, must be sordid. For ourselves, we are ready to acknowledge that money payment for work done is the best and most honest test of success. We are sure that it is so felt by young barristers and young doctors, and we do not see why rejoicing on such realisation of long-cherished hope should be more vile with the literary aspirant than with them. "What do you think I'll do first with it!?" she said. We thought she meant to send something to her lover, and we told her so. "I'll buy mamma a bonnet to go to church in. I didn't tell you before, but she hasn't been these three Sundays because she hasn't one fit to be seen." I changed the cheque for her, and she went off and bought the bonnet.

Though I was successful for her in regard to the two stories, I could not go beyond that. We could have filled pages of periodicals with her writing had we been willing that she should work without remuneration. She herself was anxious for such work, thinking that it would lead to something better. But we opposed it, and, indeed, would not permit it, believing that work so done can be serviceable to none but those who accept it that pages may be filled without cost.

During the winter, while she was thus working, she was in a state of alarm about her lover. Her hope was ever that when warm weather came he would again be well and strong. We know nothing sadder than such hope founded on such source. For does not the winter follow the summer, and then again comes the kill-

ing spring? At this time she used to read us passages from his letters, in which he seemed to speak of little but his own health. In
her literary ambition he never seemed to have taken part since
she had declared her intention of writing profane novels. As regarded him, his sole merit to us seemed to be in his truth to her.
He told her that in his opinion they two were as much joined
together as though the service of the Church had bound them;
but even in saying that he spoke ever of himself and not of her.
Well; — May came, dangerous, doubtful, deceitful May, and he
was worse. Then, for the first time, the dread word, Consump-
tion, passed her lips. It had already passed ours, mentally, a score
of times. We asked her what she herself would wish to do. Would
she desire to go down to Dorsetshire and see him? She thought
awhile, and said that she would wait a little longer.

The novel went on, and at length, in June, she was writing
the actual words on which, as she thought, so much depended.
She had really brought the story into some shape in the arrangement of her chapters; and sometimes even I began to hope.
There were moments in which with her hope was almost certainty. Towards the end of June Mr. Donne declared himself to
be better. He was to have a holiday in August, and then he intended to run up to London and see his betrothed. He still gave
details, which were distressing to us, of his own symptoms; but
it was manifest that he himself was not desponding, and she was
governed in her trust or in her despair altogether by him. But
when August came the period of his visit was postponed. The
heat had made him weak, and he was to come in September.

Early in August we ourselves went away for our annual recre-
ation; — not that we shoot grouse, or that we have any strong
opinion that August and September are the best months in the
year for holiday-making; — but that everybody does go in August.
We ourselves are not specially fond of August. In many places to
which one goes a-touring mosquitoes bite in that month. The
heat, too, prevents one from walking. The inns are all full, and
the railways crowded. April and May are twice pleasanter months
in which to see the world and the country. But fashion is everything, and no man or woman will stay in town in August for
whom there exists any practicability of leaving it. We went on
the 10th, — just as though we had a moor, and one of the last

things we did before our departure was to read and revise the last-written chapter of Mary's story.

About the end of September we returned, and up to that time the lover had not come to London. Immediately on our return we wrote to Mary, and the next morning she was with us. She had seated herself on her usual chair before she spoke, and we had taken her hand and asked after herself and her mother. Then, with something of mirth in our tone, we demanded the work which she had done since our departure. "He is dying," she replied.

She did not weep as she spoke. It was not on such occasions as this that the tears filled her eyes. But there was in her face a look of fixed and settled misery which convinced us that she at least did not doubt the truth of her own assertion. We muttered something as to our hope that she was mistaken. "The Doctor, there, has written to tell mamma that it is so. Here is his letter." The doctor's letter was a good letter, written with more of assurance than doctors can generally allow themselves to express. "I fear that I am justified in telling you," said the doctor, "that it can only be a question of weeks." We got up and took her hand. There was not a word to be uttered.

"I must go to him," she said, after a pause.

"Well; — yes. It will be better."

"But we have no money." It must be explained now that offers of slight, very slight, pecuniary aid had been made by us both to Mary and to her mother on more than one occasion. These had been refused with adamantine firmness, but always with something of mirth, or at least of humour, attached to the refusal. The mother would simply refer to the daughter, and Mary would declare that they could manage to see the twelvemonth through and go back to Cornboro, without becoming absolute beggars. She would allude to their joint wardrobe, and would confess that there would not have been a pair of boots between them but for that twelve guineas; and indeed she seemed to have stretched that modest incoming so as to cover a legion of purchases. And of these things she was never ashamed to speak. We think there must have been at least two grey frocks, because the frock was always clean, and never absolutely shabby. Our girls at home declared that they had seen three. Of her frock, as it happened, she never spoke to us, but the new boots and the new gloves, "and ever so many things that I can't tell you about, which we really couldn't have gone without," all came out of the twelve guineas. That she had taken, not only with delight, but with triumph. But pecuniary assistance from ourselves she had always refused. "It would be a gift," she would say.

"Have it as you like."

"But people don't give other people money."

"Don't they? That's all you know about the world."

"Yes; to beggars. We hope we needn't come to that." It was thus that she always answered us, — but always with something of laughter in her eye, as though their poverty was a joke. Now, when the demand upon her was for that which did not concern her personal comfort, which referred to a matter felt by her to be vitally important, she declared, without a minute's hesitation, that she had not money for the journey.

"Of course you can have money," we said. "I suppose you will go at once?"

"Oh yes; — at once. That is in a day or two, — after he shall have received my letters. Why should I wait?" We sat down to write a cheque, and she, seeing what we were doing, asked how much it was to be. "No; — half that will do," she said. "Mamma will not go. We have talked it over and decided it. Yes; I know all about that. I am going to see my lover, — my dying lover; and I have to beg for the money to take me to him. Of course I am a young girl; but in such a condition am I to stand upon ceremony of being taken care of? A housemaid wouldn't want to be taken care of at eighteen." We did exactly as she bade us, and then attempted to comfort her while the young man went to get money for the cheque. What consolation was possible? It was simply necessary to admit with frankness that sorrow had come from which there could be no present release. "Yes," she said. "Time will cure it, — in a way. One dies in time, and then of course it is all cured." "One hears of this kind of thing often," she said afterwards, still leaning forward in her chair, still with something of the old expression in her eyes, — something almost of humour in spite of her grief; "but it is the girl who dies. When it is the girl, there isn't, after all, so much harm done. A man goes about the world and can shake it off; and then, there are plenty of girls." We could not tell her how infinitely more important, to our thinking, was her life than that of him whom she was going to see now for the last time; but there did spring up within our mind a feeling, greatly opposed to that conviction which formerly we had endeavoured to impress upon herself, — that she was destined to make for herself a successful career.

She went, and remained by her lover's bed-side for three weeks. She wrote constantly to her mother, and once or twice to ourselves. She never again allowed herself to entertain a gleam of hope, and she spoke of her sorrow as a thing accomplished. In her last interview with us she had hardly alluded to her novel, and in her letters she never mentioned it. But she did say one word which made us guess what was coming. "You will find me greatly changed in one thing," she said; "so much changed that I need never have troubled you." The day for her return to London was twice postponed, but at last she was brought to leave him. Stern necessity was too strong for her. Let her pinch herself as she might, she must live down in Dorsetshire, — and could not live on his means, which were as narrow as her own. She left him; and on the day after her arrival in London she walked across from Euston Square to our office.

"Yes," she said, "it is all over. I shall never see him again on this side of heaven's gates." I do not know that we ever saw a tear in her eyes produced by her own sorrow. She was possessed of some wonderful strength which seemed to suffice for the bearing of any burden. Then she paused, and we could only sit silent, with our eyes fixed upon the rug. "I have made him a promise," she said at last. Of course we asked her what was the promise, though at the moment we thought we knew. "I will make no more attempt at novel writing."

"Such a promise should not have been asked, — or given," we said vehemently.

"It should have been asked, — because he thought it right," she answered. "And of course it was given. Must he not know better than I do? Is he not one of God's ordained priests? In all the world is there one so bound to obey him as I?" There was nothing to be said for it at such a moment as that. There is no enthusiasm equal to that produced by a death-bed parting. "I grieve greatly," she said, "that you should have had so much vain labour with a poor girl who can never profit by it."

"I don't believe the labour will have been vain," we answered, having altogether changed those views of ours as to the futility of the pursuit which she had adopted.

"I have destroyed it all," she said.

"What; — burned the novel?"

"Every scrap of it. I told him that I would do so, and that he should know that I had done it. Every page was burned after I got home last night, and then I wrote to him before I went to bed."

"Do you mean that you think it wicked that people should write novels?" we asked.

"He thinks it to be a misapplication of God's gifts, and that has been enough for me. He shall judge for me, but I will not judge for others. And what does it matter? I do not want to write a novel now."

They remained in London till the end of the year for which the married curate had taken their house, and then they returned to Cornboro. We saw them frequently while they were still in town, and despatched them by the train to the north just when the winter was beginning. At that time the young clergyman was still living down in Dorsetshire, but he was lying in his grave when Christmas came. Mary never saw him again, nor did she attend his funeral. She wrote to us frequently then, as she did for years afterwards. "I should have liked to have stood at his grave," she said; "but it was a luxury of sorrow that I wished to enjoy, and they who cannot earn luxuries should not have them. They were going to manage it for me here, but I knew I was right to refuse it." Right, indeed! As far as we knew her, she never moved a single point from what was right.

All things happened many years ago. Mary Gresley, on her return to Cornboro, apprenticed herself, as it were, to the married curate there, and called herself, I think, a female Scripture reader. I know that she spent her days in working hard for the religious aid of the poor around her. From time to time we endeavoured to instigate her to literary work; and she answered our letters by sending us wonderful little dialogues between Tom the Saint and Bob the Sinner. We are in no humour to criticise them now; but we can assert, that though that mode of religious teaching is most distasteful to us, the literary merit shown even in such works as these was very manifest. And there came to be apparent in them a gleam of humour which would sometimes make us think that she was sitting opposite to us and looking at us, and that she was Tom the Saint, and that we were Bob the Sinner. We said what we could to turn her from her chosen path, throwing into our letters all the eloquence and all the thought of which we were masters; but our eloquence and our thought were equally in vain.

At last, when eight years had passed over her head after the death of Mr. Donne, she married a missionary who was going out to some forlorn country on the confines of African colonization; and there she died. We saw her on board the ship in which she sailed, and before we parted there had come that tear into her eyes, the old look of supplication on her lips, and then the gleam of mirth across her face. We kissed her once, — for the first and only time, — as we bade God bless her!

"Mary Gresley" appeared first in the November issue of *Saint Pauls Magazine* for 1869.

The Panjandrum

Part I. — Hope

E HARDLY FEEL CERTAIN that we are justified in giving the following little story to the public as an Editor's Tale, because at the time to which it refers, and during the circumstances with which it deals, no editorial power was, in fact, within our grasp. As the reader will perceive, the ambition and the hopes, and something of a promise of the privileges, were there; but the absolute chair was not mounted for us. The great WE was not, in truth, ours to use. And, indeed, the interval between the thing we then so cordially desired, and the thing as it has since come to exist, was one of so many years, that there can be no right on our part to connect the two periods. We shall, therefore, tell our story, as might any ordinary individual, in the first person singular, and speak of such sparks of editorship as did fly up around us as having created but a dim coruscation, and as having been quite insufficient to justify the delicious plural.

It is now just thirty years ago since we determined to establish the "Panjandrum" Magazine. The "we" here spoken of is not an editorial we, but a small set of human beings who shall be personally introduced to the reader. The name was intended to be delightfully meaningless, but we all thought that it was euphonious, graphic, also, — and sententious, even though it conveyed no definite idea. The question of a name had occupied us a good deal, and had almost split us into parties. I, — for I will now speak of myself as I, — I had wished to call it by the name of a very respectable young publisher who was then commencing business, and by whom we intended that the trade part of our enterprise should be undertaken. "Colburn's" was an old affair in those days, and I doubt whether "Bentley's" was not already in existence. "Blackwood's" and "Fraser's" were at the top of the tree, and, as I think, the "Metropolitan" was the only magazine then in much vogue not called by the name of this or that enterprising publisher. But some of our colleagues would not hear of this, and were ambitious of a title that should describe our future energies and excellences. I think we should have been called the "Pandrastic," but that the one lady who joined our party absolutely declined the name. At one moment we had almost carried "Panurge." The "Man's" Magazine was thought of, not as opposed to womanhood, but as intended to trump the "Gentleman's." But a hint was given to us that we might seem to imply that our periodical was not adapted for the perusal of females. We meant the word "man" in the great generic sense; — but the somewhat obtuse outside world would not have so taken it. "The H.B.P." was for a time in the ascendant, and was favoured by the lady, who drew for us a most delightful little circle containing the letters illustrated; — what would now be called a monogram, only that the letters were legible. The fact that nobody would comprehend that "H.B.P." intended to express the general opinion of the shareholders that "Honesty is the Best Policy," was felt to be a recommendation rather than otherwise. I think it was the enterprising young publisher who objected to the initials, — not, I am sure, from any aversion to the spirit of the legend. Many other names were tried, and I shall never forget the look which went round our circle when one young and gallant, but too indiscreet reformer, suggested that were it not for offence, whence offence should not come, the "Purge" was the very name for us; — from all which it will be understood that it was our purpose to put right many things that were wrong. The matter held us in discussion for some months, and then we agreed to call the great future lever of the age, — the "Panjandrum."

When a new magazine is about to be established in these days, the first question raised will probably be one of capital. A very considerable sum of money, running far into four figures, — if not going beyond it, — has to be mentioned, and made familiar to the ambitious promoters of the enterprise. It was not so with us. Nor was it the case that our young friend the publisher agreed to find the money, leaving it to us to find the wit. I think we selected our young friend chiefly because, at that time, he had no great business to speak of, and could devote his time to the interests of the "Panjandrum." As for ourselves, we were all poor; and in the way of capital a set of human beings more absurdly inefficient for any purpose of trade could not have been brought together. We found that for a sum of money which we hoped that we might scrape together among us, we could procure paper and print for a couple of thousand copies of our first number; — and, after that, we were to obtain credit for the second number by the reputation of the first. Literary advertising, such as is now common to us, was then unknown. The cost of sticking up "The Panjandrum" at railway stations on the tops of the omnibuses, certainly would not be incurred. Of railway stations there were but few in the country, and even omnibuses were in their infancy. A few modest announcements in the weekly periodicals of the day were thought to be sufficient; and, indeed, there pervaded us all an assurance that the coming of the "Panjandrum" would be known to all men, even before it had come. I doubt whether our desire was not concealment rather than publicity. We measured the importance of the "Panjandrum" by its significance to ourselves, and by the amount of heart which we intended to throw into it. Ladies and gentlemen who get up magazines in the present day are wiser. It is not heart that is wanted, but very big letters on very big boards, and plenty of them.

We were all heart. It must be admitted now that we did not bestow upon the matter of literary excellence quite so much attention as that branch of the subject deserves. We were to write and edit our magazine and have it published, not because we were good at writing or editing, but because we had ideas which we wished to promulgate. Or it might be the case with some of us that we only thought that we had ideas. But there was certainly present to us all a great wish to do some good. That, and a not altogether unwholesome appetite for a reputation which should not be personal, were our great motives. I do not think that we dreamed of making fortunes; though no doubt there might be present to the mind of each of us an idea that an opening to the profession of literature might be obtained through the pages of the "Panjandrum." In that matter of reputation we were quite agreed that fame was to be sought, not for ourselves, not for this or that name, but for the "Panjandrum." No man or woman was to declare himself to be the author of this or that article; — nor indeed was any man or woman to declare himself to be connected with the magazine. The only name to be known to a curious public was that of the young publisher. All intercourse between the writers and the printers was to be through him. If contributions should come from the outside world, — as come they would, — they were to be addressed to the Editor of the "Panjandrum," at the publisher's establishment. It was within the scope of our plan to use any such contribution that might please us altogether; but the contents of the magazine were, as a rule, to come from ourselves. A magazine then, as now, was expected to extend itself through something over a hundred and twenty pages; but we had no fear as to our capacity for producing the required amount. We feared rather that we might jostle each other in our requirements for space.

We were six, and, young as I was then, I was to be the editor. But to the functions of the editor was to be attached very little editorial responsibility. What should and what should not appear in each monthly number was to be settled in conclave. Upon one point, however, we were fully agreed, — that no personal jealousy should ever arise among us so as to cause quarrel or even embarrassment. As I had already written some few slight papers for the press, it was considered probable that I might be able to correct proofs, and do the fitting and dovetailing. My editing was not to go beyond that. If by reason of parity of numbers in voting there should arise a difficulty, the lady was to have a double vote. Anything more noble, more chivalrous, more trusting, or, I may add, more philanthropic than our scheme never was invented; and for the persons, I will say that they were noble, chivalrous, trusting, and philanthropic; — only they were so young!

Place aux dames. We will speak of the lady first, — more especially as our meetings were held at her house. I fear that I may, at the very outset of our enterprise, turn the hearts of my readers against her by saying that Mrs. St. Quinten was separated from her husband. I must however beg them to believe that this sep-

aration had been occasioned by no moral fault or odious misconduct on her part. I will confess that I did at the time believe that
Mr. St. Quinten was an ogre, and that I have since learned to
think that he simply laboured under a strong and, perhaps, mon-
omaniacal objection to literary pursuits. As Mrs. St. Quinten was
devoted to them, harmony was impossible, and the marriage was
unfortunate. She was young, being perhaps about thirty; but I
think that she was the eldest among us. She was good-looking,
with an ample brow, and bright eyes, and large clever mouth; but
no woman living was ever further removed from any propensity
to flirtation. There resided with her a certain Miss Collins, an
elderly, silent lady, who was present at all our meetings, and who
was considered to be pledged to secrecy. Once a week we met and
drank tea at Mrs. St. Quinten's house. It may be as well to explain that Mrs. St. Quinten really had an available income,
which was a condition of life unlike that of her colleagues,— unless as regarded one, who was a fellow of an Oxford college. She
could certainly afford to give us tea and muffins once a week; —
but, in spite of our general impecuniosity, the expense of commencing the magazine was to be borne equally by us all. I can
assure the reader, with reference to more than one of the members, that they occasionally dined on bread and cheese, abstaining from meat and pudding with the view of collecting the sum
necessary for the great day.

The idea had originated, I think, between Mrs. St. Quinten
and Churchill Smith. Churchill Smith was a man with whom,
I must own, I never felt that perfect sympathy which bound me
to the others. Perhaps among us all he was the most gifted. Such
at least was the opinion of Mrs. St. Quinten and, perhaps, of
himself. He was a cousin of the lady's, and had made himself particularly objectionable to the husband by instigating his relative
to write philosophical essays. It was his own specialty to be an
unbeliever and a German scholar; and we gave him credit for
being so deep in both arts that no man could go deeper. It had,
however, been decided among us very early in our arrangements,
— and so decided, not without great chance of absolute disrup-
tion, — that his infidelity was not to bias the magazine. He was
to take the line of deep thinking, German poetry, and unintelligible speculation generally. He used to talk of Comte, whose

name I had never heard till it fell from his lips, and was prepared
to prove that Coleridge was very shallow. He was generally dirty,
unshorn, and, as I thought, disagreeable. He called Mrs. St.
Quinten, Lydia, because of his cousinship, and no one knew how
or where he lived. I believe him to have been a most unselfish,
abstemious man, — one able to control all appetites of the flesh.
I think that I have since heard that he perished in a Russian
prison.

My dearest friend among the number was Patrick Regan, a
young Irish barrister, who intended to shine at the English Bar.
I think the world would have used him better had his name been
John Tomkins. The history of his career shows very plainly that
the undoubted brilliance of his intellect, and his irrepressible personal humour and good humour have been always unfairly
weighted by those Irish names. What attorney, with any serious
matter in hand, would willingly go to a barrister who called himself Pat Regan? And then, too, there always remained with him
just a hint of a brogue, — and his nose was flat in the middle! I
do not believe that all the Irishmen with flattened noses have
had the bone of the feature broken by a crushing blow in a street
row; and yet they look as though that peculiar appearance had
been the result of a fight with sticks. Pat has told me a score of
times that he was born so, and I believe him. He had a most
happy knack of writing verses, which I used to think quite equal
to Mr. Barham's, and he could rival the droll latinity of Father
Prout, who was coming out at that time with his "Dulcis Julia
Callage," and the like. Pat's father was an attorney at Cork; but
not prospering, I think, for poor Pat was always short of money.
He had, however, paid the fees, and was entitled to appear in wig
and gown wherever common-law barristers do congregate. He is
Attorney-General at one of the Turtle Islands this moment, with
a salary of £ 400 a year. I hear from him occasionally, and the
other day he sent me "Captain Crosbie is my name," done into
endecasyllábics. I doubt, however, whether he ever made a
penny by writing for the press. I cannot say that Pat was our
strongest prop. He sometimes laughed at "Lydia," — and then I
was brought into disgrace, as having introduced him to the company.
Bar; but, I think, never was called. Of all the men I have en-

countered in life he was certainly the most impecunious. Now he is a millionaire. He was one as to whom all who knew him, — friends and foes alike, — were decided that under no circumstances would he ever work, or by any possibility earn a penny. Since then he has applied himself to various branches of commerce, first at New York and then at San Francisco; he has laboured for twenty-four years almost without a holiday, and has shown a capability for sustained toil which few men have equalled. He had been introduced to our set by Walter Watt, of whom I will speak just now; and certainly, when I remember the brightness of his wit and the flow of his words, and his energy when he was earnest, I am bound to acknowledge that in searching for sheer intellect, — for what I may call power, — we did not do wrong to enroll Jack Hallam. He had various crude ideas in his head of what he would do for us, — having a leaning always to the side of bitter mirth. I think he fancied that satire might be his forte. As it is, they say that no man living has a quicker eye to the erection of a block of buildings in a coming city. He made a fortune at Chicago, and is said to have erected Omaha out of his own pocket. I am told that he pays income-tax in the United States on nearly a million dollars per annum. I wonder whether he would lend me five pounds if I asked him? I never knew a man so free as Jack at borrowing half-a-crown or a clean pocket-handkerchief.

Walter Watt was a fellow of _____. _____ I believe has fellows who do not take orders. It must have had one such in those days, for nothing could have induced our friend, Walter Watt, to go into the Church. How it came to pass that the dons of a college at Oxford should have made a fellow of so wild a creature was always a mystery to us. I have since been told that at _____ the reward could hardly be refused to a man who had gone out a "first" in a classics and had got the "Newdegate." Such had been the career of young Watt. And, though I say that he was wild, his moral conduct was not bad. He simply objected on principle to all authority, and was of opinion that the goods of the world should be in common. I must say of him that in regard to one individual his practice went even beyond his preaching; for Jack Hallam certainly consumed more of the fellowship than did Walter Watt himself. Jack was dark and swarthy. Walter was a fair little man, with long hair falling on the sides of his face, and cut away over his forehead, — as one sees it sometimes cut in a picture. He had round blue eyes, a well formed nose, and handsome mouth and chin. He was very far gone in his ideas of reform, and was quite in earnest in his hope that by means of the "Panjandrum" something might be done to stay the general wickedness, — or rather ugliness of the world. At that time Carlyle was becoming prominent as a thinker and writer among us, and Watt was never tired of talking to us of the hero of "Sartor Resartus." He was an excellent and most unselfish man, — whose chief fault was an inclination for the making of speeches, which he had picked up at an Oxford debating society. He now lies buried at Kensal Green. I thought to myself, when I saw another literary friend laid there some eight years since, that the place had become very quickly populated since I and Regan had seen poor Watt placed in his last home, almost amidst a desert.

Of myself, I need only say that at that time I was very young, very green, and very ardent as a politician. The Whigs were still in office; but we, who were young then, and warm in our political convictions, thought that the Whigs were doing nothing for us. It must be remembered that things and ideas have advanced so quickly during the last thirty years, that the conservatism of 1870 goes infinitely further in the cause of general reform than did the radicalism of 1840. I was regarded as a democrat because I was loud against the Corn Laws; and was accused of infidelity when I spoke against the Irish Church Endowments. I take some pride to myself that I should have seen these evils to be evils even thirty years ago. But to Household Suffrage I doubt whether even my spirit had ascended. If I remember rightly I was great upon annual parliaments; but I know that I was discriminative, and did not accept all the points of the seven-starred charter. I had an idea in those days, — I can confess it now after thirty years, — that I might be able to indite short political essays which should be terse, argumentative, and convincing, and at the same time full of wit and frolic. I never quite succeeded in pleasing even myself in any such composition. At this time I did a little humble work for the _____, but was quite resolved to fly at higher game than that.

As I began with the lady, so I must end with her. I had seen and read sheaves of her MS., and must express my conviction at this day, when all illusions are gone, that she wrote with wonderful ease and with some grace. A hard critic might perhaps say that it was slip-slop; — but still it was generally readable. I believe that in the recesses of her privacy, and under the dark and secret guidance of Churchill Smith, she did give way to German poetry and abstruse thought. I heard once that there was a paper of hers on the essence of existence, in which she answered that great question, as to personal entity, or as she put it, "What is it to be?" The paper never appeared before the Committee, though I remember the question to have been once suggested for discussion. Pat Regan answered it at once, — "A drop of something short," said he. I thought then that everything was at an end! Her translation into a rhymed verse of a play of Schiller's did come before us, and nobody could have behaved better than she did, when she was told that it hardly suited our project. What we expected from Mrs. St. Quinten in the way of literary performance, I cannot say that we ourselves had exactly realised, but we knew that she was always ready for work. She gave us tea and muffin, and bore with us when we were loud, and devoted her time to our purposes, and believed in us. She had exquisite tact in saving us from wordy quarrelling, and was never angry herself, — except when Pat Regan was too hard upon her. What became of her I never knew. When the days of the "Panjandrum" were at an end she vanished from our sight. I always hoped that Mr. St. Quinten reconciled himself to literature, and took her back to his bosom.

While we were only determining that the thing should be, all went smoothly with us. Columns, or the open page, made a little difficulty; but the lady settled it for us in favour of the double column. It is a style of page which certainly has a wiser look about it than the other; and then it has the advantage of being clearly distinguished from the ordinary empty book of the day. The word "padding," as belonging to literature, was then unknown; but the idea existed, — and perhaps the thing. We were quite resolved that there should be no padding in the "Panjandrum." I think our most ecstatic, enthusiastic, and accordant moments were those in which we resolved that it should be all good, all better than anything else, — all best. We were to struggle after excellence with an energy that should know no relaxing, — and the excellence was not to be that which might produce for us the greatest number of half-crowns, but of the sort which would increase truth in the world, and would teach men to labour hard and bear their burdens nobly, and become gods upon earth. I think our chief feeling was one of impatience in having to wait to find to what heaven death would usher us, who unfortunately had to be human before we could put on divinity. We wanted heaven at once, — and were not deterred, though Jack Hallam would borrow ninepence, and Pat Regan make his paltry little jokes.

We had worked hard for six months before we began to think of writing, or even of apportioning to each contributor what should be written for the first number. I shall never forget the delight there was in having the young publisher in to tea, and in putting him through his figures, and in feeling that it became us for the moment to condescend to matters of trade. We felt him to be an inferior being; but still it was much for us to have progressed so far towards reality as to have a real publisher come to wait upon us. It was at that time clearly understood that I was to be the editor, and I felt myself justified in taking some little lead in arranging matters with our energetic young friend. A remark that I made one evening was very mild, — simply some suggestion as to the necessity of having a more than ordinarily well-educated set of printers; — but I was snubbed infinitely by Churchill Smith. "Mr. X.," said he, "can probably tell us more about printing than we can tell him." I felt so hurt that I was almost tempted to leave the room at once. I knew very well that if I seceded Pat Regan would go with me, and that the whole thing must fall to the ground. Mrs. St. Quinten, however, threw instant oil upon the waters. "Churchill," said she, "let us live and learn. Mr. X., no doubt, knows. Why should we not share his knowledge?" I smothered my feelings in the public cause, but I was conscious of a wish that Mr. Smith might fall among the Philistines of Cursitor Street, and so of necessity be absent from our meeting. There was an idea among us that he crept out of his hiding-place, and came to our meeting by by-ways; which was confirmed when our hostess proposed that our evening should be changed from Thursday, the day first appointed, to Sunday. We all acceded willingly, led somewhat, I fear, by an idea that it was the proper thing for advanced spirits such as ours to go to work on that day which by ancient law is appointed for rest.

Mrs. St. Quinten would always open our meeting with a little speech. "Gentlemen and partners in this enterprise," she would say, "the tea is made, and the muffins are ready. Our hearts are bound together in the work. We are all in earnest in the good cause of political reform and social regeneration. Let the spirit of harmony prevail among us. Mr. Hallam, perhaps you'll take the cover off." To see Jack Hallam eat muffins was, — I will say "a caution," if the use of the slang phrase may be allowed to me for the occasion. It was presumed among us that on these days he had not dined. Indeed, I doubt whether he often did dine, — supper being his favourite meal. I have supped with him more than once, at his invitation, — when to be without coin in my own pocket was no disgrace, — and have wondered at the equanimity with which the vendors of shell-fish have borne my friend's intimation that he must owe them the little amount due for our evening entertainment. On these occasions his friend Watt was never with him, for Walter's ideas as to the common use of property were theoretical. Jack came to Mrs. St. Quinten's one evening in my best, — nay, why dally with the truth? — in my only pair of black dress trousers, which I had lent him ten days before, on the occasion, as I then believed, of a real dinner party. I almost denounced him before his colleagues. I think I should have done so had I not felt that he would in some fashion have so turned the tables on me that I should have been the sufferer. There are men with whom one comes by the worst in any contest, let justice on one's own side be ever so strong and ever so manifest.

But this is digression. After the little speech, Jack would begin upon the muffins, and Churchill Smith, — always seated at his cousin's left hand, — would hang his head upon his hand, wearing a look of mingled thought and sorrow on his brow. He never would eat muffins. We fancied that he fed himself with penny hunches of bread as he walked along the streets. As a man he was wild, unsocial, untamable; but, as a philosopher, he had certainly put himself beyond most of those wants to which Jack Hallam and others among us were still subject. "Lydia," he once said, when pressed hard to partake of the good things provided, "man cannot live by muffins alone, — no, nor by tea and muffins. That by which he can live is hard to find. I doubt we have not found it yet."

This, to me, seemed to be rank apostasy, — infidelity to the cause which he was bound to trust as long as he kept his place in that society. How shall you do anything in the world, achieve any success, unless you yourself believe in yourself? And if there be a partnership either in mind or matter, your partner must be the same to you as yourself. Confidence is so essential to the establishment of a magazine! I felt then, at least, that the "Panjandrum" would have no chance without it, and I rebuked Mr. Churchill Smith. "We know what you mean by that," said I; — "because we don't talk German metaphysics, you think we ain't worth our salt."

"So much worth it," said he, "that I trust heartily you may find enough to save you even yet."

I was about to boil over with wrath; but Walter Watt was on his legs making a speech about the salt of the earth, before I had my words ready. Churchill Smith would put up with Walter when he would endure words from no one else. I used to think him mean enough to respect the Oxford fellowship, but I have since fancied that he fancied that he had discovered a congenial spirit. In those days I certainly did despise Watt's fellowship, but in later life I have come to believe that men who get rewards have generally earned them. Watt on this occasion made a speech to which in my passion I hardly attended; but I well remember how, when I was about to rise in my wrath, Mrs. St. Quinten put her hand on my arm, and calmed me. "If you," said she, "to whom we most trust for orderly guidance, are to be the first to throw down the torch of discord, what will become of us?"

"I haven't thrown down any torch," said I.

"Neither take one up," said she, pouring out tea for me as she spoke.

"As for myself," said Regan, "I like metaphysics, — and I like them German. There is nothing so stupid and pig-headed as that insular feeling which makes us think nothing to be good that is not home-grown."

"All the same," said Jack, "whoever ate a good muffin out of

London?"

"Mr. Hallam, Mary is bringing up some more," said our hostess. She was an open-handed woman, and the supply of these delicacies never ran low as long as the "Panjandrum" was a possibility.

It was, I think, on this evening that we decided finally for columns and for a dark grey wrapper, — with a portrait of the Panjandrum in the centre; a fancy portrait it must necessarily be; but we knew that we could trust for that to the fertile pencil of Mrs. St. Quinten. I had come prepared with a specimen cover, as to which I had in truth consulted an artistic friend, and had taken with it no inconsiderable labour. I am sure, looking back over the long interval of years at my feelings on that occasion, — I am sure, I say, that I bore well the alterations and changes which were made in that design until at last nothing remained of it. But what matters a wrapper? Surely of any printed and published work it is by the interior that you should judge it. It is not that old conjurer's head that has given its success to "Blackwood," nor yet those four agricultural boys that have made the "Cornhill" what it is.

We had now decided on columns, on the cover, and the colour. We had settled on the number of pages, and had thumbed four or five specimens of paper submitted to us by our worthy publisher. In that matter we had taken his advice, and chosen the cheapest; but still we liked the thumbing of the paper. It was business. Paper was paper then, and bore a high duty. I do not think that the system of illustration had commenced in those days, though a series of portraits was being published by one distinguished contemporary. We readily determined that we would attempt nothing of that kind. There then arose a question as to the insertion of a novel. Novels were not then, as now, held to be absolutely essential for the success of a magazine. There were at that time magazines with novels and magazines without them. The discreet young publisher suggested to us that we were not able to pay for such a story as would do us any credit. I myself, who was greedy for work, with bated breath offered to make an attempt. It was received but with faint thanks, and Walter Watt, rising on his legs, with eyes full of fire and arms extended, denounced novels in the general. It was not for such purpose that he was about to devote to the production of the "Panjandrum" any erudition that he might have acquired and all the intellect that God had given him. Let those who wanted novels go for them to the writer who dealt with fiction in the open market. As for him, he at any rate would search for truth. We reminded him of Blumine. * "Tell your novel in three pages," said he, "and tell it as that is told, and I will not object to it." We were enabled, however, to decide that there should be no novel in the "Panjandrum."

Then at length came the meeting at which we were to begin our real work and divide our tasks among us. Hitherto Mr. X. had usually joined us, but a hint had been given to him that on this and a few following meetings we would not trespass on his time. It was quite understood that he, as publisher, was to have nothing to do with the preparation or arrangement of the matter to be published. We were, I think, a little proud of keeping him at a distance when we came to the discussion of that actual essence of our combined intellects which was to be issued to the world under the grotesque name which we had selected. That mind and matter should be kept separate was impressed very strongly upon all of us. Now, we were "mind," and Mr. X. was "matter." He was matter at any rate in reference to this special work, and, therefore, when we had arrived at that vital point we told him, — I had been commissioned to do so, — that we did not require his attendance just at present. I am bound to say that Mr. X. behaved well to the end, but I do not think that he ever warmed to the "Panjandrum" after that. I fancy that he owns two or three periodicals now, and hires his editors quite as easily as he does his butlers, — and with less regard to their characters.

I spent a nervous day in anticipation of that meeting. Pat Regan was with me all day, and threatened dissolution. "There isn't a fellow in the world," said he, "that I love better than Walter Watt, and I'd go to Jamaica to serve him;" — when the time came, which it did, oh, so soon! he was asked to go no further than Kensal Green; — "but _____!" and then Pat paused.

"You're ready to quarrel with him," said I, "simply because he won't laugh at your jokes."

* See "Sartor Resartus."

"There's a good deal in that," said Regan; "and when two men are in a boat together each ought to laugh at the other's jokes. But the question isn't as to our laughing. If we can't make the public laugh sometimes we may as well shut up shop. Walter is so intensely serious that nothing less austere than lay sermons will suit his conscience."

"Let him preach his sermon, and do you crack your jokes. Surely we can't be dull when we have you and Jack Hallam?"

"Jack'll never write a line," said Regan; "he only comes for the muffins. Then think of Churchill Smith, and the sort of stuff he'll expect to force down our readers' throats."

"Smith is sour, but never tedious," said I. Indeed I expected great things from Smith, and so I told my friend.

"'Lydia' will write," said Pat. We used to call her Lydia behind her back. "And so will Churchill Smith and Watt. I do not doubt that they have quires written already. But no one will read a word of it. Jack, and you, and I will intend to write, but we shall never do anything."

This I felt to be most unjust, because, as I have said before, I was already engaged upon the press. My work was not renumerative, but it was regularly done. "I am afraid of nothing," said I, "but distrust. You can move a mountain if you will only believe that you can move it."

"Just so; — but in order to avoid the confusion consequent on general motion among the mountains, I and other men have been created without that sort of faith." It was always so with my poor friend, and, consequently, he is now Attorney-General at a Turtle Island. Had he believed as I did, — he and Jack, — I still think that the "Panjandrum" might have been a great success. "Don't you look so glum," he went on to say. "I'll stick to it, and do my best. I did put Lord Bateman into rhymed Latin verse for you last night."

Then he repeated to me various stanzas, of which I still remember one; —

> "*Tuam duxi, verum est, filiam, sed merum est;*
> *Si virgo mihi data fuit, virgo tibi redditur.*
> *Venit in ephippio mihi, et concipio*
> *Satis est si triga pro reditu conceditur.*"

This cheered me a little, for I thought that Pat was good at these things, and I was especially anxious to take the wind out of the sails of "Fraser" and Father Prout. "Bring it with you," said I to him, giving him great priase. "It will raise our spirits to know that we have something ready." He did bring it; but "Lydia" required to have it all translated to her, word by word. It went off heavily, and was at last objected to by the lady. For the first and last time during our debates Miss Collins ventured to give an opinion on the literary question under discussion. She agreed, she said, with her friend, in thinking that Mr. Regan's Latin poem should not be used. The translation was certainly as good as the ballad and I was angry. Miss Collins, at any rate, need not have interfered.

At last the evening came, and we sat round the table, after the tea-cups had been removed, each anxious for his allotted task. Pat had been so far right in his views as to the diligence of three of our colleagues, that they came furnished with piles of manuscript. Walter Watt, who was afflicted with no false shame, boldly placed before him on the table a heap of blotted paper. Churchill Smith held in his hand a roll; but he did not, in fact, unroll it during the evening. He was a man very fond of his own ideas, of his own modes of thinking and manner of life, but not prone to put himself forward. I do not mind owning that I disliked him; but he had a power of self-abnegation which was, to say the least of it, respectable. As I entered the room, my eyes fell on a mass of dishevelled sheets of paper which lay on the sofa behind the chair on which Mrs. St. Quinten always sat, and I knew that these were her contributions. Pat Regan, as I have said, produced his unfortunate translation, and promised with the greatest good humour to do another when he was told that his last performance did not quite suit Mrs. St. Quinten's views. Jack had nothing ready; nor, indeed, was anything "ready" ever expected from him. I, however, had my own ideas as to what Jack might do for us. For myself, I confess that I had in my pocket from two to three hundred lines of what I conceived would be a very suitable introduction, in verse, for the first number. It was my duty, I thought, as editor, to provide the magazine with a few initiatory words. I did not, however, produce the rhymes on that evening, having learned to feel that any strong expression of self on the part of one member at that board was not gratifying to the others. I did take some pains in composing those lines, and thought at the time that I had been not unhappy in mixing the useful with the sweet. How many hours shall I say that I devoted to them? Alas, alas, it matters not now! Those words which I did love well never met any eye but my own. Though I had them then by heart, they were never sounded in any ear. It was not personal glory that I desired. They were written that the first number of the "Panjandrum" might appear becomingly before the public, and the first number of the "Panjandrum" never appeared! I looked at them the other day, thinking whether it might be too late for them to serve another turn. I will never look at them again.

But from the starting of the conception of the "Panjandrum" I had had a great idea, and that idea was discussed at length on the evening of which I am speaking. We must have something that should be sparkling, clever, instructive, amusing, philoso- cial, remarkable, and new, all at the same time! That such a thing might be achieved in literature I felt convinced. And it must be the work of three or four together. It should be some- thing that should force itself into notice, and compel attention. It should deal with the greatest questions of humanity, and deal with them wisely, — but still should deal with them in a sportive spirit. Philosophy and humour might, I was sure, be combined. Social science might be taught with witty words, and abstract politics made as agreeable as a novel. There had been the "Corn Law Rhymes," — and the *"Noctes."* It was, however, essentially necessary that we should be new, and therefore I endeavoured, — vainly endeavoured, — to get those old things out of my head. Fraser's people had done a great stroke of business by calling their editor Mr. Yorke. If I could get our people to call me Mr. Lan- caster, something might come of it. But yet it was so needful that we should be new! The idea had been seething in my brain so constantly that I had hardly eat or slept free from it for the last six weeks. If I could roll Churchill Smith and Jack Hallam into one, throw in a dash of Walter Watt's fine political eagerness, make use of Regan's ready poetical facility, and then control it all by my own literary experience, the thing would be done. But it is so hard to blend the elements!

I had spoken often of it to Pat, and he had assented. "I'll do anything into rhyme," he used to say, "if that's what you mean." It was not quite what I meant. One cannot always convey one's meaning to another; and this difficulty is so infinitely increased when one is not quite clear in one's own mind! And then Pat, who was the kindest fellow in the world, and who bore with the utmost patience a restless energy which must often have troubled him sorely, had not really his heart in it as I had. "If Churchill Smith will send me ever so much of his stuff, I'll put it into Latin or English verse, just as you please, — and I can't say more than that." It was a great offer to make, but it did not exactly reach the point at which I was aiming.

I had spoken to Smith about it also. I knew that if we were to achieve success, we must do so in a great measure by the force of his intellectual energy. I was not seeking pleasure but success, and was willing therefore to endure the probable discourtesy, or at least want of cordiality, which I might encounter from the man. I must acknowledge that he listened to me with a rapt attention. Attention so rapt is more sometimes than one desires. Could he have helped me with a word or two now and again I should have felt myself to be more comfortable with him. I am inclined to think that two men get on better together in discussing a subject when they each speak a little at random. It creates a confidence, and enables a man to go on to the end. Churchill Smith heard me without a word, and then remarked that he had been too slow quite to catch my idea. Would I explain it again? I did explain it again, — though no doubt I was flustered, and blundered. "Certainly," said Churchill Smith, "if we can all be witty and all wise, and all witty and wise at the same time, and altogether, it will be very fine." The man was so uncongenial that there was no getting anything from him. I did not dare to suggest to him that he should submit the prose exposition of his ideas to the metrical talent of our friend Regan.

As soon as we were assembled I rose upon my legs, saying that I proposed to make a few preliminary observations. It certainly was the case that at this moment Mrs. St. Quinten was rinsing the teapot, and Mary Jane had not yet brought in the muffins.

We all know that when men meet together for special dinners, the speeches are not commenced till the meal is over; — and I would have kept my seat till Jack had done his worst with the delicacies, had it not been our practice to discuss our business with our plates and cups and saucers still before us. "You can't drink your tea on your legs," said Jack Hallam. "I have no such intention," said I. "What I have to lay before you will not take a minute." A suggestion, however, came from another quarter that I should not be so formal; and Mrs. St. Quinten, touching my sleeve, whispered to me a precaution against speech-making. I sat down, and remarked in a manner that I felt to be ludicrously inefficient, that I had been going to propose that the magazine should be opened by a short introductory paper. As the reader knows, I had the introduction then in my pocket. "Let us dash into the middle of our work at once," said Walter Watt. "No one reads introductions," said Regan; — my own friend, Pat Regan! "I own I don't think an introduction would do us any particular service," said "Lydia," turning to me with that smile which was so often used to keep us in good humour. I can safely assert that it was never vainly used on me. I did not even bring the verses out of my pocket, and thus I escaped at least the tortures of that criticism to which I should have been subjected had I been allowed to read them to the company. "So be it," said I. "Let us then dash into the middle of our work at once. It is only necessary to have a point settled. Then we can progress."

After that I was silent for a while, thinking it well to keep myself in the background. But no one seemed to be ready for speech. Walter Watt fingered his manuscript uneasily, and Mrs. St. Quinten made some remark not distinctly audible as to the sheets on the sofa. "But I must get rid of the tray first," she said. Churchill Smith sat perfectly still with his roll in his pocket. "Mrs. St. Quinten and gentlemen," I said, "I am happy to tell you that I have had a contribution handed to me which will go far to grace our first number. Our friend Regan has done 'Lord Bateman' into Latin verse with a Latinity and a rhyme so excellent that it will go far to make us at any rate equal to anything else in that line." Then I produced the translated ballad, and the little episode took place which I have already described. Mrs. St. Quinten insisted on understanding it in detail, and it was rejected. "Then, upon my word, I don't know what you are to get," said I. "Latin translations are not indisposable," said Walter Watt. "No doubt we can live without them," said Pat, with a fine good humour. He bore the disgrace of having his first contribution rejected with admirable patience. There was nothing he could not bear. To this day he bears being Attorney-General at the Turtle Islands.

Something must be done. "Perhaps," said I, turning to the lady, "Mrs. St. Quinten will begin by giving us her ideas as to our first number. She will tell us what she intends to do for us herself." She was still embarrassed by the tea-things. And I acknowledge that I was led to appeal to her at that moment because it was so. If I could succeed in extracting ideas they would be of infinitely more use to us than the reading of manuscript. To get the thing "licked into shape" must be our first object. As I had on this evening walked up to the sombre street leading into the New Road in which Mrs. St. Quinten lived I had declared to myself a dozen times that to get the thing "licked into shape" was the great desideratum. In my own imaginings I had licked it into shape. I had suggested to myself my own little introductory poem as a commencement, and Pat Regan's Latin ballad as a pretty finish to the first number. Then there should be some thirty pages of dialogue, — or trialogue, — or hexalogue if necessary, between the different members of our Board, each giving, under an assumed name, his view of what a perfect magazine should be. This I intended to be the beginning of a conversational element which should be maintained in all subsequent numbers, and which would enable us in that light and airy fashion which becomes a magazine to discuss all subjects of politics, philosophy, manners, literature, social science, and even religion if necessary, without inflicting on our readers the dulness of a long unbroken essay. I was very strong about these conversations, and saw my way to a great success, if I could only get my friends to act in concert with me. Very much depended on the names to be chosen, and I had my doubts whether Watt and Churchill Smith would consent to this slightly theatrical arrangement. Mrs. St. Quinten had already given in her adhesion, but was doubting whether she would call herself "Charlotte," — partly after Charlotte Corday, and partly after the lady who cut bread and butter, or "Mrs. Freeman,"

"—that name having, as she observed, been used before as a nom-de-plume,— or "Sophronie," after Madame de Sévigné, who was pleased so to call herself among the learned ladies of Madame de Rambouillet's bower. I was altogether in favour of Mrs. Freeman, which has the merit of simplicity; — but that was a minor point. Jack Hallam had chosen his appellation. Somewhere in the Lowlands he had seen over a small shop-door the name of John Neverapeny; and "John Neverapeny" he would be. I turned it over on my tongue a score of times, and thought that perhaps it might do. Pat wanted to call himself "The O'Blazes," but was at last persuaded to adopt the quieter name of "Tipperary," in which county his family had been established since Ireland was, — settled I think he said. For myself I was indifferent. They might give me what title they pleased. I had had my own notion, but that had been rejected. They might call me "Jones" or "Walker," if they thought proper. But I was very much wedded to the idea, and I still think that had it been stoutly carried out the results would have been happy.

I was the first to acknowledge that the plan was not new. There had been the "Noctes," and some imitations even of the "Noctes." But then, what is new? The "Noctes" themselves had been imitations from older works. If Socrates and Hippias had not conversed, neither probably would Mr. North and his friends. "You might as well tell me," said I, addressing colleagues, "that we must invent a new language, find new forms of expression, print our ideas in an unknown type, and impress them on some strange paper. Let our thoughts be new," said I, "and then let us select for their manifestation the most convenient form with which experience provides us." But they didn't see it. Mrs. St. Quinten liked the romance of being "Sophronie," and to Jack and Pat there was some fun in the nicknames; but in the real thing for which I was striving they had no actual faith. "If I could only lick them into shape," I had said to myself at the last moment, as I was knocking at Mrs. St. Quinten's door.

Mrs. St. Quinten was nearer, to my way of thinking, in this respect than the others; and therefore I appealed to her while the tea-things were still before her, thinking that I might obtain from her a suggestion in favour of the conversations. The introductory poem and the Latin ballad were gone. For spilt milk what wise man weeps? My verses had not even left my pocket. Not one there knew that they had been written. And I was determined that not one should know. But my conversations might still live. Ah, if I could only blend the elements! "Sophronie," said I, taking courage, and speaking with a voice from which all sense of shame and fear of failure were intended to be banished. "Sophronie will tell us what she intends to do for us herself."

I looked into my friend's face, and saw that she liked it. But she turned to her cousin, Churchill Smith, as though for approval, — and got none. "We had better be in earnest," said Churchill Smith, without moving a muscle of his face or giving the slightest return to the glance which had fallen upon him from his cousin.

"No one can be more thoroughly in earnest than myself," I replied.

"Let us have no calling of names," said Churchill Smith. "It is inappropriate, and especially so when a lady is concerned."

"It has been done scores of times," I rejoined; "and that too in the very highest phases of civilization, and among the most discreet of matrons."

"It seems to me to be twaddle," said Walter Watt.

"To my taste it's abominably vulgar," said Churchill Smith.

"It has answered very well in other magazines," said I.

"That's just the reason we should avoid it," said Walter Watt.

"I think the thing has been about worn out," said Pat Regan.

I was now thrown upon my mettle. Rising again upon my legs, — for the tea-things had now been removed, — I poured out my convictions, my hopes, my fears, my ambitions. If we were thus to disagree on every point, how should we ever blend the elements? If we could not forbear with one another, how could we hope to act together upon the age as one great force? If there was no agreement between us, how could we have the strength of union? Then I adverted with all the eloquence of which I was master to the great objects to be attained by these imaginary conversations. "That we may work together, each using his own words, — that is my desire," I said. And I pointed out to them how willing I was to be the least among them in this contest, to content myself with simply acting as chorus, and pointing to the lessons of wisdom which would fall from out of their mouths. I must say that they listened to me on this occasion with great patience. Churchill Smith sat there, with his great hollow eyes fixed upon me; but it seemed to me, as he looked, that even he was being persuaded. I threw myself into my words, and implored them to allow me on this occasion to put them on the road to success. When I had finished speaking I looked around, and for a moment I thought they were convinced. There was just a whispered word between our Sophronie and her cousin, and then she turned to me and spoke. I was still standing, and I bent down over her to catch the sentence she should pronounce. "Give it up," she said.

And I gave it up. With what a pang this was done few of my readers can probably understand. It had been my dream from my youth upwards. I was still young, no doubt, and looking back now I can see how insignificant were the aspirations which were then in question. But there is no period in a man's life in which it does not seem to him that his ambition is then, — at that moment, — culminating for him, till the time comes in which he begins to own to himself that his life is not fit for ambition. I had believed that I might be the means of doing something, and of doing it in this way. Very vague, indeed, had been my notions; — most crude my ideas. I can see that now. What it was that my interlocutors were to say to each other I had never clearly known. But I had felt that in this way each might speak his own speech without confusion and with delight to the reader. The elements, I had thought, might be so blent. Then there came that little whisper between Churchill Smith and our Sophronie, and I found that I had failed. "Give it up," said she.

"Oh, of course," I said, as I sat down; "only just settle what you mean to do." For some few minutes I hardly heard what matters were being discussed among them, and, indeed, during the remainder of the evening I took no real share in the conversation. I was too deeply wounded even to listen. I was resolute at first to abandon the whole affair. I had already managed to scrape together the sum of money which had been named as the share necessary for each of us to contribute towards the production of the first number, and that should be altogether at their disposal. As for editing a periodical in the management of which I was not allowed to have the slightest voice, that was manifestly out of the question. Nor could I contribute when every contribution which I suggested was rejected before it was seen. My money I could give them, and that no doubt would be welcome. With these gloomy thoughts my mind was so full that I actually did not hear the words with which Walter Watt and Churchill Smith were discussing the papers proposed for the first number.

There was nothing read that evening. No doubt it was visible to them all that I was, as it were, a blighted spirit among them. They could not but know how hard I had worked, how high had been my hopes, how keen was my disappointment; — and they felt for me. Even Churchill Smith, as he shook hands with me at the door, spoke a word of encouragement. "Do not expect to do things too quickly," said he. "I don't expect to do anything," said I. "We may do something even yet," said he, "if we can be humble, and patient, and persevering. We may do something, though it be ever so little." I was humble enough certainly, and knew that I had persevered. As for patience; — well; I would endeavour even to be patient.

But, prior to that, Mrs. St. Quinten had explained to me the programme which had now been settled between the party. We were not to meet again till that day fortnight, and then each of us was to come provided with the matter that would fill twenty-one printed pages of the magazine. This, with the title-page, would comprise the whole first number. We might all do as we liked with our own pages, — each within his allotted space, — filling the whole with one essay, or dividing it into two or three short papers. In this way there might be scope for Pat Regan's verse, or for any little badinage in which Jack Hallam might wish to express himself. And in order to facilitate our work, and for the sake of general accommodation, a page or two might be lent or borrowed. "Whatever anybody writes then," I asked, "must be admitted?" Mrs. St. Quinten explained to me that this had not been their decision. The whole matter produced was of course to be read, — each contributor's paper by the contributor himself, and it was to be printed and inserted in the number, if any three would vote for its insertion. On this occasion the author, of course, would have no vote. The votes were to be handed in, written on slips of paper, so that there might be no priority in voting, — so that no one should be required to express himself before or after his neighbour. It was very complex, but I made no objection.

As I walked home all alone, — for I had no spirits to join Regan and Jack Hallam, who went in search of supper at the Haymarket, — I turned over Smith's words in my mind, and resolved that I would be humble, patient, and persevering, — so that something might be done, though it were, as he said, ever so little. I would struggle still; — though everything was to be managed in a manner adverse to my own ideas and wishes, I would still struggle. I would still hope that the "Panjandrum" might become a great fact in the literature of my country.

Part II. — Despair

A fortnight had been given to us to prepare our matter, and during that fortnight I saw none of my colleagues. I purposely kept myself apart from them in order that I might thus give a fairer chance to the scheme which had been adopted. Others might borrow or lend their pages, but I would do the work allotted to me, and would attend the next meeting as anxious for the establishment and maintenance of the "Panjandrum" as I had been when I had hoped that the great consideration which I had given personally to the matter might have been allowed to have some weight. And gradually, as I devoted the first day of my fortnight to thinking of my work, I taught myself to hope again, and to look forward to a time when, by the sheer weight of my own industry and persistency, I might acquire that influence with my companions of which I had dreamed of becoming the master. After all, could I blame them for not trusting me, when as yet I had given them no ground for such confidence? What had I done that they should be willing to put their thoughts, their aspirations, their very brains and inner selves under my control? But something might be done which would force them to regard me as their leader. So I worked hard at my twenty-one pages, and during the fortnight spoke no word of the "Panjandrum" to any human being.

But my work did not get itself done without very great mental distress. The choice of a subject had been left free to each contributor. For myself I would almost have preferred that someone should have dictated to me the matter to which I should devote myself. How would it be with our first number if each of us were to write a political essay of exactly twenty-one pages, or a poem of that length in blank verse, or a humorous narrative? Good heavens! How were we to expect success with the public if there were no agreement between ourselves as to the nature of our contributions, no editorial power in existence for our mutual support? I went down and saw Mr. X., and found him to be almost indifferent as to the magazine. "You see, sir," said he, "the matter isn't in my hands. If I can give any assistance, I shall be very happy; but it seems to me that you want someone with experience." "I could have put them right if they'd have let me," I replied. He was very civil, but it was quite clear to me that Mr. X.'s interest in the matter was over since the day of his banishment from Mrs. St. Quinten's tea-table. "What do you think is a good sort of subject," I asked him, — as it were cursorily; "with a view, you know, to the eye of the public, just at the present moment?" He declined to suggest any subject, and I was thrown back among the depths of my own feelings and convictions. Now, could we have blended our elements together, and discussed all this in really amicable council, each would have corrected what there might have been of rawness in the other, and in the freedom of conversation our wits would have grown from the warmth of mutual encouragement. Such, at least, was my belief then. Since that I have learned to look at the business with eyes less enthusiastic. Let a man have learned the trick of the pen, let him not smoke too many cigars over night, and let him get into his chair within half an hour after breakfast, and I can tell you almost to a line how much of a magazine article he will produce in three hours. It does not much matter what the matter be, — only this, that if his task be that of reviewing, he may be expected to supply a double quantity. Three days, three out of the fourteen, passed by, and I could think of no fitting subject on which to begin the task I had appointed myself of teaching the British public. Politics at the moment were rather dull, and no very great question was agitating the minds of men. Lord Melbourne was Prime Minister, and had in the course of the Session been subjected to the usual party attacks. We intended to go a great deal further than Lord Melbourne in advocating liberal measures, and were disposed to regard him and his colleagues as antiquated fogies in state-craft; but, nevertheless, as against Sir Robert Peel, we should have given him the benefit of our defence. I did not, however, feel any special call to write up Lord Melbourne. Lord John was just then our pet minister; but even on his behalf I did not find myself capable of filling twenty-one closely-printed pages with matter which should really stir the public mind. In a first number, to stir the public mind is everything. I didn't think that my colleagues sufficiently realised that fact, — though I had indeed endeavoured to explain it to them. In the second, third, or fourth publications you may descend gradually to an ordinary level; you may become, — not exactly dull, — for fulness in a magazine should be avoided, — but what I may perhaps call "*adagio*" as compared with the "*con forza*" movement with which the publication certainly should be opened. No reader expects to be supplied from month to month with the cayenne pepper and shallot style of literature; but in the preparation of a new literary banquet, the first dish cannot be too highly spiced. I knew all that, — and then turned it over in mind whether I could not do something about the ballot.

It had never occurred to me before that there could be any difficulty in finding a subject. I had to reject the ballot because at that period of my life I had, in fact, hardly studied the subject. I was liberal, and indeed radical, in all my political ideas. I was ready to "go in" for anything that was undoubtedly liberal and radical. In a general way I was as firm in my politics as any member of the House of Commons, and had thought as much on public subjects as some of them. I was an eager supporter of the ballot. But when I took pen in my hand there came upon me a feeling that, —that, —that I didn't exactly know how to say anything about it that other people would care to read. The twenty-one pages loomed before me as a wilderness, which, with such a staff, I could never traverse. It had not occurred to me before that it would be so difficult for a man to evoke from his mind ideas on a subject with which he supposed himself to be familiar. And, such thoughts as I had, I could clothe in no fitting words. On the fifth morning, driven to despair, I did write a page or two upon the ballot; and then, — sinking back in my chair, I began to ask myself a question, as to which doubt was terrible to me. Was this the kind of work to which my gifts were applicable? The pages which I had already written were manifestly not adapted to stir the public mind. The sixth and seventh days I passed altogether within my room, never once leaving the house. I drank green tea. I ate meat very slightly cooked. I debarred myself from food for several hours, so that the flesh might be kept well under. I sat up one night, nearly till daybreak, with a wet towel round my head. On the next I got up, and lit my own fire, at four o'clock. Thinking that I might be stretching the cord too tight, I took to reading a novel, but could not remember the words as I read them, so painfully anxious was I to produce the work I had undertaken to perform. On the morning of the eighth day I was still without a subject.

I felt like the man who undertook to play the violin at a dance for five shillings and a dinner, — the dinner to be paid in advance; but who, when making his bargain, had forgotten that he had never learned a note of music! I had undertaken even to lead the band, and, as it seemed, could not evoke a sound. A horrid idea came upon me that I was struck, as it were, with sudden idiocy. My mind had absolutely fled from me. I sat in my arm-chair, looking at the wall, counting the pattern on the paper, and hardly making any real effort to think. I went on muttering to myself, "No, the ballot won't do;" as though there were nothing else but the ballot with which to stir the public mind. On the eighth morning I made a minute and quite correct calculation of the number of words that were demanded of me, — taking the whole at forty-two pages, because of the necessity of recopying, — and I found that about four hours a day would be required for the mere act of writing. The paper was there, and the pen and ink; — but beyond that there was nothing ready. I had thought to rack my brain, but I began to doubt whether I had a brain to rack. Of all those matters of public interest which had hitherto been to me the very salt of my life, I could not remember one which could possibly be converted into twenty-one pages of type. Unconsciously I kept on muttering words about the ballot. "The ballot be _____!" I said, aloud to myself in my agony.

On that Sunday evening I began to consider what excuse I might best make to my colleagues. I might send and say I was very sick. I might face them, and quarrel with them, — because of their ill-treatment of me. Or I might tell only half a lie, keeping within the letter of the truth, and say that I had not yet finished my work. But no. I would not lie at all. Late on that Sunday evening there came upon me a grand idea. I would stand up before them and confess my inability to do the work I had undertaken. I arranged the words of my little speech, and almost took delight in them. "I, who have intended to be a teacher, am now aware that I have hardly as yet become a pupil." In such case, the "Panjandrum" would be at an end. The elements had not been happily blended; but without me they could not, I was sure, be kept in any concert. The "Panjandrum" — which I had already learned to love as a mother loves her first-born, — the dear old "Panjandrum" must perish before its birth. I felt the pity of it! The thing itself, — the idea and theory of it, had been very good. But how shall a man put forth a magazine when he finds himself unable to write a page of it within the compass of a week? The meditations of that Sunday were very bitter, but perhaps they were useful. I had long since perceived that mankind are divided into two classes, — those who shall speak, and those who shall listen to the speech of others. In seeing clearly the existence of such a division I had hitherto always assumed myself to belong to the first class. Might it not be probable that I had made a mistake, and that it would become me modestly to take my allotted place in the second!

On the Monday morning I began to think that I was ill, and resolved that I would take my hat and go out into the park, and breathe some air, — let the "Panjandrum" live or die. Such another week as the last would, I fancied, send me to Hanwell. It was now November, and at ten o'clock, when I looked out, there was a light drizzling rain coming down, and the pavement of the street was deserted. It was just the morning for work, were work possible. There still lay on the little table in the corner of the room the square single sheet of paper, with its margin doubled down, all fitted for the printer, — only that the sheet was still blank. I looked at the page, and I rubbed my brow, and I gazed into the street, — and then determined that a two hours' ring round the Regent's Park was the only chance left for me.

As I put on my thick boots and old hat and prepared myself for a thorough wetting, I felt as though at last I had hit upon the right plan. Violent exercise was needed, and then inspiration might come. Inspiration would come the sooner if I could divest myself from all effort in searching for it. I would take my walk and employ my mind, simply, in observing the world around me. For some distance there was but little of the world to observe. I was lodging at this period in a quiet and eligible street not far from Theobald's Road. Thence my way lay through Bloomsbury Square, Russell Square, and Gower Street, and as I went I found the pavement to be almost deserted. The thick soft rain came down, not with a splash and various currents, running off and leaving things washed though wet, but gently insinuating itself everywhere, and covering even the flags with mud. I cared nothing for the mud. I went through it all with a happy scorn for the poor creatures who were endeavouring to defend their clothes with umbrellas. "Let the heavens do their worst to me," I said to myself as I spun along with eager steps; and I was conscious of a feeling that external injuries could avail me nothing if I could only cure the weakness that was within.

The park too was nearly empty. No place in London is ever empty now, but thirty years ago the population was palpably thinner. I had not come out, however, to find a crowd. A damp boy sweeping a crossing, or an old woman trying to sell an apple, were sufficient to fill my mind with thoughts as to the affairs of my fellow creatures. Why should it have been allotted to that old woman to sit there, placing all her hopes on the chance sale of a few apples, the cold rain entering her very bones and driving rheumatism into all her joints, while another old woman, of whom I had read a paragraph that morning, was appointed to entertain royalty, and go about the country with five or six carriages and four? Was there injustice in this, — and if so, whence had the injustice come? The reflection was probably not new; but, if properly thought out, might it not suffice for the one-and-twenty pages? "Sally Brown, the barrow-woman *v.* the Duchess of _____!" Would it not be possible to make the two women plead against each other in some imaginary court of justice, beyond the limits of our conventional life, — some court in which the duchess should be forced to argue her own case, and in which the barrow-woman would decidedly get the better of her? If this could be done how happy would have been my walk through the mud and slush!

As I was thinking of this I saw before me on the pathway a stout woman, — apparently middle-aged, but her back was towards me, — leading a girl who might perhaps be ten or eleven years old. They had come up one of the streets from the New Road to the Park, and were hurrying along so fast that the girl, who held the woman by the arm, was almost running. The woman was evidently a servant, but in authority, — an upper nurse perhaps, or a housekeeper. Why she should have brought her charge out in the rain was a mystery; but I could see from the elasticity of the child's step that she was happy and very eager. She was a well-made girl, with long well-rounded legs, which came freely down beneath her frock, with strong firm boots, a straw hat, and a plaid shawl wound carefully round her throat and waist. As I followed them those rapid legs of hers seemed almost to twinkle in their motion as she kept pace with the stout woman who was conducting her. The mud was all over her stockings; but still there was about her an air of well-to-do comfort which made me feel that the mud was no more than a joke. Every now and then I caught something of a glimpse of her face as she half turned herself round in talking to the woman. I could see, or at least I could fancy that I saw that she was fair, with large round eyes and soft light brown hair. Children did not then wear wigs upon their backs, and I was driven to exercise my fancy as to her locks. At last I resolved that I would pass them and have one look at her, — and I did so. It put me to my best pace to do it, but gradually I overtook them and could hear that the girl never ceased talking as she ran. As I went by them I distinctly heard her words, "Oh, Anne, I do so wonder what he's like!" "You'll see, miss," said Anne. I looked back and saw that she was exactly as I had thought, — a fair, strong, healthy girl, with round eyes and large mouth, broad well-formed nose, and light hair. Who was the "he," as to whom her anxiety was so great, — the "he" whom she was tripping along through the rain and mud to see, and kiss and love, and wonder at? And why hadn't she been taken in a cab? Would she be allowed to take off those very dirty stockings before she was introduced to her new-found brother, or wrapped in the arms of her stranger-father?

I saw no more of them, and heard no further word; but I

thought a great deal of the girl. Ah me, if she could have been a young unknown, newly-found sister of my own, how warmly would I have welcomed her! How closely would I have folded her in my arms; how anxious would I have been with Anne as to those damp clothes; what delight would I have had in feeding her, coaxing her, caressing her, and playing with her! There had seeemed to belong to her a wholesome strong health, which it had made me for the moment happy even to witness. And then the sweet, eloquent anxiety of her voice, — "Oh, Anne, I do so wonder what he's like!" While I heard her voice I had seemed to hear and know so much of her! And then she had passed out of my ken for ever!

I thought no more about the duchess and the apple-woman, but devoted my mind entirely to the girl and her brother. I was persuaded that it must be a brother. Had it been a father there would have been more of awe in her tone. It certainly was a brother. Gradually, as the unforced imagination came to play upon the matter, a little picture fashioned itself in my mind. The girl was my own sister, — a sister whom I had never seen till she was thus brought to me for protection and love; but she was older, just budding into womanhood, instead of running beside her nurse with twinkling legs. There, however, was the same broad, honest face, the same round eyes, the same strong nose and mouth. She had come to me for love and protection, having no other friend in the world to trust. But, having me, I proudly declared to myself that she needed nothing further. In two short months I was nothing to her, — or almost nothing. I had a friend, and in two little months my friend had become so much more than I ever could have been!

These wondrous castles in the air never get themselves well built, when the mind, with premeditated skill and labour, sets itself to work to build them. It is when they come uncalled for that they stand erect and strong before the mind's eye, with every mullioned window perfect, the rounded walls all there, the embrasures cut, the fosse dug, and the drawbridge down. As I had made this castle for myself, as I had sat with this girl by my side, calling her the sweetest names, as I had seen her blush when my friend came near her, and had known at once, with a mixed agony and joy, how the thing was to be, I swear that I never once thought of the "Panjandrum." I walked the whole round of the Regent's Park, perfecting the building; — and I did perfect it, took the girl to church, gave her away to my friend Walker, and came back and sobbed and sputtered out my speech at the little breakfast, before it occurred to me to suggest to myself that I might use the thing.

Churchill Smith and Walter Watt had been dead against a novel; and, indeed, the matter had been put to the vote, and it had been decided that there should be no novel. But, what is a novel? The purport of that vote had been to negative a long serial tale, running on from number to number, in a manner which has since become well understood by the reading public. I had thought my colleagues wrong, and so thinking, it was clearly my duty to correct their error, if I might do so without infringing that loyalty and general obedience to expressed authority which are so essential to such a society as ours. Before I had got back to Theobald's Road I had persuaded myself that a short tale would be the very thing for the first number. It might not stir the public mind. To do that I would leave to Churchill Smith and Walter Watt. But a well-formed little story, such as that of which I had now the full possession, would fall on the readers of the "Panjandrum" like sweet rain in summer, making things fresh and green and joyous. I was quite sure that it was needed. Walter Watt might say what he pleased, and Churchill Smith might look at me as sternly as he would, sitting there silent with his forehead on his hand; but I knew at least as much about a magazine as they did. At any rate, I would write my tale. That very morning it had seemed to me to be impossible to get anything written. Now, as I hurried up-stairs to get rid of my wet clothes, I felt that I could not take the pen quickly enough into my hand. I had a thing to say, and I would say it. If I could complete my story, — and I did not doubt its completion from the very moment in which I realised its conception, — I should be saved, at any rate, from the disgrace of appearing empty-handed in Mrs. St. Quinten's parlour. Within a quarter of an hour of my arrival at home I had seated myself at my table and written the name of the tale, — "The New Inmate."

I doubt whether any five days in my life were ever happier than those which were devoted to this piece of work. I began it that

Monday afternoon, and finished it on the Friday night. While I was at the task all doubt vanished from my mind. I did not care a fig for Watt or Smith, and was quite sure that I should carry Mrs. St. Quinten with me. Each night I copied fairly what I had written in the day, and I came to love the thing with an extreme love. There was a deal of pathos in it, — at least so I thought, — and I cried over it like a child. I had strained all my means to prepare for the coming of the girl, — I am now going back for a moment to my castle in the air, — and had furnished for her a little sitting-room and as pretty a white-curtained chamber as a girl ever took pleasure in calling her own. There were books for her, and a small piano, and a low sofa, and all little feminine belongings. I had said to myself that everything should be for her, and I had sold my horse, — the horse of my imagination, the reader will understand, for I had never in truth possessed such an animal, — and told my club friends that I should no longer be one of them. Then the girl had come, and had gone away to Walker, — as it seemed to me at once, — to Walker, who still lived in lodgings, and had not even a second sitting-room for her comfort, — to Walker, who was, indeed, a good fellow in his way, but possessed of no particular attractions either in wit, manners, or beauty! I wanted them to change with me, and to take my pretty home. I should have been delighted to go to a garret, leaving them everything. But Walker was proud, and would not have it so; and the girl protested that the piano and the white dimity curtains were nothing to her. Walker was everything; — Walker, of whom she had never heard, when she came but a few weeks since to me as the only friend left to her in the world! I worked myself up to such a pitch of feeling over my story that I could hardly write it for my tears. I saw myself standing all alone in that pretty sitting-room after they were gone, and I pitied myself with an exceeding pity. *"Si vis me fiere, dolendum est primum libi ipsi."* If success was to be obtained by obeying that instruction, I might certainly expect success.

The way in which my work went without a pause was delightful. When the pen was not in my hand I was longing for it. While I was walking, eating, or reading, I was still thinking of my story. I dreamt of it. It came to me to be a matter that admitted of no doubt. The girl with the muddy stockings, who had thus provided me in my need, was to me a blessed memory. When I kissed my sister's brow, on her first arrival, she was in my arms, —palpably. All her sweetnesses were present to me, as though I had her there, in the little turning out of Theobald's Road. To this moment I can distinguish the voice in which she spoke to me that little whispered word, when I asked her whether she cared for Walker. When one thinks of it, the reality of it all is appalling. What need is there of a sister or a friend in the flesh, — a sister or a friend with probably so many faults, — when by a little exercise of the mind they may be there, at your elbow, faultless? It came to pass that the tale was more dear to me than the magazine. As I read it through for the third or fourth time on the Sunday morning, I was chiefly anxious for the "Panjandrum," in order that "The New Inmate" might see the world.

We were to meet that evening at eight o'clock, and it was understood that the sitting would be prolonged to a late hour, because of the readings. It would fall to my lot to take the second reading, as coming next to Mrs. St. Quinten, and I should, at any rate, not be subjected to a weary audience. We had, however, promised each other to be very patient; and I was resolved that, even to the production of Churchill Smith, who would be the last, I would give an undivided and eager attention. I determined also in my joy that I would vote against the insertion of no colleague's contribution. Were we not in a boat together, and would not each do his best? Even though a paper might be dull, better a little dulness than the crushing of a friend's spirit. I fear that I thought "The New Inmate" might atone for much dulness. I dined early on that day; then took a walk round the Regent's Park, to renew my thoughts on the very spot on which they had first occurred to me, and after that, returning home, gave a last touch to my work. Though it had been written after so hurried a fashion, there was not a word in it which I had not weighed and found to be fitting.

I was the first at Mrs. St. Quinten's house, and found that lady very full of the magazine. She asked, however, no questions as to my contribution. Of her own she at once spoke to me. "What do you think I have done at last?" she said. In my reply to her question I made some slight allusion to "The New Inmate," but I don't think she caught the words. "I have reviewed Bishop

Berkeley's whole Theory on Matter," said she. What feeling I expressed by my gesture I cannot say, but I think it must have been one of great awe. "And I have done it exhaustively," she continued; "so that the subject need not be continued. Churchill does not like continuations." Perhaps it did not signify much. If she were heavy, I at any rate was light. If her work should prove difficult of comprehension, mine was easy. If she spoke only to the wise and old, I had addressed myself to babes and sucklings. I said something as to the contrast, again naming my little story. But she was too full of Bishop Berkeley to heed me. If she had worked as I worked, of course she was full of Bishop Berkeley. To me, "The New Inmate" at that moment was more than all the bishops.

The other men soon came in, clustering together, and our number was complete. Regan whispered to me that Jack Hallam had not written a line. "And you?" I asked. "Oh, I am all right," said he. "I don't suppose they'll let it pass; but that's their affair; — not mine." Watt and Smith took their places almost without speaking, and preparation was made for the preliminary feast of the body. The after-feast was matter of such vital importance to us that we hardly possessed our customary light-hearted elasticity. There was, however, an air of subdued triumph about our "Lydia," — of triumph subdued by the presence of her cousin. As for myself, I was supremely happy. I said a word to Watt, asking him as to his performance. "I don't suppose you will like it," he replied; "but it is at any rate a fair specimen of that which it has been my ambition to produce." I assured him with enthusiasm that I was thoroughly prepared to approve, and that, too, without carping criticism. "But we must be critics," he observed. Of Churchill Smith I asked no question.

When we had eaten and drunk we began the work of the evening by giving in the names of our papers, and describing the nature of the work we had done. Mrs. St. Quinten was the first, and read her title from a scrap of paper. "A Review of Bishop Berkeley's Theory." Churchill Smith remarked that it was a very dangerous subject. The lady begged him to wait till he should hear the paper read. "Of course I will hear it read," said her cousin. To me it was evident that Smith would object to this essay without any scruple, if he did not in truth approve of it. Then it was my turn, and I explained in the quietest tone which I could assume that I had written a little tale called "The New Inmate." It was very simple, I said, but I trusted it might not be rejected on that score. There was silence for a moment and I prompted Regan to proceed; but I was interrupted by Walter Watt. "I thought," said he, "that we had positively decided against 'prose fiction.'" I protested that the decision had been given against novels, against long serial stories to be continued from number to number. This was a little thing, completed within my twenty-one allotted pages. "Our vote was taken as to prose fiction," said Watt. I appealed to Hallam, who at once took my part, — as also did Regan. "Walter is quite correct as to the purport of our decision," said Churchill Smith. I turned to Mrs. St. Quinten. "I don't see why we shouldn't have a short story," she said. I then declared that with their permission I would at any rate read it, and again requested Regan to proceed. Upon this Walter Watt rose upon his feet, and made a speech. The vote had been taken, and could not be rescinded. After such a vote it was not open to me to read my story. The story, no doubt, was very good, — he was pleased to say so, — but it was not matter of the sort which they intended to use. Seeing the purpose which they had in view, he thought that the reading of the story would be waste of time. "It will clearly be waste of time," said Churchill Smith. Walter Watt went on to explain to us that if from one meeting to another we did not allow ourselves to be bound by our own decisions, we should never appear before the public.

I will acknowledge that I was enraged. It seemed to me impossible that such folly should be allowed to prevail, or that after all my efforts I should be treated by my own friends after such a fashion. I also got upon my legs and protested loudly that Mr. Watt and Mr. Smith did not even know what had been the subject under discussion, when the vote adverse to novels had been taken. No record was kept of our proceedings; and, as I clearly showed to them, Mr. Regan and Mr. Hallam were quite as likely to hold correct views on this subject as were Mr. Watt and Mr. Smith. All calling of men Pat, and Jack, and Walter, was for the moment over. Watt admitted the truth of this argument, and declared that they must again decide whether my story of "The New Inmate" was or was not a novel in the sense intended when the previous vote was taken. If not, — if the decision on that point should be in my favour, — then the privilege of reading would at any rate belong to me. I believed so thoroughly in my own work that I desired nothing beyond this. We went to work, therefore, and took the votes on the proposition, — Was or was not the story of "The New Inmate" debarred by the previous resolution against the admission of novels.

The decision manifestly rested with Mrs. St. Quinten. I was master, easily master, of three votes. Hallam and Regan were altogether with me, and in a matter of such import I had no hesitation in voting for myself. Had the question been the acceptance or rejection of the story for the magazine, then, by the nature of our constitution, I should have had no voice in the matter. But this was not the case, and I recorded my own vote in my own favour without a blush. Having done so I turned to Mrs. St. Quinten with an air of supplication in my face of which I myself was aware, and of which I became at once ashamed. She looked round at me almost furtively, keeping her eyes otherwise fixed upon Churchill Smith's immovable countenance. I did not condescend to speak a word to her. What words I had had to say, I had spoken to them all, and was confident in the justice of my cause. I quickly dropped that look of supplication and threw myself back in my chair. The moment was one of intense interest, almost of agony, but I could not allow myself to think that in very truth my work would be rejected by them before it was seen. If such were to be their decision, how would it be possible that the "Panjandrum" should ever be brought into existence? Who could endure such ignominy and still persevere?

There was silence among us, which to me in the intensity of my feelings seemed to last for minutes. Regan was the first to speak. "Now, Mrs. St. Quinten," he said, "it all rests with you." An idea shot across my mind at the moment, of the folly of which we had been guilty in placing our most vital interests in the hands of a woman merely on the score of gallantry. Two votes had been given to her as against one of ours simply because, — she was a woman. It may be that there had been something in the arrangement of compensation for the tea and muffins; but, if so, how poor was the cause for so great an effect! She sat there the arbiter of our destinies. "You had better give your vote," said Smith roughly. "You think it is a novel?" she said, appealing to him. "There can be no doubt of it," he replied; "a novel is not a novel because it is long or short. Such is the matter which we intended to declare that we would not put forth in our magazine." "I protest," said I, jumping up, — "I protest against this interference."

Then there was a loud and very angry discussion whether Churchill Smith was justified in his endeavour to bias Mrs. St. Quinten; and we were nearly brought to a vote upon that. I myself was very anxious to have that question decided, — to have any question decided in which Churchill Smith could be shown to be in the wrong. But no one would back me, and it seemed to me as though even Regan and Jack Hallam were falling off from me, — though Jack had never yet restored to me that article of clothing to which allusion was made in the first chapter of this little history; and I had been almost as anxious for Pat's Latin translation as for my own production. It was decided without a vote that any amount of free questioning as to each other's opinions, and of free answering, was to be considered fair. "I tell her my opinion. You can tell her yours," said Churchill Smith. "It is my opinion," said I, "that you want to dictate to everybody and to rule the whole thing." "I think we did mean to exclude all story-telling," said Mrs. St. Quinten, and so the decision was given against me.

Looking back at it I know that they were right on the exact point then under discussion. They had intended to exclude all stories. But, — heaven and earth, — was there ever such folly as that of which they had been guilty in coming to such a resolution! I have often suggested to myself since, that had "The New Inmate" been read on that evening, the "Panjandrum" might have become a living reality, and that the fortieth volume of the publication might now have been standing on the shelves of many a well-filled library. The decision, however, had been given against me, and I sat like one stricken dumb, paralysed, or turned to stone. I remember it as though it were yesterday. I did not speak a word, but simply moving my chair an inch or two, I faced my face away from the lady who had thus blasted all my hopes. I fear that my eyes were wet, and that a hot tear trickled down each cheek. No note of triumph was sounded, and I verily believe they all suffered in my too conspicuous sufferings. To both Watt and Smith it had been a matter of pure conscience. Mrs. St. Quinten, woman-like, had obeyed the man in whose strength she trusted. There was silence for a few moments, and then Watt invited Regan to proceed. He had divided his work into three portions, but what they were called, whether they were verse or prose, translations or original, comic or serious, I never knew. I could not listen then. For me to continue my services to the "Panjandrum" was an impossibility. I had been crushed, — so crushed that I had not vitality left me to escape from the room, or I should not have remained there. Pat Regan's papers were nothing to me now. Watt I knew had written an essay called "The Real Aristocrat," which was published elsewhere afterwards. Jack Hallam's work was not ready. There was something said of his delinquency, but I cared not what. I only wished that my work also had been unready. Churchill Smith also had some essay, "On the Basis of Political Right." That, if I remember rightly, was its title. I often talked the matter over in after days with Pat Regan, and I know that from the moment in which my consternation was made apparent to them, the thing went very heavily. At the time, and for some hours after the adverse decision, I was altogether unmanned and unable to collect my thoughts. Before the evening was over there occurred a further episode in our affairs which awakened me.

The names of the papers had been given in, and Mrs. St. Quinten began to read her essay. Nothing more than the drone of her voice reached the tympanum of my ears. I did not look at her, or think of her, or care to hear a word that she uttered. I believe I almost slept in my agony; but sleeping or waking I was turning over in mind, wearily and incapably, the idea of declining to give any opinion as to the propriety of inserting or rejecting the review of Bishop Berkeley's theory, on the score that my connection with the "Panjandrum" had been severed. But the sound of the reading went on, and I did not make up my mind. I hardly endeavoured to make it up, but sat dreamily revelling in my own grievance, and pondering over the suicidal folly of the "Panjandrum" Company. The reading went on and on without interruption, without question, and without applause. I know I slept during some portion of the time, for I remember that Regan kicked my shin. And I remember, also, a feeling of compassion for the reader, who was hardly able to rouse herself up to the pitch of spirit necessary for the occasion, — but allowed herself to be quelled by the cold, steady gaze of her cousin Churchill. Watt sat immovable, with his hands in his trousers pockets, leaning back in his chair, the very picture of dispassionate criticism. Jack Hallam amused himself by firing paper pellets at Regan, sundry of which struck me on the head and face. Once Mrs. Quinten burst forth in offence. "Mr. Hallam," she said, "I am sorry to be so tedious." "I like it of all things," said Jack. It was certainly very long. Half comatose, as I was, with my own sufferings, I had begun to ask myself before Mrs. St. Quinten had finished her task whether it would be possible to endure three other readings lengthy as this. Ah! if I might have read "My New Inmate," how different would the feeling have been! Of what the lady said about Berkeley, I did not catch a word; but the name of the philosophical bishop seemed to be repeated usque ad nauseam. Of a sudden I was aware that I had snored, — a kick from Pat Regan wounded my shin; a pellet from Jack Hallam fell on my nose; and the essay was completed. I looked up, and could see that drops of perspiration were standing on the lady's brow.

There was a pause, and even I was now aroused to attention. We were to write our verdicts on paper, — simply the words, "Insert" or "Reject," — and what should I write? Instead of doing so, should I declare at once that I was severed from the "Panjandrum" by the treatment I had received? That I was severed, in fact, I was very sure. Could any human flesh and blood have continued its services to any magazine after such humiliation as I had suffered. Nevertheless it might perhaps be more manly were I to accept the responsibility of voting on the present occasion, — and if so, how should I vote? I had not followed a single sentence, and yet I was convinced that matter such as that would never stir the British public mind. But as the thing went, we were not called upon for our formal verdicts. "Lydia," as soon as she had done reading, turned at once to her cousin. She cared for no verdict but his. "Well," said she, "what do you think of it?" At first he did not answer. "I know I read it badly," she continued, "but I hope you caught my meaning."

"It is utter nonsense," he said, without moving his head.

"Oh, Churchill!" she exclaimed.

"It is utter nonsense," he repeated. "It is out of the question that it should be published." She glanced her eyes round the company, but ventured on no spoken appeal. Jack Hallam said something about unnecessary severity and want of courtesy. Watt simply shook his head. "I say it is trash," said Smith, rising from his chair. "You shall not disgrace yourself. Give it to me." She put her hand upon the manuscript, as though to save it. "Give it to me," he said sternly, and took it from her unresisting grasp. Then he stalked to the fire, and tearing the sheets in pieces, thrust them between the bars.

Of course there was a great commotion. We were all up in a moment, standing around her as though to console her. Miss Collins came and absolutely wept over her ill-used friend. In the instant I had forgotten "The New Inmate," as though it had never been written. She was deluged in tears, hiding her face upon the table; but she uttered no word of reproach, and ventured not a syllable in defence of her essay. "I didn't think it was so bad as that." she murmured, amidst her sobs. I did not dare to accuse the man of cruelty. I myself had become so small among them that my voice would have had no weight. But I did think him cruel, and hated him on her account as well as on my own. Jack Hallam remarked that for this night, at least, our work must be considered to be over. "It is over altogether," said Churchill Smith. "I have known that for weeks past; and I have known, too, what fools we have been to make the attempt. I hope, at least, that we may have learnt a lesson that will be of service to us. Perhaps you had better go now, and I'll just say a word or two to my cousin before I leave her."

How we got out of the room I hardly remember. There was, no doubt, some leave-taking between us four and the unfortunate Lydia, but it amounted, I think, to no more than mere decency required. To Churchill Smith I know that I did not speak. I never saw either of the cousins again; nor, as has been already told, did I ever distinctly hear what was their fate in life. And yet how intimately connected with them had I been for the last six or eight months! For not calling upon her, so that we might have mingled the tears of our disappointment together, I much blamed myself; but the subject which we must have discussed, — the failure, namely, of the "Panjandrum," — was one so sore and full of sorrow, that I could not bring myself to face the interview. Churchill Smith, I know, made various efforts to obtain literary employment; but never succeeded, because he would yield no inch in the expression of his own violent opinions. I doubt whether he ever earned as much as £10 by his writings. I heard of his living, — and almost starving, — still in London, and then that he had gone to fight for Polish freedom. It is believed that he died in a Russian prison, but I could never find anyone who knew with accuracy the circumstances of his fate. He was a man who could go forth with his life in his hand, and in meeting death could feel that he encountered only that which he had expected. She certainly vanished during the next summer from the street in which she had bestowed upon us so many muffins, and what became of her I never heard.

On that evening Pat Regan and I consoled ourselves together as best we might, Jack Hallam and Walter Watt having parted from us under the walls of Marylebone Workhouse. Pat and I walked down to a modest house of refreshment with which we were acquainted in Leicester Square, and there arranged the obsequies of the "Panjandrum" over a pint of stout and a baked potato. Pat's equanimity was marvellous. It had not even yet been ruffled, although the indignities thrown upon him had almost surpassed those inflicted on myself. His "Lord Bateman" had been first rejected; and, after that, his subsequent contributions had been absolutely ignored, merely because Mr. Churchill Smith had not approved his cousin's essay on Bishop Berkeley! "It was rot; real rot," said Pat alluding to Lydia's essay, and apologising for Smith. "But why not have gone on and heard yours?" said I. "Mine would have been rot, too," said Pat. "It isn't so easy, after all, to do this kind of thing."

We agreed that the obsequies should be very private; — indeed, as the "Panjandrum" had as yet not had a body of its own, it was hardly necessary to open the earth for purposes of interment. We agreed simply to say nothing about it to any one. I would go to Mr. X. and tell him that we had abandoned our project, and there would be an end of it. As the night advanced, I offered to read "The New Inmate" to my friend; but he truly remarked that of reading aloud they had surely had enough that night. When he reflected that but for the violence of Mr. Smith's proceedings we might even then, at that moment, have been listening to an essay upon the "Basis of Political Rights," I think that he rejoiced that the "Panjandrum" was no more.

On the following morning I called on Mr. X., and explained to him that portion of the occurrence of the previous evening with which it was necessary that he should be made acquainted. I thought that he was rather brusque; but I cannot complain that he was, upon the whole, unfriendly. "The truth is, sir," he said, "you none of you exactly knew what you wanted to be after. You were very anxious to do something grand, but hadn't got this grand thing clear before your eye. People, you know, may have too much genius, or may have too little." Which of the two he thought was our case he did not say; but he did promise to hear my story of "The New Inmate" read, with reference to its possible insertion in another periodical publication with which he had lately become connected. Perhaps some of my readers may remember its appearance in the first number of the "Marble Arch," where it attracted no little attention, and was supposed to have given assistance, not altogether despicable, towards the establishment of that periodical.

Such was the history of the "Panjandrum."

"The Panjandrum" appeared first in the January and February issues of *Saint Pauls Magazine* for 1870.

Mrs. General Talboys

WHY MRS. GENERAL TALBOYS first made up her mind to pass the winter of 1859 at Rome I never clearly understood. To myself she explained her purposes, soon after her arrival at the Eternal City, by declaring, in her own enthusiastic manner, that she was inspired by a burning desire to drink fresh at the still living fountains of classical poetry and sentiment. But I always thought that there was something more than this in it. Classical poetry and sentiment were doubtless very dear to her; but so also, I imagine, were the substantial comforts of Hardover Lodge, the General's house in Berkshire; and I do not think that she would have emigrated for the winter had there not been some slight domestic misunderstanding. Let this, however, be fully made clear, — that such misunderstanding, if it existed, must have been simply an affair of temper. No impropriety of conduct has, I am very sure, ever been imputed to the lady. The General, as all the world knows, is hot; and Mrs. Talboys, when the sweet rivers of her enthusiasm are unfed by congenial waters, can, I believe, make herself disagreeable.

But be this as it may, in November, 1859, Mrs. Talboys came among us English at Rome, and soon succeeded in obtaining for herself a comfortable footing in our society. We all thought her more remarkable for her mental attributes than for physical perfection; but, nevertheless, she was, in her own way, a sightly woman. She had no special brilliance, either of eye or complexion, such as would produce sudden flames in susceptible hearts; nor did she seem to demand instant homage by the form and step of a goddess; but we found her to be a good-looking woman of some thirty or thirty-three years of age, with soft peach-like cheeks — rather too like those of a cherub, with sparkling eyes which were hardly large enough, with good teeth, a white forehead, a dimpled chin and a full bust. Such, outwardly, was Mrs. General Talboys. The description of the inward woman is the purport to which these few columns will be devoted.

There are two qualities to which the best of mankind are much subject, which are nearly related to each other, and as to which the world has not yet decided whether they are to be classed among the good or evil attributes of our nature. Men and women are under the influence of them both, but men oftenest undergo the former and women the latter. They are ambition and enthusiasm. Now Mrs. Talboys was an enthusiastic woman.

As to ambition, generally, as the world agrees with Mark Antony in stigmatizing it as a grievous fault, I am myself clear that it is a virtue; but with ambition at present we have no concern. Enthusiasm also, as I think, leans to virtue's side; or, at least, if it be a fault, of all faults it is the prettiest. But then, to partake at all of virtue, or even to be in any degree pretty, the enthusiasm must be true.

Bad coin is known from good by the ring of it; and so is bad enthusiasm. Let the coiner be ever so clever at his art, in the coining of enthusiasm the sound of true gold can never by imparted to the false metal. And I doubt whether the cleverest she in the world can make false enthusiasm palatable to the taste of man. To the taste of any woman the enthusiasm of another woman is never very palatable.

We understood at Rome that Mrs. Talboys had a considerable family, four or five children, we were told; but she brought with her only one daughter, a little girl about twelve years of age. She had torn herself asunder, as she told me, from the younger nurselings of her heart, and had left them in the care of a devoted female attendant, whose love was all but maternal. And then she said a word or two about the General, in terms which made me almost think that this quasi-maternal love extended itself beyond the children. The idea, however, was a mistaken one, arising from the strength of her language, to which I was then unaccustomed. I have since become aware that nothing can be more decorous than old Mrs. Upton, the excellent head nurse at Hardover Lodge; and no gentleman more discreet in his conduct than General Talboys.

And I may as well here declare, also, that there could be no more virtuous woman than the General's wife. Her marriage vow was to her paramount to all other vows and bonds whatever. The General's honour was quite safe when he sent her off to Rome by herself; and he no doubt knew that it was so. *Illi robur et aes triplex,* of which I believe no weapons of any assailant could get the better. But, nevertheless, we used to fancy that she had no repugnance to impropriety in other women, — to what the world generally calls impropriety. Invincibly attached herself to the marriage tie, she would constantly speak of it as by no means necessarily binding on others; and, virtuous herself as any griffin of propriety, she constantly patronised, at any rate, the theory of infidelity in her neighbours. She was very eager in denouncing the prejudices of the English world, declaring that she had found existence among them to be no longer possible for herself. She was hot against the stern unforgiveness of British matrons, and equally eager in reprobating the stiff conventionalities of a religion in which she said that none of its votaries had faith, though they all allowed themselves to be enslaved.

We had at that time a small set at Rome, consisting chiefly of English and Americans, who habitually met at each other's rooms, and spent many of our evening hours in discussing Italian politics. We were, most of us, painters, poets, novelists, or sculptors; — perhaps I should say would-be painters, poets, novelists, and sculptors — aspirants, hoping to become some day recognized; and among us Mrs. Talboys took her place naturally enough on account of a very pretty taste she had for painting. I do not know that she ever originated anything that was grand; but she made some nice copies, and was fond, at any rate, of art conversation. She wrote essays, too, which she showed in confidence to various gentlemen, and had some idea of taking lessons in modelling.

In all our circle Conrad Mackinnon, the American, was, perhaps, the person most qualified to be styled its leader. He was one who absolutely did gain his living, and an ample living, too, by his pen, and was regarded on all sides as a literary lion, justified by success in roaring at any tone he might please. His usual roar was not exactly that of a sucking-dove or a nightingale; but it was a good-humoured roar, not very offensive to any man, and apparently acceptable enough to some ladies. He was a big burly man, near to fifty, as I suppose, somewhat awkward in his gait, and somewhat loud in his laugh. But though nigh to fifty and thus ungainly, he liked to be smiled on by pretty women, and liked, as some said, to be flattered by them also. If so he should have been happy, for the ladies at Rome at that time made much of Conrad Mackinnon.

Of Mrs. Mackinnon no one did make very much, and yet she was one of the sweetest, dearest, quietest little creatures that ever made glad a man's fireside. She was exquisitely pretty, always in good humour, never stupid, self-denying to a fault, and yet she was generally in the background. She would seldom come forward of her own will, but was contented to sit behind her tea-pot and hear Mackinnon do his roaring. He was certainly much given to what the world and Rome called flirting, but this did not in the least annoy her. She was twenty years his junior, and yet she never flirted with any one. Women would tell her — good-natured friends — how Mackinnon went on; but she received such tidings as an excellent joke, observing that he had always done the same, and no doubt always would till he was ninety. I do believe that she was a happy woman, and yet I used to think that she should have been happier. There is, however, no knowing the inside of another man's house, or reading the riddles of another man's joy and sorrow.

We had also there another lion—a lion cub, —entitled to roar a little, and of him also I must say something. Charles O'Brien was a young man, about twenty-five years of age, who had sent out from his studio in the preceding year a certain bust, supposed by his admirers to be unsurpassed by any effort of ancient or modern genius. I am no judge of sculpture, and will not, therefore pronounce an opinion; but many who considered themselves to be judges declared that it was a "goodish head and shoulders," and nothing more. I merely mention the fact, as it was on the strength of that head and shoulders that O'Brien seperated himself from a throng of others such as himself in Rome, walked solitary during the days, and threw himself at the feet of various ladies when the days were over. He had ridden on the shoulders of his bust into a prominent place in our circle, and there encountered much feminine admiration — from Mrs. General Talboys and others.

Some eighteen or twenty of us used to meet every Saturday evening in Mrs. Mackinnon's drawing-room. Many of us, indeed, were in the habit of seeing each other daily, and of visiting together the haunts in Rome which are best loved by art-loving strangers; but here, in this drawing-room, we were sure to come together, and here before the end of November Mrs. Talboys might always be found, not in any accustomed seat, but moving about the room as the different male mental attractions of our society might chance to move themselves. She was at first greatly taken by Mackinnon, — who also was, I think, a little stirred by her admiration, though he stoutly denied the charge. She became, however, very dear to us all before she left us, and certainly we owed to her our love, for she added infinitely to the joys of our winter.

"I have come here to refresh myself," she said to Mackinnon one evening — to Mackinnon and myself, for we were standing together.

"Shall I get you tea?" said I.

"And will you have something to eat?" Mackinnon asked.

"No, no, no;" she answered. "Tea, yes; but, for heaven's sake, let nothing solid dispel the associations of such a meeting as this."

"I thought you might have dined early," said Mackinnon. Now Mackinnon was a man whose own dinner was very dear to him. I have seen him become hasty and unpleasant, even under the pillars of the Forum, when he thought that the party were placing his fish in jeopardy by their desire to linger there too long.

"Early! Yes. No; I know not when it was. One dines and sleeps in obedience to that dull clay which weighs down so generally the particle of our spirit. But the clay may sometimes be forgotten. Here I can always forget it."

"I thought you asked for refreshment," I said. She only looked at me, whose small attempts at prose composition had up to that time been altogether unsuccessful, and then addressed herself in reply to Mackinnon.

"It is the air which we breathe that fills our lungs and gives us life and light. It is that which refreshes us if pure, or sinks us into stagnation if it be foul. Let me, for a while, inhale the breath of an invigorating literature. Sit down, Mr. Mackinnon; I have a question that I must put to you." And then she succeeded in carrying him off into a corner; as far as I could see he went willingly enough at that time, though he soon became averse to any long retirement in company with Mrs. Talboys.

We none of us quite understood what were her exact ideas on the subject of revealed religion. Somebody, I think, had told her that there were among us one or two whose opinions were not exactly orthodox according to the doctrines of the established English church. If so, she was determined to show us that she also was advanced beyond the prejudices of an old and dry school of theology. "I have thrown down all the barriers of religion," she said to poor Mrs. Mackinnon, "and am looking for the sentiments of a pure Christianity."

"Thrown down all the barriers of religion!" said Mrs. Mackinnon, in a tone of horror which was not appreciated.

"Indeed, yes," said Mrs. Talboys, with an exulting voice; "are not the days for such trammels gone by!?"

"But yet you hold by Christianity?"

"A pure Christianity, unstained by blood and perjury, by hypocrisy and verbose genuflection. Can I not worship and say my prayers among the clouds?" and she pointed to the lofty ceiling and the handsome chandelier.

"But Ida goes to church," said Mrs. Mackinnon. Ida Talboys was her daughter. Now, it may be observed that many who throw down the barriers of religion, so far as those barriers may affect themselves, still maintain them on behalf of their children. "Yes," said Mrs. Talboys, "dear Ida! her soft spirit is not yet adapted to receive the perfect truth. We are obliged to govern children by the strength of their prejudices." And then she moved away, for it was seldom that Mrs. Talboys remained long in conversation with any lady.

Mackinnon, I believe, soon became tired of her. He liked her flattery, and at first declared that she was clever and nice; but her niceness was too purely celestial to satisfy his mundane tastes. Mackinnon himself can revel among the clouds in his own writings, and can leave us sometimes in doubt whether he ever means to come back to earth; but when his foot is on *terra firma,* he loves to feel the earthly substratum which supports his weight. With women he likes a hand that can remain an unnecessary moment within his own, an eye that can glisten with the sparkle of champagne, a heart weak enough to make its owner's arm tremble within his own beneath the moonlight gloom of the Coliseum arches. A dash of sentiment the while makes all these things the sweeter; but the sentiment alone will not suffice for him. Mrs. Talboys did, I believe, drink her glass of champagne, as do other ladies; but with her it had no such pleasing effect. It loosened only her tongue, but never her eye. Her arm, I think, never trembled, and her hand never lingered. The General was always safe, and happy, perhaps, in his solitary safety.

It so happened that we had unfortunately among us two artists who had quarrelled with their wives. O'Brien, whom I have before mentioned, was one of them. In his case, I believe him to have been almost as free from blame as a man can be, whose marriage was in itself a fault. However he had a wife in Ireland, some ten years older than himself; and though he might sometimes almost forget the fact, his friends and neighbours were well aware of it. In the other case the whole fault probably was with the husband. He was an ill-tempered, bad-hearted man, clever enough, but without principle; and he was continually guilty of the great sin of speaking evil of the woman whose name he should have been anxious to protect. In both cases our friend Mrs. Talboys took a warm interest, and in each of them she sympathized with the present husband against the absent wife.

Of the consolation which she offered in the latter instance we used to hear something from Mackinnon. He would repeat to his wife, and to me and my wife, the conversations which she had with him. "Poor Brown," she would say, "I pity him, with my very heart's blood."

"You are aware that he has comforted himself in his desolation," Mackinnon replied.

"I know very well to what you allude. I think I may say that I am conversant with all the circumstances of this heart-blighting sacrifice." Mrs. Talboys was apt to boast of the thorough confidence reposed in her by all those in whom she took an interest. "Yes, he has sought such comfort in another love as the hard, cruel world would allow him."

"Or perhaps something more than that," said Mackinnon. "He has a family here in Rome, you know; two little babies."

"I know it, I know it," she said. "Cherub angels!" and as she spoke, she looked up into the ugly face of Marcus Aurelius; for they were standing at the moment under the figure of the great horseman in the Campidoglio. "I have seen them, and they are the children of innocence. If all the blood of all the Howards ran in their veins, it could not make their birth more noble!"

"Not if their father and mother had never been married," said Mackinnon.

"What; that from you Mr. Mackinnon!" said Mrs. Talboys, turning her back with energy upon the equestrian statue, and looking up into the faces, first of Pollux and then of Castor, as though from them she might gain some inspiration on the subject which Marcus Aurelius in his coldness had denied to her. "From you, who have so nobly claimed for mankind the divine attributes of free action! From you, who have taught my mind to soar above the petty bonds which one man in his littleness contrives for the subjection of his brother. Mackinnon! you who are so great!" And she now looked up into his face. "Mackinnon, unsay those words."

"They are illegitimate," said he; "and if there was any landed property — "

"Landed property! and that from an American!"

"The children are English, you know."

"Landed property! The time will shortly come — ay, and I see it coming — when that hateful word shall be expunged from the calendar; when landed property shall be no more. What! shall the free soul of a God-born man submit itself for ever to such trammels as that? Shall we never escape from the clay which so long has manacled the subtler particles of the divine spirit? Ay, yes, Mackinnon;" and then she took him by the arm, and led him to the top of the huge steps which lead down from the Campidoglio into the streets of modern Rome. "Look down upon that countless multitude." Mackinnon looked down and saw three groups of French soldiers, with three or four little men in each group; he saw a couple of dirty friars, and three priests very slowly beginning the side ascent to the church of the Ara Coeli. "Look down upon that countless multitude," said Mrs. Talboys, and she stretched her arms out over the half-deserted city. "They are escaping now from these trammels — now, now — now that I am speaking."

"They have escaped long ago from all such trammels as that," said Mackinnon.

"Ay, and from all terrestrial bonds," she continued, not exactly remarking the pith of his last observation; "from bonds quasi-terrestrial and quasi-celestial. The full-formed limbs of the present age, running with quick streams of generous blood, will no longer bear the ligatures which past times have woven for the decrepit. Look down upon that multitude, Mackinnon; they shall all be free." And then, still clutching him by the arm, and still standing at the top of those stairs, she gave forth her prophecy with the fury of a Sybil.

"They shall all be free. Oh, Rome, thou eternal one, thou who hast bowed thy neck to imperial pride and priestly craft; thou who hast suffered sorely, even to this hour, from Nero down to Pio Nono, — the days of thy oppression are over. Gone from thy enfranchised ways for ever is the clang of Praetorian cohorts, and the more odious drone of meddling monks!" And yet, as Mackinnon observed, there still stood the dirty friars and the small French soldiers; and there still toiled the slow priests, wending their tedious way up to the church of the Ara Coeli. But that was the mundane view of the matter, a view not regarded by Mrs. Talboys in her ecstacy. "O Italia," she continued, "O Italia una, one and indivisible in thy rights, and indivisible also in thy wrongs! to us is it given to see the accomplishment of thy glory. A people shall arise around thine altars greater in the annals of the world than thy Scipios, thy Gracchi, or thy Caesars. Not in torrents of blood, or with screams of bereaved mothers, shall thy new triumphs be stained. But mind shall dominate over matter; and doomed, together with Popes and Bourbons, with cardinals, diplomatists, and police spies, ignorance and prejudice shall be driven from thy smiling terraces. And then Rome shall again become the fair capital of the fairest region of Europe. Hither shall flock the artisans of the world, crowding into thy marts all that God and man can give. Wealth, beauty, and innocence shall meet in thy streets, — "

"There will be a considerable change before that takes place," said Mackinnon.

"There shall be a considerable change," she answered. "Mackinnon, to thee it is given to read the signs of the time; and hast thou not read? Why have the fields of Magenta and Solferino been piled with the corpses of dying heroes? Why have the waters of the Mincio run red with the blood of martyrs? That Italy might be united and Rome immortal. Here, standing on the Capitolium of the ancient city, I say that it shall be so; and thou, Mackinnon, who hearest me, knowest that my words are true."

There was not then in Rome—I may almost say there was not in Italy—an Englishman or an American, who did not wish well to the cause for which Italy was and is still contending; as also there is hardly one who does not now regard that cause as well nigh triumphant; but, nevertheless, it was almost impossible to sympathise with Mrs. Talboys. As Mackinnon said, she flew so high that there was no comfort in flying with her.

"Well," said he, "Brown and the rest of them are down below. Shall we go and join them?"

"Poor Brown! How was it that, in speaking of his troubles, we were led on to this heart-stirring theme? Yes, I have seen them, the sweet angels; and I tell you also that I have seen their mother. I insisted on going to her when I heard her history from him."

"And what is she like, Mrs. Talboys!"

"Well: education has done more for some of us than for others; and there are those from whose morals and sentiments we might thankfully draw a lesson, whose manners and outward gestures are not such as custom has made agreeable to us. You, I know, can understand that. I have seen her, and feel sure that she is pure in heart and high in principle. Has she not sacrificed herself, and is not self-sacrifice the surest guarantee for true nobility of character? Would Mrs. Mackinnon object to my bringing them together?"

Mackinnon was obliged to declare that he thought his wife would object; and from that time forth he and Mrs. Talboys ceased to be very close in their friendship. She still came to the

house every Saturday evening, still refreshed herself at the fountains of his literary rills; but her special prophecies from henceforth were poured into other ears. And it so happened that
O'Brien now became her chief ally. I do not remember that she
troubled herself much further with the cherub angels or with
their mother; and I am inclined to think that taking up warmly,
as she did, the story of O'Brien's matrimonial wrongs, she forgot
the little history of the Browns. Be that as it may, Mrs. Talboys
and O'Brien now became strictly confidential, and she would en-
large by the half-hour together on the miseries of her friend's position to any one whom she could get to hear her.

"I'll tell you what, Fanny," Mckinnon said to his wife one day;
— to his wife and to mine, for we were all together; "we shall
have a row in the house if we don't take care. O'Brien will be
making love to Mrs. Talboys."

"Nonsense," said Mrs. Mackinnon. "You are always thinking
that somebody is going to make love to some one."

"Somebody always is," said he.

"She's old enough to be his mother," said Mrs. Mackinnon.

"What does that matter to an Irishman?" said Mackinnon.
"Besides I doubt if there is more than five years' difference between them."

"There must be more than that," said my wife. "Ida Talboys is
twelve, I know, and I am not quite sure that Ida is the eldest."

"If she had a son in the Guards it would make no difference,"
said Mackinnon. "There are men who consider themselves
bound to make love to a woman under certain circumstances, let
the age of the lady be what it may. O'Brien is such a one; and if
she sympathizes with him much oftener he will mistake the matter, and go down on his knees. You ought to put him on his
guard," he said, addressing himself to his wife.

"Indeed I shall do no such thing," said she; "if they are two
fools, they must, like other fools, pay the price of their folly." As
a rule there could be no softer creature than Mrs. Mackinnon;
but it seemed to me that her tenderness never extended itself in
the direction of Mrs. Talboys.

Just at this time, towards the end, that is, of November, we
made a party to visit the tombs which lie along the Appian way,
beyond that most beautiful of all sepulchres, the tomb of Cedilia

Metella. It was a delicious day, and we had driven along this road for a couple of miles beyond the walls of the city, enjoying the most lovely view which the neighbourhood of Rome affords — looking over the wondrous ruins of the old aqueducts, up towards Tivoli and Palestrina. Of all the environs of Rome this is, on a fair clear day, the most enchanting; and here, perhaps, among a world of tombs, thoughts and almost memories of the old, old days come upon one with the greatest force. The grandeur of Rome is best seen and understood from beneath the walls of the Coliseum, and its beauty among the pillars of the Forum and the arches of the Sacred Way; but its history and fall become more palpable to the mind, and more clearly realized, out here among the tombs, where the eyes rest upon the mountains whose shades were cool to the old Romans as to us — than anywhere within the walls of the city. Here we look out at the same Tivoli and the same Praeneste, glittering in the sunshine, enbowered among the far off valleys, which were dear to them; and the blue mountains have not crumbled away into ruins. Within Rome itself we can see nothing as they saw it.

Our party consisted of some dozen or fifteen persons, and as a hamper with luncheon in it had been left on the grassy slope at the back of the tomb of Cedilia Metella, the expedition had in it something of the nature of a pic-nic. Mrs. Talboys was of course with us, and Ida Talboys. O'Brien also was there. The hamper had been prepared in Mrs. Mackinnon's room, under the immediate eye of Mackinnon himself, and they therefore were regarded as the dominant spirits of the party. My wife was leagued with Mrs. Mackinnon, as was usually the case; and there seemed to be a general opinion among those who were closely in confidence together that something would happen in the O'Brien-Talboys matter. The two had been inseparable on the previous evening, for Mrs. Talboys had been urging on the young Irishman her counsels respecting his domestic troubles. Sir Cresswell Cresswell, she had told him, was his refuge. "Why should his soul submit to bonds which the world had now declared to be intolerable? Divorce was no longer the privilege of the dissolute rich. Spirits which were incompatible need no longer be compelled to fret beneath the same couples." In short she had recommended him to go to England and get rid of his wife, as she would, with a little encouragement, have recommended any man to get rid of anything. I am sure that had she been skilfully brought on to the subject, she might have been induced to pronounce a verdict against such ligatures for the body as coats, waistcoats, and trousers. Her aspirations for freedom ignored all bounds, and, in theory, there were no barriers which she was not willing to demolish.

Poor O'Brien, as we all now began to see, had taken the matter amiss. He had offered. to make a bust of Mrs. Talboys, and she had consented, expressing a wish that it might find a place among those who had devoted themselves to the enfranchisement of their fellow-creatures. I really think she had but little of a woman's customary personal vanity. I know she had an idea that her eye was lighted up in her warmer moments by some special fire, that sparks of liberty shone round her brow, and that her bosom heaved with glorious aspirations; but all these feelings had reference to her inner genius, not to any outward beauty. But O'Brien misunderstood the woman, and thought it necessary to gaze into her face, and sigh as though his heart were breaking. Indeed he declared to a young friend, that she was perfect in her style of beauty, and began the bust with this idea. It was gradually becoming clear to us all that he would bring himself to grief; but in such a matter who can caution a man?

Mrs. Mackinnon had contrived to separate them in making the carriage arrangements on this day, but such an arrangement only added fuel to the fire which was now burning within O'Brien's bosom. I believe that he really did love her, in his easy, eager, susceptible, Irish way. That he would get over the little episode without any serious injury to his heart no one doubted; but, then, what would occur when the declaration was made? How would Mrs. Talboys hear it?

"She deserves it," said Mrs. Mackinnon.

"And twice as much," my wife added. Why is it that women are so spiteful to each other?

Early in the day Mrs. Talboys clambered up to the top of a tomb, and made a little speech, holding a parasol over her head. Beneath her feet, she said, reposed the ashes of some bloated senator, some glutton of the empire, who had swallowed into his maw the provision necessary for a tribe. Old Rome had fallen through such selfishness as that; but new Rome would not forget the lesson. All this was very well, and then O'Brien helped her down; but after this there was no separating them. For her own part she would sooner have had Mackinnon at her elbow. But Mackinnon now had found some other elbow. "Enough of that was as good as a feast," he had said to his wife. And therefore Mrs. Talboys, quite unconscious of evil, allowed herself to be engrossed by O'Brien.

And then, about three o'clock, we returned to the hamper. Luncheon under such circumstances always means dinner, and we arranged ourselves for a very comfortable meal. To those who know the tomb of Cecilia Metella no description of the scene is necessary, and to those who do not, no description will convey a fair idea of its reality. It is itself a large low tower of great diameter but of beautiful proportion, standing far outside the city, close on to the side of the old Roman way. It has been embattled on the top by some latter day baron, in order that it might be used for protection to the castle which has been built on and attached to it. If I remember rightly this was done by one of the Frangipani, and a very lovely ruin he has made of it. I know no castellated old tumble-down residence in Italy more picturesque than this baronial adjunct to the old Roman tomb, or which better tallies with the ideas engendered within our minds by Mrs. Radcliffe and the Mysteries of Udolpho. It lies along the road, protected on the side of the city by the proud sepulchre of the Roman matron, and up to the long ruined walls of the back of the building stretches a grassy slope at the bottom of which are the remains of an old Roman circus. Beyond that is the long, thin, graceful line of the Claudian aqueduct, with Soracte in the distance to the left, and Tivoli, Palestrina, and Frascati lying among the hills which bound the view. That Frangipani baron was in the right of it, and I hope he got the value of his money out of the residence which he built for himself. I doubt, however, that he did but little good to those who lived in his close neighbourhood.

We had a very comfortable little banquet seated on the broken lumps of stone which lie about under the walls of the tomb. I wonder whether the shade of Cecilia Metella was looking down upon us. We have heard much of her in these latter days, and yet we know nothing about her, nor can conceive why she was honoured with a bigger tomb than any other Roman matron. There were those then among our party who believed that she might still come back among us, and with due assistance from some cognate susceptible spirit explain to us the cause of her widowed husband's liberality. Alas, alas! if we judge of the Romans by ourselves the true reason for such sepulchral grandeur would redound little to the credit of the lady Cecilia Metella herself, or to that of Crassus, her bereaved and desolate lord.

She did not come among us on the occasion of this banquet, possibly because we had no tables there to turn in preparation for her presence; but, had she done so, she could not have been more eloquent of things of the other world than was Mrs. Talboys. I have said that Mrs. Talboys' eye never glanced brighter after a glass of champagne, but I am inclined to think that on this occasion it may have done so. O'Brien enacted Ganymede, and was, perhaps, more liberal than other latter-day Ganymedes to whose services Mrs. Talboys had been accustomed. Let it not, however, be suspected by any one that she exceeded the limits of a discreet joyousness. By no means! The generous wine penetrated, perhaps, to some inner cells of her heart, and brought forth thoughts in sparkling words, which otherwise might have remained concealed; but there was nothing in what she thought or spoke calculated to give umbrage either to an anchorite or to a vestal. A word or two she said or sung about the flowing bowl, and once she called for Falernian; but beyond this her converse was chiefly of the rights of man and the weakness of women; of the iron ages that were past and of the golden time that was to come.

She called a toast, and drank to the hopes of the latter lustrums of the nineteenth century. Then it was that she bade O'Brien "Fill high the bowl with Samian wine." The Irishman took her at her word, and she raised the bumper and waved it over her head before she put it to her lips. I am bound to declare that she did not spill a drop. "The true Falernian grape," she said, as she deposited the empty beaker on the grass beneath her elbow. Viler champagne I do not think I ever swallowed; but it was the theory of the wine, not its palpable body present there, as it were, in the flesh, which inspired her. There was really something grand about her on that occasion, and her enthusiasm almost amounted to reality.

Mackinnon was amused and encouraged her, as I must confess, did I also. Mrs. Mackinnon made useless little signs to her husband, really fearing that the Falernian would do its good offices too thoroughly. My wife, getting me apart as I walked round the circle distributing viands, remarked that "the woman was a fool, and would disgrace herself." But I observed that after the disposal of that bumper she worshipped the rosy god in theory only, and therefore saw no occasion to interfere. "Come, Bacchus," she said, "and come, Silenus, if thou wilt; I know that ye are hovering round the graves of your departed favourites. And ye, too, nymphs of Egeria," and she pointed to the classic grove which was all but close to us as we sat there. "In olden days ye did not always despise the abodes of men. But why should we invoke the presence of the gods, — we, who can become godlike ourselves! We ourselves are the deities of the present age. For us shall the tables be spread with ambrosia! for us shall the nectar flow."

Upon the whole it was very good fooling — for a while; and as soon as we were tired of it we arose from our seats, and began to stroll about the place. It was beginning to be a little dusk and somewhat cool, but the evening air was pleasant, and the ladies, putting on their shawls, did not seem inclined at once to get into the carriages. At any rate, Mrs. Talboys was not so inclined, for she started down the hill towards the long low wall of the old Roman circus at the bottom; and O'Brien, close at her elbow, started with her.

"Ida, my dear, you had better remain here," she said to her daughter; "you will be tired if you come as far as we are going."

"Oh, no, mamma, I shall not," said Ida. "You get tired much quicker than I do."

"Oh, yes, you will; besides I do not wish you to come." There was an end of it for Ida, and Mrs. Talboys and O'Brien walked off together, while we all looked into each other's faces.

"It would be a charity to go with them," said Mackinnon.

"Do you be charitable, then," said his wife.

"It should be a lady," said he.

"It is a pity that the mother of the spotless cherubim is not here for the occasion," said she. "I hardly think that any one less gifted will undertake such a self-sacrifice." Any attempt of the kind would, however, now have been too late, for they were already at the bottom of the hill. O'Brien certainly had drunk freely of the pernicious contents of those long-necked bottles; and though no one could fairly accuse him of being tipsy, nevertheless that which might have made others drunk had made him bold, and he dared to do — perhaps more than might become a man. If under any circumstances he could be fool enough to make an avowal of love to Mrs. Talboys, he might be expected, as we all felt, to do it now.

We watched them as they made for a gap in the wall which led through into the large enclosed space of the old circus. It had been an arena for chariot games, and they had gone down with the avowed purpose of searching where might have been the *meta,* and ascertaining how the drivers could have turned when at their full speed. For a while we had heard their voices — or rather her voice especially. "The heart of a man, O'Brien, should suffice for all emergencies," we had heard her say. She had assumed a strange habit of calling men by their simple names, as men address each other. When she did this to Mackinnon who was much older than herself, we had been all amused by it, and other ladies of our party had taken to call him "Mackinnon" when Mrs. Talboys was not by; but we had felt the comedy to be less safe with O'Brien, especially when, on one occasion, we heard him address her as Arabella. She did not seem to be in any way struck by his doing so, and we supposed, therefore, that it had become frequent between them. What reply he made at the moment about the heart of a man I do not know; — and then in a few minutes they disappeared through the gap in the wall.

None of us followed them, though it would have seemed the most natural thing in the world to do so had nothing out of the way been expected. As it was we remained there round the tomb, quizzing the little foibles of our dear friend, and hoping that O'Brien would be quick in what he was doing. That he would undoubtedly get a slap in the face — metaphorically — we all felt certain, for none of us doubted the rigid propriety of the lady's intentions. Some of us strolled into the buildings, and some of us got out on to the road; but we all of us were thinking that O'Brien was very slow a considerable time before we saw Mrs. Talboys reappear through the gap.

At last, however, she was there, and we at once saw that she was alone. She came on, breasting the hill with quick steps, and when she drew near we could see that there was a frown as of injured majesty on her brow. Mackinnon and his wife went forward to meet her. If she were really in trouble it would be fitting in some way to assist her; and of all women Mrs. Mackinnon was the last to see another woman suffer from ill usage without attempting to aid her. "I certainly never liked her," Mrs. Mackinnon said afterwards; "but I was bound to go and hear her tale, when she really had a tale to tell."

And Mrs. Talboys now had a tale to tell — if she chose to tell it. The ladies of our party declared afterwards that she would have acted more wisely had she kept to herself both O'Brien's words to her and her answer. "She was well able to take care of herself," Mrs. Mackinnon said; "and, after all, the silly man had taken an answer when he got it." Not, however, that O'Brien had taken his answer quite immediately, as far as I could understand from what we heard of the matter afterwards.

At the present moment Mrs. Talboys came up the rising ground all alone, and at a quick pace. "The man has insulted me," she said aloud, as well as her panting breath would allow her, and as soon as she was near enough to Mrs. Mackinnon to speak to her.

"I am sorry for that," said Mrs. Mackinnon. "I suppose he had taken a little too much wine."

"No; it was a premeditated insult. The base-hearted churl has failed to understand the meaning of true honest sympathy."

"He will forget all about it when he is sober," said Mackinnon, meaning to comfort her.

"What care I what he remembers or what he forgets!" she said, turning upon poor Mackinnon indignantly. "You men grovel so in your ideas — " "And yet," as Mackinnon said afterwards, "she had been telling me that I was a god for the last three weeks." — "You men grovel so in your ideas, that you cannot understand the feelings of a true-hearted woman. What can his forgetfulness or his remembrance be to me? Must not I remember this insult? Is it possible that I should forget it?"

Mr. and Mrs. Mackinnon only had gone forward to meet her; but, nevertheless, she spoke so loud that all heard her who were still clustered round the spot on which we had dined.

"What has become of Mr. O'Brien?" a lady whispered to me.

I had a field-glass with me, and, looking round, I saw his hat as he was walking inside the walls of the circus in the direction towards the city. "And very foolish he must feel," said the lady.

"No doubt he's used to it," said another.

"But considering her age, you know," said the first, who might herself have been perhaps three years younger than Mrs. Talboys, and who was not herself averse to the excitement of a moderate flirtation. But then why should she have been averse, seeing that she had not as yet become subject to the will of any imperial lord?

"He would have felt much more foolish," said the third, "if she had listened to what he said to her."

"Well I don't know," said the second; "nobody would have known anything about it then, and in a few weeks they would have gradually become tired of each other in the ordinary way."

But in the meantime Mrs. Talboys was among us. There had been no attempt at secrecy, and she was still loudly inveighing against the grovelling propensities of men. "That's quite true, Mrs. Talboys," said one of the elder ladies; "but then ladies are not always so careful as they should be. Of course I do not mean to say that there has been any fault on your part."

"Fault on my part! Of course there has been fault on my part. No one can make any mistake without fault to some extent. I took him to be a man of sense, and he is a fool. Go to Naples indeed!"

"Did he want you to go to Naples?" asked Mrs. Mackinnon.

"Yes; that was what he suggested. We were to leave by the train for Civita Vecchia at six to-morrow morning, and catch the steamer which leaves Leghorn to-night. Don't tell me of wine. He was prepared for it!" And she looked round about on us with an air of injured majesty in her face which was almost insupportable.

"I wonder whether he took the tickets over-night," said Mackinnon.

"Naples;" she said, as though now speaking exclusively to herself, "the only ground in Italy which has as yet made no struggle on behalf of freedom — a fitting residence for such a dastard!"

"You would have found it very pleasant at this season," said the unmarried lady, who was three years her junior.

My wife had taken Ida out of the way when the first complaining note from Mrs. Talboys had been heard ascending the hill. But now, when matters began gradually to become quiescent, she brought her back, suggesting, as she did so, that they might begin to think of returning.

"It is getting very cold, Ida, dear, is it not?" said she.

"But where is Mr. O'Brien?" said Ida.

"He has fled, — as poltroons always fly," said Mrs. Talboys. I believe in my heart that she would have been glad to have had him there in the middle of the circle, and to have triumphed over him publicly among us all. No feeling of shame would have kept her silent for a moment.

"Fled!" said Ida, looking up into her mother's face.

"Yes, fled, my child." And she seized her daughter in her arms and pressed her closely to her bosom. "Cowards always fly."

"Is Mr. O'Brien a coward?" Ida asked.

"Yes, a coward, a very coward! And he has fled before the glance of an honest woman's eye. Come, Mrs. Mackinnon, shall we go back to the city? I am sorry that the amusement of the day should have received this check." And she walked forward to the carriage and took her place in it with an air that showed that she was proud of the manner in which she had conducted herself.

"She is a little conceited about it after all," said that unmarried lady. "If poor Mr. O'Brien had not shown so much premature energy with reference to that little journey to Naples things might have gone quietly after all."

But the unmarried lady was wrong in her judgment. Mrs. Talboys was proud and conceited in the matter — but not proud of having excited the admiration of her Irish lover. She was proud of her own subsequent conduct, and gave herself credit for coming out strongly as a noble-minded matron. "I believe she thinks," said Mrs. Mackinnon, "that her virtue is quite Spartan and unique; and if she remains in Rome she'll boast of it through the whole winter,"

"If she does she may be certain that O'Brien will do the same," said Mackinnon. "And in spite of his having fled from the field it is upon the cards that he may get the best of it. Mrs. Talboys is a very excellent woman. I am sure, indeed, she has proved it.

But, nevertheless, she is susceptible of ridicule."

We all felt a little anxiety to hear O'Brien's account of the matter, and after having deposited the ladies at their homes, Mackinnon and I went off to his lodgings. At first he was denied to us, but after a while we got his servant to acknowledge that he was at home, and then we made our way up to his studio. We found him seated behind a half-formed model, or rather a mere lump of clay punched into something resembling the shape of a head, with a pipe in his mouth, and a bit of stick in his hand. He was pretending to work, though we both knew that it was out of the question that he should do anything in his present frame of mind.

"I think I heard my servant tell you that I was not at home," said he.

"Yes, he did," said Mackinnon, "and would have sworn to it too if we would have let him. Come, don't pretend to be surly."

"I am very busy, Mr. Mackinnon."

"Completing your head of Mrs. Talboys, I suppose, before you start for Naples."

"You don't mean to say that she has told you all about it," and he turned away from his work, and looked up into our faces with a comical expression, half of fun and half of despair.

"Every word of it," said I. "When you want a lady to travel with you, never ask her to get up so early in winter."

"But, O'Brien, how could you be such an ass?" said Mackinnon. "As it has turned out, there is no very great harm done. You have insulted a respectable middle-aged woman, the mother of a family, and the wife of a general officer, and there is an end of it; — unless, indeed, the general officer should come out from England to call you to account."

"He is welcome," said O'Brien, haughtily.

"No doubt, my dear fellow," said Mackinnon; "that would be a dignified and pleasant ending to the affair. But what I want to know is this — what would you have done if she had agreed to go?"

"He never calculated on the possibility of such a contingency," said I.

"By heavens, then, I thought she would like it," said he.

"And to oblige her you were content to sacrifice yourself," said

Mackinnon.

"Well, that was just it. What the deuce is a fellow to do when a woman goes on in that way. She told me down there, upon the old racecourse you know, that matrimonial bonds were made for fools and slaves. What was I to suppose that she meant by that? But to make all sure, I asked her what sort of a fellow the General was. 'Dear old man,' she said, clasping her hands together. 'He might, you know, have been my father.' 'I wish he were,' said I, 'because then you'd be free.' 'I am free,' said she, stamping on the ground and looking up at me as much as to say that she cared for no one. 'Then,' said I, 'accept all that is left of the heart of Wenceslaus O'Brien,' and I threw myself before her in her path. 'Hand,' said I, 'I have none to give, but the blood which runs red through my veins is descended from a double line of kings.' I said that because she is always fond of riding a high horse. I had gotten close under the wall, so that none of you should see me from the tower."

"And what answer did she make?" said Mackinnon.

"Why she was pleased as Punch—gave me both her hands and declared that we would be friends for ever. It is my belief, Mackinnon, that that woman never heard anything of the kind before. The General, no doubt, did it by letter."

"And how was it that she changed her mind?"

"Why; I got up, put my arm round her waist, and told her that we would be off to Naples. I'm blessed if she didn't give me a knock in the ribs that nearly sent me backwards. She took my breath away, so that I couldn't speak to her."

"And then—"

"Oh, there was nothing more. Of course I saw how it was. So she walked off one way and I the other. On the whole I consider that I am well out of it."

"And so do I," said Mackinnon, very gravely. "But if you will allow me to give you my advice, I would suggest that it would be well to avoid such mistakes in future."

"Upon my word," said O'Brien, excusing himself, "I don't know what a man is to do under such circumstances. I give you my honour that I did it all to oblige her."

We then decided that Mackinnon should convey to the injured lady the humble apology of her late admirer. It was settled that no detailed excuses should be made. It should be left to her to consider whether the deed which had been done might have been occasioned by wine, or by the folly of a moment, — or by her own indiscreet enthusiasm. No one but the two were present when the message was given, and therefore we were obliged to trust to Mackinnon's accuracy for an account of it.

She stood on very high ground indeed, he said, — at first refusing to hear anything that he had to say on the matter. "The foolish young man," she declared, "was below her anger, and below her contempt."

"He is not the first Irishman that has been made indiscreet by beauty," said Mackinnon.

"A truce to that," she replied, waving her hand with an air of assumed majesty. "The incident, contemptible as it was, has been unpleasant to me. It will necessitate my withdrawal from Rome."

"Oh, no, Mrs. Talboys; that will be making too much of him."

"The greatest hero that lives," she answered, "may have his house made uninhabitable by a very small insect." Mackinnon swore that those were her own words. Consequently a *sobriquet* was attached to O'Brien of which he by no means approved. And from that day we always called Mrs. Talboys "the hero."

Mackinnon prevailed at last with her, and she did not leave Rome. She was even induced to send a message to O'Brien, conveying her forgiveness. They shook hands together with great *éclat* in Mrs. Mackinnon's drawing-room; but I do not suppose that she ever again offered to him sympathy on the score of his matrimonial troubles.

"Mrs. General Talboys" appeared first in the February 2 issue of the *London Review* for 1861.

117

The Spotted Dog

Part I. — The Attempt

SOME FEW YEARS SINCE we received the following letter; —

"Dear Sir,

"I write to you for literary employment, and I implore you to provide me with it if it be within your power to do so. My capacity for such work is not small, and my acquirements are considerable. My need is very great, and my views in regard to remuneration are modest. I was educated at _____, and was afterwards a scholar of _____ College, Cambridge. I left the university without a degree, in consequence of a quarrel with the college tutor. I was rusticated, and not allowed to return. After that I became for a while a student for the Chancery Bar. I then lived for some years in Paris, and I understand and speak French as though it were my own language. For all purposes of literature I am equally conversant with German. I read Italian. I am, of course, familiar with Latin. In regard to Greek I will only say that I am less ignorant of it than nineteen twentieths of our national scholars. I am well read in modern and ancient history. I have especially studied political economy. I have not neglected other matters necessary to the education of an enlightened man, — unless it be natural philosophy. I can write English, and can write it with rapidity. I am a poet; — at least, I so esteem myself. I am not a believer. My character will not bear investigation; — in saying which, I mean you to understand, not that I steal or cheat, but that I live in a dirty lodging, spend many of my hours in a public-house, and cannot pay tradesmen's bills where tradesmen have been found to trust me. I have a wife and four children, — which burden forbids me to free myself from all care by a bare bodkin. I am just past forty, and since I quarrelled with my family, because I could not understand The Trinity, I have never been the owner of a ten-pound note. My wife was not a lady. I married her because I was determined to take refuge from the conventional thraldom of so-called 'gentlemen' amidst the liberty of the lower orders. My life, of course, has been a mistake. Indeed, to live at all, — is it not a folly?

"I am at present employed on the staff of two or three of the 'Penny Dreadfuls.' Your august highness in literature has perhaps never heard of a 'Penny Dreadful.' I write for them matter, which we among ourselves call 'blood and nastiness,' — and which is copied from one to another. For this I am paid forty-five shillings a week. For thirty shillings a week I will do any work that you may impose upon me for the term of six months. I write this letter as a last effort to rescue myself from the filth of my present position, but I entertain no hope of any success. If you ask it I will come and see you; but do not send for me unless you mean to employ me, as I am ashamed of myself. I live at No. 3, Cucumber Court, Gray's Inn Lane; — but if you write, address to the care of Mr. Grimes, the Spotted Dog, Liquorpond Street. Now I have told you my whole life, and you may help me if you will. I do not expect an answer.

"Yours truly,
"Julius Mackenzie."

Indeed he had told us his whole life, and what a picture of a life he had drawn! There was something in the letter which compelled attention. It was impossible to throw it, half read, into the wastepaper basket, and to think of it not at all. We did read it, probably twice, and then put ourselves to work to consider how much of it might be true and how much false. Had the man been a boy at _____, and then a scholar of his college? We concluded that, so far, the narrative was true. Had he abandoned his dependence on wealthy friends from conscientious scruples, as he pretended; or had other and less creditable reasons caused the severance? On that point we did not quite believe him. And then, as to those assertions made by himself in regard to his own capabilities, — how far did they gain credence with us? We think that we believed them all, making some small discount, — with the exception of that one in which he proclaimed himself to be a poet. A man may know whether he understands French, and be quite ignorant whether the rhymed lines which he produces are or are not poetry. When he told us that he was an infidel, and that his character would not bear investigation, we went with him altogether. His allusion to suicide we regarded as a foolish boast. We gave him credit for the four children, but were not certain about the wife. We quite believed the general assertion of his impecuniosity. That stuff about "conventional thraldom" we hope we took at its worth. When he told us that his life had been a mistake he spoke to us Gospel truth.

Of the "Penny Dreadfuls," and of "blood and nastiness," so called, we had never before heard, but we did not think it remarkable that a man so gifted as our correspondent should earn forty-five shillings a week by writing for the cheaper periodicals. It did not, however, appear to us probable that any one so remunerated would be willing to leave that engagement for another which should give him only thirty shillings. When he spoke of the "filth of his present position," our heart began to bleed for him. We know what it is so well, and can fathom so accurately the degradation of the educated man who, having been ambitious in the career of literature, falls into that slough of despond by which the profession of literature is almost surrounded. There we were with him, as brothers together. When we came to Mr. Grimes and the Spotted Dog, in Liquorpond Street, we thought that we had better refrain from answering the letter, — by which decision on our part he would not, according to his own statement, be much disappointed. Mr. Julius Mackenzie! Perhaps at this very time rich uncles and aunts were buttoning up their pockets against the sinner because of his devotion to the Spotted Dog. There are well-to-do people among the Mackenzies. It might be the case that that heterodox want of comprehension in regard to The Trinity was the cause of it; but we have observed that in most families, grievous as are doubts upon such sacred subjects, they are not held to be cause of hostility so invincible

121

as is a thoroughgoing devotion to a Spotted Dog. If the Spotted Dog had brought about these troubles, any interposition from ourselves would be useless.

For twenty-four hours we had given up all idea of answering the letter; but it then occurred to us that men who have become disreputable as drunkards do not put forth their own abominations when making appeals for aid. If this man were really given to drink he would hardly have told us of his association with the public-house. Probably he was much at the Spotted Dog, and hated himself for being there. The more we thought of it the more we fancied that the gist of his letter might be true. It seemed that the man had desired to tell the truth as he himself believed it.

It so happened that at that time we had been asked to provide an index to a certain learned manuscript in three volumes. The intended publisher of the work had already procured an index from a professional compiler of such matters; but the thing had been so badly done that it could not be used. Some knowledge of the classics was required, though it was not much more than a familiarity with the names of Latin and Greek authors, to which perhaps should be added some acquaintance, with the names also, of the better-known editors and commentators. The gentleman who had had the task in hand had failed conspicuously, and I had been told by my enterprising friend Mr. X _____, the publisher, that £25 would be freely paid on the proper accomplishment of the undertaking. The work, apparently so trifling in its nature, demanded a scholars's acquirements, and could hardly be completed in less than two months. We had snubbed the offer, saying that we should be ashamed to ask an educated man to give his time and labour for so small a remuneration; — but to Mr. Julius Mackenzie £25 for two months' work would manifestly be a godsend. If Mr. Julius Mackenzie did in truth possess the knowledge for which he gave himself credit; if he was, as he said, "familiar with Latin," and was "less ignorant of Greek than nineteen twentieths of our national scholars," he might perhaps be able to earn this £25. We certainly knew no one else who could and who would do the work properly for that money. We therefore wrote to Mr. Julius Mackenzie, and requested his presence. Our note was short, cautious, and also courteous. We regretted that a man so gifted should be driven by stress of circumstances to such need. We could undertake nothing, but if it would not put him to too much trouble to call upon us, we might perhaps be able to suggest something to him. Precisely at the hour named Mr. Julius Mackenzie came to us.

We well remember his appearance, which was one unutterably painful to behold. He was a tall man, very thin, — thin we might say as a whipping-post, were it not that one's idea of a whipping-post conveys erectness and rigidity, whereas this man, as he stood before us, was full of bends and curves and crookedness. His big head seemed to lean forward over his miserably narrow chest. His back was bowed, and his legs were crooked and tottering. He had told us that he was over forty, but we doubted, and doubt now, whether he had not added something to his years, in order partially to excuse the wan, worn weariness of his countenance. He carried an infinity of thick, ragged, wild, dirty hair, dark in colour, though not black, which age had not yet begun to grizzle. He wore a miserable attempt at a beard, stubbly, uneven, and half-shorn, — as though it had been cut down within an inch of his chin with blunt scissors. He had two ugly projecting teeth, and his cheeks were hollow. His eyes were deep set, but very bright, illuminating his whole face; so that it was impossible to look at him and to think him to be one wholly insignificant. His eyebrows were large and shaggy, but well-formed, not meeting across the brow, with single, stiffly projecting hairs, — a pair of eyebrows which added much strength to his countenance. His nose was long and well-shaped, — but red as a huge carbuncle. The moment we saw him we connected that nose with the Spotted Dog. It was not a blotched nose, not a nose covered with many carbuncles, but a brightly red, smooth, well-formed nose, one glowing carbuncle in itself. He was dressed in a long brown great-coat, which was buttoned up round his throat, and which came nearly to his feet. The binding of the coat was frayed, the buttons were half-uncovered, the button-holes were tattered, the velvet collar had become party-coloured with dirt and usage. It was in the month of December, and a great-coat was needed; but this great-coat looked as though it were worn because other garments were not at his command. Not an inch of linen or even of flannel shirt was visible. Below his coat we could only see his bro-

ken boots and the soiled legs of his trousers, which had reached
that age which in trousers defies description. When we looked at
him we could not but ask ourselves whether this man had been
born a gentleman and was still a scholar. And yet there was that
in his face which prompted us to believe the account he had
given of himself. As we looked at him we felt sure that he possessed keen intellect, and that he was too much of a man to boast
of acquirements which he did not believe himself to possess. We
shook hands with him, asked him to sit down, and murmured
something of our sorrow that he should be in distress.

"I am pretty well used to it," said he. There was nothing mean
in his voice; — there was indeed a touch of humour in it, and in
his manner there was nothing of the abjectness of supplication.
We had his letter in our hands, and we read a portion of it again
as he sat opposite to us. We then remarked that we did not understand how he, having a wife and family dependent on him,
could offer to give up a third of his income with the mere object
of changing the nature of his work. "You don't know what it is,"
said he, "to write for the 'Penny Dreadfuls.' I'm at it seven hours
a day, and hate the very words that I write. I cursed myself afterwards for sending that letter. I know that to hope is to be an ass.
But I did send it, and here I am."

We looked at his nose and felt that we must be careful before
we suggested to our learned friend, Dr. _____, to put his
manuscript into the hands of Mr. Julius Mackenzie. If it had been
a printed book the attempt might have been made without much
hazard, but our friend's work, which was elaborate, and very
learned, had not yet reached the honours of the printing-house,
We had had our own doubts whether it might ever assume the
form of a real book; but our friend, who was a wealthy as well as
a learned man, was, as yet, very determined. He desired, at any
rate, that the thing should be perfected, and his publisher had
therefore come to us offering £25 for the codification and index.
Were anything other than good to befall his manuscript, his lam-
entations would be loud, not on his own score, — but on behalf
of learning in general. It behoved us therefore to be cautious. We
pretended to read the letter again, in order that we might gain
time for a decision, for we were greatly frightened by that gleam-
ing nose.

124

Let the reader understand that the nose was by no means Bardolphian. If we have read Shakespeare aright, Bardolph's nose was a thing of terror from its size as well as its hue. It was a mighty vat, into which had ascended all the divinest particles distilled from the cellars of the hostelrie in Eastcheap. Such at least is the idea which stage representations have left upon all our minds. But the nose now before us was a well-formed nose, would have been a commanding nose, — for the power of command shows itself much in the nasal organ, — had it not been for its colour. While we were thinking of this, and doubting much as to our friend's manuscript, Mr. Mackenzie interrupted us. "You think I am a drunkard," said he. The man's mother-wit had enabled him to read our inmost thoughts.

As we looked up the man had risen from his chair, and was standing over us. He loomed upon us very tall, although his legs were crooked, and his back bent. Those piercing eyes, and that nose which almost assumed an air of authority as he carried it, were a great way above us. There seemed to be an infinity of that old brown great-coat. He had divined our thoughts, and we did not dare to contradict him. We felt that a weak, vapid, unmanly smile was creeping over our face. We were smiling as a man smiles who intends to imply some contemptuous assent with the self-depreciating comment of his companion. Such a mode of expression is in our estimation most cowardly, and most odious. We had not intended it, but we knew that the smile had pervaded us. "Of course you do," said he. "I was a drunkard, but I am not one now. It doesn't matter; — only I wish you hadn't sent for me. I'll go away at once."

So saying, he was about to depart, but we stopped him. We assured him with much energy that we did not mean to offend him. He protested that there was no offence. He was too well used to that kind of thing to be made "more than wretched by it." Such was his heartbreaking phrase. "As for anger, I've lost all that long ago. Of course you take me for a drunkard, and I should still be a drunkard, only _____ "

"Only what?" I asked.

"It don't matter," said he. "I need not trouble you with more than I have said already. You haven't got anything for me to do, I suppose?" Then I explained to him that I had something he might do, if I could venture to entrust him with the work. With some trouble I got him to sit down again, and to listen while I explained to him the circumstances. I had been grievously afflicted when he alluded to his former habit of drinking, — a former habit, as he himself now stated, — but I entertained no hesitation in raising questions as to his erudition. I felt almost assured that his answers would be satisfactory, and that no discomfiture would arise from such questioning. We were quickly able to perceive that we at any rate could not examine him in classical literature. As soon as we mentioned the name and nature of the work he went off at score, and satisfied us amply that he was familiar at least with the title-pages of editions. We began, indeed, to fear whether he might not be too caustic a critic on our own friend's performance. "Dr. _____ is only an amateur himself," said we, deprecating in advance any such exercise of the red-nosed man's too severe erudition. "We never get much beyond dilettantism here," said he, "as far as Greek and Latin are concerned." What a terrible man he would have been could he have got upon the staff of the *Saturday Review,* instead of going to the Spotted Dog!

We endeavoured to bring the interview to an end by telling him that we would consult the learned Doctor from whom the manuscript had emanated; and we hinted that a reference would be of course acceptable. His impudence, — or, perhaps we should rather call it his straightforward sincere audacity, — was unbounded. "Mr. Grimes of the Spotted Dog knows me better than any one else," said he. We blew the breath out of our mouth with astonishment. "I'm not asking you to go to him to find out whether I know Latin and Greek," said Mr. Mackenzie. "You must find that out for yourself." We assured him that we thought we had found that out. "But he can tell you that I won't pawn your manuscript." The man was so grim and brave that he almost frightened us. We hinted, however, that literary reference should be given. The gentlemen who paid him forty-five shillings a week, — the manager, in short, of the "Penny Dreadful," might tell us something of him. Then he wrote for us a name on a scrap of paper, and added to it an address in the close vicinity of Fleet Street, at which we remembered to have seen the title of a periodical which we now knew to be a "Penny Dreadful."

Before he took his leave he made us a speech, again standing up over us, though we also were on our legs. It was that bend in his neck, combined with his natural height, which gave him such an air of superiority in conversation. He seemed to overshadow us, and to have his own way with us, because he was enabled to look down upon us. There was a footstool on our hearth-rug, and we remember to have attempted to stand upon that, in order that we might escape this supervision: but we stumbled, and had to kick it from us, and something was added to our sense of inferiority by this little failure. "I don't expect much from this," he said, "I never do expect much. And I have misfortunes independent of my poverty which make it impossible that I should be other than a miserable wretch."

"Bad health?" we asked.

"No; — nothing absolutely personal; — but never mind. I must not trouble you with more of my history. But if you can do this thing for me, it may be the means of redeeming me from utter degradation." We then assured him that we would do our best, and he left us with a promise that he would call again on that day week.

The first step which we took on his behalf was one the very idea of which had at first almost moved us to ridicule. We made inquiry respecting Mr. Julius Mackenzie, of Mr. Grimes, the landlord of the Spotted Dog. Though Mr. Grimes did keep the Spotted Dog, he might be a man of sense and, possibly, of conscience. At any rate he would tell us something, or confirm our doubts by refusing to tell us anything. We found Mr. Grimes seated in a very neat little back parlour, and were peculiarly taken by the appearance of a lady in a little cap and black silk gown, whom we soon found to be Mrs. Grimes. Had we ventured to employ our intellect in personifying for ourselves an imaginary Mrs. Grimes as the landlady of a Spotted Dog public-house in Liquorpond Street, the figure we should have built up for ourselves would have been the very opposite of that which this lady presented to us. She was slim, and young, and pretty, and had pleasant little tricks of words, in spite of occasional slips in her grammar, which made us almost think that it might be our duty to come very often to the Spotted Dog to inquire about Mr. Julius Mackenzie. Mr. Grimes was a man about forty, — fully ten years the senior of his wife, — with a clear grey eye, and a mouth and chin from which we surmised that he would be competent to clear the Spotted Dog of unruly visitors after twelve o'clock, whenever it might be his wish to do so. We soon made known our request. Mr. Mackenzie had come to us for literary employment. Could they tell us anything about Mr. Mackenzie.

"He's as clever an author, in the way of writing and that kind of thing, as there is in all London," said Mrs. Grimes with energy. Perhaps her opinion ought not to have been taken for much, but it had its weight. We explained, however, that at the present moment we were specially anxious to know something of the gentleman's character and mode of life. Mr. Grimes, whose manner to us was quite courteous, sat silent, thinking how to answer us. His more impulsive and friendly wife was again ready with her assurance. "There ain't an honester gentleman breathing; — and I say he is a gentleman, though he's that poor he hasn't sometimes a shirt to his back."

"I don't think he's ever very well off for shirts," said Mr. Grimes.

"I wouldn't be slow to give him one of yours, John, only I know he wouldn't take it," said Mrs. Grimes. "Well now, look here, sir; — we've that feeling for him that our young woman there would draw anything for him he'd ask, — money or no money. She'd never venture to name money to him if he wanted a glass of anything, — hot or cold, beer or spirits. Isn't that so, John?"

"She's fool enough for anything as far as I know," said Mr. Grimes.

"She ain't no fool at all; and I'd do the same if I was there; — and so'd you, John. There is nothing Mackenzie'd ask as he wouldn't give him," said Mrs. Grimes, pointing with her thumb over her shoulder to her husband, who was standing on the hearth-rug; — "that is, in the way of drawing liquor, and refreshments, and such like. But he never raised a glass to his lips in this house as he didn't pay for, nor yet took a biscuit out of that basket. He's a gentleman all over, is Mackenzie."

It was strong testimony; but still we had not quite got at the bottom of the matter. "Doesn't he raise a great many glasses to his lips?" we asked.

"No, he don't," said Mrs. Grimes, — "only in reason."

"He's had misfortunes," said Mr. Grimes.

"Indeed and he has," said the lady, — "what I call the very troublesomest of troubles. If you was troubled like him, John, where'd you be?"

"I know where you'd be," said John.

"He's got a bad wife, sir; the worst as ever was," continued Mrs. Grimes. "Talk of drink; — there is nothing that woman wouldn't do for it. She'd pawn the very clothes off her children's back in mid-winter to get it. She'd rob the food out of her husband's mouth for a drop of gin. As for herself, — she ain't no woman's notions left of keeping herself any way. She'd as soon be picked out of the gutter as not; — and as for words out of her mouth or clothes on her back, she hasn't got, sir, not an item of a female's feelings left about her."

Mrs. Grimes had been very eloquent and had painted the "troublesomest of all troubles" with glowing words. This was what the wretched man had come to by marrying a woman who was not a lady in order that he might escape the "conventional thraldom" of gentility! But still the drunken wife was not all. There was the evidence of his own nose against himself, and the additional fact that he had acknowledged himself to have been formerly a drunkard. "I suppose he has drunk, himself?" we said.

"He has drunk, in course," said Mrs. Grimes.

"The world has been pretty rough with him, sir," said Mr. Grimes.

"But he don't drink now," continued the lady. "At least if he do, we don't see it. As for her, she wouldn't show herself inside our door."

"It ain't often that man and wife draws their milk from the same cow," said Mr. Grimes.

"But Mackenzie is here every day of his life," said Mrs. Grimes. "When he's got a sixpence to pay for it, he'll come in here and have a glass of beer and a bit of something to eat. We does make him a little extra welcome, and that's the truth of it. We knows what he is, and we knows what he was. As for book learning, sir; — it don't matter what language it is, it's all as one to him. He knows 'em all round just as I know my catechism."

"Can't you say fairer than that for him, Polly?" asked Mr. Grimes.

"Don't you talk of catechisms, John; nor yet of nothing else as a man ought to set his mind to; — unless it is keeping the Spotted Dog. But as for Mackenzie; — he knows off by heart whole books full of learning. There was some furreners here as came from, — I don't know where it was they came from, only it wasn't France, nor yet Germany, and he talked to them just as though he hadn't been born in England at all. I don't think there ever was such a man for knowing things. He'll go on with poetry out of his own head till you think it comes from him like web from a spider." We could not help thinking of the wonderful companionship which there must have been in that parlour while the reduced man was spinning his web and Mrs. Grimes, with her needle-work lying idle in her lap, was sitting by, listening with rapt admiration. In passing by the Spotted Dog one would not imagine such a scene to have its existence within. But then so many things do have existence of which we imagine nothing!

"Don't you talk of catechisms, John; nor yet of nothing else as a man ought to set his mind to; — unless it is keeping the Spotted Dog. But as for Mackenzie; — he knows off by heart whole books full of learning. There was some furreners here as came from, — I don't know where it was they came from, only it wasn't France, nor yet Germany, and he talked to them just as though he hadn't been born in England at all. I don't think there ever was such a man for knowing things. He'll go on with poetry out of his own head till you think it comes from his like web from a spider." We could not help thinking of the wonderful companionship which there must have been in that parlour while the reduced man was spinning his web and Mrs. Grimes, with her needle-work lying idle in her lap, was sitting by, listening with rapt admiration. In passing by the Spotted Dog one would not imagine such a scene to have its existence within. But then so many things do have existence of which we imagine nothing!

Mr. Grimes ended the interview. "The fact is, sir, if you can give him employment better than what he has now, you'll be helping a man who has seen better days, and who only wants help to see 'em again. He's got it all there," and Mr. Grimes put his finger up to his head.

"He's got it all here too," said Mrs. Grimes, laying her hand upon her heart. Hereupon we took our leave, suggesting to these excellent friends that if it should come to pass that we had further dealings with Mr. Mackenzie we might perhaps trouble them again. They assured us that we should always be welcome, and Mr. Grimes himself saw us to the door, having made profuse offers of such good cheer as the house afforded. We were upon the whole much taken with the Spotted Dog.

From thence we went to the office of the "Penny Dreadful," in the vicinity of Fleet Street. As we walked thither we could not but think of Mrs. Grimes' words. The troublesomest of troubles! We acknowledged to ouselves that they were true words. Can there be any trouble more troublesome than that of suffering from the shame inflicted by a degraded wife? We had just parted from Mr. Grimes, — not, indeed, having seen very much of him in the course of our interview; — but little as we had seen, we were sure that he was assisted in his position by a buoyant pride in that he called himself the master, and owner, and husband of Mrs. Grimes. In the very step with which he passed in and out of his own door you could see that there was nothing that he was ashamed of about his household. When abroad he could talk of his "missus," with a conviction that the picture which the word would convey to all who heard him would redound to his honour. But what must have been the reflections of Julius Mackenzie when his mind dwelt upon his wife? We remembered the words of his letter. "I have a wife and four children, which burden forbids me to free myself from all care with a bare bodkin." As we thought of them, and of the story which had been told to us at the Spotted Dog, they lost that tone of rhodomontade with which they had invested themselves when we first read them. A wife who is indifferent to being picked out of the gutter, and who will pawn her children's clothes for gin, must be a trouble than which none can be more troublesome.

We did not find that we ingratiated ourselves with the people at the office of the periodical for which Mr. Mackenzie worked; and yet we endeavoured to do so, assuming in our manner and tone something of the familiarity of a common pursuit. After much delay we came upon a gentleman sitting in a dark cupboard, who twisted round his stool to face us while he spoke to us. We believe that he was the editor of more than one "Penny Dreadful," and that, as many as a dozen serial novels were being issued to the world at the same time under his supervision. "Oh!" said he, "so you're at that game, are you?" We assured him that we were at no game at all, but were simply influenced by a desire to assist a distressed scholar. "That be blowed," said our brother. "Mackenzie's doing as well here as he'll do anywhere. He's a drunken blackguard, when all's said and done. So you're going to buy him up, are you? You won't keep him long, —and then he'll have to starve." We assured the gentleman that we had no desire to buy up Mr. Mackenzie; we explained our ideas as to the freedom of the literary profession, in accordance with which Mr. Mackenzie could not be wrong in applying to us for work; and we especially deprecated any severity on our brother's part towards the man, more especially begging that nothing might be decided, as we were far from thinking it certain that we could provide Mr. Mackenzie with any literary employment. "That's all right," said our brother, twisting back his stool. "He can't work for both of us; — that's all. He has his bread here regular, week after week; and I don't suppose you'll do as much as that for him." Then we went away, shaking the dust off our feet, and wondering much at the great development of literature which latter years have produced. We had not even known of the existence of these papers; — and yet there they were, going forth into the hands of hundreds of thousands of readers, all of whom were being, more or less, instructed in their modes of life and manner of thinking by the stories which were thus brought before them.

But there might be truth in what our brother had said to us. Should Mr. Mackenzie abandon his present engagement for the sake of the job which we proposed to put in his hands, might he not thereby injure rather than improve his prospects? We were acquainted with only one learned doctor desirous of having his manuscripts codified and indexed at his own expense. As for writing for the periodical with which we were connected, we knew enough of the business to be aware that Mr. Mackenzie's gifts of erudition would very probably not so much assist him in attempting such work as would his late training act against him. A man might be able to read and even talk a dozen languages, — "just as though he hadn't been born in England at all," — and yet not write the language with which we dealt after the fashion which suited our readers. It might be that he would fly much above our heads, and do work infinitely too big for us. We did not regard our own heads as being very high. But, for such altitude as they held, a certain class of writing was adapted. The gentleman whom we had just left would require, no doubt, altogether another style. It was probable that Mr. Mackenzie had already fitted himself to his present audience. And, even were it not so, we could not promise him forty-five shillings a week, or even that thirty shillings for which he asked. There is nothing more dangerous than the attempt to befriend a man in middle life by transplanting him from one soil to another.

When Mr. Mackenzie came to us again, we endeavoured to explain all this to him. We had in the meantime seen our friend the Doctor, whose beneficence of spirit in regard to the unfortunate man of letters was extreme. He was charmed with our account of the man, and saw with his mind's eye the work, for the performance of which he was pining, perfected in a manner that would be a blessing to the scholars of all future ages. He was at first anxious to ask Julius Mackenzie down to his rectory, and, even after we had explained to him that this would not at present be expedient, was full of a dream of future friendship with a man who would be able to discuss the digamma with him, who would have studied Greek metres, and have an opinion of his own as to Porson's canon. We were in possession of the manuscript, and had our friend's authority for handing it over to Mr. Mackenzie.

He came to us according to appointment, and his nose seemed to be redder than ever. We thought that we discovered a discouraging flavour of spirits in his breath. Mrs. Grimes had declared that he drank, — only in reason; but the ideas of the wife of a publican, — even though that wife were Mrs. Grimes, — might be very different from our own as to what was reasonable in that matter. And as we looked at him he seemed to be more rough, more ragged, almost more wretched than before. It might be that, in taking his part with my brother of the "Penny Dreadful," with the Doctor, and even with myself in thinking over his claims, I had endowed him with higher qualities than I had been justified in giving to him. As I considered him and his appearance I certainly could not assure myself that he looked like a man worthy to be trusted. A policeman, seeing him at a street corner, would have had an eye upon him in a moment. He rubbed himself together within his old coat, as men do when they come out of gin-shops. His eye was as bright as before, but we thought that his mouth was meaner, and his nose redder. We were almost disenchanted with him. We said nothing to him at first about the Spotted Dog, but suggested to him our fears that if he undertook work at our hands he would lose the much more permanent employment which he got from the gentleman whom we had seen in the cupboard. We then explained to him that we could promise to him no continuation of employment.

The violence with which he cursed the gentleman who had sat in the cupboard appalled us, and had, we think, some effect in bringing back to us the feeling of respect for him which we had almost lost. It may be difficult to explain why we respected him because he cursed and swore horribly. We do not like cursing and swearing, and were any of our younger contributors to indulge themselves after that fashion in our presence we should, at the very least, — frown upon them. We did not frown upon Julius Mackenzie, but stood up, gazing into his face above us, again feeling that the man was powerful. Perhaps we respected him because he was not in the least afraid of us. He went on to assert that he cared not, — not a straw, we will say, — for the gentleman in the cupboard. He knew the gentleman in the cupboard very well; and the gentleman in the cupboard knew him. As long as he took his work to the gentleman in the cupboard, the gentleman in the cupboard would be only too happy to purchase that work at the rate of sixpence for a page of manuscript containing two hundred and fifty words. That was his rate of payment for prose fiction, and at that rate he could earn forty-five shillings a week. He wasn't afraid of the gentleman in the cupboard. He had some words with the gentleman in the cupboard before now, and they two understood each other very well. He hinted, moreover, that there were other gentlemen in other cupboards; but with none of them could he advance beyond forty-five shillings a week. For this he had to sit, with his pen in his hand, seven hours seven days a week, and the very paper, pens, and ink came to fifteenpence out of the money. He had struck for wages once, and for a halcyon month or two had carried his point of sevenpence halfpenny a page; but the gentlemen in the cupboards had told him that it could not be. They, too, must live. His matter was no doubt attractive; but any price above sixpence a page unfitted it for their market. All this Mr. Julius Mackenzie explained to us with much violence of expression. When I named Mrs. Grimes to him the tone of his voice was altered. "Yes;" said he, — "I thought they'd say a word for me. They're the best friends I've got now. I don't know that you ought quite to believe her, for I think she'd perhaps tell a lie to do me a service." We assured him that we did believe every word Mrs. Grimes had said to us.

After much pausing over the matter, we told him that we were empowered to trust him with our friend's work, and the manuscript was produced upon the table. If he would undertake the work and perform it, he should be paid £8:6s.:8d. for each of the three volumes as they were completed. And we undertook, moreover, on our own responsibility, to advance him money in small amounts through the hands of Mrs. Grimes, if he really settled himself to the task. At first he was in ecstasies, and, as we explained to him the way in which the index should be brought out and the codification performed, he turned over the pages rapidly, and showed us that he understood at any rate the nature of the work to be done. But when we came to details he was less happy. In what workshop was this new work to be performed? There was a moment in which we almost thought of telling him to do the work in our own room; but we hesitated, luckily, remembering that his continual presence with us for two or three months would probably destroy us altogether. It appeared that his present work was done sometimes at the Spotted Dog, and sometimes at home in his lodgings. He said not a word to us about his wife, but we could understand that there would be periods in which to work at home would be impossible to him. He did not pretend to deny that there might be danger on that score, nor did he ask permission to take the entire manuscript at once away to his abode. We knew that if he took part he must take the whole, as the work could not be done in parts. Counter references would be needed. "My circumstances are bad; — very bad indeed," he said. We expressed the great trouble to which we should be subjected if any evil should happen to the manuscript. "I will give it up," he said, towering over us again, and shaking his head. "I cannot expect that I should be trusted." But we were determined that it should not be given up. Sooner than give the matter up we would make some arrangement by hiring a place in which he might work. Even though we were to pay ten shillings a week for a room for him out of the money, the bargain would be a good one for him. At last we determined that we would pay a second visit to the Spotted Dog, and consult Mr. Grimes. We felt that we should have a pleasure in arranging together with Mrs. Grimes any scheme of benevolence on behalf of this unfortunate and remarkable man. So we told him that we would think over the matter, and send a letter to his address at the Spotted Dog, which he should receive on the following morning. He then gathered himself up, rubbed himself together again inside his coat, and took his departure.

As soon as he was gone we sat looking at the learned Doctor's manuscript, and thinking of what we had done. There lay the work of years, by which our dear and venerable old friend expected that he would rank among the great commentators of modern times. We, in truth, did not anticipate for him all the glory to which he looked forward. We feared that there might be disappointment. Hot discussion on verbal accuracies or on rules of metre are perhaps not so much in vogue now as they were a hundred years ago. There might be disappointment and great sorrow; but we could not with equanimity anticipate the prevention of this sorrow by the possible loss or destruction of the manuscript which had been entrusted to us. The Doctor himself had seemed to anticipate no such danger. When we told him of Mackenzie's learning and misfortunes, he was eager at once that the thing should be done, merely stipulating that he should have an interview with Mr. Mackenzie before he returned to his rectory.

That same day we went to the Spotted Dog, and found Mrs. Grimes alone. Mackenzie had been there immediately after leaving our room, and had told her what had taken place. She was full of the subject and anxious to give every possible assistance. She confessed at once that the papers would not be safe in the rooms inhabited by Mackenzie and his wife. "He pays five shillings a week," she said, "for a wretched place round in Cucumber Court. They are all huddled together, any way; and how he manages to do a thing at all there, — in the way of author-work, — is a wonder to everybody. Sometimes he can't, and then he'll sit for hours together at the little table in our tap-room." We went

136

into the tap-room and saw the little table. It was a wonder indeed that any one should be able to compose and write tales of imagination in a place so dreary, dark, and ill-omened. The little table was hardly more than a long slab or plank, perhaps eighteen inches wide. When we visited the place there were two brewer's draymen seated there, and three draggled, wretched-looking women. The carters were eating enormous hunches of bread and bacon, which they cut and put into their mouths slowly, solemnly, and in silence. The three women were seated on a bench, and when I saw them had no signs of festivity before them. It must be presumed that they had paid for something, or they would hardly have been allowed to sit there. "It is empty now," said Mrs. Grimes, taking no immediate notice of the men or of the women; "but sometimes he'll sit writing in that corner, when there's such a jabber of voices as you wouldn't hear a cannon go off over at Reid's, and that thick with smoke you'd a'most cut it with a knife. Don't he, Peter?" The man whom she addressed endeavoured to prepare himself for answer by swallowing at the moment three square inches of bread and bacon, which he had just put into his mouth. He made an awful effort, but failed; and, failing, nodded his head three times. The "moles" had then returned within his jaws and was masticated with slow and satisfactory precision. "They all know him here, sir;" continued Mrs. Grimes. "He'll go on writing, writing, writing, for hours together; and nobody'll say nothing to him. Will they, Peter?" Peter, who was now half way through the work he had laid out for himself, muttered some inarticulate grunt of assent.

We then went back to the snug little room inside the bar. It was quite clear to me that the man could not manipulate the Doctor's manuscript, of which he would have to spread a dozen sheets before him at the same time, in the place I had just visited. Even could he have occupied the chamber alone, the accommodation would not have been sufficient for the purpose. It was equally clear that he could not be allowed to use Mrs. Grimes' snuggery. "How are we to get a place for him?" said I, appealing to the lady. "He shall have a place," she said, "I'll go bail; he shan't lose the job for want of a workshop." Then she sat down and began to think it over. I was just about to propose the hiring of some decent room in the neighbourhood, when she made a suggestion, which I acknowledge startled me. "I'll have a big table put into my own bed-room," said she, "and he shall do it there. There ain't another hole or corner about the place as 'd suit; and he can lay the gentleman's papers all out on the bed, square and clean and orderly. Can't he now? And I can see after 'em, as he don't lose 'em. Can't I now?"

By this time there had sprung up an intimacy between ourselves and Mrs. Grimes which seemed to justify an expression of the doubt which I then threw on the propriety of such a disarrangement of her most private domestic affairs. "Mr. Grimes will hardly approve of that," we said.

"Oh, John won't mind. What'll it matter to John as long as Mackenzie is out in time for him to go to bed? We ain't early birds, morning or night, — that's true. In our line folks can't be early. But from ten to six there's the room, and he shall have it. Come up and see, sir." So we followed Mrs. Grimes up the narrow staircase to the marital bower. "It ain't large, but there'll be room for the table, and for him to sit at it; — won't there now?"

It was a dark little room, with one small window looking out under the low roof, and facing the heavy high dead wall of the brewery opposite. But it was clean and sweet, and the furniture in it was all solid and good, old-fashioned, and made of mahogany. Two or three of Mrs. Grimes' gowns were laid upon the bed, and other portions of her dress were hung on pegs behind the doors. The only untidy article in the room was a pair of "John's" trousers, which he had failed to put out of sight. She was not a whit abashed, but took them up and folded them and patted them, and laid them in the capacious wardrobe. "We'll have all these things away," she said, "and then he can have all his papers out upon the bed just as he pleases."

We own that there was something in the proposed arrangement which dismayed us. We also were married, and what would our wife have said had we proposed that a contributor, — even a contributor not red-nosed and seething with gin, — that any best disciplined contributor should be invited to write an article within the precincts of our sanctum! We could not bring ourselves to believe that Mr. Grimes would authorise the proposition. There is something holy about the bed-room of a married couple; and there would be a special desecration in the continued presence of Mr. Julius Mackenzie. We thought it better that we should explain something of all this to her. "Do you know," we said, "this seems to be hardly prudent?"

"Why not prudent?" she asked.

"Up in your bed-room, you know! Mr. Grimes will be sure to dislike it."

"What, — John! Not he. I know what you're a-thinking of, Mr. ＿＿＿＿＿ ," she said. "But we're different in our ways than what you are. Things to us are only just what they are. We haven't time, nor yet money, nor perhaps edication, for seemings and thinkings as you have. If you was travelling out amongst the wild Injeans, you'd ask any one to eat a bit in your bed-room as soon as look at 'em, if you'd got a bit for 'em to eat. We're travelling among wild Injeans all our lives, and a bed-room ain't no more to us than any other room. Mackenzie shall come up here, and I'll have the table fixed for him, just there by the window." I hadn't another word to say to her, and I could not keep myself from thinking for many an hour afterwards, whether it may not be a good thing for men, and for women also, to believe that they are always travelling among wild Indians.

When we went down Mr. Grimes himself was in the little parlour. He did not seem at all surprised at seeing his wife enter the room from above accompanied by a stranger. She at once began her story, and told the arrangement which she proposed, — which she did, as I observed, without any actual request for his sanction. Looking at Mr. Grimes' face, I thought that he did not quite like it; but he accepted it, almost without a word, scratching his head and raising his eyebrows. "You know, John, he could no more do it at home than he could fly," said Mrs. Grimes.

"Who said he could do it at home?"

"And he couldn't do it in the tap-room; — could he? If so, there ain't no other place, and so that's settled." John Grimes again scratched his head, and the matter was settled. Before we left the house Mackenzie himself came in, and was told in our presence of the accommodation which was to be prepared for him. "It's just like you, Mrs. Grimes," was all he said in the way of thanks. Then Mrs. Grimes made her bargain with him somewhat sternly. He should have the room for five hours a day, — ten till three, or twelve till five; but he must settle which, and then stick to his hours. "And I won't have nothing up there in the way of drink," said John Grimes.

"Who's asking to have drink there?" said Mackenzie.

"You're not asking now, but maybe you will. I won't have it, that's all."

"That shall be all right, John," said Mrs. Grimes, nodding her head.

"Women are that soft, — in the way of judgment, — that they'll go and do a'most anything, good or bad, when they've got their feelings up." Such was the only rebuke which in our hearing Mr. Grimes administered to his pretty wife. Mackenzie whispered something to the publican, but Grimes only shook his head. We understood it all thoroughly. He did not like the scheme, but he would not contradict his wife in an act of real kindness. We then made an appointment with the scholar for meeting our friend and his future patron at our rooms, and took our leave of the Spotted Dog. Before we went, however, Mrs. Grimes insisted on producing some cherry-bounce, as she called it, which, after sundry refusals on our part, was brought in on a small round shining tray, in a little bottle covered all over with gold sprigs, with four tiny glasses similarly ornamented. Mrs. Grimes poured out the liquor, using a very sparing hand when she came to the glass which was intended for herself. We find it, as a rule, easier to talk with the Grimeses of the world than to eat with them or drink with them. When the glass was handed to us we did not know whether or no we were expected to say something. We waited, however, till Mr. Grimes and Mackenzie had been provided with their glasses. "Proud to see you at the Spotted Dog, Mr. _____," said Grimes. "That we are," said Mrs. Grimes, smiling at us over her almost imperceptible drop of drink. Julius Mackenzie just bobbed his head, and swallowed the cordial at a gulp, — as a dog does a lump of meat; leaving the impression on his friends around him that he has not got from it half the enjoyment which it might have given him had he been a little more patient in the process. I could not but think that had Mackenzie allowed the cherry-bounce to trickle a little in his palate, as I did myself, it would have gratified him more than it did in being chucked down his throat with all the impetus which his elbow could give to the glass. "That's tidy tipple," said Mr. Grimes, winking his eye. We acknowledged that it was tidy. "My mother made it, as used to keep the Pig and Magpie, at Colchester." said Mrs. Grimes. In this way we learned a good deal of Mrs. Grimes' history. Her very earliest years had been passed among wild Indians.

Then came the interview between the Doctor and Mr. Mackenzie. We must confess that we greatly feared the impression which our younger friend might make on the elder. We had of course told the Doctor of the red nose, and he had accepted the information with a smile. But he was a man who would feel the contamination of contact with a drunkard, and who would shrink from an unpleasant association. There are vices of which we habitually take altogether different views in accordance with the manner in which they are brought under our notice. This vice of drunkenness is often a joke in the mouths of those to whom the thing itself is a horror. Even before our boys we talk of it as being rather funny, though to see one of them funny himself would almost break our hearts. The learned commentator had accepted our account of the red nose as though it were simply a part of the undeserved misery of the wretched man; but should he find the wretched man to be actually redolent of gin his feelings might be changed. The Doctor was with us first, and the volumes of the MS. were displayed upon the table. The compiler of them, as he lifted here a page and there a page, handled them with the gentleness of a lover. They had been exquisitely arranged, and were very fair. The pagings, and the margins, and the chapterings, and all the complementary paraphernalia of authorship, were perfect. "A life-time, my friend; just a life-time!" the Doctor had said to us, speaking of his own work while we were waiting for the man to whose hands was to be entrusted the result of so much labour and scholarship. We wished at that moment that we had never been called on to interfere in the matter.

Mackenzie came, and the introduction was made. The Doctor was a gentleman of the old school, very neat in his attire, — dressed in perfect black, with knee-breeches and black gaiters, with a closely shorn chin, and an exquisitely white cravat. Though he was in truth simply the rector of his parish, his parish was one which entitled him to call himself a dean, and he wore a clerical rosette on his hat. He was a well-made, tall, portly gentleman, with whom to take the slightest liberty would have been impossible. His well-formed full face was singularly expressive of benevolence, but there was in it too an air of command which created an involuntary respect. He was a man whose means were ample, and who could afford to keep two curates, so that the appanages of a Church dignitary did in some sort belong to him. We doubt whether he really understood what work meant, — even when he spoke with so much pathos of the labour of his life: but he was a man not at all exacting in regard to the work of others, and who was anxious to make the world as smooth and rosy to those around him as it had been to himself. He came forward, paused a moment, and then shook hands with Mackenzie. Our work had been done, and we remained in the background during the interview. It was now for the Doctor to satisfy himself with the scholarship, — and, if he chose to take cognizance of the matter, with the morals of his proposed assistant.

Mackenzie himself was more subdued in his manner than he had been when talking with ourselves. The Doctor made a little speech, standing at the table with one hand on one volume and the other on another. He told of all his work, with a mixture of modesty as to the thing done, and self-assertion as to his interest in doing it, which was charming. He acknowledged that the sum proposed for the aid which he required was inconsiderable; — but it had been fixed by the proposed publisher. Should Mr. Mackenzie find that the labour was long he would willingly increase it. Then he commenced a conversation respecting the Greek dramatists, which had none of the air or tone of an examination, but which still served the purpose of enabling Mackenzie to show his scholarship. In that respect there was no doubt that the ragged, red-nosed, disreputable man, who stood there longing for his job, was the greater proficient of the two. We never discovered that he had had access to books in later years; but his memory of the old things seemed to be perfect. When it was suggested that references would be required, it seemed that he did know his way into the library of the British Museum. "When I wasn't quite so shabby," he said boldly, "I used to be there." The Doctor instantly produced a ten-pound note, and insisted that it should be taken in advance. Mackenzie hesitated, and we suggested that it was premature; but the Doctor was firm. "If an old scholar mayn't assist one younger than himself," he said, "I don't know when one man may aid another. And this is no alms. It is simply a pledge for work to be done." Mackenzie took the money, muttering something of an assurance that as far as his ability went, the work should be done well. "It should certainly," he said, "be done diligently."

When money had passed, of course the thing was settled; but in truth the bank-note had been given, not from judgment in settling the matter, but from the generous impulse of the moment. There was, however, no receding. The Doctor expressed by no hint a doubt as to the safety of his manuscript. He was by far too fine a gentleman to give the man whom he employed pain in that direction. If there were risk, he would now run the risk. And so the thing was settled.

We did not, however, give the manuscript on that occasion into Mackenzie's hands, but took it down afterwards, locked in an old despatch-box of our own, to the Spotted Dog, and left the box with the key of it in the hands of Mrs. Grimes. Again we went up into that lady's bed-room, and saw that the big table had been placed by the window for Mackenzie's accommodation. It so nearly filled the room, that, as we observed, John Grimes could not get round at all to his side of the bed. It was arranged that Mackenzie was to begin on the morrow.

Part II. — The Result

During the next month we saw a good deal of Mr. Julius Mackenzie, and made ourselves quite at home in Mrs. Grimes's bed-room. We went in and out of the Spotted Dog as if we had known that establishment all our lives, and spent many a quarter of an hour with the hostess in her little parlour, discussing the prospects of Mr. Mackenzie and his family. He had procured for himself decent, if not exactly new, garments out of the money so liberally provided by my learned friend the Doctor, and spent much of his time in the library of the British Museum. He certainly worked very hard, for he did not altogether abandon his old engagement. Before the end of the first month the index of the first volume, nearly completed, had been sent down for the inspection of the Doctor, and had been returned with ample eulogium and some little criticism. The criticisms Mackenzie answered by letter, with true scholarly spirit, and the Doctor was delighted. Nothing could be more pleasant to him than a correspondence, prolonged almost indefinitely, as to the respective merits of a τὸ or a τοῦ, or on the demand for a spondee or an iamb. When he found that the work was really in industrious hands, he ceased to be clamorous for early publication, and gave us to understand privately that Mr. Mackenzie was not to be limited to the sum named. The matter of remuneration was, indeed, left very much to ourselves, and Mackenzie had certainly found a most efficient friend in the author whose works had been confided to his hands.

All this was very pleasant, and Mackenzie throughout that month worked very hard. According to the statements made to me by Mrs. Grimes he took no more gin than what was necessary for a hard-working man. As to the exact quantity of that cordial which she imagined to be beneficial and needful, we made no close inquiry. He certainly kept himself in a condition for work, and so far all went on happily. Nevertheless, there was a terrible skeleton in the cupboard, — or rather out of the cupboard, for the skeleton could not be got to hide itself. A certain portion of his prosperity reached the hands of his wife, and she was behaving herself worse than ever. The four children had been covered with decent garments under Mrs. Grimes's care, and then Mrs. Mackenzie had appeared at the Spotted Dog, loudly demanding a new outfit for herself. She came not only once, but often, and Mr. Grimes was beginning to protest that he saw too much of the family. We had become very intimate with Mrs. Grimes, and she did not hesitate to confide to us her fears lest "John should cut up rough," before the thing was completed. "You see," she said, "it is against the house, no doubt, that woman coming nigh it." But still she was firm, and Mackenzie was not disturbed in the possession of the bed-room. At last Mrs. Mackenzie was provided with some articles of female attire; — and then, on the very next day, she and the four children were again stripped almost naked. The wretched creature must have steeped herself in gin to the shoulders, for in one day she made a sweep of everything. She then came in a state of furious intoxication to the Spotted Dog, and was removed by the police under the express order of the landlord.

We can hardly say which was the most surprising to us, the loyalty of Mrs. Grimes or the patience of John. During that night, as we were told two days afterwards by his wife, he stormed with passion. The papers she had locked up in order that he should not get at them and destroy them. He swore that everything should be cleared out on the following morning. But when the morning came he did not even say a word to Mackenzie, as the wretched, downcast, broken-hearted creature passed up-stairs to his work. "You see I knows him, and how to deal with him," said Mrs. Grimes. "There ain't another like himself nowheres; — he's that good. A softer-hearteder man there ain't in the public line. He can speak dreadful when his dander is up, and can look —————————; oh, laws, he just can look at you! But he could no more put his hands upon a woman, in the way of hurting, — no more than be an archbishop." Where could be the man, thought we to ourselves as this was said to us, who could have put a hand, — in the way of hurting, — upon Mrs. Grimes?

On that occasion, to the best of our belief, the policeman contented himself with depositing Mrs. Mackenzie at her own lodgings. On the next day she was picked up drunk in the street, and carried away to the lock-up house. At the very moment in which the story was being told to us by Mrs. Grimes, Mackenzie had gone to the police office to pay the fine, and to bring his wife home. We asked with dismay and surprise why he should interfere to rescue her, — why he did not leave her in custody as long as the police would keep her? "Who'd there be to look after the children?" asked Mrs. Grimes, as though she were offended at our suggestion. Then she went on to explain that in such a household as that of poor Mackenzie the wife is absolutely a necessity, even though she be an habitual drunkard. Intolerable as she was, her services were necessary to him. "A husband as drinks is bad," said Mrs. Grimes, — with something, we thought, of an apologetic tone for the vice upon which her own prosperity was partly built, — "but when a woman takes to it, it's the ————— devil." We thought that she was right, as we pictured to ourselves that man of letters satisfying the magistrate's demand for his wife's misconduct, and taking the degraded, half-naked creature once more home to his children.

We saw him about twelve o'clock on that day, and he had then, too evidently, been endeavouring to support his misery by

145

the free use of alcohol. We did not speak of it down in the parlour; but even Mrs. Grimes, we think, would have admitted that he had taken more than was good for him. He was sitting up in the bed-room with his head hanging upon his hand, with a swarm of our learned friend's papers spread on the table before him. Mrs. Grimes, when he entered the house, had gone up-stairs to give them out to him; but he had made no attempt to settle himself to his work. "All this kind of thing must come to an end," he said to us with a thick, husky voice. We muttered something to him as to the need there was that he should exert a manly courage in his troubles. "Manly!" he said. "Well, yes; manly. A man should be a man, of course. There are some things which a man can't bear. I've borne more than enough, and I'll have an end of it."

We shall never forget that scene. After a while he got up, and became almost violent. Talking of bearing! Who had borne half as much as he? There were things a man should not bear. As for manliness, he believed that the truly manly thing would be to put an end to the lives of his wife, his children, and himself at one swoop. Of course the judgment of a mealy-mouthed world would be against him, but what would that matter to him when he and they had vanished out of this miserable place into the infinite realms of nothingness? Was he fit to live, or were they? Was there any chance for his children but that of becoming thieves and prostitutes? And for that poor wretch of a woman, from out of whose bosom even her human instincts had been washed by gin, — would not death to her be, indeed, a charity? There was but one drawback to all this. When he should have destroyed them, how would it be with him if he should afterwards fail to make sure work with his own life? In such case it was not hanging that he would fear, but the self-reproach that would come upon him in that he had succeeded in sending others out of their misery, but had flinched when his own turn had come. Though he was drunk when he said these horrid things, or so nearly drunk that he could not perfect the articulation of his words, still there was a marvellous eloquence with him. When we attempted to answer, and told him of that canon which had been set against self-slaughter, he laughed us to scorn. There was something terrible to us in the audacity of the arguments which he used, when he asserted for himself the right to shuffle off from his shoulders a burden which they had not been made broad enough to bear. There was an intensity and a thorough hopelessness of suffering in his case, an openness of acknowledged degradation, which robbed us for the time of all that power which the respectable ones of the earth have over the disreputable. When we came upon him with our wise saws, our wisdom was shattered instantly, and flung back upon us in fragments. What promise could we dare to hold out to him that further patience would produce any result that could be beneficial? What further harm could any such doing on his part bring upon him? Did we think that were he brought out to stand at the gallows' foot with the knowledge that ten minutes would usher him into what folks called eternity, his sense of suffering would be as great as it had been when he conducted that woman out of court and along the streets to his home, amidst the jeering congratulations of his neighbours? "When you have fallen so low," said he, "that you can fall no lower, the ordinary trammels of the world cease to bind you." Though his words were knocked against each other with the dulled utterances of intoxication, his intellect was terribly clear, and his scorn for himself, and for the world that had so treated him, was irrepressible.

We must have been over an hour with him up there in the bedroom, and even then we did not leave him. As it was manifest that he could do no work on that day, we collected the papers together, and proposed that he should take a walk with us. He was patient as we shovelled together the Doctor's pages, and did not object to our suggestion. We found it necessary to call up Mrs. Grimes to assist us in putting away the "Opus magnum," and were astonished to find how much she had come to know about the work. Added to the Doctor's manuscript there were now the pages of Mackenzie's indexes, — and there were other pages of reference, for use in making future indexes, — as to all of which Mrs. Grimes seemed to be quite at home. We have no doubt that she was familiar with the names of Greek tragedians, and could have pointed out to us in the print the performances of the chorus. "A little fresh air'll do you a deal of good, Mr. Mackenzie," she said to the unfortunate man, — "only take a biscuit in your pocket." We got him out into the street, but he angrily refused to take the biscuit which she endeavoured to force into his hands.

That was a memorable walk. Turning from the end of Liquor-pond Street up Gray's Inn Lane towards Holborn, we at once came upon the entrance into a miserable court. "There," said he; "it is down there that I live. She is sleeping it off now, and the children are hanging about her, wondering whether mother has got money to have another go at it when she rises. I'd take you down to see it all, only it'd sicken you." We did not offer to go down the court, abstaining rather for his sake than for our own. The look of the place was of a spot squalid, fever-stricken, and utterly degraded. And this man who was our companion had been born and bred a gentleman, —had been nourished with that soft and gentle care which comes of wealth and love combined, —had received the education which the country gives to her most favoured sons, and had taken such advantage of that education as is seldom taken by any of those favoured ones; —and Cucumber Court, with a drunken wife and four half-clothed, half-starved children, was the condition to which he had brought himself! The world knows nothing higher nor brighter than had been his outset in life, —nothing lower nor debased than the result. And yet he was one whose time and intellect had been employed upon the pursuit of knowledge, —who even up to this day had high ideas of what should be a man's career, —who worked very hard and had always worked, —who as far as we knew had struck upon no rocks in the pursuit of mere pleasure. It had all come to him from that idea of his youth that it would be good for him "to take refuge from the conventional thraldom of so-called gentlemen amidst the liberty of the lower orders." His life, as he had himself owned, had indeed been a mistake.

We passed on from the court, and crossing the road went through the squares of Gray's Inn, down Chancery Lane, through the little iron gate into Lincoln's Inn, round, through the old square, —than which we know no place in London more conducive to suicide, and the new square, —which has a gloom of its own, not so potent, and savouring only of madness, till at last we found ourselves in the Temple Gardens. I do not know why we had thus clung to the purlieus of the Law, except it was that he was telling us how in his early days, when he had been sent away from Cambridge, —as on this occasion he acknowledged to us, for an attempt to pull the tutor's nose, in revenge for a supposed insult, — he had intended to push his fortunes as a barrister. He pointed up to a certain window in a dark corner of that suicidal old court, and told us that for one year he had there sat at the feet of a great Gamaliel in Chancery, and had worked with all his energies. Of course we asked him why he had left a prospect so alluring. Though his answers to us were not quite explicit, we think that he did not attempt to conceal the truth. He learned to drink, and that Gamaliel took upon himself to rebuke the failing, and by the end of that year he had quarrelled irreconcilably with his family. There had been great wrath when he expressed his opinion upon certain questions of religious faith, and wrath to the final severance of all family relations when he told the chosen Gamaliel that he should get drunk as often as he pleased. After that he had "taken refuge among the lower orders," and his life, such as it was, had come of it.

In Fleet Street, as we came out of the Temple, we turned into an eating-house and had some food. By this time the exercise and the air had carried off the fumes of the liquor which he had taken, and I knew that it would be well that he should eat. We had a mutton chop and a hot potato and a pint of beer each, and sat down to table for the first and last time as mutual friends. It was odd to see how in his converse with us on that day he seemed to possess a double identity. Though the hopeless misery of his condition was always present to him, was constantly on his tongue, yet he could talk about his own career and his own character as though they belonged to a third person. He could even laugh at the wretched mistake he had made in life, and speculate as to its consequences. For himself he was well aware that death was the only release that he could expect. We did not dare to tell him that if his wife should die, then things might be better with him. We could only suggest to him that work itself, if he would do honest work, would console him for many sufferings. "You don't know the filth of it," he said to us. Ah, dear; how well we remember the terrible word, and the gesture with which he pronounced it, and the gleam of his eyes as he said it! His manner to us on this occasion was completely changed, and we had a gratification in feeling that a sense had come back upon him of his old associations. "I remember this room so well," he said, — "when I used to have friends and money." And, indeed, the room

149

was one which has been made memorable by Genius. "I did not think ever to have found myself here again." We observed, however, that he could not eat the food that was placed before him. A morsel or two of the meat he swallowed, and struggled to eat the crust of his bread, but he could not make a clean plate of it, as we did — regretting that the nature of chops did not allow of ampler dimensions. His beer was quickly finished, and we suggested to him a second tankard. With a queer, half-abashed twinkle of the eye, he accepted our offer, and then the second pint disappeared also. We had our doubts on the subject, but at last decided against any further offer. Had he chosen to call for it he must have had a third; but he did not call for it. We left him at the door of the tavern, and he then promised that in spite of all that he had suffered and all that he had said he would make another effort to complete the Doctor's work. "Whether I go or stay," he said, "I'd like to earn the money that I've spent." There was something terrible in that idea of his going! Whither was he to go?

The Doctor heard nothing of the misfortune of these three or four inauspicious days; and the work was again going on prosperously when he came up again to London at the end of the second month. He told us something of his banker, and something of his lawyer, and murmured a word or two as to a new curate whom he needed; but we knew that he had come up to London because he could not bear a longer absence from the great object of his affections. He could not bear to be thus parted from his manuscript, and was again childishly anxious that a portion of it should be in the printer's hands. "At sixty-five, sir," he said to us, "a man has no time to dally with his work." He had been dallying with his work all his life, and we sincerely believed that it would be well with him if he could be contented to dally with it to the end. If all that Mackenzie said of it was true, the Doctor's erudition was not equalled by his originality, or by his judgment. Of that question, however, we could take no cognisance. He was bent upon publishing, and as he was willing and able to pay for his whim and was his own master, nothing that we could do would keep him out of the printer's hands.

He was desirous of seeing Mackenzie, and was anxious once even to see him at his work. Of course he could meet his assistant in our editorial room, and all the papers could easily be brought backwards and forwards in the old dispatch-box. But in the interest of all parties we hesitated in taking our revered and reverend friend to the Spotted Dog. Though we had told him that his work was being done at a public-house, we thought that his mind had conceived the idea of some modest inn, and that he would be shocked at being introduced to a place which he would regard simply as a gin-shop. Mrs. Grimes, or if not Mrs. Grimes, then Mr. Grimes, might object to another visitor to their bed-room; and Mackenzie himself would be thrown out of gear by the appearance of those clerical gaiters upon the humble scene of his labours. We, therefore, gave him such reasons as were available for submitting, at any rate for the present, to having the papers brought up to him at our room. And we ourselves went down to the Spotted Dog to make an appointment with Mackenzie for the following day. We had last seen him about a week before, and then the task was progressing well. He had told us that another fortnight would finish it. We had inquired also of Mrs. Grimes about the man's wife. All she could tell us was that the woman had not again troubled them at the Spotted Dog. She expressed her belief, however, that the drunkard had been more than once in the hands of the police since the day on which Mackenzie had walked with us through the squares of the Inns of Courts.

It was late when we reached the public-house on the occasion to which we now allude, and the evening was dark and rainy. It was then the end of January, and it might have been about six o'clock. We knew that we should not find Mackenzie at the public-house; but it was probable that Mrs. Grimes could send for him, or, at least, could make the appointment for us. We went into the little parlour, where she was seated with her husband, and we could immediately see, from the countenance of both of them, that something was amiss. We began by telling Mrs. Grimes that the Doctor had come to town. "Mackenzie ain't here, sir," said Mrs. Grimes, and we almost thought that the very tone of her voice was altered. We explained that we had not expected to find him at that hour, and asked if she could send for him. She only shook her head. Grimes was standing with his back to the fire, and his hands in his trousers-pockets. Up to this moment he had not spoken a word. We asked if the man was drunk. She again shook her head. Could she bid him to come to us tomorrow, and bring the box and the papers with him. Again she shook her head.

"I've told her that I won't have no more of it," said Grimes; "nor yet I won't. He was drunk this morning, — as drunk as an owl."

"He was sober, John, as you are, when he came for the papers this afternoon at two o'clock." So the box and the papers had all been taken away!

"And she was here yesterday rampaging about the place, without as much clothes on as would cover her nakedness," said Mr. Grimes. "I won't have no more of it. I've done for that man what his own flesh and blood wouldn't do. I know that; and I won't have no more of it. Mary Anne, you'll have that table cleared out after breakfast to-morrow." When a man, to whom his wife is usually Polly, addresses her as Mary Anne, then it may be surmised that that man is in earnest. We knew that he was in earnest, and she knew it also.

"He wasn't drunk, John, — no, nor yet in liquor, when he come and took away that box this afternoon." We understood this reiterated assertion. It was in some sort excusing to us her own breach of trust in having allowed the manuscript to be withdrawn from her own charge, or was assuring us that, at the worst, she had not been guilty of the impropriety of allowing the man to take it away when he was unfit to have it in his charge. As for blaming her, who could have thought of it? Had Mackenzie at any time chosen to pass down-stairs with the box in his hands, it was not to be expected that she should stop him violently. And now that he had done so, we could not blame her; but we felt that a great weight had fallen upon our own hearts. If evil should come to the manuscript would not the Doctor's wrath fall upon us with a crushing weight? Something must be done at once. And we suggested that it would be well that somebody should go round to Cucumber Court. "I'd go as soon as look," said Mrs. Grimes, "but he won't let me."

"You don't stir a foot out of this to-night; — not that way," said Mr. Grimes.

"Who wants to stir?" said Mrs. Grimes.

We felt that there was something more to be told than we had yet heard, and a great fear fell upon us. The woman's manner to us was altered, and we were sure that this had come not from altered feelings on her part, but from circumstances which had frightened her. It was not her husband that she feared, but the truth of something that her husband had said to her. "If there is anything more to tell, for God's sake tell it," we said, addressing ourselves rather to the man than to the woman. Then Grimes did tell us his story. On the previous evening Mackenzie had received three or four sovereigns from Mrs. Grimes, being, of course, a portion of the Doctor's payments; and early on that morning all Liquorpond Street had been in a state of excitement with the drunken fury of Mackenzie's wife. She had found her way into the Spotted Dog, and was being actually extruded by the strength of Grimes himself, — of Grimes, who had been brought down from his bed-room by the row when he was only half-dressed, — when Mackenzie himself, equally drunk, appeared upon the scene. "No, John; — not equally drunk," said Mrs. Grimes. "Bother!" exclaimed her husband, going on with his story. The man had struggled to take the woman by the arm, and the two had fallen and rolled in the street together. "I was looking out of the window, and it was awful to see," said Mrs. Grimes. We felt that it was "awful to hear." A man, — and such a man, rolling in the gutter with a drunken woman, — himself drunk, — and that woman his wife! "There ain't to be no more of it at the Spotted Dog; that's all," said John Grimes, as he finished his part of the story.

Then, at last, Mrs. Grimes became voluble. All this had occurred before nine in the morning. "The woman must have been at it all night," she said. "So must the man," said John. "Anyways he came back about dinner, and he was sober then. I asked him not to go up, and offered to make him a cup of tea. It was just as you'd gone out after dinner, John."

"He won't have no more tea here," said John.

"And he didn't have any then. He wouldn't, he said to me, but went up-stairs. What was I to do? I couldn't tell him as he shouldn't. Well; — during the row in the morning John had said something as to Mackenzie not coming about the premises any more."

"Of course I did," said Grimes.

"He was a little cut, then, no doubt," continued the lady; "and I didn't think as he would have noticed what John had said."

"I mean it to be noticed now."

"He had noticed it then, sir, though he wasn't just as he should be at that hour of the morning. Well; — what does he do? He goes upstairs and packs up all the papers at once. Leastways, that's as I suppose. They ain't there now. You can go and look if you please, sir. Well; when he came down, whether I was in the kitchen, — though it isn't often as my eyes is off the bar, or in the tap-room, or busy drawing, which I do do sometimes, sir, when there are a many calling for liquor, I can't say; — but if I ain't never to stand upright again, I didn't see him pass out with the box. But Miss Wilcox did. You ask her." Miss Wilcox was the young lady in the bar, whom we did not think ourselves called upon to examine, feeling no doubt whatever as to the fact of the box having been taken away by Mackenzie. In all this Mrs. Grimes seemed to defend herself, as though some serious charge was to be brought against her; whereas all that she had done had been done out of pure charity; and in exercising her charity towards Mackenzie she had shown an almost exaggerated kindness towards ourselves.

"If there's anything wrong, it isn't your fault," we said.

"Nor yet mine," said John Grimes.

"No, indeed," we replied.

"It ain't none of our faults," continued he; "only this; — you can't wash a blackamoor white, nor it ain't no use trying. He don't come here any more, that's all. A man in drink we don't mind. We has to put up with it. And they ain't that tarnation desperate as is a woman. As long as a man can keep his legs he'll try to steady hisself; but there is women who, when they've liquor, get a fury for rampaging. There ain't a many as can beat this one, sir. She's that strong, it took four of us to hold her; though she can't hardly do a stroke of work, she's all that weak when she's sober."

We had now heard the whole story, and, while hearing it, had determined that it was our duty to go round into Cucumber Court and seek the manuscript and the box. We were unwilling to pry into the wretchedness of the man's home; but something was due to the Doctor; and we had to make that appointment for the morrow, if it were still possible that such an appointment should be kept. We asked for the number of the house, remembering well the entrance into the court. Then there was a whisper between John and his wife, and the husband offered to accompany us. "It's a roughish place," he said, "but they know me." "He'd better go along with you," said Mrs. Grimes. We, of course, were glad of such companionship, and glad also to find that the landlord, upon whom we had inflicted so much trouble, was still sufficiently our friend to take this trouble on our behalf.

"It's a dreary place enough," said Grimes, as he led us up the narrow archway. Indeed it was a dreary place. The court spread itself a little in breadth, but very little, when the passage was passed, and there were houses on each side of it. There was neither gutter nor, as far as we saw, drain, but the broken flags were slippery with moist mud, and here and there, strewed about between the houses, there were the remains of cabbages and turnip-tops. The place swarmed with children, over whom one ghastly gas-lamp at the end of the court threw a flickering and uncertain light. There was a clamour of scolding voices, to which it seemed that no heed was paid; and there was a smell of damp, rotting nastiness, amidst which it seemed to us to be almost impossible that life should be continued. Grimes led the way, without further speech, to the middle house on the left hand of the court, and asked a man who was sitting on the low threshold of the door whether Mackenzie was within. "So that be you, Muster Grimes; be it?" said the man, without stirring. "Yes; he's there I guess, but they've been and took her." Then we passed on into the house. "No matter about that," said the man, as we apologised for kicking him in our passage. He had not moved, and it had been impossible to enter without kicking him.

It seemed that Mackenzie held the two rooms on the ground floor, and we entered them at once. There was no light, but we could see the glimmer of a fire in the grate; and presently we became aware of the presence of children. Grimes asked after Mackenzie, and a girl's voice told us that he was in the inner room. The publican then demanded a light, and the girl, with some hesitation, lit the end of a farthing candle, which was fixed in a small bottle. We endeavoured to look round the room by the glimmer which this afforded, but could see nothing but the presence of four children, three of whom seemed to be seated in apathy on the floor. Grimes, taking the candle in his hand, passed at once into the other room, and we followed him. Holding the bottle something over his head he contrived to throw a gleam of light upon one of the two beds with which the room was fitted, and there we saw the body of Julius Mackenzie stretched in the torpor of dead intoxication. His head lay against the wall, his body was across the bed, and his feet dangled on to the floor. He still wore his dirty boots, and his clothes as he had worn them in the morning. No sight so piteous, so wretched, and at the same time so eloquent had we ever seen before. His eyes were closed, and the light of his face was therefore quenched. His mouth was open, and the slaver had fallen upon his beard. His dark, clotted hair had been pulled over his face by the unconscious movement of his hands. There came from him a stertorous sound of breathing, as though he were being choked by the attitude in which he lay; and even in his drunkenness there was an uneasy twitching as of pain about his face. And there sat, and had been sitting for hours past, the four children in the other room, knowing the condition of the parent whom they most respected, but not even endeavouring to do anything for his comfort. What could they do? They knew, by long training and through experience, that a fit of drunkenness had to be got out of by sleep. To them there was nothing shocking in it. It was but a periodical misfortune. "She'll have to own he's been and done it now," said Grimes, looking down upon the man, and alluding to his wife's good-natured obstinacy. He handed the candle to us, and, with a mixture of tenderness, and roughness, of which the roughness was only in the manner and the tenderness was real, he raised Mackenzie's head and placed it on the bolster, and lifted the man's legs on to the bed. Then he took off the man's boots, and the old silk handkerchief from the neck, and pulled the trousers straight, and arranged the folds of the coat. It was almost as though he were laying out one that was dead. The eldest girl was now standing by us, and Grimes asked her how long her father had been in that condition. "Jack Hoggart brought him in just afore it was dark," said the girl. Then it was explained to us that Jack Hoggart was the man whom we had seen sitting on the door-step.

"And your mother?" asked Grimes.

"The perlice took her afore dinner."

"And you children; — what have you had to eat?" In answer to this the girl only shook her head. Grimes took no immediate notice of this, but called the drunken man by his name, and shook his shoulder, and looked round to a broken ewer which stood on the little table, for water to dash upon him; — but there was no water in the jug. He called again, and repeated the shaking, and at last Mackenzie opened his eyes, and in a dull, half-conscious manner looked up at us. "Come, my man," said Grimes, "shake this off and have done with it."

"Hadn't you better try to get up?" we asked.

There was a faint attempt at rising, then a smile, — a smile which was terrible to witness, so sad was all which it said; then a look of utter, abject misery, coming as we thought from a momentary remembrance of his degradation; and after that he sank back in the dull, brutal, painless, death-like apathy of absolute unconsciousness.

"It'll be morning afore he'll move," said the girl.

"She's about right," said Grimes. "He's got it too heavy for us to do anything but just leave him. We'll take a look for the box and the papers."

And the man upon whom we were looking down had been born a gentleman, and was a finished scholar, — one so well educated, so ripe in literary acquirement, that we knew few whom we could call his equal! Judging of the matter by the light of our reason, we cannot say that the horror of the scene should have been enhanced to us by these recollections. Had the man been a shoemaker or a coalheaver there would have been enough of tragedy in it to make an angel weep, — that sight of the child standing by the bedside of her drunken father, while the other parent was away in custody, — and in no degree shocked at what she saw, because the thing was so common to her! But the thought of what the man had been, of what he was, of what he might have been, and the steps by which he had brought himself to the foul degradation which we witnessed, filled us with a dismay which we should hardly have felt had the gifts which he had polluted and the intellect which he had wasted been less capable of noble uses.

Our purpose in coming to the court was to rescue the Doctor's papers from danger, and we turned to accompany Grimes into the other room. As we did so the publican asked the girl if she knew anything of a black box which her father had taken away from the Spotted Dog. "The box is here," said the girl.

"And the papers?" asked Grimes. Thereupon the girl shook her head, and we both hurried into the outer room. I hardly know who first discovered the sight which we encountered, or whether it was shown to us by the child. The whole fire-place was strewn with half-burnt sheets of manuscript. There were scraps of pages of which almost the whole had been destroyed, others which were hardly more than scorched, and heaps of paper-ashes all lying tumbled together about the fender. We went down on our knees to examine them, thinking at the moment that the poor creature might in his despair have burned his own work and have spared that of the Doctor. But it was not so. We found scores of charred pages of the Doctor's elaborate handwriting. By this time Grimes had found the open box, and we perceived that the sheets remaining in it were tumbled and huddled together in absolute confusion. There were pages of the various volumes mixed with those which Mackenzie himsef had written, and they were all crushed, and rolled, and twisted, as though they had been thrust thither as waste-paper, — out of the way. " 'Twas mother as done it," said the girl, "and we put 'em back again when the perlice took her."

There was nothing more to learn, — nothing more by the hearing which any useful clue could be obtained. What had been the exact course of the scenes which had been enacted there that morning it little booted us to inquire. It was enough and more than enough that we knew that the mischief had been done. We went down on our knees before the fire, and rescued from the ashes with our hands every fragment of manuscript that we could find. Then we put the mass altogether into the box, and gazed upon the wretched remnants almost in tears. "You'd better go and get a bit of some'at to eat," said Grimes, handing a coin to the elder girl. "It's hard on them to starve 'cause their father's drunk, sir." Then he took the closed box in his hand, and we followed him out into the street. "I'll send or step up and look after him to-morrow," said Grimes, as he put us and the box into a cab. We little thought that when we made to the drunkard that foolish request to arise, that we should never speak to him again.

As we returned to our office in the cab that we might deposit the box there ready for the following day, our mind was chiefly occupied in thinking over the undeserved grievances which had fallen upon ourselves. We had been moved by the charitable desire to do service to two different persons, — to the learned Doctor, and to the red-nosed drunkard, and this had come of it! There had been nothing for us to gain by assisting either the one or the other. We had taken infinite trouble, attempting to bring together two men who wanted each other's services, — working in sheer benevolence; — and what had been the result? We had spent half-an-hour on our knees in the undignified and almost disreputable work of raking among Mrs. Mackenzie's cinders, and now we had to face the anger, the dismay, the reproach, and, — worse than all, — the agony of the Doctor. As to Mackenzie, — we asserted to ourselves again and again that nothing further could be done for him. He had made his bed, and he must lie upon it; but, oh! why, — why had we attempted to meddle with a being so degraded? We got out of the cab at our office door, thinking of the Doctor's countenance as we should see it on the morrow. Our heart sank within us, and we asked ourselves, if it was so bad with us now, how it would be with us when we returned to the place on the following morning.

But on the following morning we did return. No doubt each individual reader to whom we address ourselves has at some period felt that indescribable load of personal, short-lived care, which causes the heart to sink down into the boots. It is not great grief that does it; — nor is it excessive fear; but the unpleasant operation comes from the mixture of the two. It is the anticipation of some imperfectly understood evil that does it, — some evil out of which there might perhaps be an escape if we could only see the way. In this case we saw no way out of it. The Doctor was to be with us at one o'clock, and he would come with smiles, expecting to meet his learned colleague. How should we break it to the Doctor? We might indeed send to him, putting off the meeting, but the advantage coming from that would be slight, if any. We must see the injured Grecian sooner or later; and we had resolved, much as we feared, that the evil hour should not be postponed. We spent an hour that morning in arranging the fragments. Of the first volume about a third had been destroyed. Of the second nearly every page had been either burned or mutilated. Of the third but little had been injured. Mackenzie's own work had fared better than the Doctor's; but there was no comfort in that. After what had passed I thought it quite improbable that the Doctor would make any use of Mackenzie's work. So much of the manuscript as could still be placed in continuous pages, we laid out upon the table, volume by volume, — that in the middle sinking down from its original goodly bulk almost to the dimensions of a poor sermon; — and the half-burned bits we left in the box. Then we sat ourselves down at our accustomed table, and pretended to try to work. Our ears were very sharp, and we heard the Doctor's step upon our stairs within a minute or two of the appointed time. Our heart went to the very toes of our boots. We shuffled in our chair, rose from it, and sat down again, — and were conscious that we were not equal to the occasion. Hitherto we had, after some mild literary form, patronised the Doctor, — as a man of letters in town will patronise his literary friend from the country; — but we now feared him as a truant school-boy fears his master. And yet it was so necessary that we should wear some air of self-assurance!

In a moment he was with us, wearing that bland smile, which we knew so well, and which at the present moment almost overpowered us. We had been sure that he would wear that smile, and had especially feared it. "Ah," said he, grasping us by the hand, "I thought I should have been late. I see that our friend is not here yet."

"Doctor." we replied, "a great misfortune has happened."

"A great misfortune! Mr. Mackenzie is not dead?"

"No; — he is not dead. Perhaps it would have been better that he had died long since. He has destroyed your manuscript." The Doctor's face fell, and his hands at the same time, and he stood looking at us. "I need not tell you, Doctor, what my feelings are, and how great my remorse."

"Destroyed it!" Then we took him by the hand and led him to the table. He turned first upon the appetizing and comparatively uninjured third volume, and seemed to think that we had hoaxed him. "This is not destroyed," he said, with a smile. But before I could explain anything, his hands were among the fragments in the box. "As I am a living man, they have burned it!" he exclaimed. "I — I — I — " Then he turned from me, and walked twice the length of the room, backwards and forwards, while we stood still, patiently waiting the explosion of his wrath. "My friend," he said, when his walk was over, "a great man underwent the same sorrow. Newton's manuscript was burned. I will take it home with me, and we will say no more about it." I never thought very much of the Doctor as a divine, but I hold him to have been as good a Christian as I ever met.

But that plan of his of saying no more about it could not quite be carried out. I was endeavouring to explain to him, as I thought it necessary to do, the circumstances of the case, and he was protesting his indifference to any such details, when there came a knock at the door, and the boy who waited on us below ushered Mrs. Grimes into the room. As the reader is aware, we had, during the last two months become very intimate with the landlady of the Spotted Dog, but we had never hitherto had the pleasure of seeing her outside her own house. "Oh, Mr. _____" she began, and then she paused, seeing the Doctor.

We thought it expedient that there should be some introduction. "Mrs. Grimes," we said, "this is the gentleman whose invaluable manuscript has been destroyed by that unfortunate drunkard."

"Oh, the; — you're the Doctor, sir?" The Doctor bowed and smiled. His heart must have been very heavy, but he bowed politely and smiled sweetly. "Oh, dear," she said, "I don't know how to tell you!"

"To tell us what?" asked the Doctor.

"What has happened since?" we demanded. The woman stood shaking before us, and then sank into a chair. Then arose to us at the moment some idea that the drunken woman, in her mad rage, had done some great damage to the Spotted Dog, — had set fire to the house, or injured Mr. Grimes personally, or perhaps run amuck amidst the jugs and pitchers, window glass, and gas lights. Something had been done which would give the Grimeses a pecuniary claim on me or on the Doctor, and the woman had been sent hither to make the first protest. Oh, — when should I see the last of the results of my imprudence in having attempted to befriend such a one as Julius Mackenzie! "If you have anything to tell, you had better tell it," we said, gravely.

"He's been, and—"

"Not destroyed himself?" asked the Doctor.

"Oh yes, sir. He have indeed, —from ear to ear, —and is now a lying at the Spotted Dog!"

And so, after all, that was the end of Julius Mackenzie! We need hardly say that our feelings, which up to that moment had been very hostile to the man, underwent a sudden revulsion. Poor, over-burdened, struggling, ill-used, abandoned creature! The world had been hard upon him, with a severity which almost induced one to make complaint against omnipotence. The poor wretch had been willing to work, had been industrious in his calling, had had capacity for work; and he had also struggled gallantly against his evil fate, had recognised and endeavoured to perform his duty to his children and to the miserable woman who had brought him to his ruin! And that sin of drunkenness had seemed to us to be in him rather the reflex of her vice than the result of his own vicious tendencies. Still it might be doubtful whether she had not learned the vice from him. They had both in truth been drunkards as long as they had been known in the neighbourhood of the Spotted Dog; but it was stated by all who had known them there that he was never seen to be drunk unless when she had disgraced him by the public exposure of her own abomination. Such as he was he had now come to his end! This was the upshot of his loud claims for liberty from his youth upwards; liberty as against his father and family; liberty as against his college tutor; liberty as against all pastors, masters, and instructors; liberty as against the conventional thraldom of the world! He was now lying a wretched corpse at the Spotted Dog, with his throat cut from ear to ear, till the coroner's jury should have decided whether or not they would call him a suicide!

Mrs. Grimes had come to tell us that the coroner was to be at the Spotted Dog at four o'clock, and to say that her husband hoped that we would be present. We had seen Mackenzie so lately, and had so much to do with the employment of the last days of his life, that we could not refuse this request though it came accompanied by no legal summons. Then Mrs. Grimes again became voluble, and poured out to us her biography of Mackenzie as far as she knew it. He had been married to the woman ten years, and certainly had been a drunkard before he married her. "As for her, she'd been well-nigh suckled on gin," said Mrs. Grimes, "though he didn't know it, poor fellow." Whether this was true or not, she had certainly taken to drink soon after her marriage, and then his life had been passed in alternate fits of despondency and of desperate efforts to improve his own condition and that of his children. Mrs. Grimes declared to us that when the fit came on them, — when the woman had begun and the man had followed, — they would expend upon drink in two days what would have kept the family for a fortnight. "They say as how it was nothing for them to swallow forty shillings' worth of gin in forty-eight hours." The Doctor held up his hands in horror. "And it didn't, none of it, come our way," said Mrs. Grimes. "Indeed, John wouldn't let us serve it for 'em."

She sat there for half-an-hour, and during the whole time she was telling us of the man's life; but the reader will already have heard more than enough of it. By what immediate demon the woman had been instigated to burn the husband's work almost immediately on its production within her own home, we never heard. Doubtless there had been some terrible scene in which the man's sufferings must have been carried almost beyond endurance. "And he had feelings, sir, he had," said Mrs. Grimes; "he knew as a woman should be decent, and a man's wife especial; I'm sure we pitied him so, John and I, that we could have cried over him. John would say a hard word to him at times, but he'd have walked round London to do him a good turn. John ain't to say edicated hisself, but he do respect learning."

When she told us all, Mrs. Grimes went, and we were left alone with the Doctor. He at once consented to accompany us to the Spotted Dog, and we spent the hour that still remained to us in discussing the fate of the unfortunate man. We doubt whether an allusion was made during the time to the burned manuscript. If so, it was certainly not made by the Doctor himself. The tragedy which had occurred in connection with it had made him feel it to be unfitting even to mention his own loss. That such a one should have gone to his account in such a manner, without hope, without belief, and without fear, — as Burley said to Bothwell, and Bothwell boasted to Burley, — that was the theme of the Doctor's discourse. "The mercy of God is infinite," he said, bowing his head, with closed eyes and folded hands. To threaten while the life is in the man is human. To believe in the execution of those threats when the life has passed away is almost beyond the power of humanity.

At the hour fixed we were at the Spotted Dog, and found there a crowd assembled. The coroner was already seated in Mrs. Grimes's little parlour, and the body as we were told had been laid out in the tap-room. The inquest was soon over. The fact that he had destroyed himself in the low state of physical suffering and mental despondency which followed his intoxication was not doubted. At the very time that he was doing it, his wife was being taken from the lock-up house to the police office in the police van. He was not penniless, for he had sent the children out with money for their breakfasts, giving special caution as to the youngest, a little toddling thing of three years old; — and then he had done it. The eldest girl, returning to the house, had found him lying dead upon the floor. We were called upon for our evidence, and went into the tap-room accompanied by the Doctor. Alas! the very table which had been dragged up-stairs into the landlady's bed-room with the charitable object of assisting Mackenzie in his work, — the table at which we had sat with him conning the Doctor's pages, — had now been dragged down again and was used for another purpose. We had little to say as to the matter, except that we had known the man to be industrious and capable, and that we had, alas! seen him utterly prostrated by drink on the evening before his death.

The saddest sight of all on this occasion was the appearance of Mackenzie's wife, — whom we had never before seen. She had been brought by a policeman, but whether she was still in custody we did not know. She had been dressed, either by the decency of the police or by the care of her neighbours, in an old black gown, which was a world too large and too long for her. And on her head there was a black bonnet which nearly enveloped her. She was a small woman, and, as far as we could judge from the glance we got of her face, pale, and worn, and wan. She had not such outward marks of the drunkard's career as those which poor Mackenzie always carried with him. She was taken up to the coroner, and what answers she gave to him were spoken in so low a voice that they did not reach us. The policeman, with whom we

spoke, told us that she did not feel it much, — that she was cal-
lous now and beyond the power of mental suffering. "She's frightened just this minute, sir; but it isn't more than that," said the
policeman. We gave one glance along the table at the burden
which it bore, but we saw nothing beyond the outward lines of
that which had so lately been the figure of a man. We should
have liked to see the countenance once more. The morbid curi-
osity to see such horrid sights is strong with most of us. But we
did not wish to be thought to wish to see it, — especially by our
friend the Doctor, — and we abstained from pushing our way to
the head of the table. The Doctor himself remained quiescent in
the corner of the room the farthest from the spectacle. When the
matter was submitted to them, the jury lost not a moment in
declaring their verdict. They said that the man had destroyed
himself while suffering under temporary insanity produced by
intoxication. And that was the end of Julius Mackenzie, the
scholar.

On the following day the Doctor returned to the country, taking with him our black box, to the continued use of which, as a
sarcophagus, he had been made very welcome. For our share in
bringing upon him the great catastrophe of his life, he never uttered to us, either by spoken or written word, a single reproach.
That idea of suffering as the great philosopher had suffered
seemed to comfort him. "If Newton bore it, surely I can," he said
to us, with his bland smile, when we renewed the expression of
our regret. Something passed between us, coming more from us
than from him, as to the expediency of finding out some youthful
scholar who could go down to the rectory, and reconstruct from
its ruins the edifice of our friend's learning. The Doctor had given
us some encouragement, and we begun to make inquiry, when we
received the following letter; —

"_____ Rectory,_____ _____, 18__.

"Dear Mr. _____ , — You were so kind as to say that
you would endeavour to find me an assistant in arranging and re-
constructing the fragments of my work on The Metres of the
Greek Dramatists. Your promise has been an additional kindness." Dear, courteous, kind old gentleman! For we knew well
that no slightest sting of sarcasm was intended to be conveyed in
these words. "Your promise has been an additional kindness; but

looking upon the matter carefully, and giving to it the best consideration in my power, I have determined to relinquish the design. That which has been destroyed cannot be replaced; and it may well be that it was not worth replacing. I am old now, and never could do again that which perhaps I was never fitted to do with any fair prospect of success. I will never turn again to the ashes of my unborn child; but will console myself with the memory of my grievance, knowing well, as I do so, that consolation from the severity of harsh but just criticism might have been more difficult to find. When I think of the end of my efforts as a scholar, my mind reverts to the terrible and fatal catastrophe of one whose scholarship was infinitely more finished and more ripe than mine.

"Whenever it may suit you to come into this part of the country, pray remember that it will give very great pleasure to myself and to my daughter to welcome you at our parsonage.

"Believe me to be,
"My dear Mr. —————,
"Yours very sincerely,
"————— —————."

We never have found the time to accept the Doctor's invitation, and our eyes have never again rested on the black box containing the ashes of the unborn child to which the Doctor will never turn again. We can picture him to ourselves standing, full of thought, with his hand upon the lid, but never venturing to turn the lock. Indeed we do not doubt but that the key of the box is put away among other secret treasures, a lock of his wife's hair, perhaps, and the little shoe of the boy who did not live long enough to stand at his father's knee. For a tender, soft-hearted man was the Doctor, and one who fed much on the memories of the past.

We often called upon Mr. and Mrs. Grimes at the Spotted Dog, and would sit there talking of Mackenzie and his family. The woman soon vanished out of the neighbourhood, and no one there knew what was the fate of her or of her children. And then also Mr. Grimes went and took his wife with him. But they could not be said to vanish. Scratching his head one day, he told me with a dolorous voice that he had — made his fortune. "We've got as snug a little place as ever you see, just two mile out of

166

Colchester," said Mrs. Grimes, triumphantly, — "with thirty acres of land just to amuse John. And as for the Spotted Dog, I'm that sick of it, another year'd wear me to a dry bone." We looked at her, and saw no tendency that way. And we looked at John, and thought that he was not triumphant.

Who followed Mr. and Mrs. Grimes at the Spotted Dog we have never visited Liquorpond Street to see.

"The Spotted Dog" appeared first in the March and April issues of *Saint Pauls Magazine* for 1870.

Mrs. Brumby

WE THINK THAT WE ARE JUSTIFIED in asserting that of all the persons with whom we have been brought in contact in the course of our editorial experiences, men or women, boys or girls, Mrs. Brumby was the most hateful and the most hated. We are sure of this, — that for some months she was the most feared, during which period she made life a burden to us, and more than once induced us to calculate whether it would not be well that we should abandon our public duties and retire to some private corner into which it would be impossible that Mrs. Brumby should follow us. Years have rolled on since then, and we believe that Mrs. Brumby has gone before the Great Judge and been called upon to account for the injuries she did us. We know that she went from these shores to a distant land when her nefarious projects failed at home. She was then by no means a young woman. We never could find that she left relative or friend behind her, and we know of none now, except those close and dearest friends of our own who supported us in our misery, who remember even that she existed. Whether she be alive or whether she be dead, her story shall be told, — not in a spirit of revenge, but with strict justice.

What there was in her of good shall be set down with honesty; and indeed there was much in her that was good. She was energetic, full of resources, very brave, constant, devoted to the interests of the poor creature whose name she bore, and by no means a fool. She was utterly unscrupulous, dishonest, a liar, cruel, hard as a nether mill-stone to all the world except Lieutenant Brumby, — harder to him than to all the world besides when he made any faintest attempt at rebellion, — and as far as we could judge, absolutely without conscience. Had she been a man and had circumstances favoured her, she might have been a prime minister, or an archbishop, or a chief justice. We intend no silly satire on present or past holders of the great offices indicated; but we think that they have generally been achieved by such a combination of intellect, perseverance, audacity, and readiness as that which Mrs. Brumby certainly possessed. And that freedom from the weakness of scruple, — which in men who have risen in public life we may perhaps call adaptability to compromise, — was in her so strong, that had she been a man, she would have trimmed her bark to any wind that blew, and certainly have sailed into some port. But she was a woman, — and the ports were not open to her.

Those ports were not open to her which had she been a man would have been within her reach; but, — fortunately for us and for the world at large as to the general question, though so very unfortunately as regarded this special case, — the port of literature is open to women. It seems to be the only really desirable harbour to which a female captain can steer her vessel with much hope of success. There are the Fine Arts, no doubt. There seems to be no reason why a woman should not paint as well as Titian. But they don't. With the pen they hold their own, and certainly run a better race against men on that course than on any other. Mrs. Brumby, who was very desirous of running a race and winning a place, and who had seen all this, put on her cap and jacket and boots, chose her colours, and entered her name. Why, oh why, did she select the course upon which we, wretched we, were bound by our duties to regulate the running?

We may as well say at once that though Mrs. Brumby might have made a very good prime minister, she could not write a paper for a magazine, or produce literary work of any description that was worth paper and ink. We feel sure that we may declare without hesitation that no perseverance on her part, no labour however unswerving, no training however long, would have enabled her to do in a fitting manner even a review for the "Literary

Curricle." There was very much in her, but that was not in her. We find it difficult to describe the special deficiency under which she laboured; — but it existed and was past remedy. As a man suffering from a chronic stiff joint cannot run, and cannot hope to run, so was it with her. She could not combine words so as to make sentences, or sentences so as to make paragraphs. She did not know what style meant. We believe that had she ever read, Johnson, Gibbon, Archdeacon Coxe, Mr. Grote, and Macaulay would have been all the same to her. And yet this woman chose literature as her profession, and clung to it for a while with a per-sistence which brought her nearer to the rewards of success than many come who are at all points worthy to receive them.

We have said that she was not a young woman when we knew her. We cannot fancy her to have been ever young. We cannot bring our imagination to picture to ourselves the person of Mrs. Brumby surrounded by the advantages of youth. When we knew her she may probably have been forty or forty-five, and she then possessed a rigidity of demeanour and a sternness of presence which we think must have become her better than any softer guise or more tender phase of manner could ever have done in her earlier years. There was no attempt about her to disguise or modify her sex, such as women have made since those days. She talked much about her husband, the lieutenant, and she wore a double roll of very stiff dark brown curls on each side of her face, — or rather over her brows, — which would not have been worn by a woman meaning to throw off as far as possible her feminity. Whether those curls were or were not artificial we never knew. Our male acquaintances who saw her used to swear that they were false, but a lady who once saw her, assured us that they were real. She told us that there is a kind of hair growing on the heads of some women, thick, short, crisp, and shiny, which will main-tain its curl unbroken and unruffled for days. She told us, also, that women blessed with such hair are always pachydermatous and strong-minded. Such certainly was the character of Mrs. Brumby. She was a tall, thin, woman, not very tall or very thin. For aught that we can remember, her figure may have been good; — but we do remember well that she never seemed to us to have any charm of womanhood. There was a certain fire in her dark eyes, — eyes which were, we think, quite black, — but it was the fire of contention and not of love. Her features were well-formed, her nose somewhat long, and her lips thin, and her face too narrow, perhaps, for beauty. Her chin was long, and the space from her nose to her upper lip long. She always carried a well-wearing brown complexion; — a complexion with which no man had a right to find fault, but which, to a pondering, speculative man, produced unconsciously a consideration whether, in a matter of kissing, an ordinary mahogany table did not offer a preferable surface. When we saw her she wore, we think always, a dark stuff dress, — a fur tippet in winter and a most ill-arranged shawl in summer, — and a large commanding bonnet, which grew in our eyes till it assumed all the attributes of a helmet, — inspiring that reverence and creating that fear which Minerva's head-gear is intended to produce. When we add our conviction that Mrs. Brumby trusted nothing to female charms, that she neither suffered nor enjoyed anything from female vanity, and that the lieutenant was perfectly safe, let her roam the world alone, as she might, in search of editors, we shall have said enough to introduce the lady to our readers.

Of her early life, or their early lives, we know nothing; but the unfortunate circumstances which brought us into contact with Mrs. Brumby, made us also acquainted with the lieutenant. The lieutentant, we think, was younger than his wife; — a good deal younger we used to imagine, though his looks may have been deceptive. He was a confirmed invalid, and there are phases of ill-health which give an appearance of youthfulness rather than of age. What was his special ailing we never heard, — though, as we shall mention further on we had our own idea on that subject; but he was always spoken of in our hearing as one who always had been ill, who always was ill, who always would be ill, and who never ought to think of getting well. He had been in some regiment called the Duke of Sussex's Own, and his wife used to imagine that her claims upon the public as a woman of literature were enhanced by the royalty of her husband's corps. We never knew her attempt to make any other use whatever of his services. He was not confined to his bed, and could walk at any rate about the house; but she never asked him, or allowed him to do anything. Whether he ever succeeded in getting his face outside the door we do not know. He used to wear an old dressing-gown and slippers. He was a pale, slight, light-haired man, and we fancy that he took a delight in novels. We have heard her, however, rebuke him for reading, and fancy that he was compelled to pass the greater portion of his time in mental as well as bodily inactivity.

Their settled income consisted of his half-pay and some very small property which belonged to her. Together they might perhaps have possessed £150 per annum. When we knew them they had lodgings in Harpur Street, near Theobald's Road, and she had resolved to push her way in London as a woman of literature. She had been told that she would have to deal with hard people, and that she must herself be hard; — that advantage would be taken of her weakness, and that she must therefore struggle vehemently to equal the strength of those with whom she would be brought in contact; — that editors, publishers, and brother authors would suck her brains and give her nothing for them, and that, therefore, she must get what she could out of them, giving them as little as possible in return. It was an evil lesson that she had learned; but she omitted nothing in the performance of the duties which that lesson imposed upon her.

She first came to us with a pressing introduction from an acquaintance of ours who was connected with a weekly publication called the "Literary Curricle." The "Literary Curricle" was not in our estimation a strong paper, and we will own that we despised it. We did not think very much of the acquaintance by whom the strong introductory letter was written. But Mrs. Brumby forced herself into our presence with the letter in her hand, and before she left us extracted from us a promise that we would read a manuscript which she pulled out of a bag which she carried with her. Of that first interview a short account shall be given, but it must first be explained that the editor of the "Literary Curricle" had received Mrs. Brumby with another letter from another editor, whom she had first taken by storm without any introduction whatever. This first gentleman, whom we had not the pleasure of knowing, had, under what pressure we who knew the lady can imagine, printed three or four short paragraphs from Mrs. Brumby's pen. Whether they reached publication we never could learn, but we saw the printed slips. He, however, passed her on to the "Literary Curricle," — which dealt almost exclusively in the reviewing of books, — and our friend at the office of that influential "organ" sent her to us with an intimation that her very peculiar and well-developed talents were adapted rather for the creation of tales, or the composition of orginal treatises, than for reviewing. The letter was very strong, and we learned afterwards that Mrs. Brumby had consented to abandon her connection with the "Literary Curricle" only on the receipt of a letter in her praise that should be very strong indeed. She rejected the two first offered to her, and herself dictated the epithets with which the third was loaded. On no other terms would she leave the office of the "Literary Curricle."

We cannot say that the letter, strong as it was, had much effect upon us; but this effect it had perhaps, — that after reading it we could not speak to the lady with that acerbity which we might have used had she come to us without it. As it was we were not very civil, and began our intercourse by assuring her that we could not avail ourselves of her services. Having said so, and observing that she still kept her seat, we rose from our chair, being well aware how potent a spell that movement is wont to exercise upon visitors who are unwilling to go. She kept her seat and argued the matter out with us. A magazine such as that which we then conducted must, she surmised, require depth of erudition, keenness of intellect, grasp of hand, force of expression, and lightness of touch, That she possessed all these gifts she had, she alleged, brought to us convincing evidence. There was the letter from the editor of the "Literary Curricle," with which she had been long connected, declaring the fact! Did we mean to cast doubt upon the word of our own intimate friend? For the gentleman at the office of the "Literary Curricle" had written to us as "Dear _____," though as far as we could remember we had never spoken half a dozen words to him in our life. Then she repeated the explanation, given by her godfather, of the abrupt termination of the close connection which had long existed between her and the "Curricle." She could not bring herself to waste her energies in the reviewing of books. At that moment we certainly did believe that she had been long engaged on the "Curricle," though there was certainly not a word in our correspondent's letter absolutely stating that to be the fact. He declared to us her capabilities and excellences, but did not say that he had ever used them himself. Indeed he told us that great as they were they were hardly suited for his work. She, before she had left us on that occasion, had committed herself to positive falsehoods. She boasted of the income she had earned from two periodicals, whereas up to that moment she had never received a shilling for what she had written.

We find it difficult, even after so many years, — when the shame of the thing has worn off together with the hairs of our head, — to explain how it was that we allowed her to get, in the first instance, any hold upon us. We did not care a brass farthing for the man who had written from the "Literary Curricle." His letter to us was an impertinence, and we should have stated as much to Mrs. Brumby had we cared to go into such matter with her. And our first feelings with regard to the lady herself were feelings of dislike, — and almost of contempt even, though we did believe that she had been a writer for the press. We disliked her nose, and her lips, and her bonnet, and the colour of her face. We didn't want her. Though we were very much younger than we are now, we had already learned to set our backs up against strong-minded female intruders. As we said before, we rose from our chair with the idea of banishing her, not absolutely uncivilly, but altogether unceremoniously. It never occurred to us during that meeting that she could be of any possible service to us, or that we should ever be of any slightest service to her. Nevertheless she had extracted from us a great many words, and had made a great many observations herself before she left us.

When a man speaks a great many words it is impossible that he should remember what they all were. That we told Mrs. Brumby on that occasion that we did not doubt but that we would use the manuscript which she left in our hands, we are quite sure was not true. We never went so near making a promise in our lives, — even when pressed by youth and beauty, — and are quite sure that what we did say to Mrs. Brumby was by no means near akin to this. That we undertook to read the manuscript we think probable, and therein lay our first fault, — the unfortunate slip from which our future troubles sprang, and grew to such terrible dimensions. We cannot now remember how the hated parcel, the abominable roll, came into our hands. We do remember the face and form and figure of the woman as she brought it out of the large reticule which she carried, and we remember also how we put our hands behind us to avoid it, and would not have it; — and yet it came into our hands! We think that it must have been placed close to our elbow, and that being used to such playthings, we took it up. We know that it was in our hands, and that we did not know how to rid ourselves of it when she began to tell us the story of the lieutenant. We were hard-hearted enough to inform her, — as we have, under perhaps lesser compulsion, informed others since, — that the distress of the man or of the woman should never be accepted as a reason for publishing the works of the writer. She answered us gallantly enough that she had never been weak enough or foolish enough so to think. "I base my claim to attention," she said, "on quite another ground. Do not suppose, sir, that I am appealing to your pity. I scorn to do so. But I wish you should know my position as a married woman, and that you should understand that my husband, though unfortunately an invalid, has been long attached to a regiment which is peculiarly the Duke of Sussex's own. You cannot but be aware of the connection which His Royal Highness has long maintained with literature."

Mrs. Brumby could not write, but she could speak. The words she had just uttered were absolutely devoid of sense. The absurdity of them was ludicrous and gross. But they were not without a certain efficacy. They did not fill us with any respect for her literary capacity because of her connection with the Duke of Sussex, but they did make us feel that she was able to speak up for herself. We are told sometimes that the world accords to a man that treatment which he himself boldly demands; and though the statement seems to be monstrous, there is much truth in it. When Mrs. Brumby spoke of her husband's regiment being "Peculiarly the Duke of Sussex's own," she used a tone which compelled from us more courtesy than we had hitherto shown her. We knew that the Duke was neither a man of letters nor a warrior, though he had a library, and, as we were now told, a regiment. Had he been both, his being so would have formed no legitimate claim for Mrs. Brumby upon us. But, nevertheless, the royal Duke helped her to win her way. It was not his royalty, but her audacity that was prevailing. She sat with us for more than an hour; and when she left us the manuscript was with us, and we had no doubt undertaken to read it. We are perfectly certain that at that time we had not gone beyond this in the way of promising assistance to Mrs. Brumby.

The would-be author, who cannot make his way either by intellect or favour, can hardly do better, perhaps, than establish a grievance. Let there by anything of a case of ill-usage against editor or publisher, and the aspirant, if he be energetic and unscrupulous, will greatly increase his chance of working his way into print. Mrs. Brumby was both energetic and unscrupulous, and she did establish her grievance. As soon as she brought her first visit to a close, the roll, which was still in our hands, was chucked across our table to a corner commodiously supported by the wall, so that occasionally there was accumulated in it a heap of such unwelcome manuscripts. In the doing of this, in the moment of our so chucking the parcel, it was always our conscientious intention to make a clearance of the whole heap, at the very furthest, by the end of the week. We knew that strong hopes were bound up in those various little packets, that eager thoughts were imprisoned there, the owners of which believed that they were endowed with wings fit for aerial soaring, that young hearts, —ay, and old hearts, too, sore with deferred hope, —were waiting to know whether their aspirations might now be realised, whether those azure wings might at last be released from bondage and allowed to try their strength in the broad sunlight of public favour. We think, too, that we had a conscience; and, perhaps, the heap was cleared as frequently as are the heaps of other editors. But there it would grow, in the commodious corner of our big table, too often for our own peace of mind. The aspect of each individual little parcel would be known to us, and we would allow ourselves to fancy that by certain external signs we could tell the nature of the interior. Some of them would promise well, — so well as to create even almost an appetite for their perusal. But there would be others from which we would turn with aversion, which we seemed to abhor, which, when we handled the heap, our fingers would refuse to touch, and which, thus lying there neglected and ill-used, would have the dust of many days added to those other marks which inspired disgust. We confess that as soon as Mrs. Brumby's back was turned her roll was sent in upon this heap with that determined force which a strong feeling of dislike can lend even to a man's little finger. And there it lay for,

177

— perhaps a fortnight. When during that period we extracted first one packet and then another for judgment, we would still leave Mrs. Brumby's roll behind in the corner. On such occasions a pang of conscience will touch the heart; some idea of neglected duty will be present to the mind; a silent promise will perhaps be made that it shall be the next; some momentary sudden resolve will be half formed that for the future a rigid order of succession shall be maintained, which no favour shall be allowed to infringe. But, alas, when the hand is again at work selecting, the odious ugly thing is left behind, till at last it becomes invested with strange terrors, with an absolute power of its own, and the guilty conscience will become afraid. All this happened in regard to Mrs. Brumby's manuscript. "Dear, dear, yes; — Mrs. Brumby!" we would catch ourselves exclaiming with that silent inward voice which occasionally makes itself audible to most of us. And, then, quite silently, without even whispered violence, we would devote Mrs. Brumby to the infernal gods. And so the packet remained amidst the heap, — perhaps for a fortnight.

"There's a lady waiting in your room, sir!" This was said to us one morning on our reaching our office by the lad whom we used to call our clerk. He is now managing a red-hot Tory newspaper down in Barsetshire, has a long beard, a flaring eye, a round belly, and is upon the whole the most arrogant personage we know. In the days of Mrs. Brumby he was a little wizened fellow about eighteen years old, but looking three years younger, modest, often almost dumb, and in regard to ourselves not only reverential but timid. We turned upon him in great anger. What business had any woman to be in our room in our absence? Were not our orders on this subject exact and very urgent? Was he not kept there at an expense of 14s. a week, — we did not actually throw the amount in his teeth, but such was intended to be the effect of our rebuke, — at 14s. a week, paid out of our own pocket, — nominally, indeed, as a clerk, but chiefly for the very purpose of keeping female visitors out of our room? And now, in our absence and in his, there was actually a woman among the manuscripts! We felt from the first moment that it was Mrs. Brumby.

With bated breath and downcast eyes the lad explained to us his inability to exclude her. "She walked straight in, right over me," he said; "and as for being alone, — she hasn't been alone.

I haven't left her, not a minute."

We walked at once over to our own room, feeling how fruit-
less it was to discuss the matter further with the boy in the passage, and there we found Mrs. Brumby seated in the chair
opposite to our own. We had gathered ourselves up, if we may so
describe an action which was purely mental, with a view to severity. We thought that her intrusion was altogether unwarrant-
able, and that it behoved us to let her know that such was the
case. We entered the room with a clouded brow, and intended
that she should read our displeasure in our eyes. But Mrs. Brumby
could, — "gather herself up," quite as well as we could do, and
she did so. She also could call clouds to her forehead and could
flash anger from her eyes. "Madam," we exclaimed, as we paused
for a moment, and looked at her.

But she cared nothing for our "Madam," and condescended to
no apology. Rising from her chair, she asked us why we had not
kept the promise we had made her to use her article in our next
number. We don't know how far our readers will understand all
that was included in this accusation. Use her contribution in our
next number! It had never occurred to us as probable, or hardly
as possible, that we should use it in any number. Our eye glanced
at the heap to see whether her fingers had been at work, but we
perceived that the heap had not been touched. We have always
flattered ourselves that no one can touch our heap without our
knowing it. She saw the motion of our eye, and at once understood it. Mrs. Brumby, no doubt, possessed great intelligence,
and, moreover, a certain majesty of demeanour. There was always something of the helmet of Minerva in the bonnet which
she wore. Her shawl was an old shawl, but she was never ashamed
of it; and she could always put herself forward, as though there
were nothing behind her to be concealed, the concealing of
which was a burden to her. "I cannot suppose," she said, "that
my paper has been altogether neglected!"

We picked out the roll with all the audacity we could assume,
and proceeded to explain how very much in error she was in supposing that we had ever even hinted at its publication. We never
did mention any time in making any such promise. "You named
a week, sir," said Mrs. Brumby, "and now a month has passed by.
You assured me that it would be accepted unless returned within

seven days. Of course it will be accepted now." We contradicted her flatly. We explained, we protested, we threatened. We endeavoured to put the manuscript into her hand, and made a faint attempt to stick it into her bag. She was indignant, dignified, and very strong. She said nothing on that occasion about legal proceedings, but stuck manfully to her assertion that we had bound ourselves to decide upon her manuscript within a week. "Do you think, sir," said she, "that I would entrust the very essence of my brain to the keeping of a stranger, without some such assurance as that?" We acknowledged that we had undertaken to read the paper, but again disowned the week. "And how long would you be justified in taking?" demanded Mrs. Brumby. "If a month why not a year? Does it not occur to you, sir, that when the very best of my intellect, my inmost thoughts, lie there at your disposal," and she pointed to the heap, "it may be possible that a property has been confided to you too valuable to justify neglect? Had I given you a ring to keep you would have locked it up, but the best jewels of my mind are left to the tender mercies of your charwoman." What she said was absolutely nonsense, — abominable, villainous trash; but she said it so well that we found ourselves apologizing for our own misconduct. There had perhaps been a little undue delay. In our peculiar business such would occasionally occur. When we had got to this, any expression of our wrath at her intrusion was impossible. As we entered the room we had intended almost to fling her manuscript at her head. We now found ourselves handling it almost affectionately while we expressed regret for our want of punctuality. Mrs. Brumby was gracious, and pardoned us, but her forgiveness was not of the kind which denotes the intention of the injured one to forget as well as forgive the trespass. She had suffered from us a great injustice; but she would say no more on that score now, on the condition that we would at once attend to her essay. She thrice repeated the words, "at once," and she did so without rebuke from us. And then she made us a proposition, the like of which never reached us before or since. Would we fix an hour within the next day or two at which we would call upon her in Harpur Street and arraange as to terms! The lieutenant, she said, would be delighted to make our acquaintance. Call upon her; — upon Mrs. Brumby! Travel to Harpur Street, Theobald's Road, on the business of a chance bit of scribbling, which was wholly indifferent to us except in so far as it was a trouble to us! And then we were invited to make arrangements as to terms! Terms!! Had the owner of the most illustrious lips in the land offered to make us known in those days to the partner of her greatness, she could not have done so with more assurance that she was conferring on us an honour, than was assumed by Mrs. Brumby when she proposed to introduce us to the lieutenant.

When many wrongs are concentrated in one short speech, and great injuries inflicted by a few cleverly combined words, it is generally difficult to reply so that some of the wrongs shall not pass unnoticed. We cannot always be so happy as was Mr. John Robinson, when in saying that he hadn't been "dead at all," he did really say everything that the occasion required. We were so dismayed by the proposition that we should go to Harpur Street, so hurt in our own personal dignity, that we lost ourselves in endeavouring to make it understood that such a journey on our part was quite out of the question. "Were we to do that, Mrs. Brumby, we should live in cabs and spend our entire days in making visits." She smiled at us as we endeavoured to express our indignation, and said something as to circumstances being different in different cases; — something also, if we remember right, she hinted as to the intelligence needed for discovering the differences. She left our office quicker than we had expected, saying that as we could not afford to spend our time in cabs she would call again on the day but one following. Her departure was almost abrupt, but she went apparently in good humour. It never occurred to us at the moment to suspect that she hurried away before we should have had time to repudiate certain suggestions which she had made.

When we found ourselves alone with the roll of paper in our hands, we were very angry with Mrs. Brumby, but almost more angry with ourselves. We were in no way bound to the woman, and yet she had in some degree substantiated a claim upon us. We piqued ourselves specially on never making any promise beyond the vaguest assurance that this or that proposed contribution should receive consideration at some altogether undefined time; but now we were positively pledged to read Mrs. Brumby's effusion and have our verdict ready by the day after tomorrow.

We were wont, too, to keep ourselves much secluded from strangers; and here was Mrs. Brumby, who had already been with us twice, positively entitled to a third audience. We had been scolded, and then forgiven, and then ridiculed by a woman who was old, and ugly, and false! And there was present to us a conviction that though she was old, and ugly, and false, Mrs. Brumby was no ordinary woman. Perhaps it might be that she was really qualified to give us valuable assistance in regard to the magazine, as to which we must own we were sometimes driven to use matter that was not quite so brilliant as, for our readers' sakes, we would have wished it to be. We feel ourselves compelled to admit that old and ugly women, taken on the average, do better literary work than they who are young and pretty. I did not like Mrs. Brumby, but it might be that in her the age would find another De Stael. So thinking, we cut the little string, and had the manuscript open in our own hands. We cannot remember whether she had already indicated to us the subject of the essay, but it was headed, "Costume in 18 — ." There was perhaps thirty closely filled pages, of which we read perhaps a third. The hand-writing was unexceptionable, orderly, clean, and legible; but the matter was undeniable twaddle. It proffered advice to women that they should be simple, and to men that they should be cleanly in their attire. Anything of less worth for the purpose of amusement or of instruction could not be imagined. There was, in fact, nothing in it. It has been our fate to look at a great many such essays, and to cause them at once either to be destroyed or returned. There could be no doubt at all as to Mrs. Brumby's essay.

She came punctual as the clock. As she seated herself in our chair and made some remark as to her hope that we were satisfied, we felt something like fear steal across our bosom. We were about to give offence, and dreaded the arguments that would follow. It was, however, quite clear that we could not publish Mrs. Brumby's essay on costume, and therefore, though she looked more like Minerva now than ever, we must go through our task. We told her in half-a-dozen words that we had read the paper, and that it would not suit our columns.

"Not suit your columns!" she said, looking at us by no means in sorrow, but in great anger. "You do not mean to trifle with me

like that after all you have made me suffer?" We protested that
we were responsible for none of her sufferings. "Sir," she said,
"when I was last here you owned the wrong you had done me."
We felt that we must protest against this, and we rose in our
wrath. There were two of us angry now.

"Madam," we said, "you have kindly offered us your essay, and
we have courteously declined it. You will allow us to say that this
must end the matter." There were allusions here to kindness and
courtesy, but the reader will understand that the sense of the
words was altogether changed by the tone of the voice.

"Indeed, sir, the matter will not be ended so. If you think that
your position will enable you to trample upon those who make
literature really a profession, you are very much mistaken."

"Mrs. Brumby," we said, "we can give you no other answer,
and as our time is valuable —"

"Time valuable!" she exclaimed, — and as she stood up an artist might have taken her for a model of Minerva had she only
held a spear in her hand. "And is no time valuable, do you think,
but yours? I had, sir, your distinct promise that the paper should
be published if it was left in your hands above a week."

"That is untrue, madam."

"Untrue, sir?"

"Absolutely untrue." Mrs. Brumby was undoubtedly a woman,
and might be very like a goddess, but we were not going to allow
her to palm off upon us without flat contradiction so absolute a
falsehood as that. "We never dreamed of publishing your paper."

"Then why, sir, have you troubled yourself to read it, — from
the beginning to the end?" We had certainly intimated that we
had made ourselves acquainted with the entire essay, but we had
in fact skimmed and skipped through about a third of it. "How
dare you say, sir, you have never dreamed of publishing it, when
you know that you studied it with that view?"

"We didn't read it all," we said, "but we read quite enough."

"And yet but this moment ago you told me that you had pe-
rused it carefully." The word peruse we certainly never used in
our life. We object to "perusing," as we do to "commencing" and
"performing." We "read," and we "begin," and we "do." As to
that assurance which the word "carefully" would intend to convey, we believe that we were to that extent guilty. "I think, sir,"

183

she continued, "that you had better see the lieutenant."

"With a view to fighting the gentleman?" we asked.

"No, sir. An officer in the Duke of Sussex's Own draws his sword against no enemy so unworthy of his steel." She had told me at a former interview that the lieutenant was so confirmed an invalid as to be barely able, on his best days, to drag himself out of bed. "One fights with one's equal, but the law gives redress from injury whether it be inflicted by equal, by superior, or by — INFERIOR." And Mrs. Brumby, as she uttered the last word, wagged her helmet at us in a manner which left no doubt as to the position which she assigned to us.

It became clearly necessary that an end should be put to an intercourse which had become so very unpleasant. We told our Minerva very plainly that we must beg her to leave us. There is, however, nothing more difficult to achieve than the expulsion of a woman who is unwilling to leave the place she occupies. We remember to have seen a lady take possession of a seat in a mail coach to which she was not entitled, and which had been booked and paid for by another person. The agent for the coaching business desired her with many threats to descend, but she simply replied that the journey to her was a matter of such moment that she felt herself called upon to keep her place. The agent sent the coachman to pull her out. The coachman threatened, — with his hands as well as with his words, — and then set the guard at her. The guard attacked her with inflamed visage and fearful words about Her Majesty's mails, and then set the ostlers at her. We thought the ostlers were going to handle her roughly, but it ended by their scratching their heads, and by a declaration on the part of one of them that she was "the rummest go he'd ever seen." She was a woman, and they couldn't touch her. A policeman was called upon for assistance and offered to lock her up, but he could only do so if allowed to lock up the whole coach as well. It was ended by the production of another coach, by an exchange of the luggage and passengers, by a delay of two hours, and an embarrassing possession of the original vehicle by the lady in the midst of a crowd of jeering boys and girls. We could tell Mrs. Brumby to go, and we could direct our boy to open the door, and we could make motions indicatory of departure with our left hand, but we could not forcibly turn her out of the room. She asked us for the name of our lawyer, and we did write down for her on a slip of paper the address of a most respectable firm, whom we were pleased to regard as our attorneys, but who had never yet earned six and eightpence from the magazine. Young Sharp, of the firm of Sharp and Butterwell, was our friend, and would no doubt see to the matter for us should it be necessary; — but we could not believe that the woman would be so foolish. She made various assertions to us as to her position in the world of literature, and it was on this occasion that she brought out those printed slips which we have before mentioned. She offered to refer the matter in dispute between us to the arbitration of the editor of the "Curricle;" and when we indignantly declined such interference, protesting that there was no matter in dispute, she again informed us that if we thought to trample upon her we were very much mistaken. Then there occurred a little episode which moved us to laughter in the midst of our wrath. Our boy, in obedience to our pressing commands that he should usher Mrs. Brumby out of our presence, did lightly touch her arm. Feeling the degradation of the assault, Minerva swung round upon the unfortunate lad and gave him a box on the ear which we'll be bound the editor of the "West Barsetshire Gazette" remembers to this day. "Madam," we said, as soon as we had swallowed down the first involuntary attack of laughter, "if you conduct yourself in this manner we must send for the police."

"Do, sir, if you dare," replied Minerva, "and every man of letters in the metropolis shall hear of your conduct." There was nothing in her threat to move us, but we confess that we were uncomfortable. "Before I leave you, sir," she said, "I will give you one more chance. Will you perform your contract with me, and accept my contribution."

"Certainly not," we replied. She afterwards quoted this answer as admitting a contract.

We are often told that everything must come to an end, — and there was an end at last to Mrs. Brumby's visit. She went from us with an assurance that she should at once return home, pick up the lieutenant, — hinting that the exertion, caused altogether by our wickedness, might be the death of that gallant officer, — and go with him direct to her attorney. The world of literature should hear of the terrible injustice which had been done to her, and the courts of law should hear of it too.

We confess that we were grievously annoyed. By the time that Mrs. Brumby had left the premises, our clerk had gone also. He had rushed off to the nearest police-court to swear an information against her on account of the box on the ear which she had given him, and we were unable to leave our desk till he had returned. We found that for the present the doing of any work in our line of business was quite out of the question. A calm mind is required for the critical reading of manuscripts, and whose mind could be calm after such insults as those we had received? We sat in our chair, idle, reflective, indignant, making resolutions that we would never again open our lips to a woman coming to us with a letter of introduction and a contribution, till our lad returned to us. We were forced to give him a sovereign before we could induce him to withdraw his information. We object strongly to all bribery, but in this case we could see the amount of riducule which would be heaped upon our whole establishment if some low-conditioned lawyer were allowed to cross-examine us as to our intercourse with Mrs. Brumby. It was with difficulty that the clerk arranged the matter the next day at the police-office, and his object was not effected without the further payment by us of £1 2s. 6d. for costs. It was then understood between us and the clerk that on no excuse whatever should Mrs. Brumby be again admitted to my room, and I thought that the matter was over. "She shall have to fight her way through if she does get in," said the lad. "She ain't going to knock me about any more, — woman or no woman." "O, dea, certe," we exclaimed. "It shall be a dear job to her if she touches me again," said the clerk, catching up the sound.

We really thought we had done with Mrs. Brumby, but at the end of four or five days there came to us a letter, which we have still in our possession, and which we will now venture to make public. It was as follows. It was addressed not to ourselves, but to Messrs. X., Y., and Z., the very respectable proprietors of the periodical which we were managing on their behalf.

"Pluck Court, Gray's Inn, 31st March, 18—.
"GENTLEMEN,
"We are instructed by our client, Lieutenant Brumby, late of the Duke of Sussex's own Regiment, to call upon you for payment

of the sum of twenty-five guineas due to him for a manuscript essay on Costume, supplied by his wife to the _____ Magazine which is, we believe, your property, by special contract with Mr. _____, the Editor. We are also directed to require from you and from Mr. _____ a full apology in writing for the assault committed on Mrs. Brumby in your Editor's room on the 27th instant; and an assurance also that the columns of your periodical shall not be closed against that lady because of this transaction. We request that £1 13s. 8., our costs, may be forwarded to us, together with the above named sum of twenty-five guineas.

> "We are, Gentlemen,
> "Your obedient servants,
> "BADGER AND BLISTER.
"Messrs. X., Y., Z., Paternoster Row."

We were in the habit of looking in at the shop in Paternoster Row on the first of every month, and on that inauspicious first of April the above letter was handed to us by our friend Mr. X. "I hope you haven't been and put our foot in it at all," and we told him the whole story. "Don't let us have a law-suit, whatever you do," said Mr. X. "The magazine isn't worth it." We ridiculed the idea of a law-suit, but we took away with us Messrs. Badger and Blister's letter and showed it to our legal adviser, Mr. Sharp. Mr. Sharp was of opinion that Badger and Blister meant fighting. When we pointed out to him the absolute absurdity of the whole thing, he merely informed us that we did not know Badger and Blister. "They'll take up any case," said he, "however hopeless, and work it with superhuman energy, on the mere chance of getting something out of the defendant. Whatever is got out of him becomes theirs. They never disgorge." We were quite confident that nothing could be got out of the magazine on behalf of Mrs. Brumby, and we left the case in Mr. Sharp's hands, thinking that our trouble in the matter was over.

A fortnight elapsed, and then we were called upon to meet Mr. Sharp in Paternoster Row. We found our friend Mr. X. with a somewhat unpleasant visage. Mr. X. was a thriving man, usually just, and sometimes generous; but he didn't like being "put upon." Mr. Sharp had actually recommended that some trifle should be paid to Mrs. Brumby, and Mr. X. seemed to think that this expense would, in case that advice were followed, have been incurred through fault on our part. "A ten pound note will set it all right," said Mr. Sharp.

"Yes; — a ten pound note, — just flung into the gutter. I wonder that you allowed yourself to have anything to do with such a woman." We protested against this injustice, giving Mr. X. to know that he didn't understand and couldn't understand our business. "I'm not so sure of that," said Mr. X. There was almost a quarrel, and we began to doubt whether Mrs. Brumby would not be the means of taking the very bread from our mouths. Mr. Sharp at last suggested that in spite of what he had seen from Mrs. Brumby, the lieutenant would probably be a gentleman. "Not a doubt about it," said Mr. X., who was always fond of officers and of the army, and at the moment seemed to think more of a paltry lieutenant than of his own Editor.

Mr. Sharp actually pressed upon us and upon Mr. X. that we should call upon the lieutenant and explain matters to him. Mrs. Brumby had always been with us at twelve o'clock. "Go at noon," said Mr. Sharp, "and you'll certainly find her out." He instructed us to tell the lieutenant "just the plain truth," as he called it, and to explain that in no way could the proprietors of a magazine be made liable to payment for an article because the Editor in discharge of his duty had consented to read it. "Perhaps the lieutenant doesn't know that his name has been used at all," said Mr. Sharp. "At any rate, it will be well to learn what sort of a man he is."

"A high-minded gentleman, no doubt," said Mr. X., the name of whose second boy was already down at the Horse Guards for a commission.

Though it was sorely against the grain, and in direct opposition to our own opinion, we were constrained to go to Harpur Street, Theobald's Road, and to call upon Lieutenant Brumby. We had not explained to Mr. X. as to Mr. Sharp, what had passed between Mrs. Brumby and ourselves when she suggested such a visit, but the memory of the words which we and she had then spoken was on us as we endeavoured to dissuade our lawyer and our publisher. Nevertheless, at their instigation, we made the visit. The house in Harpur Street was small, and dingy, and old.

The door was opened for us by the normal lodging-house maid-of-all-work, who, when we asked for the lieutenant, left us in the passage, that she might go and see. We sent up our name, and in a few minutes were ushered into a sitting-room up two flights of stairs. The room was not untidy, but it was as comfortless as any chamber we ever saw. The lieutenant was lying on an old horse-hair sofa, but we had been so far lucky as to find him alone. Mr. Sharp had been correct in his prediction as to the customary absence of the lady at that hour in the morning. In one corner of the room we saw an old ram-shackle desk, at which, we did not doubt, were written those essays on Costume and other subjects, in the disposing of which the lady displayed so much energy. The lieutenant himself was a small grey man, dressed, or rather enveloped, in what I supposed to be an old wrapper of his wife's. He held in his hands a well-worn volume of a novel, and when he rose to greet us he almost trembled with dismay and bashfulness. His feet were thrust into slippers which were too old to stick on them, and round his throat he wore a dirty, once white, woollen comforter. We never learned what was the individual character of the corps which specially belonged to H.R.H. the Duke of Sussex; but if it was conspicuous for dash and gallantry, Lieutenant Brumby could hardly have held his own among his brother officers. We knew, from his wife, that he had been invalided, and as an invalid we respected him. We proceeded to inform him that we had been called upon to pay him a sum of twenty-five guineas, and to explain how entirely void of justice any such claim must be. We suggested to him that he might be made to pay some serious sum by the lawyers he employed, and that the matter to us was an annoyance and a trouble, — chiefly because we had no wish to be brought into conflict with any one so respectable as Lieutenant Brumby. He looked at us with imploring eyes, as though begging us not to be too hard upon him in the absence of his wife, trembled from head to foot, and muttered a few words which were nearly inaudible. We will not state as a fact that the lieutenant had taken to drinking spirits early in life, but that certainly was our impression during the only interview we ever had with him. When we pressed upon him as a question which he must answer whether he did not think that he had better withdraw his claim, he fell back upon his sofa, and began to sob.

While he was thus weeping Mrs. Brumby entered the room. She had in her hand the card which we had given to the maid-of-all-work, and was therefore prepared for the interview. "Sir," she said, "I hope you have come to settle my husband's just demands."

Amidst the husband's wailings there had been one little sentence which reached our ears. "She does it all," he had said, throwing his eyes up piteously towards our face. At that moment the door had been opened, and Mrs. Brumby had entered the room. When she spoke of her husband's "just demands," we turned to the poor prostrate lieutenant, and were deterred from any severity towards him by the look of supplication in his eye. "The lieutenant is not well this morning," said Mrs. Brumby, "and you will therefore be pleased to address yourself to me." We explained that the absurd demand for payment had been made on the proprietors of the magazine in the name of Lieutenant Brumby, and that we had therefore been obliged, in the performance of a most unpleasant duty, to call upon that gentleman; but she laughed our argument to scorn. "You have driven me to take legal steps," she said, "and as I am only a woman I must take them in the name of my husband. But I am the person aggrieved, and if you have any excuse to make you can make it to me. Your safer course, sir, will be to pay me the money that you owe me."

I had come there on a fool's errand, and before I could get away was very angry both with Mr. Sharp and Mr. X. I could hardly get a word in amidst the storm of indignant reproaches which was bursting over my head during the whole of the visit. One would have thought from hearing her that she had half filled the pages of the magazine for the last six months, and that we, individually, had pocketed the proceeds of her labour. She laughed in our face when we suggested that she could not really intend to prosecute the suit, and told us to mind our own business when we hinted that the law was an expensive amusement. "We, sir," she said, "will have the amusement, and you will have to pay the bill." When we left her she was indignant, defiant, and self-confident.

And what will the reader suppose was the end of all this? The whole truth has been told as accurately as we can tell it. As far as we know our own business we were not wrong in any single step we took. Our treatment of Mrs. Brumby was courteous, customary, and conciliatory. We had treated her with more consideration than we had perhaps ever before shown to an unknown, would-be contributor. She had been admitted thrice to our presence. We had read at any rate enough of her trash to be sure of its nature. On the other hand we had been insulted, and our clerk had had his ears boxed. What should have been the result? We will tell the reader what was the result. Mr. X. paid £10 to Messrs. Badger and Blister on behalf of the lieutenant; and we, under Mr. Sharp's advice, wrote a letter to Mrs. Brumby, in which we expressed deep sorrow for our clerk's misconduct, and our own regret that we should have delayed, — "the perusal of her manuscript." We could not bring ourselves to write the words ourselves with our own fingers, but signed the document which Mr. Sharp put before us. Mr. Sharp had declared to Messrs. X., Y., and Z., that unless some such arrangement were made, he thought that we should be cast for a much greater sum before a jury. For one whole morning in Paternoster Row we resisted this infamous tax, not only on our patience but, — as we then felt it, — on our honour. We thought that our very old friend Mr. X. should have stood to us more firmly and not have demanded from us a task that was so peculiarly repugnant to our feelings. "And it is peculiarly repugnant to my feelings to pay £10 for nothing," said Mr. X., who was not, we think, without some little feeling of revenge against us; "but I prefer that to a law-suit." And then he argued that the simple act on our part of signing such a letter as that presented to us, could cost us no trouble and ought to occasion us no sorrow. "What can come of it? Who'll know it?" said Mr. X. "We've got to pay £10, and that we shall feel." It came to that at last, that we were constrained to sign the letter, — and did sign it. It did us no harm, and can have done Mrs. Brumby no good; but the moment in which we signed it was perhaps the bitterest we ever knew.

That in such a transaction Mrs. Brumby should have been so thoroughly successful, and that we should have been so shamefully degraded, has always appeared to us to be an injury too deep to remain unredressed for ever. Can such wrongs be, and the heavens not fall! Our greatest comfort has been in the reflection that neither the lieutenant or his wife ever saw a shilling of the £10. That, doubtless, never went beyond Badger and Blister.

"Mrs. Brumby" appeared first in the May issue of *Saint Pauls Magazine* for 1870.

The Misfortunes of
Frederic Pickering

T HERE WAS SOMETHING ALMOST GRAND in
the rash courage with which Fred Pickering married his young
wife, and something quite grand in her devotion in marrying
him. She had not a penny in the world, and he, when he married
her, had two hundred and fifty pounds, —and no profession. She
was the daughter of parents whom she had never seen, and had
been brought up by the kindness of an aunt, who died when she
was eighteen. Distant friends then told her that it was her duty
to become a governess; but Fred Pickering intervened, and Mary
Crofts became Mary Pickering when she was nineteen years old.
Fred himself, our hero, was six years older, and should have
known better and have conducted his affairs with more wisdom.
His father had given him a good education, and had articled him
to an attorney at Manchester. While at Manchester he had written three or four papers in different newspapers, and had succeeded in obtaining admission for a poem in the *Free Trader*, a
Manchester monthly magazine which was expected to do great
things as the literary production of Lancashire. These successes,
joined, no doubt, to the natural bent of his disposition, turned
him against the law, and when he was a little more than twenty-

five, having then been four years in the office of the Manchester attorney, he told his father that he did not like the profession chosen for him, and that he must give it up. At that time he was engaged to marry Mary Crofts; but of this fact he did not tell his father. Mr. Pickering, who was a stern man, — one not given at any time to softnesses with his children, — when so informed by his son, simply asked him what were his plans. Fred replied that he looked forward to a literary career, — that he hoped to make literature his profession. His father assured him that he was a silly fool. Fred replied that on that subject he had an opinion of his own by which he intended to be guided. Old Pickering then declared that in such circumstances he should withdraw all pe- cuniary assistance; and young Pickering upon this wrote an un- gracious epistle, in which he expressed himself quite ready to take upon himself the burden of his own maintenance. There was one and only one further letter from his father, in which he told his son that the allowance made to him would be henceforth stopped. Then the correspondence between Fred and the Ex-gov- ernor, as Mary used to call him, was brought to a close.

Most unfortunately there died at this time an old maiden aunt, who left four hundred pounds apiece to twenty nephews and nieces, of whom Fred Pickering was one. The possession of this sum of money strengthened him in his rebellion against his father. Had he had nothing on which to begin, he might proba- bly even yet have gone to the old house at home, and have had something of a fatted calf killed for him, in spite of the ungra- ciousness of his letter. As it was he was reliant on the resources which Fortune had sent to him, thinking that they would suffice till he had made his way to a beginning of earning money. He thought it all over for full half-an-hour, and then came to a de- cision. He would go to Mary, — his Mary, — who was about to enter the family of a very vulgar tradesman as governess to six young children with a salary of twenty-five pounds per annum, and ask her to join him in throwing all prudence to the wind. He did go to Mary; and Mary at last consented to be as imprudent as himself, and she consented without any of that confidence which animated him. She consented simply because he asked her to do so, knowing that she was doing a thing so rash that no father or mother would have permitted it.

"Fred," she had said, half laughing as she spoke, "I am afraid we shall starve if we do."

"Starving is bad," said Fred; "I quite admit that; but there are worse things than starving. For you to be a governess at Mrs. Boullem's is worse. For me to write lawyers' letters all full of lies is worse. Of course we may come to grief. I dare say we shall come to grief. Perhaps we shall suffer awfully, — be very hungry and very cold. I am quite willing to make the worst of it. Suppose that we.die in the street! Even that, — the chance of that with the chance of success on the other side, is better than Mrs. Boullem's. It always seems to me that people are too much afraid of being starved."

"Something to eat and drink is comfortable," said Mary. "I don't say that it is essential."

"If you will dare the consequences with me, I will gladly dare them with you," said Fred, with a whole rhapsody of love in his eyes. Mary had not been proof against this. She had returned the rhapsody of his eyes with a glance of her own, and then, within six weeks of that time, they were married. There were some few things to be bought, some little bills to be paid, and then there was the fortnight of honeymooning among the Lakes in June. "You shall have that, though there were not another shot in the locker," Fred had said, when his bride that was to be had urged upon him the prudence of settling down into a small lodging the very day after their marriage. The fortnight of honeymooning among the Lakes was thoroughly enjoyed, almost without one fearful look into the future. Indeed Fred, as he would sit in the late evening on the side of a mountain, looking down upon the lakes, and watching the fleeting brightness of the clouds, with his arm round his loving wife's waist and her head upon his shoulder, would declare that he was glad that he had nothing on which to depend except his own intellect and his own industry. "To make the score off his own bat; that should be a man's ambition, and it is that which Nature must have intended for a man. She could never have meant that we should be bolstered up, one by another, from generation to generation." "You shall make the score off your own bat," Mary had said to him. Though her own heart might give way a little as she thought, when alone, of the danger of the future, she was always brave before him. So she en-

joyed the fortnight of her honeymooning, and when that was
over set herself to her task with infinite courage. They went up
to London in a third-class carriage, and, on their arrival there,
went at once to lodgings which had been taken for them by a
friend in Museum-street. Museum-street is not cheering by any
special merits of its own; but lodgings there were found to be
cheap, and it was near to the great library by means of which,
and the treasures there to be found, young Pickering meant to
make himself a famous man.

He had had his literary successes at Manchester, as has been
already stated, but they had not been of a remunerative nature.
He had never yet been paid for what he had written. He reaped,
however, this reward, that the sub-editor of a Manchester newspaper gave him a letter to a gentleman connected with a London
periodical, which might probably be of great service to him. It is
at any rate a comfort to a man to know that he can do something
towards a commencement of the work that he has in hand, —
that there is a step forward which he can take. When Fred and
Mary sat down to their tea and broiled ham on the first night,
the letter of introduction was a great comfort to them, and much
was said about it. The letter was addressed to Roderick Billings,
Esq., Office of the *Lady Bird*, 99 Catherine-Street, Strand. By
ten o'clock on the following morning Fred Pickering was at the
office of the *Lady Bird*, and there learned that Mr. Billings never
came to the office, or almost never. He was on the staff of the
paper, and the letter should be sent to him. So Fred Pickering
returned to his wife; and as he was resolved that no time should
be lost, he began a critical reading of *Paradise Lost*, with a note
book and pencil beside him, on that very day.

They were four months in London, during which they never
saw Mr. Billings or any one else connected with the publishing
world, and these four months were very trying to Mrs. Pickering.
The study of Milton did not go on with unremitting ardour. Fred
was not exactly idle, but he changed from one pursuit to another,
and did nothing worthy of note except a little account of his honeymooning tour in verse. In this poem the early loves of a young
married couple were handled with much delicacy and some pathos of expression, so that Mary thought that her husband would
assuredly drive Tennyson out of the field. But no real good had

come from the poem by the end of the four months, and Fred Pickering had sometimes been very cross. Then he had insisted more than once or twice, more than four times or five times, on going to the theatre; and now at last his wife had felt compelled to say that she would not go there with him again. They had not means, she said, for such pleasures. He did not go without her, but sometimes of an evening he was very cross. The poem had been sent to Mr. Billings, with a letter, and had not as yet been sent back. Three or four letters had been written to Mr. Billings, and one or two very short answers had been received. Mr. Billings had been out of town. "Of course all the world is out of town in September," said Fred; "what fools we were to think of beginning just at this time of the year!" Nevertheless he had urged plenty of reasons why the marriage should not be postponed till after June. On the first of November, however, they found that they had still a hundred and eighty pounds left. They looked their affairs in the face cheerfully, and Fred taking upon his own shoulders all the blame for their discomfiture up to the present moment, swore that he would never be cross with his darling Molly again. After that he went out with a letter of introduction from Mr. Billings to the sub-editor of a penny newspaper. He had never seen Mr. Billings; but Mr. Billings thus passed him on to another literary personage. Mr. Billings in his final very short note communicated to Fred his opinion that he would find "work on the penny daily press easier got."

For months Fred Pickering hung about the office of the *Morning Comet*. November went, and December and January, and he was still hanging about the office of the *Daily Comet*. He did make his way to some acquaintance with certain persons on the staff of the *Comet*, who earned their bread, if not absolutely by literature, at least by some work cognate to literature. And when he was asked to sup with one Tom Wood on a night in January, he thought that he had really got his foot upon the threshold. When he returned home that night, or I should more properly say on the following morning, his wife hoped that many more such preliminary suppers might not be necessary for his success. At last he did get employment at the office of the *Daily Comet*. He attended there six nights a week, from ten at night till three in the morning, and for this he received twenty shillings a week.

His work was almost altogether mechanical, and after three nights disgusted him greatly. But he stuck to it, telling himself that as the day was still left to him for work he might put up with drudgery during the night. That idea, however, of working day and night soon found itself to be a false one. Twelve o'clock usually found him still in bed. After his late breakfast he walked out with his wife, and then; — well, then he would either write a few verses or read a volume of an old novel.

"I must learn shorthand writing," he said to his wife, one morning when he came home

"Well, dear, I have no doubt you would learn it very quickly."

"I don't know that; I should have begun younger. It's a thousand pities that we are not taught anything useful when we are at school. Of what use is Latin and Greek to me?"

" I heard you say once that it would be of great use to you some day."

"Ah, that was when I was dreaming of what will never come to pass; when I was thinking of literature as a high vocation." It had already come to him to make such acknowledgements as this. "I must think about mere bread now. If I could report I might, at any rate, gain a living. And there have been reporters who have risen high in the profession. Dickens was a reporter. I must learn, though I suppose it will cost me twenty pounds."

He paid his twenty pounds and did learn shorthand writing. And while he was so doing he found he might have learned just as well by teaching himself out of a book. During the period of his tuition in this art he quarrelled with his employers at the *Daily Comet,* who, as he declared, treated him with an indignity which he could not bear. "They want me to fetch and carry, and be a menial," he said to his wife. He thereupon threw up his employment there. "But now you will get an engagement as a reporter," his wife said. He hoped that he might get an engagement as a reporter; but, as he himself acknowledged, the world was all to begin again. He was at last employed, and made his first appearance at a meeting of discontented tidewaiters, who were anxious to petition Parliament for some improvement in their position. He worked very hard in his efforts to take down the words of the eloquent leading tidewaiter; whereas he could see that two other reporters near him did not work at all. And yet he failed. He struggled at this work for a month, and failed at last. "My hand is not made for it," he said to his wife, almost in an agony of despair. "It seems to me as though nothing would come within my reach." "My dear," she said, "a man who can write the *Braes of Birken*" — the *Braes of Birken* was the name of his poem on the joys of honeymooning — "must not be ashamed of himself because he cannot acquire a small mechanical skill." "I am ashamed of myself all the same," said Fred.

Early in April they looked their affairs in the face again, and found that they had still in hand something just over a hundred pounds. They had been in London nine months, and when they had first come up they had expressed to each other their joint conviction that they could live very comfortably on forty shillings a week. They had spent nearly double that over and beyond what he had earned, and after all they had not lived comfortably. They had a hundred pounds left on which they might exist for a year, putting aside all idea of comfort; and then; — and then would come that starving of which Fred had once spoken so gallantly, unless some employment could in the meantime be found for him. And, by the end of the year, the starving would have to be done by three, — a development of events on which he had not seemed to calculate when he told his dearest Mary that after all there were worse things in the world than starving.

But before the end of this month there came upon them a gleam of comfort, which might be cherished and fostered till it should become a whole midday sun of nourishing heat. His friend of the *Manchester Free Trader* had become the editor of the *Salford Reformer*, a new weekly paper which had been established with the view of satisfying certain literary and political wants which the public of Salford had long experienced, and among these wants was an adequate knowledge of what was going on in London. Fred Pickering was asked whether he would write the London letter, once a week, at twenty shillings a week. Write it! Ay, that he would. There was a whole heaven of joy in the idea. This was literary work. This was the sort of thing that he could do with absolute delight. To guide the public by his own wit and discernment, as it were from behind a mask, — to be the motive power and yet unseen, — this had ever been his ambition. For three days he was in an ecstacy, and Mary was ecstatic with him. For the first time it was a joy to him that the baby was coming. A pound a week earned would of itself prolong their means of support for two years, and a pound a week so earned would surely bring other pounds. "I knew it was to be done," he said, in triumph, to his wife, "if one only had the courage to make the attempt." The morning of the fourth day somewhat damped his joy, for there came a long letter of instruction from the Salford editor, in which there were hints of certain difficulites. He was told in this letter that it would be well that he should belong to a London club. Such work as was now expected from him could hardly be done under favourable circumstances unless he did belong to a club. "But as everybody now-a-days does belong to a club, you will soon get over that difficulty." So said the editor. And then the editor in his instructions greatly curtailed that liberty of the pen which Fred specially wished to enjoy. He had anticipated that in his London letter he might give free reins to his own political convictions, which were of a very liberal nature, and therefore suitable to the *Salford Reformer*. And he had a theological bias of his own, by the putting forward of which in strong language among the youth of Salford, he had intended to do much towards the clearing away of prejudice and the emancipation of truth. But the editor told him that he should hardly touch politics at all in his London letter, and never lay a finger on religion. He was to tell the people of Salford what was coming out at the different theatres, how the Prince and Princess looked on horseback, whether the Thames embankment made proper progress, and he was to keep his ears especially open for matters of social interest, private or general. His style was to be easy and colloquial, and above all things he was to avoid being heavy, didactive, and profound. Then there was sent to him, as a model, a column and a half cut out from a certain well-known newspaper, in which the names of people were mentioned very freely. "If you can do that sort of thing," said the editor, "we shall get on together like a house on fire."

"It is a farrago of ill-natured gossip," he said, as he chucked the fragment over to his wife.

"But you are so clever, Fred," said his wife. "You can do it without the ill nature."

"I will do my best," he said; "but as for telling them about this woman and that, I cannot do it. In the first place where am I to learn it all?" Nevertheless, the London letter to the *Salford Reformer* was not abandoned. Four or five such letters were written, and four or five sovereigns were paid into his little exchequer in return for so much work. Alas! after the four or five there came a kindly-worded message from the editor to say that the articles did not suit. Nothing could be better than Pickering's language, and his ideas were manly and for the most part good. But the *Salford Reformer* did not want that sort of thing. The *Salford Reformer* felt that Fred Pickering was too good for the work required. Fred for twenty-four hours was broken-hearted. After that he was able to resolve that he would take the thing up in the right spirit. He wrote to the editor, saying that he thought that the editor was right. The London letter required was not exactly within the compass of his ability. Then he enclosed a copy of the *Braes of Birken*, and expressed an opinion that perhaps that might suit a column in the *Salford Reformer*, — one of those columns which were furthest removed from the corner devoted to the London letter. The editor replied that he would publish the *Braes of Birken* if Pickering wished; but that they never paid for poetry. Anything being better than silence Pickering permitted the editor to publish the *Braes of Birken* in the gratuitous manner suggested.

At the end of June, when they had just been twelve months in London, Fred was altogether idle as far as any employment was concerned. There was no going to the theatre now; and it had come to that with him, in fear of his coming privations, that he would discuss within his own heart the expediency of taking this or that walk with reference to the effect it would have upon his shoes. In those days he strove to work hard, going on with his Milton and his note-book, and sitting for two or three hours a day over heavy volumes in the reading-room at the Museum. When he first resolved upon doing this there had come a difficulty as to the entrance. It was necessary that he should have permission to use the library, and for a while he had not known how to obtain it. Then he had written a letter to a certain gentleman well known in the literary world, an absolute stranger to him, but of whom he had heard a word or two among his newspaper acquaintances, and had asked this gentleman to give him, or to get for him, the permission needed. The gentleman having made certain inquiry, having sent for Pickering and seen him, had done as he was asked, and Fred was free of the library.

"What sort of a man is Mr. Wickham Webb?" Mary asked him, when he returned from the club at which, by Mr. Webb's appointment, the meeting had taken place.

"According to my ideas he is the only gentleman whom I have met since I have been in London," said Fred, who in these days was very bitter.

"Was he civil to you?"

"Very civil. He asked me what I was doing up in London, and I told him. He said that literature is the hardest profession in the world. I told him that I thought it was, but, at the same time, the most noble."

"What did he say to that?"

"He said that the nobler the task, it was always the more difficult; and that, as a rule, it was not well that men should attempt work too difficult for their hands because of its nobility."

"What did he mean by that, Fred?"

"I knew what he meant very well. He meant to tell me that I had better go and measure ribbons behind a counter; and I don't know but what he was right."

"But yet you liked him?"

"Why should I have disliked him for giving me good advice? I liked him because his manner was kind, and because he strove hard to say an unpleasant thing in the pleasantest words that he could use. Besides, it did me good to speak to a gentleman once again."

Throughout July not a shilling was earned, nor was there any prospect of the earning of a shilling. People were then still in town, but in another fortnight London would have emptied itself of the rich and prosperous. So much Pickering had learned, little as he was qualified to write the London letter for the *Salford Reformer*. In the last autumn he had complained to his wife that circumstances had compelled him to begin at the wrong period of the year, — in the dull months when there was nobody in London who could help him. Now the dull months were coming round again, and he was as far as ever from any help. What was he to do? "You said that Mr. Webb was very civil," suggested his wife; "could you not write to him and ask him to help us?" "He is a rich man, and that would be begging," said Fred. "I would not ask him for money," said Mary; "but perhaps he can tell you how you can get employment."The letter to Mr. Webb was written, with many throes, and the destruction of much paper. Fred found it very difficult to choose words which should describe with sufficient force the extreme urgency of his position, but which should have no appearance of absolute begging. "I hope you will understand," he said, in his last paragraph, "that what I want is simply work for which I may be paid, and that I do not care how hard I work, or how little I am paid, so that I and my wife may live. If I have taken an undue liberty in writing to you, I can only beg you to pardon my ignorance."

This letter led to another interview between our hero and Mr. Wickham Webb. Mr. Webb sent his compliments and asked Mr. Pickering to come and breakfast with him. This kindness, though it produced some immediate pleasure, created fresh troubles. Mr. Wickham Webb lived in a grand house near Hyde Park, and poor Fred was badly off for good clothes. "Your coat does not look at all amiss," his wife said to him, comforting him; "and as for a hat, why don't you buy a new one?" "I sha'n't breakfast in my hat," said Fred; "but look here;" and Fred exhibited his shoes. "Get a new pair," said Mary. "No," said he; "I've sworn to have nothing new till I've earned the money. Mr. Webb won't expect to see me very bright, I dare say. When a man writes to beg for employment, it must naturally be supposed that he will be rather seedy about his clothes." His wife did the best she could for him, and he went out to his breakfast.

Mrs. Webb was not there. Mr. Webb explained that she had already left town. There was no third person at the table, and before his first lamb chop was eaten, Fred had told the pith of his story. He had a little money left, just enough to pay the doctor who must attend upon his wife, and carry him through the winter; — and then he would be absolutely bare. Upon this Mr. Webb asked as to his relatives. "My father has chosen to quarrel with me," said Fred. "I did not wish to be an attorney, and therefore he has cast me out." Mr. Webb suggested that a reconciliation might be possible; but when Fred said at once that it was impossible, he did not recur to the subject.

When the host had finished his own breakfast, he got up from his chair, and, standing on the rug, spoke such words of wisdom as were in him. It should be explained that Pickering, in his letter to Mr. Webb, had enclosed a copy of the *Braes of Birken*, another little poem in verse, and two of the London letters which he had written for the *Salford Reformer*. "Upon my word, Mr. Pickering, I do not know how to help you. I do not indeed."

"I am sorry for that, sir."

"I have read what you sent me, and am quite ready to acknowledge that there is enough, both in the prose and verse, to justify you in supposing it to be possible that you might hereafter live by literature as a profession; but all who make literature a profession should begin with independent means."

"That seems to be hard on the profession as well as on the beginner."

"It is not the less true; and is, indeed, true of most other professions as well. If you had stuck to the law your father would have provided you with the means of living till your profession had become profitable."

"Is it not true that many hundred men in London live on literature?" said our hero.

"Many hundred do so, no doubt. They are of two sorts, and you can tell yourself whether you belong to either. There are they who have learned to work in accordance with the directions of others; the great bulk of what comes out to us almost hourly in the shape of newspapers is done by them. Some are very highly paid, many are paid liberally, and a great many are paid scantily. There is that side of the profession, and you say that you have tried it and do not like it. Then there's those who do their work independently; — who write either books or articles which find acceptance in magazines."

"It is that which I would try if the opportunity were given me."

"But you have to make your own opportunity," said Mr. Wickham Webb. "It is the necessity of the position that it should be so. What can I do for you?"

"You know the editors of magazines."

"Granted that I do, can I ask a man to buy what he does not want because he is my friend?"

"You could get your friend to read what I write."

It ended in Mr. Webb strongly advising Fred Pickering to go back to his father, and in his writing two letters of introduction for him, — one to the editor of the *International*, a weekly gazette of mixed literature, and the other to Messrs. Brook and Boothby, publishers in St. James's-street. Mr. Webb, though he gave the letters open to Fred, read them to him with the view of explaining to him how little and how much they meant. "I do not know that they can do you the slightest service," said he; "but I give them to you, because you ask me. I strongly advise you to go back to your father; but if you are still in town next spring, come and see me again." Then the interview was over, and Fred returned to his wife, glad to have the letters; but still with a sense of bitterness against Mr. Webb. When one word of encouragement would have made him so happy, might not Mr. Webb have spoken it? Mr. Webb had thought that he had better not speak any such word. And Fred, when he read the letters of introduction over to his wife, found them to be very cold. "I don't think I'll take them," he said.

But he did take them, — of course, on the very next day, and saw Mr. Boothby, the publisher, after waiting for half-an-hour in the shop. He swore to himself that the time was an hour and a half, and became sternly angry at being so treated. It did not occur to him that Mr. Boothby was obliged to attend to his own business, and that he could not put his other visitors under the counter, or into the cupboards, in order to make way for Mr. Pickering. The consequence was that poor Fred was seen at his worst, and that the Boothbyan heart was not much softened towards him. "There are so many men of this kind who want work," said Mr. Boothby, "and so very little work to give them!"

"It seems to me," said Pickering, "that the demand for the work is almost unlimited." As he spoke, he looked at a hole in his boot, and tried to speak in a tone that should show that he was above his boots.

"It may be so," said Boothby; "but if so, the demands do not run in my way. I will, however, keep Mr. Webb's note by me, and if I find I can do anything for you, I will. Good-morning." Then Mr. Boothby got up from his chair, and Fred Pickering understood that he was told to go away. He was furious in his abuse of Boothby as he described the interview to his wife that evening.

The editor of the *International* he could not get to see; but he got a note from him. The editor sent his compliments and would be glad to read the article to which Mr. W. W. had alluded. As Mr. W. W. had alluded to no article, Fred saw that the editor was not inclined to take much trouble on his behalf. Nevertheless, an article should be sent. An article was written to which Fred gave six weeks of hard work, and which contained an elaborate criticism on the *Samson Agonistes*. Fred's object was to prove that Milton had felt himself to be a superior Samson, —blind, indeed, in the flesh, as Samson was blind, but not blind in the spirit as was Samson when he crushed the Philistines. The poet had crushed his Philistines with all his intellectual eyes about him. Then there was a good deal said about the Philistines of those days as compared with the other Philistines, in all of which Fred thought that he took much higher ground than certain other writers in magazines on the same subject. The editor sent back his compliments, and said that the *International* never admitted reviews of old books. "Insensate idiot!" said Fred, tearing the note asunder, and then tearing his own hair, on both sides of his head. "And these are the men who make the world of letters! Idiot! thick-headed idiot!"

"I suppose he has not read it," said Mary.

"Then why hasn't he read it? Why doesn't he do the work for which he is paid? If he has not read it, he is a thief as well as an idiot." Poor Fred had not thought much of his chance from the *International* when he first got the editor's note; but as he had worked at his Samson he had become very fond of it, and golden dreams had fallen on him, and he had dared to whisper to himself words of wondrous praise which might be forthcoming, and to tell himself of inquiries after the unknown author of the great article about the Philistines. As he had thought of this, and as the dreams and the whispers had come to him, he had rewritten his essay from the beginning, making it grander, bigger, more eloquent than before. He became very eloquent about the Philistines, and mixed with his eloquence some sarcasm which could not, he thought, be without effect even in dull-brained heavy-livered London. Yes; he had dared to hope. And then his essay, — such an essay as this, — was sent back to him with a notice that the *International* did not insert reviews of old books! Hideous, brainless, meaningless idiot! Fred in his fury tore his article into a hundred fragments; and poor Mary was employed, during the whole of the next week, in making another copy of it from the original blotted sheets, which had luckily been preserved. "Pearls before swine!" Fred said to himself, as he slowly made his way up to the library of the Museum on the last day of that week.

That was in the end of October. He had not then earned a single shilling for many months, and the nearer prospect of that starvation of which he had once spoken so cheerily was becoming awfully frightful to him. He had said that there were worse fates than to starve. Now, as he looked at his wife, and thought of the baby that was to be added to them, and counted the waning heaps of sovereigns, he began to doubt whether there was in truth anything worse than to starve. And now, too, idleness made his life more wretched to him than it had ever been. He could not bring himself to work when it seemed to him that his work was to have no result; literally none.

"Had you not better write to your father?" said Mary. He made no reply, but went out and walked up and down Museum-street.

He had been much disgusted by the treatment he had received from Mr. Boothby the publisher; but in November he brought himself to write to Mr. Boothby, and ask him whether some employment could not be found. "You will perhaps remember Mr. Wickham Webb's letter," wrote Fred, "and the interview which I had with you last July." His wife had wished him to speak more civilly, and to refer to the pleasure of the interview. But Fred had declined to condescend so far. There were still left to them some thirty pounds.

A fortnight afterwards, when December had come, he got a reply from Mr. Boothby, in which he was asked to call at a certain hour at the shop in St. James's-street. This he did, and saw the great man again. The great man asked him whether he could make an index to an historical work. Fred of course replied that he could do that, — that or anything else. He could make the index; or, if need was, write the historical work itself. That, no doubt, was his feeling. Ten pounds would be paid for the index, if it was approved. Fred was made to understand that payment was to depend altogether on approval of the work. Fred took away the sheets confided to him without any doubt as to the ultimate approval. It would be odd indeed if he could not make an index. "That young man will never do any good," said Mr. Boothby to his foreman, as Fred took his departure. "He thinks he can do everything, and I doubt very much whether he can do anything as it should be done."

Fred worked very hard at the index, and the baby was born to him as he was doing it. A fortnight, however, finished the index, and if he could earn money at the rate of ten pounds a fortnight he might still live. So he took his index to St. James's-street, and left it for approval. He was told by the foreman that if he would call again in a week's time he should hear the result. Of course he called on that day week. The work had not yet been examined, and he must call again after three days. He did call again, and Mr. Boothby told him that his index was utterly useless, — that, in fact, it was not an index at all. "You couldn't have looked at any other index, I think," said Mr. Boothby.

"Of course you need not take it," said Fred; "but I believe it to be as good an index as was ever made." Mr. Boothby, getting up from his chair, declared that there was nothing more to be said. The gentleman for whom the work had been done begged that Mr. Pickering should receive five pounds for his labour, — which unfortunately had been thus thrown away. And in saying this Mr. Boothby tendered a five pound note to Fred. Fred pushed the note away from him, and left the room with a tear in his eye. Mr. Boothby saw the tear, and ten pounds was sent to Fred on the next day, with the gentleman's compliments. Fred sent the ten pounds back. There was still a shot in the locker, and he could not as yet take money for work that he had not done.

By the end of January Fred had retreated with his wife and child to the shelter of a single small bedroom. Hitherto there had been a sitting-room and a bedroom; but now there was but five pounds between him and that starvation which he had once almost coveted, and every shilling must be strained to the utmost. His wife's confinement had cost him much of his money, and she was still ill. Things were going very badly with him, and among all the things that were bad with him, his own idleness was probably the worst. When starvation was so near to him, he could not seat himself in the Museum library and read to any good purpose. And, indeed, he had no purpose. Milton was nothing to him now, as his lingering shillings became few, and still fewer. He could only sit brooding over his misfortunes, and cursing his fate. And every day, as he sat eating his scraps of food over the morsel of fire in his wife's bedroom, she would implore him to pocket his pride and write to his father. "He would do something for us, so that baby should not die," Mary said to him. Then he went into Museum-street, and bethought himself whether it would not be a manly thing for him to cut his throat. At any rate there would be much relief in such a proceeding.

One day as he was sitting over the fire while his wife still lay in bed, the servant of the house brought up word that a gentleman wanted to see him. "A gentleman! what gentleman?" The girl could not say who was the gentleman, so Fred went down to receive his visitor at the door of the house. He met an old man of perhaps seventy years of age, dressed in black, who with much politeness asked him whether he was Mr. Frederic Pickering. Fred declared himself to be that unfortunate man, and explained that he had no apartment in which to be seen. "My wife is in bed upstairs, ill; and there is not a room in the house to which I can ask you." So the old gentleman and Fred walked up Museum-street and had their conversation on the pavement. "I am Mr. Burnaby, for whose book you made an index," said the old man. Mr. Burnaby was an author well known in those days, and Fred, in the midst of his misfortunes, felt that he was honoured by the visit.

"I was sorry that my index did not suit you," said Fred.

"It did not suit at all," said Mr. Burnaby. "Indeed it was no index. An index should comprise no more than words and figures. Your index conveyed opinions, and almost criticism."

"If you suffered inconvenience, I regret it much," said Fred. "I was punished at any rate by my lost labour."

"I do not wish you to be punished at all," said Mr. Burnaby, "and therefore I have come to you with the price in my hand. I am quite sure that you worked hard to do your best." Then Mr. Burnaby's fingers went into his waistcoat pocket, and returned with a crumpled note.

"Certainly not, Mr. Burnaby," said Fred. "I can take nothing that I have not earned."

"Now, my dear young friend, listen to me. I know that you are poor."

"I am very poor."

"And I am rich."

"That has nothing to do with it. Can you put me in the way of earning anything by literature? I will accept any such kindness as that at your hand; but nothing else."

"I cannot. I have no means of doing so."

"You know so many authors; — and so many publishers."

"Though I knew all the authors and all the publishers, what can I do? Excuse me if I say that you have not served the apprenticeship that is necessary."

"And do all authors serve apprenticeships?"

"Certainly not. And it may be that you will rise to wealth and fame without apprenticeship; — but if so, you must do it without help."

After that they walked silently together half the length of the street before Fred spoke again. "You mean," said he, "that a man must be either a genius or a journeyman."

"Yes, Mr. Pickering; that, or something like it, is what I mean."

Fred told Mr. Burnaby his whole story, walking up and down Museum-street, — even to that early assurance given to his young bride that there were worse things in the world than starvation. And then Mr. Burnaby asked him what were his present intentions. "I suppose we shall try it," said Pickering, with a forced laugh.

"Try what?" said Mr. Burnaby.

"Starvation," said Fred.

"What; with your baby, — with your wife and baby? Come; you must take my ten pound note at any rate. And while you are spending it, write home to your father. Heaven and earth! is a man to be ashamed to tell his father that he has been wrong?" When Fred said that his father was a stern man, and one whose heart would not be melted into softness at the tale of a baby's sufferings, Mr. Burnaby went on to say that the attempt should at any rate be made. "There can be no doubt what duty requires of you, Mr. Pickering. And, upon my word, I do not see what other step you can take. You are not, I suppose, prepared to send your wife and child to the poor-house." Then Fred Pickering

burst into tears, and Mr. Burnaby left him at the corner of Great
Russell-street, after cramming the ten-pound note into his hand.

To send his wife and child to the poor-house! In all his misery
that idea had never before presented itself to Fred Pickering. He
had thought of starvation, or rather of some high-toned extrem-
ity of destitution, which might be borne with an admirable and
perhaps sublime magnanimity. But how was a man to bear with
magnanimity a poor-house jacket, and the union mode of hair-
cutting? It is not easy for a man with a wife and baby to starve in
this country, unless he be one to whom starvation has come very
gradually. Fred saw it all now. The police would come to him,
and take his wife and baby away into the workhouse, and he
would follow them. It might be that this was worse than starvation, but it lacked all that melodramatic grandeur to which he
had looked forward almost with satisfaction.

"Well," said Mary to him, when he returned to her bedside,
"who was it? Has he told you of anything? Has he brought you
anything to do?"

"He has given me that," said Fred, throwing the bank note on
to the bed, "—out of charity. I may as well go out into the streets
and beg now. All the pride has gone out of me." Then he sat over
the fire crying, and there he sat for hours.

"Fred," said his wife to him, "if you do not write to your father
tomorrow I will write."

He went again to every person connected in the slightest degree with literature of whom he had the smallest knowledge; to
Mr. Roderick Billings, to the teacher who had instructed him in
shorthand writing, to all those whom he had ever seen among
the newspapers, to the editor of the International, and to Mr.
Boothby. Four different visits he made to Mr. Boothby, in spite
of his previous anger, but it was all to no purpose. No one could
find him employment for which he was suited. He wrote to Mr.
Wickham Webb, and Mr. Wickham Webb sent him a five-pound
note. His heart was, I think, more broken by his inability to refuse charity than by anything else that had occurred to him.

His wife had threatened to write to his father, but she had not
carried her threat into execution. It is not by such means that a
young wife overcomes her husband. He had looked sternly at her
when she had so spoken, and she had known that she could not

bring herself to do such a thing without his permission. But when she fell ill, wanting the means of nourishment for her child, and in her illness begged of him to implore succour from his father for her baby when she should be gone, then his pride gave way, and he sat down and wrote his letter. When he went to his ink-bottle it was dry. It was nearly two months since he had made any attempt at working in that profession to which he had intended to devote himself.

He wrote to his father, drinking to the dregs the bitter cup of broken pride. It always seems to me that the prodigal son who returned to his father after feeding with the swine suffered but little mortification in his repentant submission. He does, indeed, own his unworthiness, but the calf is killed so speedily that the pathos of the young man's position is lost in the hilarity of the festival. Had he been compelled to announce his coming by post; had he been driven to beg permission to return, and been forced to wait for a reply, his punishment, I think, would have been more severe. To Fred Pickering the punishment was very severe, and indeed for him no fatted calf was killed at last. He received without delay a very cold letter from his father, in which he was told that his father would consider the matter. In the meanwhile thirty shillings a week should be allowed him. At the end of a fortnight he received a further letter, in which he was informed that if he would return to Manchester he would be taken in at the attorney's office which he had left. He must not, however, hope to become himself an attorney; he must look forward to be a paid attorney's clerk, and in the meantime his father would continue to allow him thirty shillings a week. "In the present position of affairs," said his father, "I do not feel that anything would be gained by our seeing each other." The calf which was thus killed for poor Fred Pickering was certainly by no means a fatted calf.

Of course he had to do as he was directed. He took his wife and baby back to Manchester, and returned with sad eyes and weary feet to the old office which he had in former days not only hated but despised. Then he had been gallant and gay among the other young men, thinking himself to be too good for the society of those around him; now he was the lowest of the low, if not the humblest of the humble.

He told his whole story by letters to Mr. Burnaby, and received some comfort from the kindness of that gentleman's replies. "I still mean," he said, in one of those letters, "to return some day to my old aspirations; but I will endeavour first to learn my trade as a journeyman of literature."

"The Misfortunes of Frederic Pickering" appeared first in the September issue of *Argosy* for 1866.

Josephine de Montmorenci

THE LITTLE STORY WHICH WE are about to relate
refers to circumstances which occurred some years ago, and we
desire, therefore, that all readers may avoid the fault of connect-
ing the personages of the tale, — either the Editor who suffered
so much, and who behaved, we think, so well, or the ladies with
whom he was concerned, — with any editor or with any ladies
known to such readers either personally or by name. For though
the story as told is a true story, we who tell it have used such craft
in the telling, that we defy the most astute to fix the time or to
recognise the characters. It will be sufficient if the curious will
accept it as a fact that at some date since magazines became common in the land, a certain editor, sitting in his office, came upon
the perusal of the following letter, addressed to him by name;

"19, King-Charles Street,
"1st May, 18—.
"Dear Sir,
"I think that literature needs no introduction, and, judging of
you by the character which you have made for yourself in its
paths, I do not doubt but you will feel as I do. I shall therefore
write to you without reserve. I am a lady not possessing that modesty which should make me hold a low opinion of my own talents, and equally free from that feeling of self-belittlement which
induces so many to speak humbly while they think proudly of

their own acquirements. Though I am still young, I have written much for the press, and I believe I may boast that I have sometimes done so successfully. Hitherto I have kept back my name, but I hope soon to be allowed to see it on the title-page of a book which shall not shame me.

"My object in troubling you is to announce the fact, agreeable enough to myself, that I have just completed a novel in three volumes, and to suggest to you that it should make its first appearance to the world in the pages of the magazine under your control. I will frankly tell you that I am not myself fond of this mode of publication; but Messrs. X., Y., Z., of Paternoster Row, with whom you are doubtless acquainted, have assured me that such will be the better course. In these matters one is still terribly subject to the tyranny of the publishers, who surely of all cormorants are the most greedy, and of all tyrants are the most arrogant. Though I have never seen you, I know you too well to suspect for a moment that my words will ever be repeated to my respectable friends in the Row.

"Shall I wait upon you with my MS., — or will you call for it? Or perhaps it may be better that I should send it to you. Young ladies should not run about, — even after editors; and it might be so probable that I should not find you at home. Messrs. X., Y., and Z. have read the MS. — or more probably the young man whom they keep for the purpose has done so, — and the nod of approval has been vouchsafed. Perhaps this may suffice; but if a second examination be needful, the work is at your service.

"Yours faithfully, and in hopes of friendly relations,
                                "Josephine de Montmorenci.

"I am English, though my unfortunate name will sound French in your ears."

For facility in the telling of our story we will call this especial editor Mr. Brown. Mr. Brown's first feeling on reading the letter was decidedly averse to the writer. But such is always the feeling of editors to would-be contributors, though contributions are the very food on which an editor must live. But Mr. Brown was an unmarried man, who loved the rustle of feminine apparel, who delighted in the brightness of a woman's eye when it would be bright for him, and was not indifferent to the touch of a woman's hand. As editors go, or went then, he knew his business, and was

216

not wont to deluge his pages with weak feminine ware in return
for smiles and flattering speeches, — as editors have done before
now; but still he liked an adventure, and was perhaps afflicted by
some slight flaw of judgment, in consequence of which the words
of pretty women found with him something of preponderating
favour. Who is there that will think evil of him because it was so?

He read the letter a second time, and did not send that curt,
heartrending answer which is so common to editors, — "The Editor's compliments and thanks, but his stock of novels is at present so great that he cannot hope to find room for the work which
has been so kindly suggested." Of King-Charles Street, Brown
could not remember that he had ever heard, and he looked it out
at once in the Directory. There was a King-Charles Street in
Camden Town, at No. 19 of which street it was stated that a Mr.
Puffle resided. But this told him nothing. Josephine de Montmorenci might reside with Mrs. Puffle in Camden Town, and yet
write a good novel, — or be a very pretty girl. And there was a
something in the tone of the letter which made him think that
the writer was no ordinary person. She wrote with confidence.
She asked no favour. And then she declared that Messrs. X., Y.,
Z., with whom Mr. Brown was intimate, had read and approved
her novel. Before he answered the note he would call in the Row
and ask a question or two.

He did call, and saw Z. Mr. Z. remembered well that the MS.
had been in their house. He rather thought that X., who was out
of town, had seen Miss Montmorenci, — perhaps on more than
one occasion. The novel had been read, and, — well, Mr. Z.
would not quite say approved: but it had been thought that there
was a good deal in it. "I think I remember X. telling me that she
was an uncommon pretty young woman," said Z., — "and there
is some mystery about her. I didn't see her myself, but I am sure
there was a mystery." Z. himself was an old family man of nearly
sixty, whereas X. was known to be over seventy. Mr. Brown made
up his mind that he would, at any rate, see the MS.

He felt disposed to go at once to Camden Town, but still had
fears that in doing so he might seem to make himself too common. There are so many things of which an editor is required to
think! It is almost essential that they who are ambitious of serving under him should believe that he is enveloped in MSS. from

217

morning to night, — that he cannot call an hour his own, — that he is always bringing out that periodical of his in a frenzy of mental exertion, — that he is to be approached only with difficulty, — and that a call from him is a visit from a god. Mr. Brown was a Jupiter willing enough on occasions to go a little out of his way after some literary Leda, or even on behalf of a Danae desirous of a price for her compositions; — but he was obliged to acknowledge to himself that the occasion had not as yet arisen. So he wrote to the young lady as follows;

"Office of the Olympus Magazine,
"4th May, 18—.
"The Editor presents his compliments to Miss de Montmorenci, and will be very happy to see her MS. Perhaps she will send it to the above address. The Editor has seen Mr. Z., of Paternoster Row, who speaks highly of the work. A novel, however, may be very clever and yet hardly suit a magazine. Should it be accepted by the 'Olympus,' some time must elapse before it appears. The Editor would be very happy to see Miss de Montmorenci if it would suit her to call any Friday between the hours of two and three."

When the note was written Mr. Brown felt that it was cold; — but then it behoves an editor to be cold. A gushing editor would ruin any publication within six months. Young women are very nice; pretty young women are especially nice; and of all pretty young women, clever young women who write novels are perhaps as nice as any; — but to an Editor they are dangerous. Mr. Brown was at this time about forty, and had had his experiences. The letter was cold, but he was afraid to make it warmer. It was sent; — and when he received the following answer, it may fairly be said that his editorial hair stood on end.

"Dear Mr. Brown,
"I hate you and your compliments. That sort of communication means nothing, and I won't send you my MS. unless you are more in earnest about it. I know the way in which rolls of paper are shoved into pigeon-holes and left there till they are musty, while the writers' hearts are being broken. My heart may be broken some day, but not in that way.

"I won't come to you between two and three on Friday. It

sounds a great deal too like a doctor's appointment, and I don't think much of you if you are only at your work one hour in the week. Indeed, I won't go to you at all. If an interview is necessary you can come here. But I don't know that it will be necessary.

"Old X. is a fool and knows nothing about it. My own approval is to me very much more than his. I don't suppose he'd know the inside of a book if he saw it. I have given the very best that is in me to my work, and I know that it is good. Even should you say that it is not I shall not believe you. But I don't think you will say so, because I believe you to be in truth a clever fellow in spite of your 'compliments' and your 'two and three o'clock on a Friday.'

"If you want to see my MS., say so with some earnestness, and it shall be conveyed to you. And please to say how much I shall be paid for it, for I am as poor as Job. And name a date. I won't be put off with your 'some time must elapse.' It shall see the light, or, at least, a part of it, within six months. That is my intention. And don't talk nonsense to me about clever novels not suiting magazines, —unless you mean that as an excuse for publishing so many stupid ones as you do.

"You will see that I am frank; but I really do mean what I say. I want it to come out in the 'Olympus;' and if we can I shall be so happy to come to terms with you.

"Yours as I find you,
"Josephine de Montmorenci."

"Thursday. —King-Charles Street."

This was an epistle to startle an editor as coming from a young lady; but yet there was something in it that seemed to imply strength. Before answering it Mr. Brown did a thing which he must be presumed to have done as man and not as editor. He walked off to King-Charles Street in Camden Town, and looked at the house. It was a nice little street, very quiet, quite genteel, completely made up with what we vaguely call gentlemen's houses, with two windows to each drawing-room, and with a balcony to some of them, the prettiest balcony in the street belonging to No. 19, near the Park, and equally removed from poverty and splendour. Brown walked down the street, on the opposite side, towards the Park, and looked up at the house. He intended to walk at once homewards, across the Park, to his own little home in St. John's Wood Road; but when he had passed half a street away from the Puffle residence, he turned to have another look, and retraced his steps. As he passed the door it was opened, and there appeared upon the step, — one of the prettiest little women he had ever seen in his life. She was dressed for walking, with that jaunty, broad, open bonnet which women then wore, and seemed, as some women do seem, to be an amalgam of soft-ness, prettiness, archness, fun, and tenderness, — and she carried a tiny blue parasol. She was fair, grey-eyed, dimpled, all alive, and dressed so nicely and yet simply, that Mr. Brown was carried away for the moment by a feeling that he would like to publish her novel, let it be what it might. And he heard her speak. "Charles," she said, "you shan't smoke." Our editor could, of course, only pass on, and had not an opportunity of even seeing Charles. At the corner of the street he turned round and saw them walking the other way. Josephine was leaning on Charles's arm. She had, however, distinctly avowed herself to be a young lady, — in other words, an unmarried woman. There was, no doubt, a mystery, and Mr. Brown felt it to be incumbent on him to fathom it. His next letter was as follows: —

"My Dear Miss de Montmorenci,

"I am sorry that you should hate me and my compliments. I had intended to be as civil and as nice as possible. I am quite in earnest, and you had better send the MS. As to all the questions you ask, I cannot answer them to any purpose till I have read the story, — which I will promise to do without subjecting it to the pigeon-holes. If you do not like Friday, you shall come on Mon-day, or Tuesday, or Wednesday, or Thursday, or Saturday, or even on Sunday, if you wish it; — and at any hour, only let it be fixed.

"Yours faithfully,
"Jonathan Brown."

"Friday."

In the course of the next week the novel came, with another short note, to which was attached no ordinary beginning or end-ing. "I send my treasure, and, remember, I will have it back in a week if you do not intend to keep it. I have not £5 left in the world, and I owe my milliner ever so much, and money at the

220

stables where I get a horse. And I am determined to go to Dieppe in July. All must come out of my novel. So do be a good man. If you are I will see you." Herein she declared plainly her own conviction that she had so far moved the editor by her correspondence, — for she knew nothing, of course, of that ramble of his through King-Charles Street, — as to have raised in his bosom a desire to see her. Indeed, she made no secret of such conviction. "Do as I wish," she said plainly, "and I will gratify you by a personal interview." But the interview was not to be granted till the novel had been accepted and the terms fixed, — such terms, too, as it would be very improbable that any editor could accord.

"Not so Black as he's Painted;" — that was the name of the novel which it now became the duty of Mr. Brown to read. When he got it home, he found that the writing was much worse than that of the letters. It was small, and crowded, and carried through without those technical demarcations which are so comfortable to printers, and so essential to readers. The erasures were numerous, and bits of the story were written, as it were, here and there. It was a manuscript to which Mr. Brown would not have given a second glance, had there not been an adventure behind it. The very sending of such a manuscript to any editor would have been an impertinence, if it were sent by any but a pretty woman. Mr. Brown, however, toiled over it, and did read it, — read it, or at least enough of it to make him know what it was. The verdict which Mr. Z. had given was quite true. No one could have called the story stupid. No Mentor experienced in such matters would have ventured on such evidence to tell the aspirant that she had mistaken her walk in life, and had better sit at home and darn her stockings. Out of those heaps of ambitious manuscripts which are daily subjected to professional readers such verdict may safely be given in regard to four fifths, — either that the aspirant should darn her stockings, or that he should prune his fruit trees. It is equally so with the works of one sex as with those of the other. The necessity of saying so is very painful, and the actual stocking, or the fruit tree itself, is not often named. The cowardly professional reader indeed, unable to endure those thorns in the flesh of which poor Thackeray spoke so feelingly, when hard-pressed for definite answers, generally lies. He has been asked to be candid, but he cannot bring himself to undertake a duty so onerous, so odious, and one as to which he sees so little reason that he personally should perform it. But in regard to these aspirations, — to which have been given so much labours, which have produced so many hopes, offsprings which are so dear to the poor parents, — the decision at least is easy. And there are others in regard to which a hopeful reader finds no difficulty, — as to which he feels assured that he is about to produce to the world the fruit of some new-found genius. But there are doubtful cases which worry the poor judge till he knows not how to trust his own judgment. At this page he says, "Yes, certainly;" at the next he shakes his head as he sits alone amidst his papers. Then he is dead against the aspirant. Again there is improvement, and he asks himself, — where is he to find anything that is better. As our editor read Josephine's novel, — he had learned to call her Josephine in that silent speech in which most of us indulge, and which is so necessary to an editor, he was divided between Yes and No throughout the whole story. Once or twice he found himself wiping his eyes, and then it was all "yes" with him. Then he found the pages ran with a cruel heaviness, which seemed to demand decisive editorial severity. A whole novel, too, is so great a piece of business! There would be such difficulty were he to accept it! How much must he cut out! How many of his own hours must he devote to the repairing of mutilated sentences, and the remodelling of indistinct scenes. In regard to a small piece an editor, when moved that way, can afford to be good-natured. He can give to it the hour or so of his own work which it may require. And if after all it be nothing, — the evil is of short duration. In admitting such a thing he has done an injury, — but the injury is small. It passes in the crowd, and is forgotten. The best Homer that ever edited must sometimes nod. But a whole novel! A piece of work that would last him perhaps for twelve-months! No editor can afford to nod for so long a period.

But then this tale, this novel of "Not so Black as he's Painted," this story of a human devil, for whose crimes no doubt some Byronic apology was made with great elaboration by the sensational Josephine, was not exactly bad. Our editor had wept over it. Some tenderhearted Medora, who on behalf of her hyena-in-love, had gone through miseries enough to kill half a regiment of heroines, had dimmed the judges' eyes with tears. What stronger proof of excellence can an editor have? But then there were those long pages of metaphysical twaddle, sure to elicit scorn and neglect from old and young. They, at any rate, must be cut out. But in the cutting of them out a very mincemeat would be made of the story. And yet Josephine de Montmorenci, with her impudent little letters, had already made herself so attractive! What was our editor to do?

He knew well the difficulty that would be before him should he once dare to accept, and then undertake to alter. She would be as a tigress to him, — as a tigress fighting for her young. That work of altering is so ungracious, so precarious, so incapable of success in its performance! The long-winded, far-fetched, high-stilted, unintelligible sentence which you elide with so much confidence in your judgment, has been the very apple of your author's eye. In it she has intended to convey to the world the fruits of her best meditation for the last twelvemonths. Thinking much over many things in her solitude, she has at last invented a truth, and there it lies. That wise men may adopt it, and candid women admire it, is the hope, the solace, and at last almost the certainty of her existence. She repeats the words to herself, and finds that they will form a choice quotation to be used in coming books. It is for the sake of that one newly invented truth, — so she tells herself, though not quite truly, — that she desires publication. You come, — and with a dash of your pen you annihilate the precious gem! Is it in human nature that you should be forgiven? Mr. Brown had had his experiences, and understood all this well. Nevertheless he loved dearly to please a pretty woman.

And it must be acknowledged that the letters of Josephine were such as to make him sure that there might be an adventure if he chose to risk the pages of his magazine. The novel had taken him four long evenings to read, and at the end of the fourth he sat thinking of it for an hour. Fortune either favoured him or the reverse, — as the reader may choose to regard the question, — in this, that there was room for the story in his periodical if he chose to take it. He wanted a novel; — but then he did not want feminine metaphysics. He sat thinking of it, wondering in his mind how that little smiling, soft creature with the grey eyes, and the dimples, and the pretty walking dress, could have written those interminable pages as to the questionable criminality of crime; whether a card-sharper might not be a hero; whether a murderer might not sacrifice his all, even the secret of his murder, for the woman he loved; whether devil might not be saint, and saint devil. At the end of the hour he got up from his chair, stretched himself, with his hands in his trousers-pocket, and said aloud, though alone, that he'd be d_____ if he would. It was an act of great self-denial, a triumph of principle over passion.

But though he had thus decided, he was not minded to throw over altogether either Josephine or her novel. He might still, perhaps, do something for her if he could find her amenable to reason. Thinking kindly of her, very anxious to know her personally, and still desirous of seeing the adventure to the end, he wrote the following note to her that evening.: —

"Cross Bank, St. John's Wood,
"Saturday Night.

"My Dear Miss de Montmorenci,

"I knew how it would be. I cannot give you an answer about your novel without seeing you. It so often happens that the answer can't be Yes or No. You said something very cruel about dear old X., but after all he was quite right in his verdict about the book. There is a great deal in it; but it evidently was not written to suit the pages of a magazine. Will you come to me, or shall I come to you; — or shall I send the MS. back, and so let there be an end of it? You must decide. If you direct that the latter course be taken, I will obey; but I shall do so with most sincere regret, both on account of your undoubted aptitude for literary work, and because I am very anxious indeed to become acquainted with my fair correspondent. You see I can be frank as you are yourself.

"Yours most faithfully,
"Jonathan Brown.

"My advice to you would be to give up the idea of publishing this tale in parts, and to make terms with X., Y., and Z., — in endeavouring to do which I shall be most happy to be of service to you."

This note he posted on the following day, and when he returned home on the next night from his club, he found three replies from the divine, but irritable and energetic, Josephine. We will give them according to their chronology.

No. 1. "Monday Morning. — Let me have my MS. back, — and, pray, without any delay. — J. de M."

No. 2. "Monday, 2 o'clock. — How can you have been so ill-natured, — and after keeping it twelve days!" — His answer had been written within a week of the receipt of the parcel at his office, and he had acted with a rapidity which nothing but some tender passion would have instigated. — "What you say about being clever, and yet not fit for a magazine, is rubbish. I know it is rubbish. I do not wish to see you. Why should I see a man who will do nothing to oblige me? If X., Y., Z. choose to buy it, at once, they shall have it. But I mean to be paid for it, and I think you have behaved very ill to me. — Josephine."

No. 3. "Monday evening. — My dear Mr. Brown, — Can you wonder that I should have lost my temper and almost my head. I have written twice before to-day, and hardly know what I said. I cannot understand you editing people. You are just like women; — you will and you won't. I am so unhappy. I had allowed myself to feel almost certain that you would take it, and have told that cross man at the stables he should have his money. Of course I can't make you publish it; — but how you can put in such yards of stupid stuff, all about nothing on earth, and then send back a novel which you say yourself is very clever, is what I can't understand. I suppose it all goes by favour, and the people who write are your uncles, and aunts, and grandmothers, and lady-loves. I can't make you do it, and therefore I suppose I must take your advice about those old hugger-muggers in Paternoster Row. But there are ever so many things you must arrange. I must have the money at once. And I won't put up with just a few pounds. I have been at work upon that novel for more than two years, and I know that it is good. I hate to be grumbled at, and complained of, and spoken to as if a publisher were doing me the greatest favour in the world when he is just going to pick my brains to make money of them. I did see old X., or old Z., or old Y., and the snuffy old fellow told me that if I worked hard I might do something some day. I have worked harder than ever he did, — sitting there and squeezing brains, and sucking the juice like an old ghoul. I suppose I had better see you, because of money and all that. I'll come, or else send some one, at about two on Wednesday. I can't put it off till Friday, and I must be home by three.

You might as well go to X., Y., Z., in the meantime, and let me
know what they say. — J. de M."

There was an unparalleled impudence in all this which
afronted, amazed, and yet in part delighted our editor. Josephine
evidently regarded him as her humble slave, who had already received such favours as entitled her to demand from him any service which she might require of him. "You might as well go to
X., Y., Z., and let me know what they say!" And then that direct
accusation against him, — that all went by favour with him! "I
think you have behaved very ill to me!" Why, — had he not gone
out of his way, very much out of his way indeed, to do her a service? Was he not taking on her behalf an immense trouble for
which he looked for no remuneration, — unless remuneration
should come in that adventure of which he had but a dim fore-
boding? All this was unparalleled impudence. But then impudence from pretty women is only sauciness; and such sauciness is
attractive. None but a very pretty woman who openly trusted in
her prettiness would dare to write such letters; and the girl whom
he had seen on the door-step was very pretty. As to his going to
X., Y., Z. before he had seen her, that was out of the question.
That very respectable firm in the Row would certainly not give
money for a novel without considerable caution, without much
talking, and a regular understanding and bargain. As a matter of
course they would take time to consider. X., Y., and Z. were not
in a hurry to make a little money to pay a milliner or to satisfy a
stable-keeper, and would have but little sympathy for such troubles; — all which it would be Mr. Brown's unpleasant duty to explain to Josephine de Montmorenci.

But though this would be unpleasant, still there might be pleasure. He could foresee that there would be a storm, with much
pouting, some violent complaint, and perhaps a deluge of tears.
But it would be for him to dry the tears and allay the storm. The
young lady could do him no harm, and must at last be driven to
admit that his kindness was disinterested. He waited, therefore,
for the Wednesday, and was careful to be at the office of his magazine at two o'clock. In the ordinary way of his business the office
would not have seen him on that day, but the matter had now
been present in his mind so long, and had been so much considered, — had assumed so large a proportion in his thoughts, — that

he regarded not at all this extra trouble. With an air of indifference he told the lad who waited upon him as half-clerk and half-
errand boy, that he expected a lady; and then he sat down, as
though to compose himself to his work. But no work was done.
Letters were not even opened. His mind was full of Josephine de
Montmorenci. If all the truth is to be told, it must be acknowledged that he did not even wear the clothes that were common
to him when he sat in his editorial chair. He had prepared himself
somewhat, and a new pair of gloves was in his hat. It might be
that circumstances would require him to accompany Josephine at
least a part of the way back to Camden Town.

At half-past two the lady was announced, — Miss de Montmorenci; and our editor, with palpitating heart, rose to welcome
the very figure, the very same pretty walking-dress, the same little blue parasol, which he had seen upon the steps of the house
in King-Charles Street. He could swear to the figure, and to the
very step, although he could not as yet see the veiled face. And
this was a joy to him; for, though he had not allowed himself to
doubt much, he had doubted a little whether that graceful houri
might or might not be his Josephine. Now she was there, present
to him in his own castle, at his mercy as it were, so that he might
dry her tears and bid her hope, or tell her that there was no hope
so that she might still weep on, just as he pleased. It was not one
of those cases in which want of bread and utter poverty are to be
discussed. A horsekeeper's bill and a visit to Dieppe were the
melodramatic incidents of the tragedy, if tragedy it must be. Mr.
Brown had in his time dealt with cases in which a starving
mother or a dying father were the motives to which appeal was
made. At worst there could be no more than a rose-water catastrophe; and it might be that triumph, and gratitude, and smiles
would come. He rose from his chair, and, giving his hand grace-
fully to his visitor, led her to a seat.

"I am very glad to see you here, Miss de Montmorenci," he
said. Then the veil was raised, and there was the pretty face half
blushing, half smiling, wearing over all a mingled look of fun and
fear.

"We are so much obliged to you, Mr. Brown, for all the trouble
you have taken," she said.

"Don't mention it. It comes in the way of my business to take

227

such trouble. The annoyance is in this, that I can so seldom do what is wanted."

"It is so good of you to do anything!"

"An editor is, of course, bound to think first of the periodical which he produces." This announcement Mr. Brown made, no doubt, with some little air of assumed personal dignity. The fact was one which no heaven-born editor ever forgets.

"Of course, sir. And no doubt there are hundreds who want to get their things taken."

"A good many there are, certainly."

"And everything can't be published," said the sagacious beauty.

"No, indeed; very much comes into our hands which cannot be published," replied the experienced editor. "But this novel of yours, perhaps, may be published."

"You think so?"

"Indeed I do. I cannot say what X., Y., and Z. may say to it. I'm afraid they will not do more than offer half profits."

"And that doesn't mean any money paid at once?" asked the lady plaintively.

"I'm afraid not."

"Ah! if that could be managed!"

"I haven't seen the publishers, and of course I can say nothing myself. You see I'm so busy myself with my uncles, and aunts, and grandmothers, and lady-loves — "

"Ah, — that was very naughty, Mr. Brown."

"And then, you know, I have so many yards of stupid stuff to arrange."

"Oh, Mr. Brown, you should forget all that."

"So I will. I could not resist the temptation of telling you of it again, because you are so much mistaken in your accusation. And now about your novel."

"It isn't mine, you know."

"Not yours?"

"Not my own, Mr. Brown."

"Then whose is it?" Mr. Brown, as he asked this question, felt that he had a right to be offended. "Are you not Josephine de Montmorenci?"

"Me an author! Oh no, Mr. Brown," said the pretty little

woman. And our editor almost thought that he could see a smile on her lips as she spoke.

"Then who are you?" asked Mr. Brown.

"I am her sister; — or rather her sister-in-law. My name is, — Mrs. Puffle." How could Mrs. Puffle be the sister-in-law of Miss de Montmorenci? Some such thought as this passed through the editor's mind, but it was not followed out to any conclusion. Relationships are complex things, and, as we all know, give rise to most intricate questions. In the half moment that was allowed to him Mr. Brown reflected that Mrs. Puffle might be the sister-in-law of a Miss de Montmorenci; or, at least, half sister-in-law. It was even possible that Mrs. Puffle, young as she looked, might have been previously married to a de Montmorenci. Of all that, however, he would not now stop to unravel the details, but endeavoured as he went on to take some comfort from the fact that Puffle was no doubt Charles. Josephine might perhaps have no Charles. And then it became evident to him that the little fair, smiling, dimpled thing before him could hardly have written "Not so Black as he's Painted," with all its metaphysics. Josephine must be made of sterner stuff. And, after all, for an adventure, little dimples and a blue parasol are hardly appropriate. There should be more of stature than Mrs. Puffle possessed, with dark hair, and piercing eyes. The colour of the dress should be black, with perhaps yellow trimmings; and the hand should not be of pearly whiteness, — as Mrs. Puffle's no doubt was, though the well-fitting little glove gave no absolute information on this subject. For such an adventure the appropriate colour of the skin would be, — we will not say sallow exactly, — but running a little that way. The beauty should be just toned by sadness; and the blood, as it comes and goes, should show itself, not in flushes, but in the mellow, changing lines of the brunette. All this Mr. Brown understood very well.

"Oh, — you are Mrs. Puffle," said Brown, after a short but perhaps insufficient pause. "You are Charles Puffle's wife?"

"Do you know Charles?" asked the lady, putting up both her little hands. "We don't want him to hear anything about this. You haven't told him?"

"I've told him nothing as yet," said Mr. Brown.

"Pray don't. It's a secret. Of course he'll know it some day. Oh,

Mr. Brown, you won't betray us. How very odd that you should know Charles!"

"Does he smoke as much as ever, Mrs. Puffle?"

"How very odd that he never should have mentioned it. Is it at his office that you see him?"

"Well, no; not at his office. How is it that he manages to get away on an afternoon as he does?"

"It's very seldom, — only two or three times in a month, — when he really has a headache from sitting at his work. Dear me, how odd! I thought he told me everything, and he never mentioned your name."

"You needn't mention mine, Mrs. Puffle, and the secret shall be kept. But you haven't told me about the smoking. Is he as inveterate as ever?"

"Of course he smokes. They all smoke. I suppose then he used always to be doing it before he married. I don't think men ever tell the real truth about things, though girls always tell everything."

"And now about your sister's novel?" asked Mr. Brown, who felt that he had mystified the little woman sufficiently about her husband.

"Well, yes. She does want to get some money so badly! And it is clever; — isn't it? I don't think I ever read anything cleverer. Isn't it enough to take your breath away when Orlando defends himself before the lords?" This referred to a very high-flown passage which Mr. Brown had determined to cut out when he was thinking of printing the story for the pages of the "Olympus." "And she will be so brokenhearted! I hope you are not angry with her because she wrote in that way."

"Not in the least. I liked her letters. She wrote what she really thought."

"That is so good of you! I told her that I was sure you were good-natured, because you answered so civilly. It was a kind of experiment of hers, you know."

"Oh, — an experiment!"

"It is so hard to get at people. Isn't it? If she'd just written, 'Dear sir, I send you a manuscript,' — you never would have looked at it; — would you?"

"We read everything, Mrs. Puffle."

"But the turn for all the things comes so slowly; doesn't it? So Polly thought — "

"Polly, — what did Polly think?"

"I mean Josephine. We call her Polly just as a nick-name. She was so anxious to get you to read it at once! And now what must we do?" Mr. Brown sat silent awhile, thinking. Why did they call Josephine de Montmorenci, Polly? But there was the fact of the MS., let the name of the author be what it might. On one thing he was determined. He would take no steps till he had himself seen the lady who wrote the novel. "You'll go to the gentlemen in Paternoster Row immediately; won't you?" asked Mrs. Puffle, with a pretty little beseeching look which it was very hard to resist.

"I think I must ask to see the authoress first," said Mr. Brown.

"Won't I do?" asked Mrs. Puffle. "Josephine is so particular. I mean she dislikes so very much to talk about her own writings and her own works." Mr. Brown thought of the tenor of the letters which he had received, and found that he could not reconcile with it this character which was given to him of Miss de Montmorenci. "She has an idea," continued Mrs. Puffle, "that genius should not show itself publicly. Of course she does not say that herself. And she does not think herself to be a genius, though I think it. And she is a genius. There are things in 'Not so Black as he's Painted' which nobody but Polly could have written."

Nevertheless Mr. Brown was firm. He explained that he could not possibly treat with Messrs. X., Y., and Z., — if any treating should become possible, — without direct authority from the principal. He must have from Miss de Montmorenci's mouth what might be the arrangements to which she would accede. If this could not be done he must wash his hands of the affair. He did not doubt, he said, but that Miss de Montmorenci might do quite as well with the publishers by herself, as she could with any aid from him. Perhaps it would be better that she should see Mr. X. herself. But if he, Brown, was to be honoured by any delegated authority, he must see the author. In saying this he implied that he had not the slightest desire to interfere further, and that he had no wish to press himself on the lady. Mrs. Puffle, with just a tear, and then a smile, and then a little coaxing twist of her lips, assured him that their only hope was in him. She would carry his message to Josephine, and he should have a further letter from that lady. "And you won't tell Charles that I have been here," said Mrs. Puffle as she took her leave.

"Certainly not. I won't say a word of it."

"It is so odd that you should have known him."

"Don't let him smoke too much, Mrs. Puffle."

"I don't intend. I've brought him down to one cigar and a pipe a day, — unless he smokes at the office."

"They all do that; — nearly the whole day."

"What; at the Post Office!"

"That's why I mention it. I don't think they're allowed at any of the other offices, but they do what they please there. I shall keep the MS. till I hear from Josephine herself." Then Mrs. Puffle took her leave with many thanks, and a grateful pressure from her pretty little hand.

Two days after this there came the promised letter from Josephine.

"Dear Mr. Brown,

"I cannot understand why you should not go to X., Y., and Z. without seeing me. I hardly ever see anybody; but, of course, you must come if you will. I got my sister to go because she is so gentle and nice, that I thought she could persuade anybody to do anything. She says that you know Mr. Puffle quite well, which seems to be so very odd. He doesn't know that I ever write a word, and I didn't think he had an acquaintance in the world whom I don't know the name of. You're quite wrong about one thing. They never smoke at the Post Office, and they wouldn't be let to do it. If you choose to come, you must. I shall be at home any time on Friday morning, — that is, after half-past nine, when Charles is away.

"Yours truly,
"J. de M.

"We began to talk about Editors after dinner, just for fun; and Charles said that he didn't know that he had ever seen one. Of course we didn't say anything about the 'Olympus;' but I don't know why he should be so mysterious." Then there was a second postscript, written down in a corner of the sheet of paper. "I know you'll be sorry you came."

Our editor was now quite determined that he would see the adventure to an end. He had at first thought that Josephine was keeping herself in the background merely that she might enhance the favour of a personal meeting when that favour should be accorded. A pretty woman believing herself to be a genius, and thinking that good things should ever be made scarce, might not improbably fall into such a foible. But now he was convinced that she would prefer to keep herself unseen if her doing so might be made compatible with her great object. Mr. Brown was not a man to intrude himself unnecessarily upon any woman unwilling to receive him; but in this case it was, so he thought, his duty to persevere. So he wrote a pretty little note to Miss Josephine saying that he would be with her at eleven o'clock on the day named.

Precisely at eleven o'clock he knocked at the door of the house in King-Charles Street, which was almost instantaneously opened for him by the fair hands of Mrs. Puffle herself. "H—sh," said Mrs. Puffle; "we don't want the servants to know anything about it." Mr. Brown, who cared nothing for the servants of the Puffle establishment, and who was becoming perhaps a little weary of the unravelled mystery of the affair, simply bowed and followed the lady into the parlour. "My sister is upstairs," said Mrs. Puffle, "and we will go to her immediately." Then she paused, as though she were still struggling with some difficulty; — "I am so sorry to say that Polly is not well. — But she means to see you," Mrs. Puffle added, as she saw that the editor, over whom they had so far prevailed, made some sign as though he was about to retreat. "She never is very well," said Mrs. Puffle, "and her work does tell upon her so much. Do you know, Mr. Brown, I think the mind sometimes eats up the body; that is, when it is called upon for such great efforts." They were now upon the stairs, and Mr. Brown followed the little lady into her drawing-room.

There, almost hidden in the depths of a low arm-chair, sat a little wizened woman, not old indeed, — when Mr. Brown came to know her better, he found that she had as yet only counted five-and-twenty summers, — but with that look of mingled youth and age which is so painful to the beholder. Who has not seen it; — the face in which the eye and the brow are young and bright, but the mouth and the chin are old and haggard? See such a one when she sleeps, — when the brightness of the eye is hidden, and all the countenance is full of pain and decay, and then the difference will be known to you between youth with that health which is generally given to it, and youth accompanied by premature decrepitude. "This is my sister-in-law," said Mrs. Puffle, introducing the two correspondents to each other. The editor looked at the little woman who made some half attempt to rise, and thought that he could see in the brightness of the eye some symptoms of the sauciness which had appeared so very plainly in her letters. And there was a smile too about the mouth, though the lips were thin and the chin poor, which seemed to indicate that the owner of them did in some sort enjoy this unravelling of her riddle, — as though she were saying to herself, "What do you think now of the beautiful young woman who has made you write so many letters, and read so long a manuscript, and come all the way at this hour of the morning to Camden Town!" Mr. Brown shook hands with her, and muttered something to the effect that he was sorry not to see her in better health.

"No," said Josephine de Montmorenci, "I am not very well. I never am. I told you that you had better put up with seeing my sister."

We say no more than the truth of Mr. Brown in declaring that he was now more ready than ever to do whatever might be in his power to forward the views of this young authoress. If he was interested before when he believed her to be beautiful, he was doubly interested for her now when he knew her to be a cripple; — for he had seen when she made that faint attempt to rise that her spine was twisted, and that when she stood up, her head sank between her shoulders. "I am very glad to make your acquaintance," he said, seating himself near her. "I should never have been satisfied without doing so."

"It is so very good of you to come," said Mrs. Puffle.

"Of course it is good of him," said Josephine; "especially after the way we wrote to him. The truth is, Mr. Brown, we were at our wit's end to catch you."

This was an aspect of the affair which our editor certainly did not like. An attempt to deceive anybody else might have been pardonable; but deceit practised against himself was odious to

him. Nevertheless, he did forgive it. The poor little creature before him had worked hard, and had done her best. To teach her
to be less metaphysical in her writings, and more straightforward
in her own practises should be his care. There is something to a
man inexpressibly sweet in the power of protecting the weak; and
no one had ever seemed to be weaker than Josephine. "Miss de
Montmorenci," he said, "we will let bygones be bygones, and will
say nothing about the letters. It is no doubt the fact that you did
write the novel yourself?"

"Every word of it," said Mrs. Puffle energetically.

"Oh, yes; I wrote it," said Josephine.

"And you wish to have it published?"

"Indeed I do."

"And you wish to get money for it?"

"That is the truest of all," said Josephine.

"Oughtn't one to be paid when one has worked so very hard?"
said Mrs. Puffle.

"Certainly one ought to be paid if it can be proved that one's
work is worth buying," replied the sage Mentor of literature.

"But isn't it worth buying?" demanded Mrs. Puffle.

"I must say that I think that publishers do buy some that are
worse," observed Josephine.

Mr. Brown with words of wisdom explained to them as well as
he was able the real facts of the case. It might be that that manuscript, over which the poor invalid had laboured for so many
painful hours, would prove to be an invaluable treasure of art,
destined to give delight to thousands of readers, and to be, when
printed, a source of large profit to publishers, booksellers, and
author. Or, again, it might be that, with all its undoubted merits,
— and that there were such merits Mr. Brown was eager in ac-
knowledging, — the novel would fail to make any way with the
public.

"A publisher," — so said Mr. Brown, — "will hardly venture to
pay you a sum of money down, when the risk of failure is so
great."

"But Polly has written ever so many things before," said Mrs.
Puffle.

"That counts for nothing," said Miss de Montmorenci. "They
were short pieces, and appeared without a name."

"Were you paid for them?" asked Mr. Brown.

"I have never been paid a halfpenny for anything yet."

"Isn't that cruel," said Mrs. Puffle, "to work, and work, and work, and never get the wages which ought to be paid for it?"

"Perhaps there may be a good time coming," said our editor. "Let us see whether we can get Messrs. X., Y., and Z. to publish this at their own expense, and with your name attached to it. Then, Miss de Montmorenci—"

"I suppose we had better tell him all," said Josephine.

"Oh, yes; tell everything. I am sure he won't be angry; he is so good-natured," said Mrs. Puffle.

Mr. Brown looked first at one, and then at the other, feeling himself to be rather uncomfortable. What was there that remained to be told? He was good-natured, but he did not like being told of that virtue. "The name you have heard is not my name," said the lady who had written the novel.

"Oh, indeed! I have heard Mrs. Puffle call you, — Polly."

"My name is , — Maryanne."

"It is a very good name," said Mr. Brown, — "so good that I cannot quite understand why you should go out of your way to assume another."

"It is Maryanne — Puffle."

"Oh; — Puffle!" said Mr. Brown.

"And a very good name, too," said Mrs. Puffle.

"I haven't a word to say against it," said Mr. Brown. "I wish I could say quite as much as to that other name, — Josephine de Montmorenci."

"But Maryanne Puffle would be quite unendurable on a title-page," said the owner of the unfortunate appellation.

"I don't see it," said Mr. Brown doggedly.

"Ever so many have done the same," said Mrs. Puffle. "There's Boz."

"Calling yourself Boz isn't like calling yourself Josephine de Montmorenci," said the editor, who could forgive the loss of beauty, but not the assumed grandeur of the name.

"And Currer Bell, and Jacob Omnium; and Barry Cornwall," said poor Polly Puffle, pleading hard for her falsehood.

"And Michael Angelo Titmarsh! That was quite the same sort of thing," said Mrs. Puffle.

Our editor tried to explain to them that the sin of which he now complained did not consist in the intention, — foolish as that had been, — of putting such a name as Josephine de Montmorenci on the title-page, but in having corresponded with him, — with him who had been so willing to be a friend, — under a false name. "I really think you ought to have told me sooner," he said.

"If we had known you had been a friend of Charles's we would have told you at once," said the young wife.

"I never had the pleasure of speaking to Mr. Puffle in my life," said Mr. Brown. Mrs. Puffle opened her little mouth, and held up both her little hands. Polly Puffle stared at her sister-in-law. "And what is more," continued Mr. Brown, "I never said that I had had that pleasure."

"You didn't tell me that Charles smoked at the Post Office," exclaimed Mrs. Puffle, — "which he swears that he never does, and that he would be dismissed at once if he attempted it?" Mr. Brown was driven to a smile. "I declare I don't understand you, Mr. Brown."

"It was his little Roland for our little Oliver," said Miss Puffle.

Mr. Brown felt that his Roland had been very small, whereas the Oliver by which he had been taken in was not small at all. But he was forced to accept the bargain. What is a man against a woman in such a matter? What can he be against two women, both young, of whom one was pretty and the other an invalid? Of course he gave way, and of course he undertook the mission to X., Y., and Z. We have not ourselves read "Not so Black as he's Painted," but we can say that it came out in due course under the hands of those enterprising publishers, and that it made what many of the reviews called quite a success.

"Josephine de Montmorenci" appeared first in the December issue of *Saint Pauls Magazine* for 1869.

THIS BOOK WAS DESIGNED BY
JUDITH OELFKE SMITH
TYPESET IN ELEVEN POINT GOUDY OLDSTYLE
BY FORT WORTH LINOTYPING COMPANY
PRINTED ON WARREN'S OLDE STYLE WOVE
BY MOTHERAL PRINTING COMPANY
AND BOUND BY UNIVERSAL BINDERY